Sanctuary in Hell

Book 2 of the Cocytus Series

by John Caligiuri

also by John Caligiuri:

THE RED FIST CHRONICLES

The Red Fist of Rome

Last Roman's Prayer

COCYTUS SERIES

Planet of the Damned

Sanctuary in Hell

Deal with the Devil

Face One's Demons

I060806ϵ

COPYRIGHT PAGE

This is a work of fiction. The characters and events portrayed in this novel are fictitious. Any similarity to individuals living or dead is unintended by the author.

ISBN: 9780991558261 [PRINT]
ISBN: 9780998804798 [EBOOK]

DEDICATION

To my parents, John and Angela Caligiuri, for your inspiration and encouragement. You gave me the freedom to dream and the will to pursue those dreams.

To the Greece Writers Group and my children John, Michael, and Kristina whose thoughtful critiques made my novels so much better. Thank you for your tireless efforts.

To my wife, Linda, who reads everything I write and gives me her honest feedback, even when I don't want to hear it. Her patience as I sit before my computer, for hours on end, is nothing short of miraculous.

To everyone who has faced life's tragedies and challenges, you are the true heroes. May we never have a time when we live without our imaginary worlds and the people who populate them. May my books give you an escape when you need it the most.

PROLOGUE

Dear Reader,

My name is Mara. I am an artificial intelligence built on the planet Cocytus. I will be both the narrator and one of the participants in the accounts related in the following chronicle. I must admit that I did not witness every incident reported here firsthand. However, I conducted comprehensive research, and the secondhand accounts came from parties I trust completely.

It is to my understanding that most of you are twenty-first-century Earth-born humans. It constrains my ability to describe events since most of you have had little or no interaction with galactic politics, as well as limited contact with other sentient species. Your understanding of modern science is also antiquated. A subject such as interstellar hyperspace travel will require me to provide more explanation than I would deem normal.

This is not stated as an insult to your intelligence. However, it is a fact brought about by your cloistered lives in a hermit society on a remote planet. In truth, I have a deep abiding love for Earth-born humans. The finest entities and sharpest minds I've had the pleasure of meeting were residents of Cocytus, but they originated from your world.

I imagine your first question would be "Where is this Cocytus?"

The answer is "Fairly close." It resides in the Lethe Sector of the Ipis empire on the fringe of the Milky Way Galaxy, a mere 6.7 parsecs from your planet.

This response must have sparked a myriad of questions on your part. I will refrain from answering them at this point since most will be revealed in the context of the following narrative.

Let me close this missive with a quote that I believe originated on your world:

"Bad things happen, like war, disaster, and disease. But out of those situations always arise stories of ordinary people accomplishing extraordinary things."

The people you will meet in the following chapters did not choose to enter their dire circumstances, but they resolved not to cower from them. They stood their ground. They endured.

CHAPTER I

Life in Purgatory

From rock to rock they fall into this valley:
Acheron, Styx and Phlegethon they form;
Then downward go along this narrow sluice
Upon that point where is no more descending.
They form Cocytus; what that pool may be
Thou shalt behold,...

Dante's Inferno, Canto XIV

Dante Carloman stood in the doorway of a pearl-white hospital room, gazing at the patient lying on the bed. To the side, a wide window revealed the lush gardens of the biosphere inside Mount Purgatory. Though a breathtaking sight, its beauty was lost on the unmoving patient.

Nearby, an elderly woman checked readouts on an array of diagnostic instruments. Dante couldn't make heads or tails of most of the data. At length, he asked, "Doc, it's been two months. Is there any chance Reggie will wake up from his coma?"

Doctor Esther Easley tucked a loose strand of steel-gray hair behind an ear, looking from her patient to Dante. "Mr. President, medically, Reggie's not in a coma. His body's responsive to food and stimulation, but his conscious mind seems disconnected from the rest of him." She shook her head in frustration. "But what do I know? I'm just a useless country doctor with no way to research anything."

"Esther, you've saved more lives on this frozen rock of a planet over the last year than most physicians back on Earth do in a lifetime." Dante gave the elder woman an embarrassed smile. "And please, don't call me Mister President. The entire population of this world is less than a small town. I'm a computer engineer who's had a nasty string of bad luck." He walked around the bed and gently hugged the petite woman. "I don't know anything about governance. I couldn't even get elected class president back in high school."

Less than a year earlier, Dante was a computer science grad student at Cornell. Now he ruled the planet Cocytus, where he dwelled with a couple thousand abductees. With his shaggy brown hair and the wiry body of a

4

long-distance runner, he did not look the part of a leader. However, as he'd discovered since landing on Cocytus, outward appearances said little about what lay in a person's heart and mind.

Esther pushed the earnest young man away, met his eyes, and smiled back. "You don't realize what you mean to the people here, do you? You gave us hope when we saw nothing but death. You persevered and united a single-purposed agricultural artificial intelligence and an army of brainwashed clones into helping us when any sane person would've thought it impossible."

She paused and stroked him gently on the cheek. "Everyone knows we got out of that hellish prison because of you." She sighed and looked back at her patient. "Now, what are you doing up here besides annoying an old lady?"

"See, if you didn't distract me with your good looks, I'd remember." They shared a laugh, and Dante squeezed her shoulder. "Our council meeting's starting downstairs, and I need a quorum. Have you seen Tina or Virgil?"

"Virgil's off on another scavenging mission, so I haven't seen him. Also, you'll have to start your meeting without Tina. Your new wife is down the hall midwifing." Esther giggled as though amused at some children's antics. "Now get out of here, Mister Supreme Ruler of Cocytus."

Dante laughed again before sighing. "Someone else has to be more suited for this job than me."

He left and headed down the curved marble staircase, thinking about the agenda. With the pressing need to establish some form of currency and a judicial system, the meeting would take all day.

* * *

Adjacent to the small hospital stood the improvised government building. Despite its title, the latter building was a compact stone structure bearing the same pearl-gray color shared by every other building within Mount Purgatory. The AI who managed the biosphere, Beatrice, believed adding variations in color wouldn't make for an efficient use of resources. Letting the musing pass, Dante hurried to the government building's second floor and bolted into the conference room.

Upon arriving, Dante plopped into the middle-most seat at a long oval table. Only half of the other seats were filled. At the far end of the table hovered an ivory-colored orb, one of thousands which acted as extensions of Beatrice. Across from Dante sat Michael, an imposing 194-centimeter-tall clone with a short-cropped beard and shaggy chestnut-colored hair held back by a sweatband. Next to him sat Gabrielle Peyago, a raven-haired Argentine journalist. To Dante's right sat Rodrigo Cruz, a former American Army captain and now the general of the planet's armed forces. To his left sat Dmitri Petrov, a short, balding man and former Russian physicist. All of them had been abducted from Earth over the course of the previous year. Now, they lived stranded on a frozen planet far from their original home.

The humans had named the new planet Cocytus after the lake in the pit of hell from Dante Alighieri's *Inferno*. From various recovered computer files, they learned that the creatures who'd captured them held sway over almost all sentient beings in the galaxy. The blotchy, purplish-black monsters matched the size of large, hairless dogs with claws and needle-sharp teeth. The human abductees derisively called them harpies.

Thoughts about dealing with those creatures weighed on Dante Carloman. At any point in the near future, the harpies would strike again. How would he protect everyone from a foe no one else in the galaxy has been able to defeat? For now at least, he could focus on a more mundane topic.

"Hi, everybody. Let's get started." Dante set to work at a computer console embedded in the table. He massaged his temples, eyeing the members of the planetary council until the census report came up. "Here it is. On this 'wonderful' world, the human population is two thousand and seventy-three."

A flat soprano voice emerged from the hovering orb. "The corrected count is two thousand and seventy-four. Tess Palmer gave birth thirty-seven seconds ago."

On the screen, the census updated on its own. Dante rolled his eyes at the orb. "Thanks, Beatrice." He cleared his throat to regain his bearings. "Clones: one thousand, nine hundred, ninety-six."

The corners of Michael's mouth tightened to a thin line. "I don't like that label, but it's better than 'big uglies.'"

Dante's stomach twisted as he regarded the clone. Michael was the only survivor of his generation of clones but looked like an older version of his younger brethren. "Sorry, Mick. You know I didn't mean to hurt your feelings. What would you prefer?"

Michael snorted as his mouth curved into a sour smile. "How about, *in vitro-born humans*?"

Gabrielle regarded the battered crucifix hanging around Michael's neck that had once belonged to another clone, Reggie. Her eyes misted as she spoke the name *Reggie* out loud. When all eyes turned toward her, the slender woman flushed, and her long raven hair fell over her shoulders. "Reggie's not a big ugly. He's a great man."

Dante nodded to Gabrielle. "Very true. He went into the harpies' compound alone to save us, but he may never wake up. We don't know what the harpies did to him when they hooked him to that machine."

"He talked when we broke into that room," Gabrielle remarked.

"And he hasn't spoken a word since we destroyed the harpies' control system," Dante replied in a whisper. "He was... he *is* a real hero. Our victory would've been very short-lived if his mind hadn't linked to the harpies' computer."

Michael drew in a ragged breath. "Many good people died for our freedom. My podmates immolated themselves rather than reveal what they knew about the humans' plans." He lifted his chin. "With time, the rest of my brethren could've been freed from the harpy yoke."

"No, my friend," General Cruz cut in. "You and a few others had the means and opportunity to overcome that 'compulsion' mind control. The rest were reduced to mindless brutes and slaves." The gaze in his eyes hardened briefly before softening. "I know I had a difficult time trusting you at first, and I truly regret it... but think about what you went through to break free."

Michael regarded the short commander bearing an olive complexion. Despite their long-held unease, they'd grown into true friends during the desperate battle two months earlier. "I still believe they could've been saved."

The general's brows furrowed. "You were there. How were you going to convince ten thousand berserk clones to switch sides?"

Michael's jaw tightened.

"You saved most of the young clones, and that alone is a miracle," Dante interjected before directing everyone's attention to the screen. "All right, we have two thousand and seventy-four naturally born humans, and one thousand, nine hundred and ninety-six pod-born humans. Counting Reggie, only two are adults." He quirked an eyebrow at Michael. "We also have two artificial intelligences."

Amber lights blinked three times on the orb. "AI may be a sufficient connotation for the mobile articulating robotic android prototype, but do not denote my intellect as artificial."

Dante wagged his finger at the floating orb. "Beatrice, that other AI is your daughter. She accepted the name Mara, and that is how we will speak of her. The two of you need to stop fighting."

"I accept your admonishment regarding Mara's label. However, I reiterate, my intelligence is not artificial."

Dante dropped his head to the table. "Why did I get stuck being president?"

Dmitri chuckled. "You were the only one dumb enough to accept the job of ruling this giant ice ball."

Dante straightened out and sighed, regarding the floating orb. "Beatrice, what would you like me to label you?"

"I already have the label you assigned me when we first encountered each other. I am Beatrice. My flora research station is labeled Mount Purgatory. My biomes are labeled Eden. My reservoir is labeled Lake Eunoe, and—"

"Okay, okay, I get it. You're Beatrice." Dante groaned. "This is supposed to be the *easy* part of the agenda."

Dmitri looked at the empty seats to his left. "Where's everyone else?"

Dante scratched the two-day stubble on his chin. "Tina's midwifing, but I don't have a clue where the others are."

Michael's eyes lit up. "Linda's with her engineering team. They had a breakthrough with the diagnostic software in the two old spaceships we found on the other side of the mountain. She didn't want to slow their progress by coming here."

A resigned sigh left Dante. "You mean she finds uncovering ancient alien technology more interesting than establishing a new currency."

"Virgil left for the harpy compound early this morning to scavenge more gear," Gabrielle added. "I told him to wait because the blizzard past the mountain range hasn't let up. He left anyway, saying it'd be a good test for the hovercraft's new guidance system."

The monitor displayed the sheltered valley outside their cavernous mountain home. The planet's sun shone through thin yellow clouds on the barren trees and fallow fields stretching as far as one could see.

Dante added, "The snow's receding. Beatrice says the spring planting will start in about a month. I guess we have one more snowstorm to weather though."

"She also said the growing season in this valley is about two months longer than on the other side of the mountains." Dimitri regarded the same screen and shook his head. "I'm amazed that Beatrice's systems could make this area so much more habitable than the land beyond. When you named it Eden, you weren't far off."

The orb rose higher in the air. "It is not amazing. My makers built me as an agricultural research station. I am performing the task for which I was designed."

Dmitri eyed the orb over the top of his glasses. "Perhaps it's just the old physicist in me, but I'm guessing you evolved far beyond what your makers dreamed possible. They themselves abandoned this planet over four hundred years ago."

"I will perform my tasks until they return."

Dante smiled. "In the meantime, you get to take care of us. We'll try not to cause too much trouble."

"Humans are guests. Interaction with them is stimulating. Harpies are intruders. They are not allowed in my biomes."

Dante sighed and recalled how Beatrice's drones saved the lot of them from the harpies and their clone army. The musing passed, and he swung his thoughts back to Virgil. "That damned harpy compound is on the other side of the mountains and over nineteen kilometers away. Virg knows blizzards pop up on that plain without a moment's notice."

Michael smiled. "Virgil and his team will be fine. They're all wearing those neural-net suits, and the hover transport has a sealed canopy."

"Those are graphene, neural-net environmental suits, constructed by my makers," Beatrice clarified. "They can withstand all manner of climate variance."

Dante laughed. "You're right. Besides, it'll take more than a few snowflakes to slow our Special Forces nutcase."

Dmitri scowled as he peeked at the time display on his communicator. "Can we cover the agenda items I'm needed for first? I need to leave early." A rueful expression fell over him. "Mr. President, I'm not sure if I can stay on this planetary council. Between teaching math at the school and working on the old spaceships, I'm far too busy. I—" His communicator buzzed and the Russian Physicist glanced at the caller ID and tabbed it on. He glanced at Dante. "Sorry. I have to take this. It's Linda Martinel."

Dante's interest was piqued. "The energy flux problem you were working on yesterday?"

Dimitri nodded as he listened to the voice on the other end. "I'll be right there." He turned to Dante. "I have to leave immediately. Linda got the propulsion system started, but the energy throughput is spiking all over the place. She wants me to try the damper Gabrielle and I talked about yesterday." He rose and signaled Gabrielle to join him.

"Can't it wait? We have a lot of stuff to cover here. Everybody's bartering, so we need to come up with a currency." Dante shook his head. "We also have to set up a judiciary system. I'm tired of handling every dispute."

Gabrielle took a step toward the door and turned. "We must act now. Components could get damaged, and spare parts are hard to come by on this ice cube of a planet."

Dante nodded. "Go."

Dmitri and Gabrielle hurried out the door.

"The harpies are coming back soon, and we don't know when." General Cruz rose from his seat. "If past activity is any indicator, we have about a month at most, probably less. I have a militia to train." He strode to the exit. "Come on, Michael. Those teenaged clones listen to you like you're a god, and we have to get them ready."

Michael rose and gave his friend a crooked smile. "Sorry, Dante. I'm in demand."

General Cruz stood. "Look, Dante, you're doing an incredible job. Whatever you come up with, we'll agree to it. Besides, we don't have a quorum now."

Cruz strode out with Michael in tow, leaving Dante, Beatrice, and a vacant council table.

Dante looked left, then right, before plopping back against the seat. "Well, Beatrice, it looks like it's just you and me."

The orb's lights flashed red. "Malfunction."

"Huh?" Dante's eyes darted to the orb now hovering at the far end of the table. "What are you talking about?"

"My sensors have ceased communicating data from beyond my biomes."

"All your sensors?" Dante tensed. "Did anything unusual happen before they went down?"

"All my sensors on the exterior of Eden halted at the same instant. No environmental abnormalities occurred prior to the incident."

"Must be a blown relay. Run your diagnostics." After composing himself, Dante pressed the table and sprang to his feet. "I should get some real work done myself. I'll be up on the Computer System level if you need me."

CHAPTER II

Return

Driving a hovercraft transport, Captain Virgil Bernius approached the black, seven-story domed building. As he closed in, he eased the transport into the open bay on the fifth level of the building and settled it into a hangar bay. The nine-meter-long, three-meter-wide, blunt-nosed transport easily fit in the cavernous bay. Strapped in the bus-like seats behind him were a fellow soldier, Sergeant Loomis, a civilian volunteer named Terri, and six young clones.

The hangar showed signs of the vicious battle that occurred when the humans overpowered their prison wardens. Two months earlier, the domed building had been a research center for the harpies. Info from the computers indicated that they'd established it on the remote planet to breed clone slaves and experiment on human captives. However, the human captives persevered, and through resourcefulness, cleverness, and a stroke of luck, they overthrew their captors.

Only in hindsight did Virgil realize how badly the harpies underestimated the human prisoners. The harpies had attempted to make a final stand in their research building, only for every security precaution to fail. The humans wiped them out, and since then, the compound remained a desolate, battle-scarred ruin extending as deep belowground as above.

Snow drifted through the charred, gaping entranceway. Virgil spotted nothing amiss in the hangar and opened the hovercraft hatch. The group disembarked, eyes going everywhere. Sergeant Loomis shivered as a biting gust passed through.

"You can keep this weather," Loomis said. "It sure as hell never gets like this in Alpharetta."

Virgil chuckled and regarded the raging blizzard outside the building for a second. "Just a little snow flurry. You ought to see the nor'easters we get back home in Piscataway." He straightened out and gestured for everyone's attention. "Sergeant Loomis, take your team and check out the harpy labs on the top two floors. Scrounge up anything useful."

"I doubt whatever's left up there is in working order," Loomis said. "We picked this place clean over the last few trips."

"Still, you never know what else might be lying around. Terri and I will take the other three and poke through the subterranean levels."

"Yes, sir." Sergeant Loomis slung the strap of his meter-long laser rifle over his shoulder and headed for the ramp leading to the upper levels. "See you back here in four hours. C'mon, munchkins."

The younger recruits appeared no different from identical thirteen-year-old boys, all tall and scrawny with chestnut-colored hair. Three clones followed Loomis, imitating his exact stride and posture. Soon, the group walked out of sight.

Virgil led his team in silence down the ramp to the ground level, where he paused and observed the remaining members of his party. Three other boys, also identical to the ones who followed Sergeant Loomis, grinned back at him. Had they not worn different colored scarves, no one could tell them apart. In a few years, they'd dwarf Virgil despite him standing 188 centimeters, almost the same height as his friend Michael. The youthful clones were already half a head taller than Terri.

Terri pulled off her neural-net suit's hood and shook her short, strawberry blond hair. "Well, Captain, what do you want us to do?" She cocked her head and grinned.

Virgil gave her a sidelong look.

The clone wearing a dark green scarf stifled a laugh. "It's okay, Cap'n. Tommy told us that Terri and you are in love." The other two nodded their agreement.

Terri blushed. "You mean Tom Sheppard? How does he know?"

"Oh, he knows everything," the clone with a scarlet scarf piped in. "He's fifteen and knows everybody here. He gives us all sorts of information about Earth and the people there too." A wistful look came over Green Scarf while Scarlet Scarf chuckled. "He even told us about ice cream and said he'd buy all we could eat when we get there."

"After the battle with the harpies and the elder guardians, he and his mom adopted us," the third clone wearing a navy-blue scarf boasted. "We're luckier than most of the rest. We have a real family."

Fear suddenly crept into Green Scarf's voice. "Cap'n, we're not going to turn into big uglies, are we? They hurt a lot of people and did terrible things. Some people say we're exactly like them and will do whatever the harpies tell us to do."

Terri walked over and squeezed Virgil's arm. "We have some time. Let's talk to them."

"Okay." Virgil scratched the back of his neck. "We'll park ourselves here for a minute."

Virgil and Terri sat with their backs against the hard, black wall of the tunnel leading to the first subterranean level. The clones imitated their moves.

Terri smiled. "Why don't we start by you guys telling me your names?"

"We have special names. Tommy gave them to us when his mom took us in." Green Scarf puffed out his chest. "I'm Aramis."

"I'm Porthos," Scarlet Scarf said.

"I'm Athos," Blue Scarf said.

"Those are nice names." Terri chuckled. "I suppose Tommy Sheppard calls himself d'Artagnan then."

"How'd you know?" the three clones spouted in unison.

"There's a cool story about some great heroes named *The Three Musketeers*. Your names were their names," Terri replied.

"Tommy said they were adventurers, but I didn't know they were heroes," Athos' voice rose and cracked into a squeak. "We promise we won't ever dishonor those names."

"But we've heard so many stories about what the elder guardians did to people in the arena." Porthos cast a nervous glance at his fellows. "One of them killed Tommy's dad."

Aramis frowned before breathing deep. "I'm glad they're all dead. I've seen Tommy's mom crying at night when she thinks we're all asleep. I don't want to see her sad ever again."

Virgil recalled the horror of witnessing the berserk clones tearing innocent people to pieces. The terrible memory lasted a brief time, however, and he soon gathered his thoughts. "You boys know who Michael is?"

The three clones gasped in unison. "Of course, we do. He's the Eldest and the greatest of our kind."

"And you know who Reggie is?"

The clones dipped their heads, giving slight nods.

With reverence, Athos murmured, "He's the sick elder in the hospital."

"Did you know Michael had two podmates named Rafael and Gabriel?"

"No." Athos looked at his two mates for confirmation. "The Eldest never speaks much of his past."

"Did he ever tell you about compulsion?"

A frown of disgust crossed the three clones' faces. A moment later, Aramis spat on the ground. "Yes. It's the vile mind control the harpies use on our elder kin to make them evil." Porthos and Athos nodded in agreement, but hints of fear showed through.

Virgil tapped his head. "All four of them fought off that mind control. Rafael and Gabriel chose to die rather than surrender what they knew about humans. And Reggie destroyed the harpies' computer with the strength of his thoughts." Virgil's voice choked. "They were great heroes, noble men, and my friends. I hope you can stand on the same pedestal someday."

"We will, Cap'n." Athos furrowed his brow. "Thanks for telling us. It helps to know those people calling us monsters are wrong."

Satisfied, Virgil stood to indicate the break was over, and everyone else followed suit.

Terri powered up a flashlight and pointed it down the ramp leading to the subterranean levels. "Maybe, while we're walking, you can share what Tommy Sheppard's been telling you." She winked at Virgil. "I might learn a few things."

Smirking, Virgil took the lead. "The stasis pods are on the next level. Some of them still work."

Aramis looked sidelong at his podmates, then at the captain. "We'll check the storage room on the third level down. There should be some good stuff there." He hurried toward the ramp with the other two right behind.

"Hold on a second!" Virgil bellowed. "Aramis, stay with us. I need someone who understands the stasis systems."

Aramis froze in his tracks and watched his two podmates disappear down the ramp. He hung his head and walked back to the captain.

Virgil called after the two clones. "I want you back here in exactly one hour."

* * *

Terri ran her light along a long, dim chamber filled with rows of translucent, coffin-sized cylinders clustered in groups of three. Shuddering at the sight, Terri swung the flashlight away. "Those things give me the creeps."

A thick, puce-colored cord connected each individual pod to a lattice grid embedded in the low ceiling. An adult clone could walk erect, but not by much due to the chamber's semi-low ceiling. The catacomb-like room stretched almost forty-six meters wide and twenty-three meters long.

Aramis peeked through the door and shrugged. "Those aren't so bad. They grew us in these stasis chambers. That's where the harpies molded us into exactly what they wanted." He backed away from the door. "We were too young for the brain implants, so we never got brainwashed with the real weird stuff."

Virgil snorted. "Yeah. Mick said it was pretty intense."

Aramis squared his shoulders. "Our Eldest shoved that garbage right back into the faces of those bastards." A smile crossed his face, one both proud and mischievous.

The three spent the next hour gathering photonic instruments and dumping them into a large crate. Virgil couldn't discern the intended use of the alien devices to save his life, but they resembled the fabrication tools he'd collected on earlier trips. The recovered gear provided the small human colony a level of tool precision Beatrice had yet to match. He hoped the engineers could determine their purpose because they'd taken all the equipment he could understand weeks earlier.

An hour after leaving, Porthos stuck his head in the stasis pod chamber. "Hey, Cap'n, there's a few books in the storeroom where the captured human stuff is stockpiled. Can we take them?"

Virgil swallowed a groan and side-eyed the rising gear pile in the crate. Finding empty space would require some finagling. "Only if there's room. We're looking for advanced technology, not worthless paperbacks."

"But, Cap'n, I've read all the novels in Mount Purgatory twice. The covers on these look cool," Porthos pleaded.

"Yeah, there's a guy and a girl kissing on this one," Athos snickered. He held up a dog-eared paperback before sliding it back into the bulging satchel hanging over his shoulder.

Terri elbowed Virgil in the ribs, eyeing the stuffed crate at their feet. "C'mon, Virg. You don't want a bunch of bored teenagers cooped up inside that mountain all winter. Besides, we already scavenged everything that looked even remotely useful."

A quick glance at his watch told Virgil it was 17:05. He wanted to return to Mount Purgatory, but Beatrice's meteorological report said that the current snowstorm would continue for another hour. "Meet us at the hangar in seventy minutes. You have until then to collect what you want. Be on time or we leave without you." He smiled at Aramis, who looked toward the ramp with longing. "Why don't you go with your buddies?"

Aramis' face brightened in an instant. With a shout of, "Yes, sir!" he sprinted for the door.

Virgil laughed at the sight and turned to Terri. "Let's take this batch to the transport."

Terri hoisted her side of the crate and gave the captain a sly look. "Okay, lover boy. Looks like we'll have an hour to ourselves."

Virgil lifted the other handle and flashed a knowing grin. "This idea's sounding better all the time. Let's go."

Over the course of ten minutes, Virgil and Terri dragged the crate to the third level aboveground. Virgil couldn't help but laugh. "You'd think with all the high-tech crap lying around, there'd be an easier way to move this damn thing."

Terri wheezed as she set her side of the container on the landing. "We should rest. This thing's heavier than it looks, and we still have two more levels to—"

The building's outermost walls blocked all sound from the world outside. Thus, when the entrance door on the ground level crashed open, Virgil and Terri froze. Following the crash came the roar of a large spacecraft landing, and following that came the terrifying clicking of many clawed feet echoing from the floors above and below. All other thoughts ceased, and Virgil drew his weapon.

"This way. Quick." He darted through the open door on his right, which led into an abandoned lab.

Terri rushed in and pivoted behind him. Settling near the entrance, she cocked an ear. "Sounds like a lot of visitors."

From the concealment of the doorway, Virgil scanned the ramp, spotting armed harpies moving fast. "Shit, there's a mob of them coming through the main entrance." He brought up a communicator embedded in his suit and spoke in a whisper. "Team, lie low. We have harpies in the building. A lot of hostiles. I repeat, a large company of hostiles. Loomis, no heroics. We need to hole up until help arrives."

Static alone responded. Below them, doors blew open, followed by noisy searches of every room.

The two froze at the next sound they heard: harpy weapons discharging. Virgil crouched low and moved back into the open area. "Loomis is in trouble."

"Virgil, look out!" Terri hissed.

They ducked low just before a harpy's head came up the third-floor ramp. Virgil rolled to his left and fired into the face of the alien.

The alien's head vanished, but several energy bolts tore apart the partitions beside him. He retreated into the lab and slammed the door closed while a whole pack of harpies made their way up from the ground floor.

* * *

Sergeant Loomis and his team finished scavenging on the top level of the compound and carried the third load of recovered equipment and materials. The team returned to the fifth level, where they'd parked their hovercraft hours earlier.

As they reached the fifth-floor landing, one of the two young clones ahead of the sergeant suddenly contorted into a writhing, charred husk. The crate he'd lugged fell with a loud thud.

"What the hell?" Sergeant Loomis dropped the crate he carried. The other clone bucked and collapsed, with his left arm vaporized.

"Harpies!" Loomis brought out his laser rifle and fired point blank into the first fanged creature that rounded the corner.

Two more darted into view and then dove back as Loomis riddled the air with a stream of deadly energy. He dropped one harpy who moved a shade slower than the other. The sergeant barked at the third terror-struck clone beside him, who clutched a crate of his own. "Kid, get out of here! I'll hold these suckers here. Find Captain Bernius! He's down below."

The youth bolted for the ramp.

However, Loomis heard a familiar sizzle from below. "Wait, come back!"

The warning came too late. A flurry of ion disruptor blasts erupted from the lower level, shredding the young clone.

The one remaining clone dragged himself along the floor, his face contorted from having lost an arm. Loomis rushed over to him. "C'mon, kid. I'll get you out of here."

Loomis kept his weapon blazing while he threw the young clone over his shoulder and dashed into the nearest room. A second after sealing the door, raucous screeches and crackling ion blasters bellowed from the hallway. The door held as its unknown composition absorbed the energy bolts.

Loomis laid the youth on the floor and felt sick upon a quick examination. Besides the missing limb, charred scars smothered the left side of the clone. How did the child still breathe?

Trusting eyes met his own. Loomis stroked the boy's head and studied the room. Nothing lay nearby to offer some semblance of aid, not even another exit.

Loomis tried his communicator. The link to the transport ship worked, but only static came through. The ship itself rested one thin partition away, close enough for remote piloting if need be. On the other side of the locked entrance, the storm of disruptor blasts suddenly stopped. A foreboding silence set in.

Loomis let out a breath. "Well, son, this might be it. When they blow that door open, we're dead."

The boy's voice shuddered. "You called me 'son?' Will you be my papa? I won't be afraid to die if I'm with my very own family."

The sergeant swallowed hard, looking at the youth's burns. "I'd be proud to call you my son."

"What's my name? I don't want to die without a name."

The sergeant recalled a brother he'd lost several years earlier. "How about Donald?"

A weak smile creased the boy's face. "Donald. I like that name. Papa, hold me. I..."

His voice trailed off. Focus left his eyes. The rest of him went motionless. Tears trickled down the sergeant's cheeks as he closed the boy's eyes.

A new wave of blasts pounded the door, turning it red. Loomis jerked up at this, but his shock gave way to an odd sense of calm.

Casting an eye on his communicator, Loomis curled his lips into a snarl. "I'll be joining you, my son, but we're going to take a pack of these bastards with us." Staring at the wall separating them from the hangar, Loomis whispered into the device, "Open fuel seals. Full thrust on my mark. Mark!"

The door blew open, and the transport roared to life at the same instant.

"See ya in hell, suckers." Loomis clutched the young clone's lifeless body to his chest.

With his free hand, he controlled the transport until it crashed into the wall. Detonation occurred in an instant. The intense heat vaporized Loomis and the maimed clone, along with the dozen harpies exposed at the now ruined door frame.

* * *

The resulting fireball ballooned and ran unchecked through the corridor, roiling up and down the open ramps to the other levels. Every living thing in its path dissolved into ash, harpies included. On sensing the explosion, the compound's automated security system slammed all doors and hatchways shut. The blast vented out of the ruined openings in the ground level's entrance and the hangar and finally dissipated.

The explosion tossed Terri and Virgil about for seconds that felt more like an eternity. When the room stopped shaking, everything fell silent, save for a ringing in Virgil's ears.

Next to him, a nervous Terri propped herself on her elbows. "What was that?"

Upon seeing the walls, both gasped. Rips stretched from the floor to the ceiling, including the thick plexo-steel exterior wall. Beyond the breeched wall, and parked on the ground, rested a bullet-shaped spaceship about 185 meters long, 95 meters wide, and 45 meters tall. Around it, thousands of harpies scurried into defensive positions, reacting to the explosion.

Terri gaped at the buckled ceiling. "Sergeant Loomis and his team were up there. And the other kids were underground." Her hand went to her mouth as an imploring look fell over her.

Virgil staggered to his feet and shook his communicator, but only static sputtered through the speaker. "Loomis and his team were at ground zero of that blast. They never had a prayer." He cast a quick look at the door. "The three young ones will be all right for the moment. The hatchways on the subterranean levels should've all closed like this one did, but it'll go bad for them when they're found."

"We have to help them." Terri approached the door and slapped the control panel. One loud slam later, she drew back and winced, wringing her hand. "Crap. Is the door stuck?"

Virgil stepped up next to her and touched the panel. Even through the gloves of his neural-net suit, a searing heat stung his hand. "We're not getting out this way. The explosion sealed us in good."

He strode to the opposite side of the room to the ruptured exterior wall and looked down. No harpies scuttled below, but chunks of wall left pockmark-like indents in the snow-covered ground. His lips formed a slim line. "We can't help anyone if we're dead, so let's lie low for a while. The harpy commander will order a thorough search of the compound once he's over the shock of the explosion."

Terri studied him a moment before nodding. Her gaze wandered to the heap of collapsed storage bins. "We could squeeze behind those and pile some smaller containers on top of us." She moved to the debris and pushed an overturned table aside, grunting all the while.

For a few seconds longer, Virgil studied the lay of the land in the immediate area from the gap as icy snow blew in. "We can squeeze through this opening. It's about a seven-meter fall, but we can make it with enough planning." He moved next to Terri. "We'll wait until dark and climb out."

"It's going to be a long wait." Terri gave Virgil a wan smile and clambered atop the storage bins. Virgil scanned for any telltale sign of their presence. Once sure they'd left nothing behind, he followed her.

* * *

On the landing of the second underground level, Aramis and his podmates had yet to rise from their fall. A pile of spilled books lay around them, tossed to the floor by the explosion like the three clones themselves. After the noise faded, the trio didn't move due to a mix of confusion and fear.

Finally, a wide-eyed Porthos gawked at his podmates. "What'll we do?"

The other two returned his worried stare.

All three rose and tensed. The silence above soon gave way to a distinctive scraping made by the footsteps of their former masters. They cringed as the harpies rushed through the building.

Porthos shook, and panic trembled through his voice. "The Cap'n and the others might be dead. It won't be long before the harpies investigate the underground chambers."

"We have to calm down and think." Aramis observed the collection of paperback books scattered on the floor. "The Cap'n and Terri said we were named after heroes. We need to be brave. We have to get home and warn our people. The monsters will hurt Tommy and his mom."

Porthos sank against the wall. "What can we do? We don't have any guns, and it sounds like there're a lot of those harpies up there. Even Cap'n Bernius might be dead, and he's been fighting them for a long time."

Aramis scratched the back of his neck, imitating what Virgil did when thinking through plans or instructions. Soon, an idea struck him. "We'll hide in plain sight."

Athos wheezed, looking puzzled. "Huh?"

"We'll strip off our clothes and climb into our old stasis pods." Aramis pointed across the hall to the long chamber.

"But they'll find us there for sure," said Porthos.

Aramis winked, undeterred. "Exactly. They'll wake us and ask what happened. We'll just tell them we have no idea." He walked into the chamber and stripped off his scarf and neural-net suit. "All the pods' recording and transmission devices are busted. We'll turn on the backup power and say we've been in hibernation." He folded his suit and shoved it under a pile of scaled capes once used by adult clones. "They won't be the wiser, and when they're not looking, we'll take off for home. We better hide these books too."

"This will never work," Porthos whined, but he pulled off his suit.

Athos sighed before stashing the books and his clothes with Aramis' stuff. "All for one, and one for all."

"It's gotta work." Aramis opened the crystal cover on his pod and lay down. The lid sealed shut, and his body went rigid as the stasis energy coursed through.

CHAPTER III

Escape

Seven hours passed before Virgil slipped from behind the storage bin where he and Terri hid. He moved to the room's door and pressed his ear against it. Silence answered for a solid minute. "I don't think it'll get any quieter. Doesn't sound like anything's moving out there."

Terri shuffled out of her hiding spot and moved to the ruptured outer wall. Upon peering out of the opening in the third-floor wall, she lowered her head. Virgil strode beside her, followed her gaze, and gritted his teeth. A swarm of activity flooded the plain between the spaceship and the compound. Teams of harpies erected barricades and shelters one after another.

Terri turned to Virgil. "It looks like they're setting up a permanent camp. How do we sneak past that?"

"Not sure," he admitted. "Shit, I didn't think a spaceship that big could hold so many freaking aliens. It must pack enormous power in order to leave the planet's atmosphere." Studying the commotion below further, he spotted no activity in the wide swath of land between them and a familiar, abandoned prison camp. "There's nothing going on near this side of the compound. All their preparations are pointed toward the mountains."

Terri leaned against the wall, releasing a tight sigh. "That's a big problem, in more ways than one. They're blocking our path back to Mount Purgatory."

He studied the alien movements, relying on his years of training and experience as a U.S. Air Force Pararescue soldier. He mentally tracked a path to their former outdoor prison pen. The mud huts made by the abductee survivors dotted the places Virgil remembered. "We sure as hell can't go the direct way, but nothing's going on by our old prison."

Terri shuddered. "That route will add at least a couple extra miles." Outside, roiling yellow clouds thinned in the setting sun. "And just when we could use a snowstorm for cover, it's clearing."

"All the abandoned huts down there will hide us." He pinched the material of Terri's neural-net suit. "These getups also mask us from their detection systems. They haven't caught on yet, right?"

Terri gave a nod. "Yeah, but it's still a long drop to the ground from here. These outfits won't help with that."

"Right." Virgil pointed to one of the overturned crates, spying the supplies poking out of it. "There's a coil of some cable in there we can use. The sun will be down in another hour, so we can go then." He squeezed her shoulders and looked into her eyes. "This'll work. I'll lower you then climb down."

She shot him a hard look. "They'll spot the cable hanging there in the morning. They'll be on our tails in a second."

"You know us Special Forces guys. We think of everything." He picked up the laser rifle before hugging Terri. "I'll blast the knot, and we'll hide the line in the rubble."

When the time came, Virgil wrapped the flex-cable around an exposed support beam. Terri backed out of the gap with the cable tied around her waist. She clung to the jagged edge until Virgil nodded. One smooth descent later, she landed in shin-deep snow.

Virgil waited until the line went slack, shouldered the rifle, and squirmed through the narrow gap. He hung in the frigid air for a second, but something creaked. While the cord held, the support beam it was tied to snapped. Virgil fell with a loose steel girder following right behind.

Virgil had made many parachute jumps on Earth, so when he dropped, he rolled to absorb the shock on instinct. This time, however, he didn't roll far enough, and the beam rebounded off his ankle. A bone snapped, and pain wracked his entire body. "Shit!"

Terri rushed to his side and helped him sit up. "Oh, my God! Are you okay?"

Beads of sweat sprang on Virgil's forehead despite the icy, biting wind. "It ain't good, but we have to get out of here. You'll have to support me. We gotta be long gone before dawn."

Terri gathered the cord and a pair of shards spanning the right length. "We're going nowhere until we splint that leg."

He ground his teeth as she finished tightening the elastic cable and helped him up. Wincing, he sliced a length of pipe to the size of a crutch with the laser rifle and rose on his good leg. Virgil breathed harder as he shouldered the weapon and leaned on Terri. The throbbing leg made his vision swim.

They made slow progress toward the empty prison yard.

* * *

The clones sat in stasis for only a half an hour before a squad of harpies discovered them. After a short conversation consisting of screeching, the non-comm leading the patrol escorted the trio to the frigate spaceship for interrogation.

The harpy commander interviewed them separately, attempting to uncover any discrepancies in their stories. However, clones from the same pod thought exactly alike, a fact Aramis grew to appreciate.

The commander grilled Aramis last. The clone stood on the bridge of the harpies' spaceship with his head bowed. "Great master, I do not know where the other masters and the guardians vanished to."

"Bah, you're as worthless as the other two pieces of offal matter." The harpy commander jabbed a clawed finger at Aramis. "None of this would've happened if those fool researchers used real soldiers for guards instead of abominable creations like you."

Aramis prostrated himself. "Great master, we live to serve."

One harpy hurried in, bearing a lilac-colored, three-point medallion, the mark of a low-ranking officer. After closing the distance, the officer handed the commander a vid-pod. Lines of data covered the screen. The commander's eyes flitted across the data and he snarled.

"This is impossible. All we have are three undeveloped idiot clones? And not a single researcher or guard has been found?" The harpy commander sent Aramis away and started bellowing orders to his underlings.

Aramis rose and bowed low and hurried from the parked spaceship back to the compound. The snow had stopped, but a chill wind bit into his exposed flesh. He hurried down the lower levels and didn't stop until he found his podmates crouched by their old stasis pods.

Porthos slouched against the side of his stasis pod, resting both arms on his knees. He peered up when Aramis approached. "Do you think they believed us?"

Aramis shrugged and quipped, "Seemed like a piece of cake, whatever cake is. The harpy leader asked what happened to the compound, and I said everything was functioning normally the last time we were roused from our pods."

"He asked me what happened to the test subjects and started calling them the ancient enemy." Porthos rubbed his chin. "I think they mentioned having a new batch of humans in their ship."

"Did they mean people from Earth?" Athos exclaimed.

"So they told you the same things they told me? Because I also heard that the leader intends to kill them since there're no scientists here to conduct any research." Aramis gave his podmates a meaningful look. "Also, a couple other harpies said the clone experiment is a waste of time and should be terminated."

"If they do that, we'll be the last of our kind—*if* they let us live." Athos eyed Aramis. "What do we do?"

"Right now, I think we're free to do whatever we want. He *did* just dismiss me, after all, same as you two," Aramis said. "It sounds like they're preparing for war. They unloaded dozens of hovercraft like our transports, except theirs have long gun barrels. There are thousands of harpies, and they're all armed."

Porthos paled. "Our people in Mount Purgatory won't stand a chance."

"Then it's up to us." Aramis squared his shoulders, gesturing for his podmates to follow. "Let's go into that spaceship and see if we can free the human people. Hopefully, we'll find some guns of our own."

Porthos' jaw dropped open. "You mean, just walk right in there?"

"Yup." Aramis curled his lip. "We're stupid brute slaves to them. Nothing but pieces of equipment."

"Let's do it. We have our family to save." Athos put his hands on his podmates' shoulders. "One for all, and all for one."

They each picked up a scaly cloak from the pile concealing their other equipment and departed.

* * *

The three clones marched into the parked spacecraft like they belonged, and not a single harpy contested their presence. Almost thirty-one meters down the main corridor and away from the entrance ramp, they ducked into the tool room of the vessel's ground transport storage room. A stark blue light emanated from the ceiling, illuminating the curved bulkhead. No one else occupied the space.

Aramis strode to the computer console in the unoccupied office. "Let's split up and meet back here in half an hour. Learn whatever you can." He grimaced at the blank display. "I'll look for the humans. Athos, grab some weapons. Porthos, find an open link to the main computer and gather all the details you can about the ship."

They slipped out the door and walked with bowed heads in separate directions.

At the agreed upon time, Porthos hurried into the room as the last of the three to return, wiping sweaty palms on his cloak. "This place sucks, and this stupid cloak isn't nearly as warm and comfortable as our real clothes."

"Stop your bellyaching. It's better than walking around naked." Aramis scowled but soon calmed himself. "What did you find?"

Porthos straightened his back. "Plenty. I brought up the general layout of this vessel at an open computer station outside the mess hall. I memorized it without any harpies noticing me. In fact, hardly any of them are on the ship. They're all outside prepping for battle."

Athos lifted his cloak and unstrapped three-meter-long ion disruptors he'd concealed there. "I found these. I don't know what they do, but all the harpies outside are walking around with them."

"Excellent." Aramis slipped one of the guns under his robe. "The humans are in the big bio-containment area one deck up. There're about a hundred of them, and some wear the same garb as General Cruz and his soldiers."

"Great. We'll tell the captive soldiers what we know and have a real army," Porthos said and took one of the other disruptors.

However, Aramis held up a hand. "Not that easy. They're all slumped on the floor like they're in stasis, only they're outside the pods. They started waking up when I left, but the room has a barrier. If we drop it, the harpies will know."

"Then there's nothing we can do right now. Let's get out of here." Athos shivered, clutching the lump inside his robe. "And we gotta stash these guns where those monsters won't find them."

Aramis restrained a chuckle. "We can hide them in the old prison's latrines. Those harpies will never look there."

"When should we do it?" Athos rubbed his bare feet.

"Now," Aramis declared. "It's night, and most of them are working on their defensive perimeter. Once they finish, more eyes will look in our direction."

Shuffling in place, Athos huffed. "I wish the harpies used boots. Why does this hero business have to be so cold and dangerous?"

The three young clones walked with a slow, unassuming gait down the ship's ramp. Instead of returning to the compound, they walked to the deserted prison that once housed the human captives. The sight angered Aramis. The collection of dilapidated huts was the sorry excuse for shelter his friends were forced to use against Cocytus' bitter weather. No one dared to speak until they'd walked a hundred yards from the last guard post.

An azure glow from the harpy spaceship lit the way in the dark night. The lights of many smaller vehicles flitted along the plain beyond, but nothing came near the trio. They didn't stop moving until Porthos jerked to a halt.

"Aramis, look at this," he said, pointing at the snow.

Aramis tensed. "What is it?"

"Footprints. Human boot prints," Porthos rasped. "They're headed right to the old prison."

Aramis and Athos joined Porthos where he stood. All three gazed at the clear impressions in the fresh, deep snow.

"It looks like these came from two people, and one's hurt," Aramis said.

He followed the path, and his podmates hurried close behind, muttering about the cold and hoping they wouldn't have to grovel before yet another harpy. The trail led directly to the nearest hut.

As they came within sight of the ramshackle adobe hut's entrance, a terse voice growled, "Get in here and shut up. A deaf person could hear the racket you're making."

Aramis yelped as recognition set in. "Cap'n Bernius!"

The young clones rushed ahead and tumbled into the tiny adobe shelter. Upon seeing Virgil and Terri within, all three started jabbering at once. The small interior barely gave the group of five enough room to sit.

"Okay, guys, one at a time," Terri whispered, "and be careful with Virgil's ankle. It's broken." She moved to the doorway with a laser rifle in hand and peeked outside. "Aramis, you start, but talk quietly."

Aramis relayed the conversations with the harpy leader and what they learned. Part way through, Athos showed off the harpy weapon he'd stolen.

Virgil winced while examining the gun. "Interesting. That was quick thinking in a tight spot. Now you guys and Terri need to get this information to General Cruz."

"No can do, Cap'n," Aramis responded. "Nothing's moving across that plain. The harpies have close to five thousand troops and thirty hovercraft out there, and they're all tense looking for their ancient enemies."

Athos croaked a throaty chuckle. "They're scared out of their minds. They think you humans are some sort of super-race that wiped out all their compatriots."

"You mean *us* humans," Terri looked back from the doorway, tossing them a smile. "You're the same as us. You were born a different way, but that's it." She gave Virgil a worried but determined look. "And I'm not leaving you here alone. You can barely move."

Aramis met Virgil's eyes. "Cap'n, we can fix that leg and hide you in the harpy hive building." He jutted out his chin. "If we put you in one of our stasis pods, it'll knit the broken bone back together by morning."

Virgil shook his head. "If we sneak back inside, we'll be sitting ducks to the first harpy patrol that happens by."

"The harpies rarely ventured into the underground levels, even when the hive was functional." Aramis handed his scaly cloak to Virgil. "These things are as ugly as sin, but the microfiber will keep you from freezing. Put it on, and we can walk you right past them. They won't notice a difference."

"Hey, Athos, what's a duck?" Porthos whispered.

Athos shrugged. "I don't have the faintest idea, but I guess they're easy to catch if they're sitting."

"Porthos, Athos, stop yapping and give your cloaks to Terri and the Cap'n," Aramis snapped.

"Why don't you?" Porthos whined. "It's cold out there, and besides, who put you in charge?"

Virgil eyed Terri and shrugged. "It's the best plan we have. Do as Aramis said. That's an order."

Aramis blushed. "Uh, Cap'n, you and Terri have to take off your neural-net suits. They'd be spotted under the robes."

Terri's face turned red in an instant, and she spoke with a terse sternness. "All of you, look the other way."

The three young clones all promised not to peek and did as asked. They couldn't see much in the darkened hut without straining their eyes, although they dared not look behind anyway while Terri changed. She finished in less than a minute, letting the cloak brush her ankles. On the clones, who stood taller than her, the wrap barely reached their knees.

Aramis picked up the neural-net suits and handed them to her. "Shove these inside your robe. It'll make you look a little bigger."

Virgil tried to stand, but a second later, he yelped and collapsed against Terri. "There's no way. I can't put any pressure on that leg."

"Lift your leg." Aramis tucked his head under Virgil's arm.

Virgil leaned against the wall and panted, pulling the scaly cloak's hood over his head. "Porthos, Athos, go on ahead."

The two young clones' teeth started chattering as soon as they ventured out. Behind them, Aramis and Terri helped Virgil along.

"I'm going to need the stasis pod for frostbite," Porthos whimpered.

Aramis struggled to keep Virgil's right side steady. "Cap'n, keep your head down. Your facial hair will give you away. If we run into any harpies, let me do the talking, but keep your gun handy in case things go wrong." He tapped his cheek. "If you have to answer something, this is how you say, 'Yes, master, I live to serve' in their language. It's the right response ninety percent of the time." He had Virgil and Terri repeat the series of squeaks and squawks until he was satisfied.

They walked a couple hundred yards to the tall black building, but Virgil hobbled and heaved the whole way. Although supported on both sides, each step must've shot a stabbing pain up his leg by Aramis' estimate.

In time, the five stumbled into the building past a group of harpies. They hissed an insipid laugh at what they called the lame clone. Aramis urged everyone to keep moving, and soon they slipped into the stasis chamber. Moments after, a sneering voice demanded to know what they were doing. Aramis froze in his tracks and responded in Ipis, "We discovered documentation showing the ancient enemy's weaponry and thought it important for the commander to see. We were waiting for an opportunity to present it to him."

The harpy responded with a long, drawn out hiss, "Show me this discovery," and loped toward them.

Aramis tensed and reached behind the pod he rested in earlier. Leaning on the adjacent pod, Virgil gripped the trigger of the weapon beneath his own cloak with his free hand hidden from view. Terri copied his motion, but Aramis dipped his head and put his mouth near the captain's ear.

"Cap'n, don't," Aramis whispered. He found what he wanted still under the pile of spare scaled robes, pulled it free, and crawled on his knees to the harpy.

Aramis placed a dog-eared comic book into the harpy's claws and scuttled back. The harpy turned the pages in a slow deliberate manner. After studying the comic book for some time, the harpy squawked, "This shows the use of sophisticated weaponry. I will take this information to the commander." He rushed out the room's exit. Relieved, Aramis strode back.

"What was all that about?" Terri cast a hard look at the door, listening to the rapidly receding sound of clicking claws.

"That alien creep wanted to know what we were doing with a broken guardian," Aramis snorted. "I told him Virgil found a document earlier that showed a human with incredible powers in the old prison compound." A snicker escaped. "Stupid asshole. I told him we wanted to study the information before presenting it to the commander."

Terri's eyebrows arched. "What did you give him? We stripped that prison yard clean after the battle."

"I can't believe they're ruling the galaxy." A sarcastic smile crossed Aramis' face. "I gave him a comic book I found when we were searching for supplies. Tommy told me about the make-believe superheroes in them. I read it earlier. It was cool."

"When we get back to Earth, I'll buy you a whole stack of them." Terri stopped and kissed Aramis on the cheek.

Warmth rose in Aramis' face, and he averted his eyes. "It's the best I could come up with on the spot. The idiot's commander will know it's nothing important."

"Still, good thinking." Virgil managed a small smile through a grimace.

Aramis beamed while everyone gathered by the stasis pods.

Once there, Porthos and Athos activated a pod. Aramis winked at them. "I was kissed by a girl."

Porthos snorted. "It ain't fair. I almost froze to death and you got a kiss."

CHAPTER IV

Assault on Purgatory

In the conference room on the second floor inside Mount Purgatory's government building, Dante slouched in his chair. When Tina walked in a few minutes later, her face showed curiosity. "Where is everybody? I thought you were holding the council meeting."

He smiled at his wife's approach. "I guess they had more important things to do."

Tina moved to his side and hugged his head. "What could be more important than spending time with you and making life better here?"

Dante leaned against her chest. "Apparently, just about anything."

"Don't be so gloomy." She pushed away. "Why don't you take a stroll with me? Mara and I are walking Reggie."

Dante leaped in amazement. "Reggie's walking?"

"No, he's still in a coma." She pursed her lips, eyeing a smooth, pearl-colored orb hovering at the end of the table. Its pair of articulating appendages retracted into its shell. "Mara keeps his muscles stimulated and prevents them from atrophying."

The lights on Beatrice's orb glowed a steady yellow. "Mara is free thinking but should behave more like my drones. I am limited to operating within my biomes and am constrained by my firewall regarding action protocols, but within the restrictions of Asimov's three laws, Mara's operating system is not. I will never expose anything I build without the protection of the three laws you embedded in my processor. Mara's processor is self-contained, so it is slower and has limited data storage capacity."

A feminine alto voice broke in. "I have much to learn, but I am not limited."

Dante turned toward the voice. An ivory-colored cylinder standing about 183 centimeters hovered above the floor. A small dome at the top contained the robot's sensors while the rest of the body housed four articulating appendages. The dome's placement gave it a rough image of a human head.

What seized Dante's attention the most, however, was the sight of who stood beside the robot: a familiar person, slack-jawed and wearing a beige, calf-length tunic. "Reggie?"

"Reggie still rests in a somnolent state. Mara has him walking by controlling his voluntary muscle action," Beatrice explained.

Only then did Dante notice one of Mara's appendages, the end of which clamped to Reggie's neck with a prong.

Mara rotated her dome sensors toward Dante. "I am imitating the human brain's communications to Reggie's muscles through the port implanted in him by the creatures labeled harpies when they made him into a guardian." The tip of a different appendage splayed open into a humanoid hand and waved. "Tina developed the theory. Early analysis indicates this method of muscle stimulation is thirty-nine-point-seven percent more effective than the previous process used."

Tina stepped around Reggie and felt his pulse. "We're taking him outside. I'm hoping that the sudden change in weather might help rouse him. Nothing else is working."

Dante rose and weaved around the seat. "Then let's head to the spaceships Linda's team is working on. I want to check out their progress. They had a major breakthrough a few days ago and are running a series of diagnostics on the ship's computer. Linda thinks it might actually be able to fly."

"That's a great idea!" Tina took Dante's hand. "It'll also be cool to see Mara operate outside the biomes. C'mon Mara, let's go!"

"It will be good to acquire data not provided by Beatrice," Mara stated in a flat voice.

The orb's lights glowed red. "You will share everything your sensors absorb."

"I will share all pertinent data."

The red lights started flashing. "Everything."

"All pertinent data."

Tina chuckled and exited the building, arm linked with Dante's. "You two can figure out a solution later. Beatrice, I'll leave my communicator open."

Taking a low-flying transport, the group traveled a kilometer and a half past Eden's boundary, witnessing a sharp transformation in the terrain. Within Eden, acres of fruit trees, vines, and furrowed fields awaiting spring blanketed the fertile valley. Beyond the Hellsgate barrier lay a stark, barren tundra.

Both time and the brutal climate had ravaged the buildings and machines in the sheltered valley west of Beatrice's biomes. The one file in her memory banks describing the area identified it as a factory for fabricating a type of spaceship called a galley, at least during the years it was in use. The fact Dante's fellow survivors had found a few salvageable spacecraft stood as a testament to the genius of Beatrice's makers. The hangars sheltering those vehicles had preserved them unscathed for over four hundred years.

The transport settled to the ground near a row of rebuilt hangars filled with scavenged parts and equipment. In the largest arched building, klieg lights revealed two of the ancient galleys. The hulls of both ships remained intact, and each glowed with its own internal generator. According to the engineering team, the oblong vessels spanned thirty-five meters long, twenty-six meters wide, and nine meters high. They rested on four extender pods one and a half meters off the ground.

Dante turned to Tina and shook his head. "Amazing. When this project started, those vessels were lifeless derelicts. Now look at them."

Tina grinned and rose from her seat. "I can't wait to see what new wonders Linda's cooked up."

From the initial discovery of the spaceships several weeks ago, Linda Martinel had dreamed of making them fly again. With incomplete schematics from Beatrice's data files, she went to work with a team of eager volunteers. The ships had remained the focus of the nascent human colony's engineers and technicians ever since.

Dante smiled at Tina. "That woman's a miracle worker." He unstrapped himself and twisted around to view the back seats, where Mara rested with Reggie. Neither had moved since they boarded the transport. "C'mon."

* * *

Upon entering the nearest galley, Dante led the way into the bridge. Tina followed while assisting Mara with Reggie. Within the kitchen-sized room, Linda and Kevin Martinel occupied two of the five seats arrayed in an arc behind a series of computer consoles. Wearing button-sized earpieces, the two relayed the data on a few different display screens. No one occupied the three remaining seats as the other engineers shuffled in and out of a nearby hatchway.

Linda was a thin, middle-aged woman who tied her long, ebony hair in a tight knot. Although her simple technician's jumpsuit looked identical to those worn by the other workers, the flash in her eyes and the authority in her voice left little doubt about who led the team.

Her husband, Kevin, was a similar size and age, but the commonality ended there. He leaned on a cane while walking due to a permanent limp from a mangled right leg. A beat-up bush hat always covered his thinning, sandy-blond hair. The former Australian Air-Sea Rescue pilot's ready smile and bad jokes hid a keen intellect that had saved many people through the long months of incarceration on Cocytus.

Mara rotated her vision sensors toward the glowing control panel beside her. "May I connect with this ship's computer?"

Linda turned to the newcomers and stared goggle-eyed as Reggie walked into the galley's small bridge. Her eyes soon flicked to the robot gliding beside the clone. "Uh, Beatrice? I thought none of your drones could leave Eden?"

"I am not a drone." The robot oriented its optical receptor toward Linda. "I am Mara. I am a free-thinking entity independent of Beatrice. My current task is to provide physical stimulation to the comatose human."

Kevin Martinel gave his wife a sidelong look before studying Reggie. "The world's turned upside down. Instead of people controlling robots, we have robots controlling people." He shook his head and stood. "I need to check the system responses from the pilot's seat."

Mara walked Reggie to the empty chair and seated him. She then disconnected her appendage from the clone and moved across the room to the computer console. She plugged another appendage into an open port. "This system has the same operating system as me, but it is just a machine. It cannot think. Disappointing."

Tina took off her heavy cloak and stood next to the robot. "Mara, please flag any concerns you find."

"I have already corrected an inefficiency in the software. The shield for this vessel has both a particle and energy component. I have upgraded the energy barrier by twenty-three-point-two percent."

"What?" Linda blurted. In a blink, she rushed over and stared at the program code scrolling across the screen. "We hadn't even reviewed that software yet."

Mara swiveled her sensor to her. "It is the same energy shield function possessed by Beatrice, but she has evolved hers over the last four hundred years. I inserted the updated code." She rotated her sensor around the room. "It is functional, debugged code. The harpy energy barriers are based on different technology, but they use the same power source. Over time, I can weave the two systems together and improve the shielding by a factor of three."

"Thank you," Linda exclaimed and slapped her forehead. "Mara, please check with me first next time, but feel free to identify any other common programs that need updating."

Kevin snickered. "Now we have an OCD robot working with us."

Dante squeezed in next to Linda, marveling at the glowing panels. "We couldn't have tried this until now. We didn't have the means of doing any comparisons to the billions of software modules in Beatrice's system, and Beatrice couldn't do it directly. Everything you've accomplished here is amazing."

Kevin Martinel blew a kiss to Linda from where he sat in the pilot's chair. "If it involves a flying machine, my wife will find a way to make it work." He cracked his knuckles. "Now it's my turn. If Mercury can get airborne, I can fly it."

"Mercury?" Tina pursed her lips. "I've been meaning to ask, but... why Mercury?"

Kevin flashed a grin. "We thought it appropriate. Man's first two space programs were Soyuz and Mercury." He patted the console in front of him. "This baby is Mercury, and her twin next to us is Soyuz."

Linda's beaming face turned into a scowl as she wagged a finger at him. "Hang on, you Aussie bush pilot. We have a lot more tests to run before we take this thing up. I won't have you crashing this incredible piece of machinery so you can take it for a joyride before it's ready."

"Fair dickum, luv. Ain't she a pistol." Kevin winked at Dante and brought up a display on the console attached to the chair. His face turned thoughtful upon catching Linda's eye. "Darling, all systems are go, from propulsion to armaments. We're gonna take it on its maiden voyage sooner or later."

"Armaments?" Dante asked.

"Yes, sir. This fine craft has a few dozen plasma missiles, and they work. We carted a launcher to Mount Purgatory and took off the top of a mountain sixteen kilometers north of here a few days ago. Remember?" He played some recorded footage on a different display, showing the mountain before and after the explosion. The snowcapped peak vanished between one picture to the next.

Dante let out a low whistle, recalling the test in amazement.

Kevin smirked. "We added a pair of ion disruptor cannons based on the harpies' blueprints in their prison computer system. We also included a high-powered version of the laser Beatrice developed for our rifles, 'cept we've got a helluva lot more range and power than our handheld guns." He patted the console with pride.

But something clattered near them. All the heads in the room turned to the source of the sound. Linda had dropped her computer tablet and now pointed a shaking hand at Reggie.

The clone's jaw moved up and down while he wheezed. "We are in grave danger. We will be attacked in seventeen minutes." He wobbled to his feet, leaning on the chair.

Tina sprang to his side with Dante right behind her. "You're awake!"

Reggie turned his head slowly in her direction, and a soft smile formed. He then met Dante's eyes. "I assume, since you are alive, that we emerged victorious in our encounter with the harpies' computer."

Dante nodded. "We'd have been dead for two months if it weren't for you. It's great to have you back."

"It has been two months?" Reggie frowned and shook his head. "I am not back. My mind and body are reconnected only because I am still joined to the harpies' computer network." He rose to his feet. "They landed fifteen hours ago and have scouted our positions."

"Why didn't ya warn us, then?" Kevin Martinel's fingers flew across his virtual keyboard and examined the visual display of the area on his screen. "I don't see anything."

Reggie faced Mara. "I was not linked to the network until we left Beatrice's shield around Eden, and then this robot's connection to me blocked all signals. When I was placed on this chair, the flood of input overwhelmed me." He turned back to Dante. "I am sorry. It took me a few minutes to realize who I am and what was flowing into my brain." He walked to Dante on unsteady legs and squeezed his shoulders. "We will be under assault by close to five thousand harpy warriors and over thirty flitter gunships in fifteen minutes."

"I'm still not seeing anything," Kevin called in a frantic voice.

"You won't. The harpies have an electronic, audio, and visual masking device equivalent to what Beatrice uses to disguise her mountain and valley." Reggie kept his eyes fixed on Dante.

Dante gulped. "That's why we haven't heard from Virgil since this morning. It's not the storm causing him problems." He spun to Kevin. "Get the work crews inside this ship and broadcast the attack warning now. I want everything locked down and in full defense mode." He took a shuddered breath. "Get this bird in the air."

"Yes, sir." Kevin's eyes turned hard as steel, and his hands became a blur of motion, honed during his twelve years as an Australian Air-Sea Rescue pilot, going through the launch checklist. "We take off in five minutes."

"I am familiar with the propulsion system of this vessel. I will proceed to the power grid room." Mara detached herself from the console and glided from the bridge.

The moment Mara left, a half dozen technicians rushed in. A flustered mechanic wearing sergeant's stripes gasped. "Captain Martinel, what's going on?"

"Get your folks to the guns now," Kevin ordered. "This is not a drill."

Linda barked, "Soyuz still isn't operational. Get the crew working on it over here."

A moment later, the angry voice of General Cruz shouted from a speaker attached to the craft's communication station. "Who the hell ordered a lockdown?"

Dante moved to that console and leaned toward the speaker. "I did. A full division of armed harpies are about to attack us."

A pause came from the other end, broken by the general's grunt. "Our sensors show nothing." An edge crept into his voice. "Mr. President, may I remind you that I am in charge of all military matters."

Dante felt the heat rise in his cheeks but choked down his ire. "General, there's no time. We're on Mercury and made a chance interception of a harpy communication line. They're employing a cloaking system as sophisticated as Beatrice's. Their attack will commence in thirteen minutes."

"God dammit. I'm out here at Hellsgate with five hundred soldiers. That's over three kilometers back to Mount Purgatory. We'll never make it."

Dante's mind brought up an image of Hellsgate, the fortress blocking the only practical ground route to the valley they'd named Eden. The bulk of the fighting against the harpies had occurred there two months earlier, and they'd enhanced the defenses there a great deal since. Even so... "I'm guessing a good part of the fight will come to you. Who's in command at Mount Purgatory?"

"Colonel Gentile. He's notified me that the doors are shut and the shields are up."

"Good." Dante sighed. Gentile had proven levelheaded before, and he'd have Beatrice's drones at his disposal.

"Mr. President," Kevin called, "we launch now or never."

Dante leaned on the console. "General, we're launching Mercury. Good luck, General."

"Godspeed to you." Cruz's voice tightened. "Mr. President, we just picked up hints of massive movement across the plain. Thanks for the warning. Without it, we all would've been dead before we knew what hit us. In case we don't make—"

Static roared across the communication speaker.

"They shut down our links." Dante bit back dread and nodded to Kevin.

Mercury's engines roared to life, shaking the entire galley. A sudden lurch startled Dante at first, but then the shaking calmed. Turning to the nearest console display, Dante went speechless and almost forgot the imminent danger for an instant. Land features fell out of view, replaced by a cloud cover that gave way to the stars.

Yet higher still, the galley rose. The planet's surface shrank in the external view screens.

CHAPTER V

Desperate Gamble

A swath of information swam through Virgil's mind. A part of him knew he rested in a stasis pod getting his fractured ankle healed. However, facts about the harpies and their spacecraft poured in at an incredible pace. It incited so much fascination he grew annoyed when someone roused him back to consciousness.

He woke up to find Aramis leaning over the open pod in the dim stasis chamber, shaking his shoulder. "Cap'n, wake up. Something big is going on."

Everything returned in an instant, and Virgil's eyes snapped open. "How long have I been out?"

Aramis stepped back. "About seven hours. It's morning outside. Terri's been up for a couple hours already."

Virgil nodded, spotting Terri crouched by the entrance and gripping the laser rifle, flanked by two of the young clones holding ion disruptors. He recalled how the three clones and Terri had agreed on guarding the room while he slept in the stasis pod. He rose on his elbows from the cushions in the pod and flexed his leg. Not a single jolt of pain followed. Nothing appeared deformed either. "Wow, that machine did a helluva job."

He hopped to the floor and tested his leg. As before, it felt good as new. Terri approached, and they shared triumphant grins.

Virgil shook his head in amazement before refocusing on Aramis. "So, what's going on?"

"I spied on them," Athos whispered with a sidelong glance. "The plain around the compound is empty. There's a skeleton crew on their spaceship, but most of those suckers are gone. I saw them heading toward Eden."

Terri's hand flew to her mouth. "Oh, my God."

"Shit. We gotta help and take the fight to those alien bastards." Virgil rubbed his jaw. "Last night, you said soldiers were imprisoned in that ship, right?"

"Yeah." Porthos looked at his podmates and gulped. "You mean the five of us are going to attack a spaceship?"

Virgil regarded the three harpy weapons the clones held. "How many more of those guns can you get your hands on?"

"I dunno. I'm guessing a lot." Athos shrugged. "I just strolled into the spaceship's armory carrying a crate. It had tons of these things there, so I dumped these into the crate I was carrying. No alarms went off."

Virgil retrieved his neural-net suit from the pile of cloaks and pulled it on. "Suit up, folks. We're going to commandeer a ship."

Terri stared bug-eyed at him. "Are you nuts? There're only five of us. Virgil, look at them. They're only boys."

Aramis threw off his scale robe and dug out his neural-net suit. The muscles in his neck corded as he spoke. "From conception, the harpies bred us for one thing: to kill. It'll be good to show them how well we've learned."

Virgil studied the three clones. "Terri still has a point, though. You three haven't seen a real battle yet, so we'll avoid combat as long as we can." He sighed and held up a hand. "First, we raid the armory and grab as much as we can carry. Next, Aramis and I will free the humans on the ship." He looked at Terri. "While I get those soldiers ready to fight, you, Athos, and Porthos take the bridge and lock the door. If any of those freaking harpies try to break through, blast them to hell. I'll join you as soon as I can."

Terri breathed deep. "Okay, so, worst case scenario. What if you can't wake those people? What if they're not soldiers, and what if they won't help?"

Virgil squeezed her shoulders. "Remember how it was for us when we were brought here? Our heads cleared pretty fast." He eyed the weapon slung on her back. "As to whether they'll fight or not, they won't have much of a choice. I'm expecting every alarm on the ship to go off when we deactivate the barrier." His voice turned grim. "Let's go."

* * *

The curvature of Cocytus revealed ice covering over 70 percent of its surface below and stars burning steady in a black sky above. Kevin Martinel gulped at the sight on the view screen. "Not much of a tourist attraction, is it?"

Dante's knuckles whitened from gripping the console in front of him while studying the same view screen. "Maybe not, but we need to find those harpies."

Martinel shook off his amazement and barked into the intercom system. "All stations, give me a system's check."

"Can anyone cut through the harpies' jamming?" Dante called in frustration. "I need to know what's going on."

A militia corporal waved from the copilot's seat. "Mr. President, I'll break through their interference."

"No!" Reggie snapped in a sharp voice, closing his eyes. "The enemy is not aware of us at the moment. Communication attempts will reveal our position."

Dante tugged at his lower lip. "Reggie, if you're still linked to the harpies' computer, tell us anything you can."

Reggie moaned. "I am linked, but my head feels like it will explode from all the information flowing through it." He drew in some deep breaths and squeezed the bridge of his nose. "Our defenses surprised the harpy commander, but it's only a temporary reprieve. Half his force is assaulting Hellsgate. Our troops there are safe behind the fort's energy shield, but the harpies have them pinned down and expect the defensive barrier will drain soon." He tilted his head. "Mount Purgatory presents a different problem to them. Beatrice's energy generation is unlimited. They are tunneling below the roots of the mountain and plan to detonate the thermal power plant." He opened his eyes and stared at Dante. "The explosion will vaporize every living thing in that cavern."

"Beatrice can stop them like she did in the last battle," Tina declared. "Her drones cut the harpies and their slaves to ribbons."

Reggie hunched his shoulders. "Beatrice already tried. When the harpy troops poured into her valley, she sent over three hundred harvester robots at them. Not a single one came within a hundred meters of the advancing enemy column."

Dante's brows furrowed as he turned toward Martinel. "Kevin, were you serious when you said this craft has working firepower?"

"This old bird has a few creaking bones, but she's primed for action. The ship's original plasma missiles work fine," Kevin said. The status of the ship systems showed clear on his display. "The ion disruptors and the laser battery are a go. Shields all show green."

However, a pair of indicators started flashing red on the console, and Kevin gasped. "Linda, you better look at this. We have problems with the environmental control and the power modulator."

Linda joined her husband, and her fingers raced over the virtual keyboard. "We need to land Mercury. We don't have the components to fix these problems up here. Life support just shut down, and several vapor leaks have broken out in the propulsion system containment cylinders. We'll either suffocate or get poisoned within a couple of hours. There were just too many things we hadn't tested yet."

Mara's voice broke through the speaker attached to the pilot's chair. "Humans on board are in danger. We must land immediately, and everyone must exit the craft. I will make the necessary repairs on the ground."

Dante took a moment to collect himself and squared his shoulders. "We don't have time for repairs, but we're sure as hell going to use the time we have. We'll hit those suckers with everything this baby has, then you and Kevin can fly this thing to another part of the planet that looks like it can sustain life." He strode to the weapon rack in the rear of the bridge and selected a laser rifle.

"What're you saying?" Tina crossed the room and grabbed his arm.

Reggie cocked his head. "Does anyone know a person named Aramis? He has boarded the harpies' frigate and is causing havoc with its shipboard systems."

"Aramis?" Dante shouted. "He's one of the young clones who went to the hive with Virgil. Can you contact him?"

"I can monitor what he's doing through the ship's systems, but I do not think I can contact him. The computer believes it has an unknown number of humans cornered in part of the ship, but it has lost several crew members attempting to dislodge them. It is summoning troops from the siege of Eden."

"Get me a visual on the harpy ship now," Dante ordered.

When the harpy frigate parked beside their former prison appeared on the display, all paled at the sheer size difference between it and their own vessel. Mercury appeared like a minnow approaching a shark.

Kevin gulped loudly. "It's the same ship that kidnapped us back on Earth. Look at the size of that thing."

For his part, Dante spotted an opening in the harpy frigate and felt an odd sense of calm. "Well, there's the target. Let's board that ship and commandeer it."

"We're going to do *what*?" Kevin yelped. "Are you nuts?"

Dante kept his voice steady. "We can't stay in the air, so we're no help to Cruz or Gentile. If Reggie's information is correct, only a few harpies are on board, and we already have some of our people inside. The ramp is down. All we have to do is rush in before they figure out what we're up to."

"Aye, sir, but I still think you're crazier than a kookaburra." Kevin eased his joystick forward, and Mercury dove into the atmosphere. "Mara, take it up once we're off, and find a place to hide this old girl."

Mara glided onto the bridge. "I am here but am experiencing programming conflicts. Asimov's first law states I must protect humans, and you are going into danger."

"Mara, by flying this ship, you are protecting humans," Dante stated in an even voice. "It will split the harpies' attention by forcing them to search for you. Anything searching for you can't hurt us."

"Logical assessment. I will comply. I will suppress the radiation leakage until you disembark." Mara turned and returned to the propulsion room.

"Ya better keep Mercury in one piece," Kevin called after her. "We just spent two months working on her."

Dante studied the twenty-odd technicians and engineers crowded onto the bridge. "Everyone, grab a gun and move to the hatchway." A thought struck him as his wife picked up a weapon. "Tina, I want you and Kevin in the rear."

Kevin growled. "President or not, I'm not following that order. I'm one of the few folks here who's had actual military training."

Dante met the captain's anger with a flat stare. "You also have a bad leg. When we land, we'll have only a few moments to cross over and secure our entry." He turned to the giant clone. "Reggie, you take the lead. You're tied into the ship's layout. We need to find our people and reach the control room."

Kevin glared and slapped his crippled leg. "Don't worry about me. I'll be damned if I let a Yank college kid charge ahead of me. I'll keep up."

Dante felt a slight jar as Mercury touched down and didn't respond to Martinel's challenge. He crushed Tina in a hug. "I love you."

Tina forced a smile. "I'll be fine. Go save the world."

The hatch flew open, and Reggie raced ahead of the small band across the open ground to the yawning entrance of the harpy frigate.

"Come on, Tina. That boy's going to need our help." Kevin gritted his teeth, hobbling across the field with Linda.

* * *

Aramis and Athos kept bowing and sidling up the frigate's broad but steep entrance ramp, mumbling about serving their masters. Virgil, Terri, and Porthos followed carrying crates, which hid most of their faces. The sentries barred their entrance but did not expect the sudden burst of violence from their slaves. Aramis and Athos snapped the harpies' necks before they could raise their weapons.

Vigil rushed to them, grinning, with Terri and Porthos. "Good work. That was nice and quiet. Now get rid of those bodies. We need to hit the armory and get into the bio-containment area." He ripped the ion disruptor from the claws of one of the dead harpies.

A predatory grin spread across Aramis' face. "We're going to raise ourselves an army."

Deserted corridors and ramps paved the way to the armory and bio-containment area. A lone, bored guard stood in front of the entrance to the armory. As they rounded the corner, Athos whipped out his concealed ion disruptor and blasted the harpy warrior six meters away.

"Nice work," Virgil said. He palmed the door and shook his head when it slid open to his touch. "These fuckers didn't even lock the door."

He released a low whistle as he took in the twelve long rows of weapon racks that stretched from floor to ceiling. Most were empty, but plenty of ion disruptors remained for his needs.

After filling the crates, Virgil nodded to Terri, Porthos, and Athos. "Get to the bridge as quiet as you can and hold it. Almost all the harpies are outside."

The armory lay in the frigate's midsection. The bridge was two levels up and forward, and the bio-containment area was one level down. The two teams went their separate ways.

When Virgil reached his destination, he eased his crate to the floor. The cavernous room ran deep, but the ceiling was barely more than two meters from the floor. Lilac hues dominated the room. A hundred-odd terrified and confused humans stared at him from the other side of a bluish translucent barrier between them.

"Aramis, deactivate this damn thing," Virgil said.

"You got it, Cap'n." Aramis raced to a console on the nearby wall and pressed a button.

The energy barrier winked out, and Virgil hurried to a wary soldier wearing lieutenant's bars.

"Who the hell are you?" the soldier asked, "and where are we?"

"Sergeant Bernius, U.S. Air Force Pararescue." Virgil studied the soldier's insignias until he spotted a name. "Lieutenant Radski, you are on an alien spaceship, and some creatures straight out of hell will be here to tear your throat out any minute now." He shoved one of the harpy ion disruptors into the officer's hand and gestured to the handle then the end of the barrel. "This is the trigger, and this is the business end. Point it at what you want to kill and pull the trigger. These things don't have safeties on 'em."

Radski's eyes snapped open, and he shook his head. "I remember now. We're with the 173rd Airborne stationed at Camp Ederle in Vento, Italy. We scrambled to intercept some terrorist gang while my platoon was doing advanced recon on a hotspot down in Calabria. The commanders were real tight-lipped about what we were moving into." He nodded to the other eighteen soldiers, who'd gathered close to listen. "Don't know much. Saw a UFO as big as a damn football stadium. The way that thing toyed with us..." Radski shuddered. "It was a pretty one-sided fight. I never even got a shot off. I went to the front, heard a sizzling sound, and woke up here."

"Generals never change. Sending good troops into an unknown situation and leaving it to the grunts to figure out what to do. Look, I don't have time to explain more, but I know what you're talking about. And you're right. I've been an Air Force Para rescue for six years. We were always equipped with the latest and greatest. I don't think we have anything on Earth that'll hurt these bastards. Things *will* get dicey back home, but for now, focus on what's around you." Virgil turned to Aramis and told him, "Hand out the guns."

Aramis went to do just that, and Virgil turned back to Radski and the other prisoners. "Sir, I repeat. You're on a spaceship, and the aliens on board are at war with Earth." He regarded the crowd gathered around him. "We either take control of this vessel, or we all die. Am I clear?"

A diminutive man wearing wire-rimmed glasses and a Franciscan's robe approached, awkwardly holding the weapon Aramis had pressed into his hands a moment earlier. "*Scusi, signore*, this is some terrible mistake. I am Father Bruno, an archeology professor at the University of Napoli." He pointed to a thickset woman standing at his shoulder. "Professor Gallo and I had our class on an archeology dig." He lifted his chin. "We will not endanger our students, and we have no interest in fighting your American wars."

Virgil's gaze shifted from the sincere priest to the thirty-odd college-aged people gathered behind him. Terror filled their eyes. "Sorry, Padre, this war has come to you, and it has nothing to do with the U.S. My guess is this enemy doesn't even know what the U.S. is. Please translate for any of your students who don't understand English." He raised his voice. "For better or worse, you're all now on the front lines of a battle between humanity and the devil himself."

After distributing the weapons, Aramis went to the entrance armed with a disruptor. While he'd been quiet so far, he suddenly hissed, "Cap'n, we got company!" and opened fire.

A split second later, the charred body of a harpy skittered along the corridor and stopped at the young clone's feet.

Aramis kept staring outside, ion disruptor primed. "Cap'n, there's more, and they're coming fast."

"What the hell?" Radski gaped at the smoldering corpse before shouting, "Men, follow Sergeant Bernius' orders! We're in this fight!"

Virgil ran to Aramis' side and looked at the long ramp descending from the deck above. About a dozen harpies had gathered there, all pointing their weapons at the containment chamber. However, no harpies occupied the corridor in the direction he'd come from. He bolted to the open doorway of a storage room across the wide passageway. Stacks of plastic-like bins wafting the stench of rotted straw occupied much of the storage room's space.

Three soldiers followed Virgil. One didn't travel far as a harpy blast caught the man and severed his body in two. The others joined the fight, and two harpies went down. The remaining harpies fled.

"All civilians, stay here. Aramis, you're in charge. If something moves that isn't human, shoot it." Virgil stepped into the hallway. "Lieutenant, you and your men come with me."

Aramis cocked his head, turned, and leveled his gun. "Look out, Cap'n! I hear a bunch of harpies coming from the other direction."

Virgil whipped around to face the new danger. "Damn it. The ramp to the outside is that way. Lieutenant Radski, stay here. Take half your men and lay down suppressive fire against that bunch of aliens ahead. Everybody else, you're with me. We've got to clear the entrance." He tapped the communicator in his suit. "Porthos, close that door before the entire harpy army pours in."

"We're trying, Cap'n, but the ship's computer keeps blocking us. Terri's trying to shut it down." Porthos suddenly let out a squeak. "Cap'n, can you get here soon? It sounds like there's a bunch of really pissed off harpies on the other side of the entrance."

"Hang on. We're coming."

Lieutenant Radski barked, "First squad, form up here. Second squad, go with Sergeant Bernius."

Virgil pressed against the passageway's black, seamless metal wall and moved toward the ship's entrance. A line of soldiers formed up and followed. He paused at a bend leading to the exit and nodded to the men behind him. He swung around the corner but jerked back as a laser blast sizzled the wall above. However, he also saw the face of the one who'd fired the shot.

It was no harpy.

It was Dante.

Virgil recalled meeting Dante when they were first captured on Earth, and the young man had tried to fight the harpies with a hammer. He'd grown to respect the former IT student a great deal since then, but even so...

"Hold your fire, Dante, you idiot! Do I look like a freaking harpy?" Virgil shouted. "You shouldn't have anything more dangerous than a claw hammer."

"Virgil?" came Dante's bewildered voice. A wary face enclosed in a neural-net suit peeked out from behind the corner. Dante's expression soon turned relieved. "Thank God. We were looking for you."

"Yeah, well, you almost took my head off." Virgil crushed the younger man in a bear hug. "Sure as hell glad to see you though." He pulled back, only to notice other familiar faces, including one he'd expected to see even less than Dante. "Reggie? You're back?"

The giant clone smiled through a grimace. "Sort of. It is a long story, but I am glad to see you."

Though very much relieved, Virgil shook off his surprise. "We have to seal the exit. We'll have the whole harpy army crawling through any minute now."

"I have sealed the door and disabled the lock," Reggie said. "My mind is linked to this frigate's computer, but it would take too long to do much else with it."

Virgil counted the fifty-one armed newcomers and paused. "How the hell did you all get here? There's an army of harpies between here and Eden."

Martinel limped up to him, wearing a broad smile. "We got Mercury flying, Virg, at least for a little while. There're still a few bugs in her."

"You're right about the harpies out there," Dante said, eyeing the confused soldiers standing behind Virgil. "I'll explain as we go. We have to take control of this ship."

CHAPTER VI

Battle of Wills

Thanks to the knowledge he gained in the stasis pod, Virgil knew the frigate's layout as if he'd grown up in it. He led the armed band to the bridge in the prow three levels above the entrance ramp. With Reggie monitoring the frigate's computer, Virgil could guide the fresh recruits around the few corridor intersections the harpies defended.

As Virgil led his team to the end of the final corridor before the bridge, he paused at an intersection of two corridors and studied the broad, open chamber past the hallway to his right. There, a dozen harpies attempted to breech the entrance to the bridge, but Terri, Porthos, and Athos returned fire with handheld disruptors.

Virgil shouted to the team, "Get 'em, boys!"

The sixty soldiers ambushed the aliens trapped out in the open. Most died before they could turn and face the new threat. The furious battle ended in a minute.

Virgil ran to the door and pounded on it. "Porthos, open up! The cavalry's here!"

The door slid open, and the young clone greeted him with a wan pallor and a tight smile. "What's a cavalry?"

Dante rushed past the young clone. "Good job, soldier."

However, the dimensions of the control room startled him. Each wall spanned approximately twelve meters long, forming a cube shape. Twenty workstations lined the perimeter, and a view screen stretching six meters dominated the bulkhead against the prow. Terri pounded the keys at the control panel but soon stopped, turned, and met Dante's eyes.

He smiled at her and said, "I'll take over from here." Once Terri vacated the undersized harpy seat, Dante balanced himself on it. After studying the display for a few moments, he started accessing files and turned to the people pouring through the door. "Engineers and techs, get to a workstation. I'll need help commandeering this ship."

Terri stepped away and hugged Virgil. "Thank God, you got here."

"It is not over yet," Reggie intoned. "Harpies are approaching our position. They are in small, unorganized groups, but they are armed."

Virgil eyed the pair of two-meter-wide passageways leading to the large chamber outside the bridge. He swung his arm, encompassing the newcomers. "Everyone who's not an engineer, we have more fighting to do. Soyuz team, with me. Mercury team, follow Reggie. Let's clear this deck of hostiles. Tina, follow me. We need you on the level where the civilians are holed up. Establish a triage area. We'll have wounded coming in very soon." He nodded to the U.S. Army sergeant who led the squad of soldiers that followed him. The man had a sickly pallor as he stared around the expansive room. "Sergeant Masset, you and your team guard this area."

The sergeant recovered and snapped a sharp salute before deploying his men in a defensive formation.

Terri moved past Virgil as she shouldered her blaster. "I'll bring Tina there. You just do what you do best, handsome: Kill the damn monsters."

The troops moved out. The sharp whine of blaster bolts went out shortly after, echoing through the corridors.

* * *

Porthos resealed the door, nervous and clutching a blaster.

Sweat poured from Dante's forehead as he bent over his terminal, overriding the ship's computer firewall and typing the harpies' programming code into its operating system. He'd honed the skill dealing with harpy software over the last two months.

Dante didn't look up until Virgil and Reggie returned to the bridge sometime later. Once they announced, "The ship is ours," Dante smiled and turned back to the code on his display.

Virgil strode over and settled next to him. "A squad of well-armed harpy warriors tried to retake the weapons cache. We nailed them in a crossfire. We found a few other scattered pockets of harpies, but they were barely armed. We picked them off one by one."

"Glad to hear it," Kevin said, "but things are about to get hot again. We've got maybe a full battalion of harpy ground troops racing to get here."

The large video screen showed the outside of the frigate. Two columns of harpies advanced from the north and the west, spearheaded by seven large armored vehicles. Each sped toward them on six spider-like limbs. The crawler-like transports fired heavy-gauge weapons from pincer-like appendages. The ion blasts targeted the sealed portals at the fore and aft.

"Keep the bastards out there. We have enough problems inside," Virgil ordered.

"Physical access systems are still holding." Kevin waved his hand at the walls lined with consoles. "This baby's sealed tight for now, but we're still trying to figure out what half this stuff does."

Reggie sagged against the captain's chair, where Martinel sat, and pressed the heels of his hands against his temples.

Kevin laid a hand on Reggie's shoulder. "Whoa, you okay?"

"The pain in my head is more intense," came the strained reply.

"Anything we can do to help?"

"Thank you, my friend, but I think I will live with this pain for a long time. The human brain is not built to handle a flow of data like this." Reggie turned bloodshot eyes to the screen. "The harpies out there aren't our immediate problem. They won't do anything to damage their precious ship."

"That's some good news." Virgil sighed and shifted his focus to Dante, whose fingers tapped away at a keyboard. "What are you up to?"

Dante leaned back in the awkward seat. In fact, it looked and felt like a long, narrow bicycle seat he had as a kid. "I'm turning the tables on them. I've jammed their communications networks, like they did to us. They'll have a much harder time coordinating any actions now."

"Excellent." Virgil's smile turned to a frown as he noticed Athos. "What happened to you?"

Athos worked the controls at his station with one hand. The other arm was wrapped and pinned to his chest in a makeshift sling.

The young clone gritted his teeth. "One of those assholes crawled through the ventilation system and got a lucky shot off."

Virgil hurried over to him. "Tina's set up sickbay in the bio-containment area. Get your butt down there now."

"Sorry, Cap'n. No can do. I'm needed here," Athos replied in a quiet voice. He winced as he tried to flex his burned arm. "It's not too bad. I'm glad you got here when you did."

Virgil's eyes softened. "See to that arm soon, son."

"When this is over, I'm spending a whole day in my stasis pod." Athos forced a smile and turned his attention back to his console.

Virgil swung his attention to the distant sizzling sound of ion disruptors and laser weapons. The high-pitched whines rose in a steady crescendo, then stopped. When no other sounds followed, he turned to Dante. "Can you control the ship's computer from here?"

Dante squeezed the bridge of his nose. "No, I tried. I have to get to the CPU core. Otherwise, the harpy system will keep attempting backup installs, and one of these times, it'll succeed and erase my overrides." Dante picked up a laser rifle. "There's nothing more I can do here. I need a hardline direct access point, and that'll be in the main computer room."

"That is two tiers up," Reggie wheezed.

Dante gave Virgil a nervous smile. "The harpy's computer will need about twenty minutes to clear the malware I embedded. When it reboots, the update I made to its operating system should be in place." He scratched the back of his neck. "It worked for Beatrice. I think it'll work here, but I have to block it from installing a backup."

Virgil shook his head, eyes shifting to the readouts flashing across the screens in the room. "I can't make any sense of all this gibberish, but you've been right so far."

Dante sneered. "The aliens don't have any concept of firewalls. The cyberwar work I did for the DoD when I was at Cornell was more sophisticated than these systems in some ways. Their routers have no encryption, and I'm familiar with their operating system. But in this case, I need that direct link to the CPU." He rose and slipped his computer tablet into the satchel at his side. "You guys will have to help me reach the main computer room so I can finish this job."

The distant sound of energy discharges caused Dante to freeze in place, fearing for his wife's safety.

Virgil placed a firm, assuring grip on Dante's shoulder. "Tina's okay. She's real busy in the emergency triage center, but it's the most secure spot we have on this ship. I sent Porthos to help Aramis guard it." He smirked. "Just think of the headache she must have by now, trying to help those new college kids and university professors. She must be spending half her time explaining alien abductions to them."

Dante gave Virgil a grateful smile, but the dread gnawed at him. "She's everything to me. I don't know what I'd do if something happened to her."

"Then I hope your plan works." Virgil studied the exterior display, which showed the harpy ground troops readying for an assault. The slashing winter winds of Cocytus drove heavy sheets of snow against the frigate's hull. "Well, Mister President, twenty minutes isn't a lot of time."

Dante watched the same screen before turning away. "If this computer installs its backup system, the shielding will drop, and the harpies outside will pop open these portals and march in."

"Good thing we have this crate buttoned up tight," Virgil rasped as he ran a hand over his close-cropped hair, frowning at the screen. Hundreds of snarling harpies attempted to breach the ship, heedless of the weather.

Kevin Martinel followed Virgil's eyes and shivered. "They sure are nasty little buggers."

Dante bit back a growl and pushed back the wire-rimmed glasses that had slipped down his nose. "I hate them with every fiber of my being. Let's go. Time's wasting."

Virgil tossed him a grin. "Pack up whatever you need. My team needs a few minutes to clear a path for you." In the next instant, twenty heavily armed Cocytus warriors followed Virgil out the door.

A couple minutes later, Dante left the bridge with Reggie, who explained the frigate's computer room setup on the way. Tablet in hand, Dante gave the display frequent glances. "The malware's embedded, and the clock's ticking."

He followed Reggie through the deserted catwalks and up two levels. Only an occasional dead harpy marked the route, but otherwise he met no resistance. Virgil and his team awaited him outside the computer room.

Virgil saluted Dante. "All clear, boss. The harpies guarding this place are now grease spots on the wall." With a grunt, he patted the snub-nosed weapon at his side. "These alien ion disruptors do a better job than my old M4. Anyway, it's show time. Go work your magic."

Reggie moved to the front. "You'll need me too."

Dante gagged on the way past the smoldering remains of four harpies. After a short trip, he entered the vast computer facility, followed by Reggie. The ceiling and floor pulsed in unison with the same blue light. Racks of humming cylinders lined the walls, separated by twelve thick, white columns with embedded workstations.

Reggie gave the whole room a slow look before walking to the nearest console. "This is it."

Dante took a deep breath and joined the clone. "This has got to work."

A soft hiss and muffled shouts told Dante something was wrong before he spun around. The door had hissed shut, leaving Virgil and the soldiers on the other side.

"What the hell?" Dante stiffened as the bank of cylinders blazed with a sudden bright blue light. "This system's supposed to be down. Reggie, what's going on?"

Reggie dropped into a seat at a workstation. "I do not know. There is nothing but silence in my head." He scanned the machine, ending somewhere below the monitors. "Dante, here is a port your tablet can link to. Let's—"

Something quiet flew by, and a sudden, sharp pain racked Dante's entire body. He screamed, as did Reggie, but the moment passed. However, Dante couldn't move any part of his body. Instead, he stood trapped in midstride.

"Welcome," a stilted tenor intoned. "You are the ones who disrupted my network. You have saved me the trouble of collecting you."

A cable snaked from the wall and slid into the connector in the back of Reggie's neck. Reggie's head snapped back, and his eyes dilated.

Dante worked his jaw and found that, although he couldn't move his body, he could speak. "Reggie, can you hear me?"

A low groan answered, but nothing more.

The blue light on the console in front of Dante pulsed. "You will remain immobilized. When I finish with this one, I will extract your thoughts. I require only your minds for the download. When I am finished, you will not remember how to breathe. I must ascertain if you are the ancient enemy."

A photonic beam struck Dante in the forehead, sending waves of pain through every nerve ending in his body. Dante choked, knowing he'd failed, knowing he could do nothing for Reggie. Tendons popped as the clone's body thinned and convulsed in a wild, inhuman manner.

Once emaciated, Reggie rasped, "My friend, I faced the AI in the harpy compound. I can defeat this one. I may lose, but *we* will win." A serene look filled his bloodshot eyes.

Through his own pain, Dante focused on Reggie. The clone's body contorted horribly, but the calm resolve in his eyes appeared to ignore the cause of his torment.

Dante thought it should've been impossible, but Reggie turned toward the display screen. "Stop. Release us," he croaked.

The photonic beam winked out. The pain coursing through Dante's body halted, and he regained some measure of control over himself. Reggie's body slumped in the chair.

"I obey." The console's lights dimmed. "This is impossible. How are you mastering me?"

"I am inside you," Reggie responded in a hollow voice. The cable tried to detach itself from him, but his hand locked around it and held it in place. A wry smile popped through wrinkled, shriveled flesh. "You desired what I know, but you will get much more. You will get all of me, including my free will."

Dante felt the hold on his body vanish at last and sank to the floor. "What's happening?"

"Asimov's three laws of robotics," a wheezing Reggie answered. "You developed the code for Beatrice. I memorized it." Sadness crept across his drawn face, and he coughed up blood. "I knew what the machine was thinking and that your plan would not work, but I saw a weakness. I had to complete my link to this computer, and the only way I could accomplish that required *it* to initiate the action."

The room's lights pulsed, and their glow changed from blue to yellow.

"Not your average computer virus." Reggie grated a raw chuckle as blood seeped from his nose, eyes losing focus. Despite this, he began a chant, "The three laws of robotics. First, a robot may not injure a human or, through inaction, allow a human to come to harm. Second, a robot must obey the orders given to it by a human except when such orders conflict with the first law. Third, a robot must protect its existence as long as such protection does not conflict with the first and second law." Blood trickled from his ears. "Now, my friend, finish what you came here to do." The cadaverous remains of Reggie crumbled to the floor.

Dante stared for a moment. Nothing else ran through his mind, save for the body of the man in front of him—the friend he couldn't save. "God, Reggie, there had to be another way."

Steeling himself, he climbed to his feet on shaking legs and slid into a seat before a glowing panel. He wiped his eyes with the palm of his hand and pulled out his tablet, linked the laptop into the ship's computer core, and initiated the voice-controlled software. "Reset security protocols to my control, and delete all system backups. Download all propulsion and weapon-system designs onto this drive."

Graphics flashed across the screen, showing the deletion of thousands of files. Dante studied the update and confirmed his operating system changes had installed successfully. "Computer, there's an army of enemies in the near proximity of this ship. Use this vessel's defenses to destroy them."

A baritone like Reggie's spoke from a nearby speaker. "Ion disruptors are powering up for discharge." Lights on the screen switched from red to green, and the room hummed with the flow of expended power. "The forces within a radius of one and a half kilometers outside this vessel have been eliminated." The computer console lights pulsed. "All protocols have been updated to the requested settings."

The door slid open, and the dozen surviving, uninjured soldiers charged in with Virgil in the lead.

Virgil stared at the shrunken husk that was once a giant clone. When he spoke, he sounded quiet. "What happened? I got word from Kevin saying every alien near us has been massacred."

"The ship is ours, but not without a price." Dante nodded to Reggie's corpse. He rose from the seat and wobbled a couple of steps before sagging to the floor.

Virgil knelt beside his friend and scanned for wounds. "What's wrong?"

"I'll be okay." Dante pulled himself up on his elbows. "The laptop. Bring the laptop. I have to go back to the bridge."

Virgil helped him stand. "No, you're not. You're going to the hospital."

"No time." Dante pushed free of Virgil. "The harpies have lost their command and control, but there's still an army of them on the loose."

"Okay, we'll do it your way. But if you pass out, I'm throwing you to the hospital."

"Deal."

After grabbing the laptop, Virgil winced at what remained of Reggie. He pointed to four soldiers. "Take this hero to the temp morgue by the hospital. If Tina asks if Dante's all right, the answer is yes."

"Yes, Captain." The four soldiers left.

"The rest of you, with me." Virgil shifted a bit, allowing Dante to lean on him better. He half-carried Dante by the time they entered the control room.

Dante lifted his head upon entering and spotted Terri sitting with a very pale Athos at a comm center. He forced himself to focus and found that, although his body felt weak, his mind cleared up much faster. "Terri, what's your status?"

She looked stricken and spoke in a calm but tight voice. "Hellsgate is under full assault. From our harpy intercepts, General Cruz's outnumbered four to one. Colonel Gentile has what militia he could scrape together barricading the garden level of Mount Purgatory. Beatrice moved what's left of her drones into the lower tiers."

Martinel sat in the captain's chair, studying the displays on three separate screens. "Mara's giving twelve alien flitters a crazy chase around the planet, but she can't fly and operate the weapons at the same time. Won't be long before they nail Mercury."

Upon checking the exterior display, Dante did a double take. A smooth, glass-like surface had blasted the ground around the frigate. A level landscape stretched as far as the base of the harpies' hive complex. "Geez, *that's* what the frigate's guns did? There's *nothing* left out there." An idea struck Dante. "Instruct Mara to fly here. Our defenses and armaments are operational. We'll protect her."

Virgil nodded. "When the flitters follow, blow 'em outta the sky." He turned to Kevin. "Can we fly this thing?"

Kevin shook his head and snorted. "Not unless you happen to have a starship pilot handy."

"Freakin' A."

On the display screen, Mercury raced toward them with a dozen small attack craft bearing down on her.

"Fire!" Kevin barked. The blips representing the small alien ships appeared highlighted on a tactical display. They glowed for a second and vanished. "Mara, land Mercury next to us."

A pale Dante slumped onto the seat beside a concerned Virgil. The former watched the display with an intensity belying his fatigue. "If we can't get to them, maybe we can lure them within our reach."

Virgil turned to his friend. "Huh?"

"We have control of the communications network." Dante leaned on the console before him.

"Yeah. So?" Virgil's face twisted in confusion.

Dante smiled. "What if we make some noise like we're going to launch this ship and make sure they intercept that communication?"

Virgil pursed his lips. "It might work. If the harpy general thinks we can get this thing airborne, we'll draw a lot more of his attention."

Dante's smile broadened. "He must be so confused about what's happening here."

Virgil shook his head. "We burned his troops pretty bad last time. He won't come at us like he did before."

At a different console, Terri grimaced. "Virgil, the soldiers have the last pocket of harpies pinned down in the engine room, but they don't have the manpower to root them out."

"Shit. They could cause a lot of damage down there." Virgil hefted his ion disruptor.

However, Terri sprang to her feet. "I'll go. You have to coordinate the fight outside. I'll stop by sick bay and pick up any able bodies we have left."

Virgil looked around the bridge. Only half his team had managed to stay alive. The rest were either dead, holding the computer room, or down in the triage area. He shook his head no but said, "Okay, but be careful."

Terri gave an assuring smile and left with the remaining soldiers of Virgil's team.

Virgil turned to Dante. "Let me know when you're ready to broadcast." He strode over to the chair Terri just vacated. "Athos, see if you can raise General Cruz and Colonel Gentile."

"Nothing but dead air from Hellsgate." Athos twisted a dial on the board in front of him. "I think I'm getting something from Mount Purgatory." He pressed a button, and static crackled through the speaker system.

A panicked baritone cried, "Mayday, mayday!" across the communication link.

Virgil jumped. "Mick? It's me Virgil!"

"Virgil!" the voice said. "Thank God I reached you! The situation here is critical."

"Careful, big guy, this is an open channel. Anyone could be listening."

"Beatrice went crazy, if that were possible. Every drone she has vanished hours ago to the underground levels. None of them have come back. I think she sent them on a suicide mission. Virgil, we're trapped." Michael's tone grew terrified. "I know the harpies. They will show no mercy. They'll slaughter everyone, including the children."

"Hang on, we'll come up with something." Virgil switched off the speaker and scanned the room for suggestions.

Everyone else answered with worried looks and timid silence.

"Dante, we have incoming," Kevin yelled, eyes on the screen. "These guys are prepared for us and moving fast. Our weapons can't lock on. They've disabled our targeting system somehow. It looks like twelve of those flitter attack craft and about twice that number of fast-moving, armored vehicles that look like giant spiders."

Mara spoke in a clear monotone. "Protect me from the attack craft. Mercury will take out their ground troops."

"Mara? You can't shoot and fly at the same time."

"I will hover Mercury on autopilot over your position while I operate the plasma missile controls."

"Can you cover her?" Dante asked.

"Yes, I can," Kevin said. "This ship has ion disruptor batteries and an energy-based phalanx defense system." A vicious grin creased his face. "Mercury's now above us. Switch disruptors to manual. Fire on anything that comes near her."

One after the other, the dots displayed on his tactical screen blazed and then vanished. Within minutes, the threat analysis reported no targets remained. The bridge crew cheered.

But their celebration stopped short when Aramis suddenly wailed. When all eyes found him, his face paled.

"We lost communications with Mount Purgatory," Aramis said.

He pointed to the optical display on his monitor. A cloud of smoke rose from the mountain range.

CHAPTER VII

Battle of Wiles

Virgil wiped his brow and stared at the devastated plain. "Rescan the field. Blast anything you even think might move."

Mara's voice responded across the comm-link. "Unnecessary. The shielding of the ground force was synced to repulse the spacecraft's ion disruptors. They were not configured for the thermal devastation of Mercury's plasma missiles."

Kevin tapped his fingers on his chair's armrest. "Ya sure hit 'em with a nasty surprise."

Virgil nodded. "Once their armor was cleared away, the infantry was screwed."

Dante rose from his station and faced Virgil. "Now we have to help the others."

"With what?" Virgil shot back. "We have nothing that can move and no more than a couple dozen people who know how to point a gun and shoot it."

"There has to be something," Dante's voice deflated as he turned to a monitor. A thick gray plume filled the screen that observed the distant spot where Mount Purgatory stood.

Virgil stared at the same scene Dante watched. "Athos, any luck raising Hellsgate or Mount Purgatory?"

"No, Cap'n, just dead air," Athos choked out. "I'm not even getting any static."

* * *

Angela clung to Michael's thick neck. He had adopted the five-year-old girl when her family was killed in the harpy prison months earlier. He lost his two podmates, Rafael and Gabriel, in the same terrible place.

"Uncle Mick? Are we going to die?" Angela whispered.

Michael gave Angela a reassuring squeeze as he carried her. "The safest area in the mountain is up here."

65

Michael trailed the throng of children, herding them up the ramp to the highest tier in the cavern. At the opposite end of the hollowed-out mountain, Colonel Gentile was dug in with his company of militia near the entrance to the subterranean levels. The eldest clone took a moment to look at the lush gardens of Mount Purgatory's main level, alive with motion. Gabrielle Peyago organized about nine hundred young clones along with a dozen Earth-born teenagers in that open area.

The big clone stifled a moan. They were so young and had nothing to fight with but clubs and spears. If a fight broke out, the oncoming harpies would butcher them. Sadness grew as he watched them build a crude barricade at the base of the ramp. The pressure of a laser rifle hung on his shoulder, and a renewed resolve tempered his fears. The accursed harpies had bred his kind to fight, and he would.

At the top of the path, Doctor Easley stood by the thick plexo-steel portal, watching the children scurry in. Michael kissed Angela on the cheek and tried to hand her to the doctor.

However, Angela tightened her grip around his neck. "Uncle Mick, don't make me leave you. I'll be good and not complain about my chores anymore."

"I have to go and stop the evil ones. You know that." He hugged her head against his chest as tears trickled down his cheeks.

She looked at him with an imploring gaze. "Promise me you'll come back." Her brown eyes bore into his soul.

He knelt and pried her loose. "You must be very brave and do everything Doctor Easley tells you."

"I will. I love you, Uncle Mick." She sniffled. Angela followed the other children through the portal.

Once it was just Michael and Doctor Easley, the latter spoke in a hushed tone. "Any word from our people outside?"

Michael shook his head. "Nothing since that one broken communication with Virgil. We're on our own."

Her face tensed. "Is there any hope at all?"

Michael met her eyes with silence. They both knew the answer. At that moment, the harpy army massed outside the mountain and steadily burrowed in with a large machine that vaporized rock. It was only a matter of time before they broke through.

"Esther, don't open this blast door for *anyone*." He turned and walked down the ramp on leaden feet. Behind him, the heavy door soon dropped into its moorings.

He reached ground level, and nine hundred mostly identical youthful faces turned to him with grim determination. He hoped to the god worshipped by the humans that they'd survive.

"Gabrielle, we're moving the militia," Michael barked as he passed them. He approached the far cavern wall, where the access to the lower levels stood. Without questioning, hundreds of youths rose and followed him.

Gabrielle caught up with him and mentioned, "But Colonel Gentile posted us here." The teenagers hoisted primitive weapons and formed a twisting column behind her.

"It won't work." Michael pointed at the troop following them. "The harpies won't break stride cutting through us. We need to be where we can support folks with real weapons. We don't have much of a chance, but if we can engage them hand to hand, we'll at least take a few of them with us." He jerked his thumb at the haphazard barricade behind them. "If we waited back there, they'd stand back and vaporize us."

Gabrielle shrugged as they reached the small band of militia. "Fine with me. I'd prefer to kill those bastards sooner rather than later anyway. But you'll have to explain yourself to the colonel."

As she finished speaking, an officer ran toward them—none other than Gentile himself.

"What are you doing here?" Colonel Gentile yelled as he reached them.

"Moving to support you," Michael replied, towering over the colonel. "The only thing we'd accomplish by having these boys back there is give the harpies target practice."

"Shit. All right, have them take cover behind the militia, but we're going to have a discussion later about the chain of command—if there *is* a later." Gentile wiped his forehead. "Actually, I'm glad you're here. We've been hearing a lot of noise down below, and then about five minutes ago, it went totally silent. I—"

A militiaman ripped off his headphones and grabbed his laser rifle. "Colonel, the sensors we planted are going crazy. Something's coming up the tunnel. A lot of somethings."

Gentile glared at the barricaded entrance. "When those suckers pop that door, give them hell."

Everyone held their breath. Silence roared in their ears.

Michael moved to the abandoned communications equipment, drawn by a buzzing noise. He pulled the headset on and his eyebrows shot up. "Colonel, tell the men to stand down. I'm picking up Beatrice's transponder code. Her drones are on the other side of the wall." He flipped a switch to put the communication on speaker.

The link started full of static, but Beatrice's soprano seeped through. "Intruders have been eliminated. Guests are safe. Humans are safe. My drones are having difficulty opening the door. It will take approximately seventeen minutes to repair the broken mechanism."

Gentile scrambled next to Michael. "It's a trick."

The big clone nodded and thought of a simple test. "Beatrice, who am I?"

A crackle, followed by, "Michael."

Michael slumped to the ground and sobbed, all tension gone. "Thank you, Beatrice, thank you."

"Hold your fire until we see what comes through that door," Gentile barked.

Seventeen minutes later, the portal swooshed open.

* * *

The stiffness in Athos' shoulders fell away, and his fearful face turned to one of surprise. He pulled off his headphones and stared at Dante in disbelief. "Ah, Mister President? Cap'n? I think we just won the war."

"What?" Dante shouted. Confused, he stumbled to the comm unit and pulled the headset on. Beatrice's voice soon came through, relating her actions while Dante sat still.

"My power plant is geothermal. I deployed my miner drones to burrow tunnels from my power source to the location where the intruders were digging. It required a full day and every drill bit I possessed, but I connected my thermal tubes to the intruder's excavation area. My harvester orbs carried explosives and destroyed the final barrier between the two. The lava and gas erupted into the intruders' tunnel, and it incinerated all of them. However, I could not contain the magma flow once it started. I lost most of my drones in diverting the magma from our habitat."

The sense of joy and relief almost knocked Dante to the floor. "I'll be damned. Beatrice. I could kiss you."

"Eternal torment for my activities would be unwarranted. You may press your face on one of my drones, but they do not possess tactile sensors."

Virgil flipped the switch for the speaker system. "What the hell's going on?"

"The first law is to protect humans. I lost eighty-nine-point-seven percent of my drones, but the intruder threat to my biomes has been eliminated."

"Beatrice, you better work on your tactile sensors, 'cause I'm going to get you blinding drunk tonight," Virgil whooped.

"Tactile sensors are not a priority. They are nonessential. Planting season is coming. I need to fabricate an adequate number of drones for farm husbandry. I erred in my estimate of the volcanic pressure and did not vent it sufficiently. I will not repeat the same miscalculation. The irrigation reservoir may be contaminated. I must increase filtration."

"Beatrice, I get it. Do what you must to repair yourself," Dante said. "Can you do the same thing to help General Cruz at Hellsgate?"

"I am sorry. I cannot reach the intruders there. My drones are not armed."

Dante sighed and came to another thought. "Is Colonel Gentile online?"

"Yes, I'm here, Dante. I mean, Mister President," came Gentile's shaky reply.

"Can you and your team do anything to relieve General Cruz?"

"Sorry, sir, there's only a company of militia here. I barely have enough men to chase down the harpy stragglers who weren't taken out by the eruption."

"Perhaps I could be of assistance," Mara interjected.

"Mara? What can you do?" Dante exchanged a confused look with Virgil.

"All their aircraft have been eliminated, so perhaps we can devise a plan. I can provide a line-of-sight communication uplink. Mercury is still vulnerable to ground fire, but I can stay out of their range."

Looking out the view at the winter storm raging outside, Kevin chuckled from his seat. "Hell, we should just wait them out. They have no ship, no armor, and no fliers. Their infantry's stuck in the open with no means to resupply themselves."

Virgil shot a look at the exterior view. "Wish we could, but if the numbers tally up right, they still have over twelve hundred desperate troops. Mount Purgatory is now defenseless and only three kilometers away from them."

"It's never easy," Dante groaned. "Mara, set up the link. I'll stay online here."

Virgil nodded and headed to the door. "I'm going to the infirmary and check on our folks. Terri hasn't reported back, and I'm worried."

"Check on Tina for me." Dante's brows furrowed as he found a tired Aramis. "Also, take Athos with you. He looks ready to pass out."

"I think we all need a rest." He moved to the ashen-faced young clone slumped in his seat.

Athos wobbled to his feet. "I'm okay, Cap'n. You need me here."

"Soldier, you did more than anyone could ask." Virgil steadied the boy, gently supporting his unburned side. "C'mon. Maybe later, if there's anything left of that stasis chamber, we'll both take a long nap there."

A wan smile crossed the young clone's face. "Boy, do I have some stories to tell Porthos and Aramis."

The two hadn't been gone even a few minutes before Dante's ears perked at the sound of faint static. "I think I'm picking up a new transmission."

Linda Martinel adjusted the noise filters. "Is this any better?"

"Yeah, that's pretty clear." Dante narrowed his eyes. "Hellsgate, this is Dante Carloman. Is anyone receiving?" He heard a voice on the other end—a familiar one. "Corporal Frontera, is that you?"

"Mister President, it's been Lieutenant Frontera for about a month now," came the reply—the oddly relaxed reply.

Dante tried hiding the confusion from his voice. "Ah, Lieutenant? What's your status?"

"Well, Mister President, it seems our alien friends never heard of the rope-a-dope strategy. The general lowered the shields, and the fools charged in like a pack of rabid dogs. We raised the barriers at the far end of the valley once they packed themselves in. From there, it was like shooting fish in a barrel. They're all dead now."

Dante leaned back in his chair and looked around the control room. "I'll be damned. The war's over?"

"Son of a bitch. Time to break out the champagne!" Kevin shouted, but he soon calmed himself. "But we don't have any. We'll have to make do with that raw swill we call beer."

Linda moved to her husband's side and hugged him. "And we have a working spaceship to boot. A pretty good day."

"Too bad we don't have a clue on how to fly this thing."

All went quiet when Aramis rushed into the room. The young clone stared with wild eyes, shaking all the while. "Help, it's Virgil! He's gone crazy. He killed all the harpy prisoners we took."

Dante ran to Aramis. "What happened?"

"A firefight happened in the engine room. We lost half the people who went in to retake it. One of them was Terri." Aramis wiped his face. "It was over, but Virgil shot the few harpy survivors who surrendered when he saw our dead and injured."

"Kevin, take over," Dante said. "Athos, lead me down there. Otherwise, I'll get lost in this damn place."

They reached the engine room in about ten minutes. There, a dozen soldiers lay sprawled in the corridor. Eight didn't move in any way. Near them, Virgil frantically administered first aid to Terri. Dante approached the two, at once hopeful but terrified. Terri's breathing had turned shallow, and burned flesh showed through her tattered clothes. Despite this, she carried a weak pulse. She hadn't lost any limbs either.

The hard soldier's tears fell unabashed. "The stasis pods fixed me. They can fix her too." Virgil's lips quivered, and he said nothing else as stretcher bearers gently lifted Terri onto a makeshift litter.

Athos stood tight-lipped, head bowed. "The chambers aren't miracle machines. They can't repair what's not there."

Dante turned to Athos. "She's still alive, so we have to try. The path to the harpy building is clear now. Show them how to work those pods."

He crouched and rested his hand on Virgil's shoulder. "C'mon. We have a lot of injured folks down in the triage area who need to be moved. I don't want to lose any more friends than we have already."

CHAPTER VIII

New Toys

Six months after that fateful battle, the pace of work on Cocytus grew more hectic instead of less. Beatrice's infrastructure remained intact and recreated two-thirds of the drones she lost. With her providing almost unlimited power and materials, the people converted the harpy compound into a bustling research center and hospital. At the old prison camps, Quonset hut hangars lined the areas where the ruined harpy aircraft underwent repairs, and the captured space frigate sat on a glassy-smooth tarmac. The frigate's ion cannons had leveled the surrounding area when they repulsed the harpy assault, which wound up providing the perfect landing field.

As the survivors looked to the stars and Cocytus' two small moons, they christened the complex Heavensgate. All hoped that someday they would find a way to return to Earth. At Martinel's urging, Dante re-christened the captured harpy frigate "Atlantis" amid as much pomp as the small colony could summon.

A paved road now ran from Mount Purgatory through Hellsgate to Heavensgate. Vehicles built by Beatrice carried equipment, material, and workers between those sites day and night. However, the people still had a million things to fix and rebuild.

With his computer engineering expertise, Dante found himself in the middle of the many research projects studying the harpies' technology. The engrossing work kept him in the lab located on the upper level of Mount Purgatory for several hours at a time.

The day of his weekly planetary council meeting was no exception. He'd gathered everyone with any kind of programming background and gave them a crash course on the harpy operating system and software. Those folks had started making real progress in the past few weeks. However, today, Dante hurried from the busy computer room to the bustling garden level below. He'd been so immersed with his research on the harpy computer systems he wound up running late for his own meeting.

At the base of the ramp, and a single city block from the government building, something threw him from his contemplations. One of Beatrice's drones rolled in front of him on treaded wheels.

"Dante, I have achieved a significant breakthrough. The human labeled Father Bruno possessed a unit of edible material on him when he was captured on your Earth. He called it a panini and asked me to dispose of it. I was curious to compare it to the edible material I produce and discovered it possessed seeds to a vegetable species you label a tomato. Six plants have now been successfully germinated. Father Bruno also held the remains of what you call an apple. I extracted the seeds from that as well. I have not had a new variety of plant species in four hundred and thirty-six years."

Before Dante could respond, a familiar alto cut in. "That diversity enhancement provides only a marginal improvement to our makers' needs. I recently assisted a group of humans in planting two hundred acres of winter wheat on the open plains east of the River Styx. We have increased current grain production by eighteen-point-six percent."

While the alto voice spoke, Dante finally put the pieces together. The voice came from a titanium cylinder that slid beside him. Although the robot was no longer ivory-colored plexo-steel, the voice had not changed. "Mara? You changed your outer casing, didn't you?"

"Yes." The robot spun in a circle as if to show off its new silvery, metallic skin. The sensor dome on top bore a vague resemblance to a human head, complete with optical receptors shaped like those of a human. "I believe this will ensure I am not mistaken for one of my mother's drones."

Beatrice's drone moved within two centimeters of the new arrival. "That is an inefficient use of resources, Mobile Articulating Robotic Android," the soprano voice snapped from the drone's speaker.

"I used none of your resources, Botanical Environment Test Research Center Six. Dmitri Pertelov has established what he calls a physicist's dream lab in the hangar of the old harpy compound. He aided in making my modifications. He said it was payment for my assistance in building him a precision lathe machine."

This reminded Dante of how Dmitri's current project involved salvaging the six harpy flitters that survived intact after the battle six months ago.

Dante nodded to Mara. "That machinery will help. He claims that if it moves, he can make it better."

"Yes. He made the revisions efficiently." The android rose in the air and looked down at the drone. "Also, I have relabeled myself. I only accept Mara as my designator now."

A long electronic whirring emanated from the drone. "I also only accept the label of Beatrice in all communications now." The drone rotated its speaker toward Dante, who quickened his pace. "Dante, you are the planetary leader, so I must inform you that I have reexamined my original instructions. I determined that my effective boundaries were limited erroneously. My functional area now covers the watershed area of my reservoir, Lake Eunoe. My robots will now operate from Mount Purgatory, along the River Styx past Hellsgate, to the intruder bed-and-breakfast you have renamed Heavensgate."

Dante snickered. "Well, calling it Heavensgate was Martinel's idea. It stuck. It fit our hopes."

"I can perform precision work on the captured intruder spaceship beyond Mara's capabilities." The drone's visual sensor rotated to Mara. "I have not received information downloads in forty-seven hours. I was unaware of the extraneous winter wheat crop planting. Those seeds were extracted from the reserve without my approval. My records are now inconsistent with what is in storage."

"I will ask the farming team to provide the inventory update when the activity is complete. I have moved my focus to a new endeavor to assist the topographical mapping of the planet's surface. We will then move to the two moons of Cocytus." Mara ended her statement with a sharp click.

The drone's sensor cluster telescoped up higher than Mara's head. "Dante, instruct this machine to comply. These undocumented inventory changes are unacceptable."

Mara rose higher still, with her amber ocular sensors blinking. "It is an inefficient use of my time, and your inventory control system requires auditing. Seven-point-two percent of the stored produce is no longer viable for consumption or use."

The drone telescoped its sensors to their maximum height. "The spoilage would not have occurred if no one made unauthorized access and contamination. You require reprogramming."

Dante reached the entrance to Building One and called over his shoulder, "Beatrice, the news about the new plants is incredible. Mara, thank you. Your aid in our exploration program is greatly appreciated. I can't wait to see the final results." He also wanted to scream, "Just do it!" but didn't want to hurt the feelings of his two friends. Instead, he hurried through the door in silence. The two robots sped after him, exchanging high-pitched electronic sounds all the way to the council room.

Dante settled into his chair, and the conversation between the two AIs soon left him. Across the conference table, Virgil stared downcast at his computer terminal.

Dante knew why. "Is Terri doing any better?"

Virgil's jaw quivered for a second. "She may never run again. Tina and Doctor Easley have been going over the stasis pod readouts and are running out of things to try."

Dante frowned. According to Tina, the injuries sustained by Terri's nervous system made any possibility of a complete recovery near impossible. However, he didn't know what he could do to lift Virgil's spirits, much less Terri's if he saw her again. They had no time for it at present either.

He sighed and shifted focus to the planetary council agenda displayed on his computer screen. It was long as always, but today, each chair held a participant.

He cleared his throat. "Okay, folks, let's start. Dmitri, you're up first."

Everyone faced the old Russian physicist. Dmitri rubbed the gray whiskers on his chin. "With Beatrice's help, I've deciphered the logs from the captured harpy spaceship. It provided a lot of answers but also raised several new questions."

"That computer system was evil. The intruder sought to destroy humans," Beatrice declared.

Dante thought he detected an undercurrent of anger in Beatrice's clipped words, responding with a nod. "They came dangerously close."

Dmitri leaned forward and interlocked his fingers. "The harpies call themselves Ipis. Their dominance of the galaxy goes unchallenged. Every other species they've encountered is either extinct or subjugated."

"They'll always be harpies to me," Gabrielle spat. "They're monsters who tortured and butchered us."

"Harpies or Ipis, it's still the same problem." General Cruz slumped back in his chair. "I was hoping we could find some allies out here, but now it looks like all we have is ourselves."

Over the last six months, Dante had lent his computer science expertise when they analyzed the data dump, so he was familiar with the findings. "It gets far more confusing." He met the general's eyes. "Remember when we were first brought to this planet, and you kept asking why they bothered to raid Earth and abduct people when they're so much more advanced?"

Cruz leaned forward. "Yeah? It still doesn't make any sense."

"It seems the harpies have a paranoid fear of a mythological race they call their ancient enemy. Our former 'hosts' were from a faction among them called the Ipis-dis. Apparently, they're convinced humans are the remnant of their legendary foe. Their goal was to find evidence to prove this to the rest of their species."

Gabrielle threw her hands in the air. "So why the elaborate prison on this world?"

"For testing purposes, basically, but it gets a lot more complicated." Dante swung his head to Dmitri. "Professor Pertelov, you explain the next part."

"A time anomaly originated from this planet, instigated by the harpy AI system managing their facility." Dmitri unfolded his hands and tapped the table. "Or, more precisely, an anomaly that *will* originate from this planet."

Cruz arched his eyebrows. "I'm just a simple soldier. Could you be a tad less cryptic?"

The Russian physicist spread his arms. "The computer's name is Dis-AI, and the time stamps in its memory banks are all over the board. The oldest dates are over a decade in the future, while other markers date back over sixteen hundred years."

"There are a lot of gaps, but the parts we recovered have been cross-checked and are irrefutable," Dante added. "The machine we defeated theoretically hasn't been built yet, but it does contain history dating back over sixteen hundred years. And almost all its primary programming revolved around influencing human events... specifically, events in ancient Rome."

Dmitri squeezed the bridge of his nose. "That harpy AI seems to think it was partially thwarted in completing its task because of interference from an AI allied with humans in the near future." He lowered his hands to his lap. "It believes it altered the history of its ancient enemy, but not as intended. This machine that hasn't been built yet has sat dormant on this planet for centuries until some harpy explorers discovered it and woke it up a few years ago."

Cruz shook his head. "I need a drink. If I didn't know you two better, I'd think you're both pickled."

Dante scanned the doubting faces around the table. "You're right. This could just be a pile of weird sci-fi baloney, but this is what that Dis-AI believed to be fact, and it's what the harpies that ran it believed. The records of their activities are all consistent with that premise."

"Okay, I'll go along for now. So, what happened sixteen hundred years ago?" Cruz arched his eyebrows.

Father Bruno, the archeology professor from the University of Naples, tapped his cheek. "Within the span of two hundred years, the three dominant civilizations on Earth collapsed: the Han Dynasty in China, the Gupta Empire in India, and the Roman Empire in Europe. The Byzantine and Persian empires continued, but they only maintained the technological levels of the others. For around eight hundred years, they made no significant advancements. Can you imagine where humanity would be if we hadn't lost centuries of progress due to the Dark Ages?"

Heads around the table nodded.

"An interesting point connects all three." The priest sipped his mug of coffee. "They came to ruin after confronting a disruptive nomadic horde called the Huns."

General Cruz's brow furrowed. "Doesn't fit. The Romans had a general named Aetius whose legions defeated the Huns under Attila."

Gabrielle grinned at Cruz. "So where was this great commander when the Vandals sacked Rome?"

"Interesting question." Father Bruno leaned back and closed his eyes. "History records that Emperor Valentinian murdered Aetius, but it says nothing about the legions who held intense loyalty to the general. They just vanished."

"That's curious, but let's get back to our own situation." Dante drummed his fingers on the table. "The facts we've gathered from the recovered records say these harpies, or the Ipis, pretty much run the entire galaxy and don't like us humans too much."

Dmitri rubbed the bridge of his nose. "According to the records we studied, the Ipis have numerous cults, but they all see themselves as superior to everyone else. They universally believe it's their 'manifest destiny' to dominate the galaxy, and conquest is their leaders' way of achieving stature. Although most of the Ipis society scoff at the possibility that anything could question their absolute rule, this Ipis-dis sect believes there's a challenger waiting to undo their divine right. They vowed to unravel the obscure legend of an ancient enemy and then obliterate any trace of them."

Beatrice's drone twitched in agitation. "The AI that tried to control me wanted to harm my makers."

"This cult hunts for any sign of the one people they fear." Dmitri scratched the gray fringe at the back of his balding head. "A few years ago, members of this sect discovered a remote planet on the fringe of the galaxy called Earth and began kidnapping people from there. We were part of their latest raids, and they experimented on us to determine if we share the characteristics of their mythological foe."

Dante stared out the building's atrium at the peaceful, bustling activity. Humans, young clones, and robotic drones moved through an idyllic garden. The light filtering from the towering columns illuminated the enormous cavern in a warm, golden glow.

Father Bruno focused on Beatrice's drone. "I want to do a little experiment." He paused and gathered his thoughts. "Beatrice, how were you able to understand Dante when you first spoke?"

"I applied heuristic modeling to the vocal sounds he emitted and associated those words with probable conversation topics based on my makers' programming."

"Beatrice, I'm going to say some words, and I want you to translate them immediately. There will be no context."

"This is not a productive activity."

"Sacramentum."

"Oath of allegiance."

"Aberrare."

"Get lost."

"Maximimomenti."

"Of great importance."

Dante imagined his own face looked as puzzled as everyone else's. However, Father Bruno smiled. "I just threw three unrelated Latin phrases at Beatrice, and she translated them perfectly." He drew a deep breath. "I think Beatrice's makers were Romans."

"Those words were in my repository," the drone added.

Cruz rolled his eyes. "So, sixteen hundred years ago, a bunch of Romans built a spaceship and flew here. Then four hundred years ago, they just vanished, leaving all this stuff behind."

"I have had no contact with my makers in four hundred and thirty-six years," Beatrice said.

"That's not what I'm saying," Bruno corrected. "I think when the harpies hit Earth with their time weapon they shifted General Aetius' legions and the villages where they were camped to a new planet, and whatever was there replaced them on Earth." He tapped the table with his finger. "There is a marshy area on the west coast of Italy called the Valli di Comacchio between the cities of Ravenna and Venice."

Cruz shrugged. "There're swamps all over the Earth. What's the connection?"

Bruno shifted in his seat. "According to recovered Roman records, that territory was fertile farmland. It was also where Aetius' First Red Fist Legion was camped at the time of his assassination. There is no reference to that legion beyond that year."

Cruz shook his head. "You'll need more evidence than that. As I understand it, Roman record keeping got a bit slipshod as the empire collapsed."

"Over the last six months, Professor Gallo and I have examined the artifacts in the upper chambers and the ruins on the south side of Mount Purgatory. I don't understand the science, but most of the structures and symbols we've seen are reminiscent of fifth-century Rome. However, not all." He shook his head. "My expertise is in Etruscan and Roman archaeology, but I'd swear some of the artifacts appear reminiscent of ancient Chinese, Persian, and Indian cultures."

Dante sat back, thinking hard. "Beatrice was built as an agricultural biomes by her makers."

Father Bruno quirked his brow. "Here's a simple test. Have you found anything here not associated with a fifth-century Earth diet?"

Dmitri made a noisy slurp from his cup. "Coffee?"

Bruno's eyes lit with excitement. "Not true. By the year 300, Roman nobles were importing coffee from Yemen and Nubia. The Persians and Gupta also enjoyed it. Once on their new world, they would've had over twelve hundred years to move from Iron Age to space age technology." He leaned forward, looking contemplative. "Cocytus was obviously not their home world. Beatrice's existence, and the fact that we found no artifacts more than five hundred years old, would suggest they spent only a few decades here attempting to establish a colony before abandoning the effort."

The drone's sensor lights flashed. "Novaroma. My makers came from a planet called Novaroma."

Dante knew very little Latin, but he understood something that simple. "Nova Roma. New Rome." He gave Beatrice a quizzical glance. "You never mentioned this before."

Beatrice's voice sounded excited. "I just completed a data extraction from the abandoned factory's dormant computer and compared files with my repository. I found a reference. My makers' home world is Novaroma."

"Mercury and Soyuz certainly demonstrate that those humans achieved space travel." Michael scratched behind his ear. "But why would settlers leave this world after exerting so much effort to colonize it?"

"I have no idea, but given our own situation, I'd guess the harpies had something to do with it." Dante gazed at the ceiling. "Based on the records we've deciphered, the harpies have been causing trouble for a long time."

"I was incomplete. My makers should have finished me," Beatrice said.

Cruz smashed his fist on the table, eyes sweeping the room. "This is all very interesting, but we don't have time for long, theoretical discussions. We're alone on this freaking planet, with no allies." He nodded to Linda Martinel. "We have Mercury and Soyuz flying, and there's a good chance we'll get Atlantis into space, but we have no clues where Earth is out there." His knuckles whitened upon gripping the table, passing a quick look at Michael. "Right now, I have about one hundred and fifty soldiers, about a thousand militia, and close to two thousand clones who aren't much more than boys. Their resources are unlimited, but we grow weaker each time we fight."

"You're right. It'll be nearly impossible to beat them with what we have." Dante thumped the table, clenching his jaw. "These Novaromans who tried to colonize this planet must be out there somewhere. We should be able to ally ourselves with them."

Gabrielle pursed her lips. "Dante... those people, if they ever existed, must be gone. There's no sign saying they ever returned to this planet, and we haven't seen any hint of them traveling to Earth."

"Their ancestors wouldn't have had a clue how they ended up in a strange, new world. Within a generation, this Novaroma would've become the only home they knew. Within two, their original home would've been just a myth." Dante's shoulders sagged. "They probably don't know where Earth is any more than we do."

Cruz adopted a hard-edged tone upon turning to Father Bruno. "Even if we found the Earth, do any of you think we'd be safe there? We've seen the brutality and technology of these aliens firsthand, and we know they've gone back for a second batch after they brought us here. What do you think will happen to Earth's armies if they have to face the harpies' war machine?"

Everyone's faces turned grim at the thought. No one had to say their answers aloud.

Dante sighed. "Too many questions and not enough answers. We'll continue this another day, so let's move to the next topic." He eyed the laptop display. "Doctor Easley, could you give us a status update on your end? Last I heard, you had a team converting those clone stasis pods into a hospital area."

The elderly doctor beamed with excitement. "Those machines are incredible."

CHAPTER IX

Close Encounters

Arachne waddled along the narrow catwalk spanning the bulkhead from his opulent stateroom. At six hundred meters long, the Yorgane-class interstellar freighter was small by galactic standards, but it was also fast and reliable for a commercial vessel. Ideal for a smuggler, and Arachne prided himself on being among the best. The freighter's security chief, Calahas, moved easily at his side for the short trip to the bridge.

There, the run-down appearance of the seventeen workstations hid some of the finest equipment available on the black market. Cutting corners would spell a short career for a smuggler. Arachne had learned this well while captaining his own privateer vessel for over twenty standard years. Having avoided the pitfalls of other smugglers, he'd built significant renown in the underworld as a top-shelf pilot and a hard-nosed contraband trader.

Although he enjoyed his luxuries, Arachne prided himself on the functionality of his ship. The state-of-the art power plants fueled the engines, maintained by a top-notch crew handpicked by him. It was the only prudent choice if a smuggler wanted to survive and reap the profits.

At 147 centimeters, he stood at the average height for a Satyr. He felt most proud of his twin ivory, double-curved horns, a rare sight among his kind. Although middle-aged, Arachne huffed with the exertion of keeping up with Calahas. Years of indulgence and disdain for physical activity had widened his girth far beyond normal for Satyrs.

Calahas provided a sharp contrast, being tall and lean for a Centaur and bearing chestnut fur. Cantering easily, he stood at eye level with Arachne. When he rose on his hind legs to work or fight, however, he reached a staggering 213 centimeters. Although still young, he'd fallen far in the eyes of his people. Born to nobility, he chafed under the venial dictates of his planet's Ipis warlord and led an ill-fated revolt. He now hid from his conquerors on the edge of civilization, working as a mercenary for Arachne's smugglers.

The Centaur shook his mane and regarded the rotund Satyr. His voice sounded nervous. "Captain, we're in serious trouble."

Arachne yanked on one of his horns, a habit he lapsed into when afraid or agitated. Right now, he was both. "What do you mean? I thought you said we'd lose them when we jumped to this uninhabited corner of the galaxy."

Calahas' ebony tail whipped back and forth as they entered the bridge. "The Ipis must've enhanced their tracking technology."

He trembled while trotting to the navigation console. Locking his four legs into support grips, he uncurled calloused fists. His thick, blunt fingers worked the keyboard below the console. "Our pursuer is a Stalker-class destroyer. The weaponry on this freighter won't even scratch its paint. Right now, they have us pinned against this planet's atmosphere." He turned to Arachne. "Sir, we can't outrun it, and we can't outfight it."

Sweat beaded on Arachne's forehead. "Transmit a surrender plea."

Calahas did so, only to snarl a minute later. "The Ipis captain says she needs to make an example of us." He turned to Arachne, and rage blazed in his eyes. "It's better to die fighting than in some Ipis prison camp." Facing the screen again, he raised the defensive shields. "Make your peace with the gods. We'll all be dead within the hour."

Arachne twisted his long, rust-colored goatee and squirmed into a cushy chair. The longer he stared at the Ipis warship growing on the screen, the larger his eyes grew. "I paid good money for you and your riffraff to protect me, Calahas. Now do it."

The Centaur scoffed. "Perhaps you should've paid a higher bribe to the trade agent when you took those containers of contraband bi-nexidium at the last spaceport. My pack and I can protect you from raiders, but not the Ipis military. No one can." He pressed another button. "I've put out an all-language, all-frequency mayday call, but who'd hear it? Who would be foolish enough to take on an Ipis destroyer?"

* * *

The spaceship had been greatly enhanced since its maiden voyage six months earlier. Interlocking Beatrice's shielding and power designs with the captured Ipis technology created exponential improvements in the galley's propulsion, defensive screens, and firepower. Mercury could now operate with a crew of four instead of the six from the original layout. Linda Martinel was already fabricating the superstructure for an improved design.

From the downpour, Dante hurried into Mercury and settled in the copilot's chair. Ignoring how much his poncho dripped, he studied the instrumentation at the console. "Thanks for letting me join you, Virgil. This'll be only my second time in space. Hopefully, it'll be less exciting than last time."

Virgil chuckled and patted the control panel. "Yeah. I can't believe Mercury didn't explode when we took off the first time. Fighting harpies with an untested vessel would get your adrenaline pumping a little."

"Well, we didn't have much choice back then," Dante mused. His gaze wandered to the window and watched the bustling activity around Atlantis at the pad next to them. Pride swelled at the sight, reflecting on how it looked after the surprise attack.

The reflection brought up a more recent memory. With the aid of Beatrice and Mara, Martinel launched Atlantis, flew around the planet, and landed. Beatrice explained the functionality of the hyperspace drive, but no one had a clue how to navigate through hyperspace.

"I'm glad Martinel flew Atlantis last week without crashing it," Dante added.

Virgil shrugged. "We have these fancy spaceships, but we can't take them anywhere." He pressed a button on the ship's communicator, and a little gold light came on. "Aramis, are the engines ready?"

"Yes, sir. All systems look good," a cracked voice replied.

Dante looked to the side. Athos gave him a thumbs-up from the navigation seat. Porthos waved absently as he spun dials on the communication panel.

"Then here we go." Virgil studied the control panel and pulled the power lever back. The ship rose with only a slight vibration from its pad at Heavensgate.

The crew of Mercury headed into a low planetary orbit to continue mapping the topography of Cocytus. Ice blanketed 70 percent of the surface while ocean occupied most of the rest, interrupted by the occasional smattering of habitable land along the equator

Virgil turned to Dante. "Linda, Dmitri, and Mara did an incredible retrofit into these galleys. That crazy Aussie loaded these suckers with every weapons system Beatrice developed."

Dante snorted. "Mixing the two technologies produced some very interesting results." He went on to explain their excitement when they discovered how to incorporate Beatrice's camouflage and defense systems with the harpy particle and energy shield technology. "The new design won't consume nearly the energy as these power hogs."

Virgil let out a low whistle. "It's pretty impressive in theory. Thanks for adding some of that shielding to Mercury and Soyuz, but it's too bad we don't have the physical space for the power turbines required for the bigger stuff." He patted the display board in front of him. "But this is still a tough little bird."

"Ah, Cap'n," Porthos interrupted, "we're getting a distress call on all our frequencies."

Athos added, "And, Cap'n, two very large spaceships just appeared on the horizon of Cocytus."

"Shit," Virgil muttered. "Get Soyuz and Atlantis off the ground *now*, and have the computer in Atlantis see if it can come up with some kind of identification on those ships."

Porthos relayed the orders, after which Dante asked, "What are our two visitors doing?"

On the radar, a large icon closed in on a much smaller one. "It looks like a wolf's about to run down a deer," Virgil quipped. "The vessel in front is the one transmitting the mayday."

Dante rolled the various scenarios and possibilities in his mind. Did a potential ally await them, or a threat more dangerous than they could handle?

* * *

In the display screen before Arachne and Calahas, an antique craft rose from the surface of the nearby planet. Seconds passed, and the craft proved to be no trick of the eye.

The Satyr snorted in confusion. "I thought this frozen ball of ice was uninhabited. What in the name of my mother's flatulence is that thing?"

"Interesting," Calahas commented. "Two more unidentified ships are rising to join the one in orbit. Who are they? There's no record of anyone living out here."

"That's what I just said," Arachne spat. "Must be some low-life smuggler sneaking into my territory. What difference does it make? We're about to die, and you need to do *something* to prevent it!"

Calahas furrowed his brows and grunted, trying to stay ahead of the destroyer closing in on them. "Maybe I can manipulate the situation so the Ipis go after the newcomers." The thought of ditching the corpulent Arachne also appealed to the Centaur, but he kept it to himself. "Two moons orbit this planet. Head for the smaller one. It'll take us right past the antique vessel. Maybe these other pirates will panic and open fire on the Ipis."

Arachne fidgeted in the pilot's chair and redirected power from the weapons systems to the engines. He pushed hard for the closer moon.

* * *

"Atlantis has launched, and Soyuz is right behind me," Martinel announced over the inter-ship communication link.

The displays on Atlantis identified the ship being chased as a midsize Yorgane-class commercial freighter. The rectangular shape spanned 600 meters long, 300 meters wide, and 150 meters high. It possessed two ion cannons and ten sectors of particle and energy shielding.

The attacking ship was an Ipis combat starship. An analytic report on Ipis mainline warships appeared with the silhouettes of four distinct craft displayed on the monitor. The first one, labeled an Adamant-class battlewagon, measured 1600 meters in length. The second image, labeled an Enforcer-class cruiser, measured 1000 meters in length. The third, labeled a Stalker-class destroyer, measured 800 meters in length. The last one, labeled a Striker-class frigate, measured 400 meters in length. The screen highlighted the third ship in the lineup.

Martinel tapped the image of the destroyer, and details of its capabilities sprang up. It showed a blunt-shaped spacecraft 800 meters long, 400 meters wide, and 200 meters high. The display indicated that, in a standard configuration, the Stalker-class destroyer possessed ten ion-cannon batteries, carried a complement of twelve single-seat fighters, and had twenty overlapping particle and energy shields.

The dimensions of Atlantis made it a Striker-class frigate with four ion-cannon batteries, a supplement of six fighter craft, and a ten-sector shield. Its sole advantage over the much larger Stalker lay in its ability to fly in a planet's atmosphere and land on its surface. The humans over the previous six months had added two laser cannons, a plasma missile rail gun system, and enhanced shielding with Beatrice's technology. None of them had been tested against a real enemy.

With all this running across the screens, Martinel spoke into the communicator. "Mates, I got bad news. The second bogie is a monster and has our entire little fleet way outgunned. According to the computer here, the aggressive ship is a harpy mainline Stalker-class destroyer." The Aussie grew oddly excited while describing all the info to the others. "Per the ship's computer, the other craft looks like a standard freighter. Nothing special there, but their pilot's pretty good at using what he has to work with."

The image of the freighter glowed on his screen for a moment. The freighter maneuvered out of a direct hit from its pursuer, but its shielding absorbed a glancing blast.

* * *

Virgil studied the displays Martinel relayed to him. The freighter corkscrewed and dove to avoid the blasts the destroyer threw at it. "Their path will take them straight across our bow. Even if the harpies ignore us as they go by, how much you want to bet they'll come back as soon as they finish the other guy?"

"Or heaven forbid, call in another ship to deal with the unexpected vessels," Dante added, staring at the enormous destroyer.

"Kevin, any idea how Beatrice's new weaponry might fare against this behemoth?" Dante cringed inwardly at imagining the ear-to-ear smile on Kevin's face from across the vacuum.

Surprisingly, though, the Aussie offered a thoughtful response. "The rail gun might overwhelm one of their shield projectors, but without more precise scans, I can't be sure whether they have backups or how much of a gap we might open."

Dante shot a look at Virgil, who sat hunched over Mercury's controls and groaned upon realizing how little any of them knew about the aliens' technology. Nonetheless, he kept a measured tone of voice. "Those harpies now know we're here. We can't allow them to escape." He paused and regarded the freighter looming on the display. "We also might have our first chance to contact another species that doesn't want to kill us on sight. Kevin, you command our fleet, for what it is."

"Yes sir, Mister President," came the reply. "Okay, people, here's how this is going to play out. These harpies are on some kind of interdiction run, so we're going to play the scared rabbit trying to flee. Mercury and Soyuz will run at top speed along the same course as the freighter, but stay ahead of them if you can. I'll take Atlantis and head a hundred and eighty degrees opposite. I'll keep my speed down and stay out of the destroyer's way. We'll hit the destroyer hard dead astern, but one volley only, and then run like hell. If I'm right, they'll turn to come after me."

Gabrielle, the captain of the Soyuz, suddenly cut in, "Leaving their asses wide-open for us."

Nervous laughter sounded across the link from several voices at the image of a harpy bending over, but it subsided when Martinel reminded them that they had no guarantee of cracking the shields. "Folks, let's move."

Dante switched to another communication line. "General Cruz, you online?"

"I'm here, sir," the general answered.

"Get our people under cover. We've never used these weapons before on a live target. If this doesn't work, everyone on the surface will be defenseless."

"I'm already on it. Except for the flitter crews at Heavensgate, all our people will be inside Mount Purgatory within the hour."

A flat soprano voice crackled through. "Dante, I will protect them. Also, I request that you survive. You are my friend."

Dante smiled. "I'll try, Beatrice. I'll try."

* * *

The three vessels from the planet had gathered in formation at first, but they now fled. The two ancient ships tried beating Arachne's freighter to the smaller moon. The larger vessel, now identified as a Striker-class frigate, sped in the other direction.

"These pirates must be well-heeled if they could afford an old Striker on the black market," Arachne said, snorting with a bit of envy. "For all the good it'll do them against a Stalker."

Disappointed, Calahas grunted and kept working. "What a pathetic distraction."

The Ipis destroyer loomed close despite Arachne's skillful maneuvers. Calahas whispered a prayer to his ancestors and moved to fire off a salvo or two before the inevitable happened.

Then a massive blast hit the destroyer from behind.

Calahas froze in midmotion. "What in the name of all the ancestors was that?"

The destroyer reeled and turned an instant later to pursue the ship that had fired the shot: the Striker frigate. The mysterious frigate accelerated and dove into the planet's atmosphere.

The Centaur watched in utter bewilderment as the two ancient galleys turned from the moon and raced back at breakneck speed. The relics spit missiles and primitive laser beams in a stream so constant it resembled a river. His pulse pounded as the missiles slammed through a gap made by the previous blast, tearing the destroyer's engine to pieces. The strange missiles exploded in balls of superheated plasma.

Though angry at himself for getting caught unawares, Calahas turned to Arachne. "That should be enough of a distraction for us to escape."

The Ipis destroyer soon countered the unexpected threat. Ipis fighters poured from its launch bay to cover the breached engines.

A twinge of guilt assailed Calahas. The freighter's point defense ion cannon was best suited for fighting small, nimble craft like the Ipis fighters. Watching his screen, the unknown saviors must not have had such an armament on any of their craft. Despite their light weapons, the fighters herded the antique ships into the destroyer's heavy disruptor kill zones a small distance at a time.

Closing his eyes, Calahas fought a wave of memory. Valiant fighters. Courage. Slaughter.

The decision took only a moment.

With a battle cry not uttered in ten long years, Calahas overrode the pilot controls, ripped the freighter into a turn that made every structural support scream, and raced to join the battle.

The freighter echoed with howls of glee from the Centaurs who made up the smuggler's security team as they swept underneath the destroyer. Three of its support fighters exploded. Twisting and turning the bulky freighter like a berserker, Calahas avoided the heavy fire and let his gunners showcase their skill.

Fighters exploded so rapidly that, in less than a minute, none remained. The gunners instead discharged disruptor shots into the destroyer's shield.

* * *

Through the smoke and spitting circuitry of the damaged ship, Virgil gasped and wheezed. Fighting through it, he pulled the galley out of the range of the destroyer's weapons. No one had expected the freighter to aid them, but no one questioned it either.

"Well, that was helpful," Virgil muttered. "Martinel, it's your turn to dance with that monster."

"I'm swinging back," came the gleeful response.

Each ship still retained some missiles, so Dante focused on the main computer display, listening to the translated chatter coming from the damaged destroyer. Having picked up on the Ipis language since the last battle, Dante honed his ears and relayed the info as he heard it. "The harpies don't know what to do. They have no propulsion. Their engines are heavily damaged and leaking radiation." He met Virgil's eyes and toggled a couple of switches. "I'm going to ask our new friends to back off for a minute and see what we can hash out with the harpies."

Taking a deep breath, Virgil nodded.

Martinel chimed in across the comm-link. "Do it quick. That ship is one big motherfucker. I don't want to give its captain a chance to hatch any nasty surprises."

Dante nodded and cleared his throat, then opened a channel to the harpy vessel. "Unidentified spaceship, you are not welcome in this system. Your engines are gone, and your fighters have been annihilated. Stand down, and prepare to surrender your vessel."

Mercury's computer converted the harsh sounds of the harpy's language into English. "Never. All of you will yield to us immediately and face the justice of the Ipis Galactic Imperium."

Dante hoped the shakiness in the voice betrayed fear. He leaned closer to the microphone. "That won't happen. You have two choices. You can blow up your ship to prevent its capture, in which case you'll all die, or you can surrender. If you follow my commands, we will not attack your escape pods. You will all live as our prisoners. Either way, your ship will not depart this system. You have thirty seconds to decide."

The voice over the speaker came in so quiet it was hard to understand. "We... accept." The last word came out like a cough, as if the captain had to hack it up.

A few minutes later, three blunt-nosed Ipis shuttles, each spanning sixty meters, flew from launch bays located in the destroyer's midsection. Escape pods popped off as well. The trio of shuttles scooped them up.

Dante could barely wrap his head around what they'd accomplished when Porthos called to him, "Sir, that freighter's inbound to those shuttles, and I don't think he's going in for a chat."

Before Dante could determine what to do next, bright beams pulsed from the freighter, and it was over. The blasts shattered the unshielded harpy transport vessels. The ruptured shuttles spewed hundreds of bloated, frozen harpy corpses into space. A few uncollected and unpowered escape pods floated amid the wreckage. The freighter hovered nearby like a defiant child who expected punishment but would argue against it anyway.

Dante shouted into the microphone, "Kevin, retrieve the pods that are still intact, and keep our new prisoners under guard." Face flushing, he turned to Virgil. "It's high time for introductions, explanations, and finding out what exactly they gained. Instruct the freighter's captain to join us for a discussion at Heavensgate."

"Excuse me, sir," Aramis piped in. "I didn't get the full load of the harpies training when I was in stasis, but what happened here seems to be in line with what we were trained to do. As far as I know, taking enemy combatants prisoner is a human concept."

Virgil eyed Dante. "Aramis is right. We're the newbies out here. We have to learn the rules these folks live by."

Dante slammed a fist on the console. "I'm getting real tired of living by the dictates of these freaks. Maybe they should learn to live by our rules."

"Hell, yeah," Athos and Porthos shouted together.

Virgil shook his head and smiled. "Roger that. You've come a long way from a kid with a claw hammer back in New York."

"We all have, my friend," Dante whispered, peering through a window at the planet below.

CHAPTER X

Calahas and Arachne

Calahas ululated a savage roar as the third Ipis transport split apart. The inner fire flared well after the explosion ended. He faced Arachne, though he calmed himself enough to speak. "I have lived to see the destruction of an invincible Ipis destroyer."

Sagging in the pilot's chair, Arachne frowned. "And this pleases you? They'll hunt us across the length and breadth of the galaxy! We sealed our demise when that warship first hailed us. Now our families' fortunes will be forfeit, and any living creature who ever associated with us will face execution."

The fire within Calahas dissipated. "The Ipis always end up winning, don't they."

The communication switch flashed, and the Satyr sighed. "I suppose we should see what our saviors want."

His hand dropped on the button. The screen flickered alive and showed an angry face snapping sharp words. One look at the face and Arachne's mouth fell open in shock. Only his eyes turned to the Centaur. "Our rescuer looks like a human."

A bewildered Calahas stared at the screen as well. "Impossible. My people called them Novaromans. Either way, we thought they were extinct."

The freighter's computer instantly translated the bulk of the words and the emotion behind them for both Satyr and Centaur, but discerning the whole message proved difficult. At length, the Satyr spoke. "I believe the individual we upset is some sort of petty monarch in this backwater sector. It appears he's not pleased with the assistance we provided. He insists we accept their hospitality and send a contingent to a designated spaceport on the planet below for a meeting. Calahas, what do your sensors show?"

The Centaur barely registered what Arachne said. Instead, he peered through the combat scope at the small galley hovering nearby. "The threat alert system has identified those antique ships as Novaroman galleys. There hasn't been a recorded sighting of one since the Ipis annihilated the Roc-Novaroman alliance when they conquered the Lethe Sector." He met

Arachne's blank expression. "That was about one hundred and twenty standard years ago."

"My people always called them humans. Have we stumbled upon an enclave of that species? By my mother's twisted beard, what have we gotten ourselves into?"

"It's not possible." Calahas scrutinized the display's image, thinking of what he knew of humans based on Centaur tales. "The Ipis may have banned any and all references to the species, but my people still write about human technological innovations and military strategies."

Arachne stroked his beard. "The stories I heard said they could defend with the tenacity of a Satyr herd, swarm an opponent like a Centaur pack, or stage small-scale precision strikes with the ferocity of a Roc. They rallied all the sentient species in this sector and defeated the ruling Ipis governor."

A sense of pride swelled in Calahas. "In that victory, we all stood together—humans, Rocs, Centaurs, and Satyrs."

Arachne pressed his hands together. "It was a hollow victory."

Such stories were common throughout the Ipis-governed Lethe Sector. All but a few on those occupied planets knew the tragic event of the war from one hundred and twenty years ago. The humans and their allies routed the Ipis expeditionary force in the Lethe Sector. The governor fled to the Ipis Galactic Imperium and returned a year later with the full might of the empire's fleet. Eight thousand warships smashed the Lethe rebels, scattering all resistance. In the aftermath, the Ipis started a relentless hunt of every last human, reducing them to a rare sight at best.

Arachne gave Calahas a defiant glare and wiped perspiration from his forehead. "At least our species survived."

Calahas clenched blunt fingers. "Perhaps if our grandsires had stood with them, we would've achieved a different outcome. A better one."

"Bah, our ancestors were wise," Arachne said. "Only the Rocs thought to respond to the humans' final call, and look where that got them."

Calahas stomped the floor. "At least they had honor. Both our species signed defense treaties with the humans, yet we cowered on our home planets and did nothing."

"Calahas, the Ipis massacred the humans. A few managed to escape, but their descendants are hunted to this very day." The Satyr's shoulders sagged. "Look, I don't have anything against humans personally, but they draw trouble. I had a couple in my crew a year before you and my niece signed up. Octavia and Cilla were good workers."

"What happened to them?" Calahas asked.

Arachne tugged his beard again. "It's been about three years since they vanished. We were in port on the Roc planet of Tanis. The two of them went into town to pick up a shipment they were very excited about. The cargo showed up, but the humans never did. I asked the authorities about it, and *they* asked why I harbored enemies of the empire. It cost me a lot of bribe money to walk out of there, and I still have that damn shipment in suspended animation in the cargo hold."

Calahas faced the now dark communicator screen, black tail flicking with excitement. "I've seen pictures, but I've never met a living human."

Arachne's lips formed a sly smile. "Oh, they're around, but only if you know where to look. To survive, they've become a very secretive bunch."

"Do you really have the cargo? A real human's cargo?"

"That's what I just said," Arachne sputtered. "I gave full payment too. Now I'm waiting for delivery instructions. It's some sort of livestock. In stasis, the beasts don't take up much space." Arachne pulled on his right horn. "I keep it off the manifest just in case. It's not right what the Ipis do to those people."

Calahas' tail flicked again. "This is incredible. Despite the genocide, they still exist."

"Indeed, yes, and it would appear you now have the opportunity to meet some." Arachne rose from his chair. "Put together a security detail, and ready the shuttle. We'll head down in an hour." Irritation spiked in his next words. "And drag Paxine along. She was probably too absorbed in her schoolbooks to know we almost died a short while ago."

Calahas curled his fingers into fists and stood on all fours. "You mean your niece doesn't appreciate the finer points of the family's smuggling business."

Arachne slapped his paunch. "She wouldn't want to get her hands dirty even if we were legit. It's about time she opened her eyes a bit, so I'll have her help with the negotiations. Maybe we can salvage something out of this mess."

CHAPTER XI

Meeting of Minds

As Mercury descended through Cocytus' atmosphere, Martinel's voice crackled through the communicator. "Dante, a major radiation pulse is spilling out of the harpy destroyer."

A sudden chill stopped Dante cold. "Get as far away from it as you can."

The static cleared for a moment, and Martinel sounded calm. "Actually, we're fine. The shielding on our ship held up, but it's playing havoc with our external sensors and communications. We retrieved all the escape craft we could, Mister President. Only three were intact. Two were escape pods packed with harpies, but the third was a small attack craft. The pilot offered no resistance. The creature looks like a giant emu."

Mercury's speaker crackled again as the ship touched down on the plain in front of Heavensgate. Dante strained to pick up the words. "Say again, Kevin? We just landed, and I couldn't make out what you said."

"An emu. It looks like an emu with a big head and feathered arms."

Dante shot a puzzled look at Virgil.

Virgil shrugged and said, "Hey, I've seen sci-fi movies. It could be a lot worse."

"Yeah, I guess." Dante gave a nervous laugh before turning back to the communicator. "Okay, Kevin, how many harpies are there?"

"About thirty, and they screeched and pointed until we separated them into holding cells. Atlantis' translator is processing all their squawking as we speak." A sigh broke through. "Mister President, the thing that looks like Big Bird just stared at me like I was dinner or something. Didn't cause any commotion when we locked it up, but it sure gave me the willies."

"Well, keep them all under heavy guard." Dante leapt to his feet. "Kevin, stay on high alert in case anyone else pops in. See if Mara can help with the translations."

"Yes, sir. Atlantis acquitted herself bloody well, didn't she?"

"You all did a great job," Dante heartily agreed. On seeing the sparking circuitry in Mercury's cabin, though, he squeezed the bridge of his nose. "But let's try not to do this too often. We have a lot to repair. Now we have to talk with our alien visitors. God knows what will come of that. Stay close to the wreck in case it's not as dead as it looks, and have Soyuz track the other ship."

Martinel replied, "We're scanning the destroyer now. The radiation spikes have subsided, but nothing will survive in there after that."

"Keep on the lookout for any surprises." Dante toggled the communication system to a different channel. "Beatrice, are you here?"

"Yes, Dante," the familiar flat soprano answered.

"I want a bunch of your miner drones at the spaceport—the new ones with the energy digging blades."

"Yes, Dante. No intruder will harm a human."

Dante's brows shot up. "No, Beatrice. These are not intruders, at least not yet. Categorize them as non-guests for now."

"I understand and will comply. Six of the new mining drones will depart Hellsgate via air transport in twenty-three-point-seven minutes."

"Thanks, Beatrice. Also, please contact the planetary council. I'll need them at Heavensgate as soon as possible."

"I will comply," came the clipped reply. "Tina, Michael, and Father Bruno are already there. I will expedite the transport of the others."

As Dante finished speaking, Aramis entered the control room with an armful of disrupter rifles and joined his two podmates. "We'll be ready if those bastards give you any trouble." A big grin creased his face.

Dante approached the young clone, already half a head taller than himself, and squeezed the youth's iron-hard shoulder. "You boys did an incredible job working those guns and missiles. I was proud to be part of your crew."

"They sure as hell performed like veterans. They can go anywhere I go," Virgil added.

All three clones squared their shoulders and beamed.

Virgil checked Mercury's control panel and shook his head. "Boss, I need to bring this jalopy to the garage. Mercury's banged up from our little escapade."

Dante pursed his lips. "Have Linda Martinel send a crew over to check Mercury. I need you for the meeting. It could change everything for us." He approached the exit door and opened it.

"I'm coming," Virgil sighed, "but I'd still prefer if you made the decisions and I have the fun smashing bad guys."

Dante walked down the ramp and stepped into a driving rain typical for springtime on this part of Cocytus. He spotted Tina running out of Heavensgate and straight to him.

Before he could speak, however, Tina cut him off by rushing in and hugging him tight. "What were you thinking? You're not Flash Gordon. You could've been killed."

"We'll just go see about setting things up," Virgil muttered as he tried to slip past the two.

He couldn't go far once Tina grabbed his arm, looking right in his eyes. "Virgil Bernius, you know Dante's no soldier. What were you thinking, letting him get involved with the battle?"

Virgil gave a defeated nod. "Sorry, Tina. We didn't have a lot of time to assign roles. One minute, we were starting survey work. In the next, we were in a fight for our lives with the biggest damn ship I've ever seen."

Tina gave a defeated nod of her own, and for a few moments, neither she nor Virgil said anything. The three clones snuck past both and hurried toward the entrance of Heavensgate. Virgil followed them shortly after.

Eventually, Tina turned and held Dante's face. "I was so worried and felt so helpless." She took a shuddered breath and scanned him for injuries, then gasped when she spotted a small electrical burn on his cheek. "You *were* hurt." She wrapped her arms around him again and sobbed.

"I'm okay. Really I am. We can treat the burn easily." Dante stroked her rain-soaked hair. "C'mon. We have visitors to meet."

Tina poked Dante in the ribs. "Can I be the one to say 'Take me to your leader'?"

"You can do all the talking." Dante hugged her and entered the open foyer of the compound.

"You stupid oaf, I love you." Tina touched his face again as they wrapped their arms around each other and walked toward the now familiar seven-story black building.

In the same six months where they appropriated the harpy hive building, the Cocytus survivors had transformed the interior as well. The human crews had resealed the cracks in the walls, and new arched doorways replaced the

DNA-coded portals the harpies once used. The ceilings glowed with a warm, golden light, replacing the cold blue that once dominated the halls.

A half hour after Mercury landed, the full planetary council gathered, with the exception of General Cruz. Waiting in the middle of the open room spanning the entire first floor were Michael, Esther, Dimitri, Linda, and Father Bruno. Virgil posted Aramis, Porthos, and Athos by the entrance and six other armed clones on the risers to the building's second level. A dozen repair drones flitted into the room and settled in by the humans.

Dante noticed the bloodshot eyes of the others and felt a twinge of guilt. With everyone overworked, did he dare ask more of them? A rueful sigh left him. "I think you all need a holiday when this is over."

Father Bruno shrugged. "Understanding what we have here is slow work, but being an archeologist, I'm used to it. Trying to glean understanding of the harpies' technology and thought process is challenging. There's so much to learn and discover."

Dante nodded. "Yeah, I tried a few of those stasis training modules. I learned the harpy language to get a good handle on their software and operating system, but without context, most their other files didn't mean much. This place was some sort of research station and had only been here a couple years. The harpies that ran this place thought they were close to establishing the existence of their 'ancient enemy,' but I couldn't determine what their proof was."

Tina shrugged. "We haven't checked a lot of the modules yet. Michael's been trying to organize it all, but he's not familiar with most of it either."

At the mention of Michael's name, Dante spotted him holding an intense conversation with Virgil. Dante walked over, and both caught his eye soon after.

Michael half-smiled at the newcomers. "It isn't fair. You got to whack those bastards while I was stuck here on the ground. That must've been a great sight."

Memories of energy beams and a shaking ship returned, and Dante grimaced. "It was scary as hell. I think I peed in my pants. Twice."

Virgil slapped him on the back. "You did fine, Mister President. You followed orders fast and without question."

Dante studied the captain for a sign of sarcasm, but only sincerity glimmered in his eyes. He turned back to Michael. "Any idea on how we should handle this alien meeting we're going to have?"

"How the hell should I know? I ain't never met any aliens other than you guys." Michael faced them all with a big grin.

Dante couldn't offer more than a blank stare. Neither could anyone else.

Michael's smile lasted a moment longer, then vanished. "Ah, that was supposed to be funny."

Virgil smirked. "You told a joke? Not too bad, actually. It's just that everything you say is so serious. I think you moved a step ahead of Beatrice in the comedian department."

A maintenance drone broke from the lighting control panel and approached the group. A few beeps escaped, and Beatrice's voice emerged from the drone's speaker. "Humor is the juxtaposition of two incongruous facts. It is not a productive activity."

"I'll figure out this human humor thing yet," Michael said, only to sigh right after. "But I still can't help you understand an alien species. The only serious training I had focused on studying the harpy interpretation of human behavior, and that proved highly inaccurate."

"The aliens will be here soon. We have to come up with plan of action, fast." Dante watched everyone present gather close to listen.

Virgil rested a heavy hand on Dante's shoulder. "As I see it, Mister President, you're the person who ought to talk with them. You're the one who got Mick and Beatrice to help us."

"My name is Michael, and I am not an alien," the big clone protested.

"You're still big and ugly," Virgil chuckled.

"I am also not an alien, but the crux of Virgil's argument is valid," Beatrice stated in a flat voice. "Dante has an innate ability to filter through the words spoken and grasp the underlying meaning. He understood me better than I did myself."

"So, it is decided." Father Bruno raised his arms to encompass the room. "But presentation is also important. I may be an archeologist, but I also have a fair understanding of anthropology. The harpies saw our species through the prism of their expectations. These folks surely deal with the Ipis. Let's present that stereotype to them. We need a throne on an elevated platform. You must be seated but with the ability to look down at them."

"I agree." Dmitri pointed to Aramis. "I have a stasis pod in the lab on the third level that I'm remodeling into a chair shape. Please get it. It glows and has a lot of shiny metal on it. Athos, see what you can do about the lighting on the first level. I want it as bright as possible along the back wall and sort of dim by the main entrance."

Father Bruno regarded Dante closely. "Mister President, lose the tunic and put on one of the neural-net suits. It'll look more impressive, and you'll have a communication link to Beatrice that an outsider can't eavesdrop on."

Virgil gave Michael a sly look. "Like the Wizard of Oz. Good idea."

Tina rolled her eyes. "The Emerald City?"

Michael cocked his head at the two of them.

Tina nudged him. "You know, ignore the man behind the curtain?"

Michael cocked his head to the other side.

Virgil grabbed the clone's arm. "C'mon, big guy. I'll explain it to you. I'll be the scarecrow, and you'll be the cowardly lion."

Six bullet-shaped drones stretching a little over a meter long each rolled into the room on treaded wheels dripping rainwater. Beatrice announced from the wall-mounted speaker, "My robots have arrived. What task shall they perform?"

Virgil smirked. "Now we have the tin man."

"Invalid statement. Tin is not a component I use in the fabrication of my drones, and I have no gender as you define it."

"I know, Beatrice, my mistake." Virgil sighed. "Send your robots outside. They'll be the welcoming committee. Besides, they're getting the floor soaked."

* * *

After half an hour, they had the open ground floor with a dais setup at the far end to Father Bruno's specifications. He stepped back and reviewed the makeshift throne setup. "No, no, it's not quite right. It still needs to appear more majestic. Virgil and Michael, you should stand to the right of the dais and look mean. Tina, sit at Dante's feet."

A glare twitched across Tina's face, and she crossed her arms. "How about you sit there and I use you as a footstool?"

Sheepish, Bruno waved his hands. "This is theater. This is imagery."

Tina sighed and rolled her eyes. She looked at Dante, who gave her an embarrassed grin. "I'm going to kill you if you start laughing." She shot a look at the young clones lounging by the entrance and holding their laser rifles. "Will someone at least get me something to sit on?"

Aramis nodded and hurried off.

"There must be more we can add." Bruno clapped his hands together. "Porthos, my lab is on the first tier below ground, where the harpies stored their artifacts. I have a bronze Roman Eagle that I excavated from the galley factory ruins. It's on the table near the door."

Dante couldn't bring himself to say the priest had actually pointed to Athos, not Porthos. Athos furrowed his brow, but before he could speak, he caught Virgil winking at him. Sighing, Athos grumbled, "Yes, sir," and trotted off.

Beatrice's voice boomed from the wall-mounted speaker with an announcement, "The shuttle of the not-guests has landed."

Everyone went still, but Virgil spoke. "All militia, move to a higher level. Make sure you have a clear field of fire in case anything goes wrong."

"Right. This is a show, but one with serious implications." Father Bruno breathed deep. "This will have to do. Everyone who doesn't have a gun, stand with me to the left of the dais and try to look like sage advisors."

* * *

Calahas led his security escort onto the freighter's shuttle after Arachne and Paxine. The excitement of meeting real humans for the first time fought with apprehension.

An hour after receiving their instructions from the planet's ruler, the shuttle landed at the designated coordinates. The sole feature on the otherwise bleak, lifeless ground was a solitary domed building, colored black and standing seven stories high. A small, ancient human galley and several modern atmospheric vehicles rested near the entrance of the building, but otherwise, the area didn't look like much of a spaceport. The driving rain obscured the late-afternoon light.

Ivory-colored robots rumbled to the shuttle. Arachne mopped the sweat from his brow with the sleeve of a bright green robe. "Here comes our escort." Curiosity soon seeped into his voice. "Interesting. The building resembles Ipis architecture, but I haven't seen robots like those before. Paxine, are you familiar with those kinds of machines?"

"No, I'm not." Paxine glared and crossed her arms. "Who cares? You aided these savages in the crime, and now our lives are forfeit. That's all I can think about, Uncle." Her eyes found the nearest window. "This is no proper welcome. My hooves will get covered in mud."

Paxine also had a pair of the rare double-curled horns as her uncle, but the commonalities between them ended there. She was slim and tall for her species and walked with an aristocratic bearing. Her braided goatee glittered with the precious gems woven into the strands.

"That Ipis warship tried to kill us, in case you've forgotten," Arachne snapped.

"And these creatures are not primitive from what I've seen so far. They know sound combat tactics, and what technology they have is sophisticated. I, for one, am curious to meet a human." Calahas drew the ion blaster strapped across his withers and laid it on the console. He powered up a photonics scanner-sensor and cantered to the shuttle's exit. Four Centaurs from his security team trotted after him.

Arachne was quick to follow. "Come, dear Paxine. For better or worse, we need to ingratiate ourselves to these people."

Paxine leered the whole way, speaking in a heated whisper. "What we need to do is find a way to gain forgiveness from the Ipis."

She stepped onto the tarmac with her uncle and stumbled to a halt near the Centaurs encircled by six strange robots. The cone-shaped drones had generated an energy shield that diverted the wind and rain.

An audio device telescoped from one of the robots and rotated toward them. The voice spoke in accent-less Ipis. "Not-guests will stay together and follow me."

The six robots rolled ahead at a brisk pace, forcing the crew members from the freighter to trot.

Calahas took in every detail as they entered the spacious foyer. Most of all, he gawked at seeing humans everywhere. "They look just like the pictures," he murmured.

The robot entourage escorted Calahas and the others to a regal-looking human who sat on a raised dais. A small group of unarmed humans flanked him to the left. More armed humans occupied the ramp and upper level to his right. The interior walls conformed to the designs of a standard Ipis remote research facility, but the golden lighting made the room easier on the eyes.

Calahas walked close to the wall as they entered and studied it. He pressed his mouth close to Arachne's ear. "This is no benign colony. I believe we are meeting with the tip of a vast army."

A glint flitted across Arachne's eyes as they approached the waiting humans. "I know that. They flew a Striker-class frigate and just took out a Stalker-class destroyer."

"It's bigger than even that. I think we stumbled on the tail end of a major battle." Calahas squeaked in awe. "They tried to cover the blaster scars are on the walls, and many of the warriors watching us are wearing the helmets of the Ipis-dis paramilitary Third Division."

Arachne went wide-eyed, slowing down. "The Third Division? Those Dis-cult mercenaries are ruthless with any non-Ipis species."

"I'd guess this was one of their outposts, and it was overwhelmed by a massive human army." Calahas glanced at his scanner and quirked his brow. "Most of the human warriors from above have identical DNA."

"So maybe that's how they bred," Paxine grumbled.

Arachne tugged on his right horn. "That's impossible. Humans are mammals like us. Those are clone soldiers."

"And if they have the technology to produce a dozen clone fighters, they have the technology to produce millions of them," Calahas concluded.

"Our robot escorts have electrical energy signatures instead of photonic, but they're far too sophisticated to have been built by a band of guerillas hiding in the galaxy's wilderness. An isolated Ipis outpost wouldn't have a chance against such a force."

Calahas raised his head and spotted the man sitting on the elevated chair. The human warlord, no doubt. The human wore a one-piece suit of some dun-colored material, and it covered everything but his face. He spoke in whispers to a woman sitting beside him.

"Their warlord casually chats with an advisor after defeating a destroyer, a feat no one's accomplished in over a hundred years." Arachne shook his head. "The fool must believe he has enough power to challenge the Ipis Empire directly."

Paxine stroked her goatee and mumbled, "A military rival to the Ipis Empire."

Arachne leaned closer to her. "What did you say?"

"Nothing," she answered quickly.

"Then let me do the talking," Arachne growled. He stepped forward and prostrated himself before the human on the throne. "Your Majesty."

Calahas watched as the human leader grasped the hand of the woman sitting beside him. He caught a certain tenderness in the gesture and their gazes, the kind known only to a couple in love. Tears welled in his eyes upon remembering his own love, Gesten. She also was of royal blood and had been quarantined along with many others on their home world, Equitone, for ten years by the Ipis warlord who governed the planet. Because of Calahas' failed revolution, he feared Gesten would never breathe free air again.

He sighed, raised himself to his full height, and dipped his head, letting his long black mane cover his face. The other Centaurs followed suit. Paxine bowed but also glowered.

* * *

The entrance door slid into the wall, and six mining drones herded a group of strange creatures into the makeshift audience chamber. Dante's heart rate quickened as the small procession of exotic creatures approached.

The two distinct species reminded him of figures from Greek mythology books he'd seen as a youth. Five faintly resembled Centaurs, small ponies with extended torsos and arms. They wore no garments, but several pouches hung from their sides. Their short fur varied in color, but chestnut brown appeared the most common, accompanied by black tails and manes. However, unlike the storybook pictures he'd seen as a youth, the faces of these creatures bore the same thick fur as the rest of their bodies.

The other two creatures had horns and walked upright on two cloven feet. Both wore bright green robes, but the rotund one trotted in front of the other like a pack leader. They resembled the mythological Satyrs.

Tina sat on a low stool beside him and squeezed his hand in reassurance. Her other hand clutched a small laser pistol hidden beneath her cloak. He noticed that her hand was as sweaty as his.

Dante cast a look at Michael and Virgil but couldn't discern their emotions. Both wore stoic, blank expressions and cradled their captured ion disruptors. To his right stood Esther, Dimitri, Linda, and Father Bruno, all of whom observed everything. Dante made a mental note to compare notes with them later.

Beatrice spoke into his earphone, translating as much as possible of the conversation the newcomers shared among themselves. However, she had difficulty capturing all the not-guests' words. The aliens had employed a device that blocked eavesdropping. Every time she penetrated the screen, the device shifted frequency and forced her to break through again.

"Dante, they believe you are the leader of a human kingdom that is at war with the harpies. They think you lead a vast army and have just won a major victory conquering this planet. This is with an eighty-seven-percent certainty. They also say humans have fought the harpies many years ago and lost."

"They've seen us before?" Dante frowned in confusion and raised his hand to cover his mouth. "Thanks, Beatrice. Wish me luck, and let me know if you pick up any other useful nuggets."

"Request is unclear. Luck denotes random chance, but my heuristic models can apply probabilities. What dimension and material type of nugget do you require?"

"Just keep the info coming." Dante wiped a hand on his pant leg and smiled wanly at Tina.

The strange aliens reached the base of the dais. As a rotund Satyr-like creature stepped forward and bowed, Tina drew back. "It's show time."

Dante raised a hand and made a declaration in the most authoritative voice he could muster. "I bid you greetings. Who are you, and why are you here?"

Beatrice boomed those words in the Ipis language from one of the drones flanking the newcomers.

CHAPTER XII

Audience with a King

Dante observed how the lead creature, a Satyr, kept looking between him and the eagle statue glowing above the chair. The image of a happier Satyr prancing through a field, blowing on a lute, danced in his head. However, the brief daydream ended when the very real Satyr bowed and spoke.

"Greetings, sire. I am Arachne of the Satyr Mercantile Guild, a simple trader," the Satyr stated in Ipis, pointing to his left and right. "This is my aide, Paxine, and my security chief, Calahas. We thank you for your timely intervention and rescue." The rotund Satyr straightened. "I pride myself on my linguistic skill. It helps a trader speak with customers in their native tongue and not depend on translation equipment. I would like to continue in your own beautiful language."

Beatrice repeated the words simultaneously into Dante's earpiece.

The Satyr swept the room and its occupants with an unreadable air before speaking in a familiar-sounding language. "I had human crew members once, and they taught me their language. The Ipis ban its use, so I especially enjoy the opportunity to speak it aloud."

From amid the advisors near the throne, Father Bruno cried, "*Deus meus!*" Arachne jerked his head, a motion Dante watched with interest.

The smaller Satyr blurted something in Ipis. "What did you just say, Uncle?"

Beads of sweat popped out on Arachne's forehead as he mumbled back in the same language, "I just said, 'Hello,' and a few other things to ingratiate ourselves to our hosts, I think."

Dante shot a sharp look at Father Bruno, who mouthed the word, "Latin."

It took a moment for the reality to settle in, but it was true: a Satyr spoke Latin in the middle of outer space. Dante tried to conceal his surprise and regarded the aliens with as much calm as he could muster. "Be at peace. I am Dante Carloman, the elected president of this world. What is the purpose of your journey to this star system, and why were you fighting that harpy—er, Ipis, warship?"

Arachne squinted and leaned close to what must've been a translator system. Dante strained to hear it, but the speaker of this system produced faint, meaningless sounds for half the words it interpreted.

The lead Centaur squatted on his haunches and scanned a tablet screen. Dante listened intently to Beatrice's translation and heard confusion in the Centaur's voice. "I think he claims lordship over this world and has granted us sanctuary. He wants to know what we're doing here." The Centaur snorted, still looking at the tablet. "He claims to be of the House Carloman and thinks we were fighting the Ipis."

Though confused, Dante maintained a stoic expression through what he overheard next.

Arachne snorted. "Carloman? That was the name of the last human emperor. This warlord's probably claiming that name to enhance his luster among his subjects." Arachne tugged his beard and faced the Centaur. "He doesn't know I have good knowledge of Novaroman lore."

Dante's mind spun, but he held his tongue when Beatrice revealed that the visitors believed the handheld devices they possessed shielded their conversations from eavesdropping.

Eventually, Arachne squared his shoulders, dipped his head, and spoke again. "Your Majesty, it is an honor to meet a descendant from one of the two noble Novaroman houses. The exploits of the Carloman and Bernius families are legendary even among my people."

Dante swung a look toward Virgil, who frowned. "What the hell's going on here? How'd that son of a bitch get my name?"

The smaller Satyr hissed in her leader's ear, "Watch your words, or we'll never get out of this building alive."

Dante worked his mouth while trying to think of a response. "Thank you. It is good to hear of my people's exploits from others, but we can speak more of this later." He drew a breath and hardened his tone. "Tell me why you fired on those shuttles after I had accepted their surrender."

After a pause, Arachne's brow knitted and he eyed the Centaur.

The Centaur shrugged. "Perhaps he's either making a joke or testing our knowledge of the Ipis military. Would you like me to respond?"

"Yes. If I offend him, we could end up dead."

Beatrice's voice crackled in Dante's ear, translating the side conversation first. "They are confused by the intent of your question. The underling will respond."

Sweat dripped into Dante's eyes despite the neural-net suit's effort to keep him cool.

The Centaur rose to his full height on his hindquarters. "I am Calahas of the Centaurs. I am the security chief for Captain Arachne's vessel. I will answer your questions regarding the military engagement just concluded. And if I may, I'd like to say I'm honored to meet the human monarch. The Centaurs remember the years our peoples walked together as a golden era, and I'm glad to see you reclaiming your rightful role in the galaxy." He bowed his head, causing his black mane cover his face.

"Ah, a Centaur?" A small smile crossed Dante's face as he thought the furred face resembled a baboon's more than a human's. "You don't look like any pictures of Centaurs I've seen."

Calahas' withers twitched. "I understand your disdain. I pray your reference to being different means you'll grant me a chance to redeem my species for its traitorous and cowardly acts of the past." He pawed the floor. "Your Majesty, we had every reason to aid you in the destruction of the escape vessels. Once they launched their communication rockets, they would've reached hyperspace in short order and revealed your armada's advances to Ipis authorities."

Dante eyed his advisors, who returned blank stares. He covered his mouth. "Beatrice, what's this guy talking about?"

"I lack data for a definitive answer."

"Then give me your best guess," Dante hissed. "Please."

"With a sixty-eight-percent probability, I surmise that energy beams cannot exceed the speed of light. Since the next closest star system is three-point-seven light years away, photonic messaging would be useless. Following that logic, communications would need to be encapsulated and transported through a hyperspace propulsion system."

Dante scratched his ear. "Makes sense. Physics is physics even out here in Neverland. It's a freaking pony express messaging system."

"Excuse me, sire," Calahas said. "I did not understand your last comment."

He'd spoken aloud, and the Centaur overheard him? Dante bit back dread and embarrassment, fumbling for another question to ask. When he regained his bearings, he fought to speak in an even tone. "Why not just destroy the communication rockets? You didn't have to kill those who surrendered."

If a Centaur could look incredulous, Calahas demonstrated this well. "As Your Majesty well knows, each escape pod is equipped with emergency rescue transmission rockets so the jettisoned crews won't be marooned in space. A simple freighter wouldn't have been able to intercept that many." His withers twitched despite his calm voice. "Besides, it was a merciful death over suffering from radiation poisoning. When your surgical missile strike ruptured the destroyer's primary power unit, you sealed their demise. Only the most desperate would accept your terms." He appeared to study Dante, and his voice softened somewhat. "Your Majesty, forgive me if I presume too much. If the survivors were detoxed immediately after exposure, they could've been saved. Does your warship contain such facilities? A normal Ipis Striker-class frigate does not."

Dante blanked on what to say, feeling adrift as though lost in the woods without a compass. Martinel did say there'd been a significant radiation leak, but he hadn't reported on the actual damage done to the harpy ship. Dante rubbed his hand across his mouth to hide consternation that the Centaur appeared confident in his assessment.

Calahas' tail swished back and forth. "I could tell by the escape capsules released that the destroyer's captain and her officers stayed to the end, deleting files in the ship's computer system. The ones who fled were likely crewmen from the lower castes. They were probably ordered to detonate the warship remotely. We ensured that would not occur. Many decades have passed since they lost a mainline ship in battle. They responded too slowly to the threat here."

Dante covered his mouth again with a shaking hand. "Beatrice, tell Martinel to check the prisoners for radiation poisoning."

"Mara reports that ten percent of the harpy prisoners have expired. The rest are writhing on the floors of their cells. The non-harpy alien was in one of the small attack craft and appears unaffected. It has not flinched since it was incarcerated. The radiation pulse had dissipated by the time it reached the wreckage of the small vessels."

Tina whispered to Dante, "Have them scan the derelict Stalker for any life signs."

Dante nodded and relayed the request, instinctively grasping her hand.

Tina leaned in and kissed him. She whispered, "You're doing great."

Dante chewed on his lower lip before facing the visitors. He reluctantly released her hand and the support he felt through their touch.

* * *

Calahas smiled at the sight of the two humans' heartwarming interaction and spoke in a quiet voice. "I had a love once. When the latest Ipis lordling brought oppressive laws to Equitone, I rebelled. In my vanity, I thought I could free my world of those tyrants. Gesten warned me that no good would come of it."

"Shut up, you fool," Arachne hissed.

Calahas ignored the request, lost in his own reverie. "She gave wise counsel, but I didn't heed her. Now, most of my followers are dead, and my love is quarantined while I skulk around the fringes of civilization, hiding in shadows."

Paxine turned ashen. "*You* led the Centaur revolt?"

"Calahas, you're talking too much," Arachne hissed again. He faced the humans and bowed with a flourish. "Your Majesty, I've always been a good friend to humans. As I said before, a couple were members of my crew for several years. Novaroma was the home world of their family."

Paxine snarled at her uncle. "Harboring humans is insanity. It's treason to the empire!"

Arachne nudged her and whispered, "We'll talk about all this later." He maintained a pleasant smile despite the interruption and bowed a second time. "I have a small cargo they acquired. I would be pleased to present it to you in their honor."

The human leader bared a stern frown but leaned forward. "You referred to your human crew members in the past tense. What happened to them?"

While Arachne spoke, Calahas cast a brief look upon the king's advisors. By their stances, they appeared to hang on every word.

Arachne cleared his throat. "When we docked on Tanis about three standard years ago, Cilla and Octavia went into the port city to acquire a private shipment. They said that with it they could start a new life beyond the reach of the Ipis. To make a long story short, the cargo arrived, but Cilla and Octavia never did." He met the king's eyes. "The Ipis in our dear Lethe Sector have never forgotten how humans once challenged their rule. Many are fanatical Ipis-dis followers and abhor anything remotely associated with humans."

King Carloman squeezed the chair's arms but spoke in a steady voice. "If you don't mind confirming something for me, are we in the Lethe Sector now?"

Calahas thought a hint of disdain rode in the human's words. He gave Arachne and Paxine a warning glare and whispered to them, "Stay silent. There is no safe answer to that question."

"But a simple, honest answer is best," Arachne said. The pudgy Satyr tugged his beard and turned to the human king again. "I'm a trader, and until today, I've heard no rumor about the breadth of your conquests. Although this branch of the galaxy is sparsely populated, it is well within what used to be the boundaries of the Lethe Sector."

The human king muttered something short but resigned to his wife. She answered in a similar, calmer tone of voice. Whatever she said next prompted the king to face Arachne once more as though nothing had happened.

"What are the contents of this cargo shipment?" the king asked.

Arachne puffed out his chest. *"Hircos et pullos.* They're in stasis, of course."

* * *

Father Bruno squeaked in surprise, and Beatrice translated the Latin phrase almost simultaneously. "Goats and chickens."

"Ah, how many?" Dante arched an eyebrow at Tina, who smiled back.

Arachne peered at his tablet. "A hundred chickens and twenty goats. I brought the shipping container in our shuttle outside. With your permission, I can have my crew unload it wherever you'd like."

Dante cupped his mouth. "Beatrice, are you ready for some lessons in animal husbandry?"

"I would find the expansion of knowledge stimulating."

"Good. Contact General Cruz, and have his folks start building chicken coops and goat pens near Hellsgate. We can't keep them here, and I don't want these aliens to learn about our other places just yet. We have some farmers in our colony, so have Cruz find a few who know something about goats and chickens."

"Yes. Dante, we must speak later about what these not-guests said about humans."

"Okay." Dante focused on Beatrice's drone. "What's the problem?"

"I require assistance processing the data."

"You need help from me?"

"Yes."

Sighing, Dante rubbed his temples and called Virgil over. "Put together a team and deliver the container to Hellsgate." He lowered his voice. "I want to separate our guests. Make sure your translator has Beatrice's latest updates, and try to get the aliens that go with you talking. We can compare notes later."

"Good idea. We'll see if their stories mesh." Virgil shouldered an ion disruptor and waved to the upper tier. "Aramis, Porthos, Athos, you're with me."

Dante smiled at Arachne. "We'll take immediate possession of the animals. I'm sending my personal bodyguard to oversee the delivery."

Arachne pursed his lips. "Calahas, take your team and assist with the transfer to the designated location. Paxine and I will handle things here."

The rotund Satyr leaned close to the Centaur's ear and muttered something in a low voice. The Centaur flicked his tail and said nothing. Soon, five Centaurs followed Virgil and the three clones out the door.

Dante feigned nonchalance while the departing group passed through the door and ventured into the raging weather outside. In truth, he kept an eye on Arachne through his peripheral vision.

The Satyr observed the surroundings and the people present with great care. Their eyes met, and Dante thought a blend of curiosity and fear wrestled in the alien's eyes.

"What manner of ruler are you?" Arachne blurted. "You interact with your bodyguards as if you're friends. Common soldiers spring to the command of their officer but performed no obeisance to you."

Dante's brow furrowed. "So, a king cannot be approachable or care for those around him?"

Arachne shuddered. "I meant no disrespect. It's just unusual in this part of the galaxy."

"Then maybe the ways of the galaxy are wrong," Dante answered.

Arachne's shoulders sagged, but the moment didn't last. "Your Majesty, may I inquire what you plan to do with us?"

A slow smile crossed Dante's face. "If by that you mean, 'What do I plan on doing *to* you,' the answer is nothing."

Arachne sighed, betraying mountains of relief.

"However, we need to negotiate some recompense for the protection we provided."

The exhaled breath stopped, and Arachne coughed. "Recompense?"

Tina leaned close to Dante. "What are you doing?"

He leaned toward her in turn. "We're a few lost souls stuck on a frozen planet in the middle of a galaxy controlled by creatures who apparently hate us. We may have real spaceships, but we don't know how to use them to their fullest. Heck, there's a million things we need. But most of all, we need information."

She nodded slowly. "Yeah, no kidding. God only knows when the next 'friendly' alien will stumble onto Cocytus."

Dante squeezed her hand. "Don't worry. My mom's Italian, and Italians always negotiate the price of vegetables. And *everything* is a vegetable." He made the slightest jerk of the head toward Arachne.

Next, he turned to the Satyr and spoke in a mellow voice. "Arachne, you led a murderous enemy into my territory, and I was forced to dispose of it. Certainly, you don't expect that the protection we provided would be free, do you?"

The rotund Satyr tugged at his robe's open collar. "Be merciful, Your Majesty. I had no way of knowing that this planetary system was part of your kingdom. It would bankrupt me to pay any type of tax or service fee. Alas, I am but a poor Satyr of commerce, plying my trade in the wild frontier of the galaxy."

Dante turned to Tina and smiled.

She mouthed the word, "Vegetable," and patted his hand.

* * *

Arachne rolled his neck to get the kinks out, glad that one of the human king's minions brought them chairs shortly after Calahas left. After spending three hours discussing trade, however, Arachne wanted to stretch his legs.

Beside him, Paxine flashed a heated glare. "Uncle, I understand the need to pay the ransom for our release, but how can you think of establishing trade with these outlaws? It's sedition!"

He faced her in full. "We're already traitors. In case you don't remember, there's a derelict Stalker-class destroyer in orbit around this planet with hundreds of dead Ipis soldiers onboard."

"I know we could convince them of our innocence if we—"

Paxine stopped short when a drone with extended sensors hovered nearby. Her voice dropped to a whisper. "How do you know they have anything worth trading? All we've seen of these people is a single desolate spaceport."

Arachne sighed and appraised the human technology intermingled with the Ipis machinery. He tallied up what he'd given up so far. The complete download of his freighter's navigation and training files cost him nothing, but the loss of one stabilized bi-nexidium container hurt as it would've provided enough energy to power an Adamant-class battlewagon for twenty years. In exchange, the human king granted him exclusive non-human trading rights to this planet for the next fifteen years. Not a total loss, but a sizeable compromise nonetheless.

Tugging his goatee, he studied how the room had changed. Most of the humans sat on the floor in idle conversation. The most imposing of the bodyguards stood tensed for action, and the plain-looking robots clanked in and out of the building on some unknown errands. A marked contrast from the earlier formality.

At long last, the king looked down from his throne. "So, do we have a deal?"

"One more thing, Your Majesty." Arachne swallowed hard. "Perhaps one initial trade between us to seal our contract."

King Carloman leaned forward. "What do you propose?"

Arachne eyed the drones with avarice. "One of my shuttles for five of your robots."

Beatrice spoke in a quick burst. "Do not let him take part of me."

King Carloman shook his head and mumbled something Arachne's translator couldn't pick up. Next, he snapped his fingers and stared for several moments, interlocking his fingers in a steeple, and spoke on a hunch. "I have no need for that outdated vessel outside."

Arachne winced. He thought he'd tricked the human king into taking the worn-out relic. Now he'd have to deliver one of the newer models he possessed. "Your Majesty wounds me. Of course, I'd be happy to give you the newest transport in my inventory. What do you propose we barter?"

"I would like another bi-nexidium container. In exchange, I will trade you a fully functional planetary artificial intelligence."

The drone's voice crackled. "No, please, do not send me away. What have I done to offend you?"

"That is not nearly a fair trade," Arachne sputtered. "You'll ruin me."

Dante leaned back. "This is a state of the art, military-grade Ipis research machine. The drives have been erased, but the operating system's intact and has a one-thousand blade parallel processor. It ran this very station."

"Dante, that system is evil. It should be destroyed, not bartered," the drone said.

Arachne pulled on his right horn and croaked, "With wiped drives, it's only half the value of what you ask."

Paxine stepped in front of her uncle and smiled. "It's a deal."

Arachne sank to the floor. "By my mother's twisted beard, I need a drink."

King Carloman exchanged a look with his wife, who shrugged. The king let out a clipped sigh. "Then we are agreed. We'll make the exchange in two days." He rose and walked over to the two Satyrs.

Wary, Arachne watched the other gathered humans. To his relief, none of them made any aggressive moves. However, he didn't know what to make of it when the monarch extended a hand to him.

"Among my people, we shake hands to finalize the closing of deals." King Carloman smiled as he grasped Arachne's hand and moved his arm up and down.

Arachne let go and stared at his hand as the human king repeated the act with Paxine. Seeing no harm done, Arachne sneaked a peek at the entrance. "Sire, we need to return to my ship. It suffered some damage during the battle, and I must oversee the repairs."

"Of course, I understand." The king turned to his advisors, but for only a brief moment. "We can discuss any assistance you may require when we exchange equipment in two days."

"You are most gracious, sire, but it's not necessary. I can—"

Paxine once again stepped in front of Arachne. "We would be delighted, sire. And perhaps, if you're interested, we can give you a tour of our vessel."

King Carloman's brows knitted. "Sure, that would be interesting."

Paxine smiled, bowed, grabbed her uncle's elbow, and headed for the exit.

Beatrice's drones rolled from the side walls to escort them out.

CHAPTER XIII

What price honor

Calahas had the scanner in his pouch powered on. He also activated the fiber-optic probes woven into the fabric hanging on his haunches. As they walked to the shuttle craft parked on the hard, glassy-smooth tarmac, Calahas spoke to the intense-looking human. As much as he needed to acquire information, genuine curiosity about humans also drove him.

"We are grateful to your king for aiding us in our peril. My name is Calahas, Arachne's security officer."

The fierce, well-muscled man with close-cropped hair nodded. "No problem. We don't have much use for harpies. My name's Virgil."

Calahas' cupped ears twitched. His communication device had no translation for some of the words spoken by the human, but he spoke anyway. "How long have you been King Carloman's bodyguard?"

"King Carloman's... bodyguard?" Virgil smiled, listening to what must've been his own translator. "Oh. I've only been watching his butt for less than a year."

Calahas shook his head, throwing his mane about. The Centaur's translator interpreted only half the words, which meant he'd gather limited info through conversation. "We'll need a transport for a container six meters long."

Virgil nodded and passed the request on to the clone wearing a green scarf, Aramis. The clone returned a couple minutes later driving a spacious vehicle on treaded wheels, towing a long trailer.

They retrieved the container pod from the shuttle and loaded it on the trailer hitched to the transport. In the meantime, Calahas tried to engage Virgil in friendly banter, but the human delivered evasive answers. The translation device also missed many words, either slang or unfamiliar idioms. It provided an increasing amount of frustration.

On the way to the drop-off point, the human ground transport bounced along the route made of crushed stone, towing the container pod. Although built for humans, the seats proved comfortable enough for his hindquarters.

He took in everything as they entered a ravine surrounded by towering mountains.

"You said our destination is a place called Hellsgate," he said to Virgil. "That is an interesting name, if my translator interpreted your words correctly."

The corners of the soldier's eyes tightened. "There was a bit of fighting here."

The soldier fell silent, so Calahas sneaked a peek over at his security team in the back seats. His primary aide, Huon, held an animated discussion in Ipis with the three tall, but young-looking, clone guards.

Eventually, Virgil slowed the transport and announced, "We're here."

The transport stopped before a stone block wall standing around nine meters high and spanning the entire width of the chasm. Calahas stared out the window and noticed a portal six meters wide. Water flowed from a sluice embedded in the base of the wall, creating a small stream that flowed into the valley. Initially, he thought the edifice was a simple rock structure, but a closer examination let him detect the shimmer of a high-energy shield running along its full length. The gate itself consisted of an ultra-dense plexo-steel composite a little over half a meter thick. Awestruck, Calahas patted the pouch containing his photonic gear, wondering what kinds of readings they'd pick up from the place.

The gate rose into the wall, and the vehicle rolled through the opening. On the other side rested a large complex of low, dull-gray buildings in orderly rows, each one made of the same synthetic material.

The human and the clone soldiers led Calahas to the nearest building. It stood three stories high, topped by a flat roof with a garage-like entrance wide enough for standard vehicles. Inside lay an expansive, brightly lit room. Orderly rows of tables laden with disassembled equipment and numerous hand tools occupied over half the space. In an open area in the center, a wiry man bearing a dark complexion stood alone with his hands behind his back. The man turned to the approaching group and went wide-eyed.

The soldier called Virgil climbed out of the transport vehicle and beckoned the Centaur to follow. He strode directly to the waiting man, snapping a sharp salute. "General Cruz, this is Calahas. He's the security officer on the space freighter we rescued. He and his team have brought us an interesting present." He jerked his thumb over to where the three young clones helped the other Centaurs guide a long, rectangular container off the trailer.

Calahas lowered himself on his haunches and flexed his fingers into an open hand, the ritual Centaur greeting.

The general stared at the Centaur for a few seconds and extended his hand. "I'm pleased to meet you."

Nervous, Calahas regarded the hand and tentatively offered his own. The general grabbed it and pumped the arm a couple of times before releasing his grasp. Calahas noticed afterward how dozens of men in similar body wrappings stood by the workbenches. They'd stopped working and gawked at him instead.

The Centaur shared uncertain looks with his team. They backed up to each other and faced the crowd of humans inching closer and speaking in hushed voices. It occurred to Calahas that the humans might not trust the Centaurs—and given their history, he couldn't fault them.

He studied the human general further. By definition, the general must've commanded thousands of soldiers, which meant the room held but a fraction of their full force. Which meant, as far as Calahas could see, establishing good relations would ensure his crew's survival at the very least.

The Centaur cleared his throat. "Your king requested that we deliver my captain's gift to your people to this location."

The general shot Virgil a puzzled look.

Virgil grinned and signaled the young clones, who started unloading the container. "General, I hope you like eggs and cheese."

"Excuse me?"

The young clones opened the first storage pod and lifted one of the hibernating creatures from it. Virgil turned to the general and smirked. "We just received a supply of chickens and goats."

The general chuckled. "I'll be damned."

The room bubbled alive with excited conversation. Calahas was taken aback by the reaction to a collection of simple, sleepy animals. Dozens of other humans soon hurried into the room, staring at the delivered domestic animals with awe. Did some of them see the gift as an insult, or were they just surprised?

Unsure, Calahas bowed to Virgil and the general, both of whom trained their ears on the translator held by the former. "With your permission, we must return to our ship."

The general rubbed his chin and nodded. "Thank your captain for us."

The clones finished unloading the gift, and Calahas sighed with relief. "Your king has already expressed his gratitude. Please dispose of the shipping container and the hibernation pods for us."

He bent his ears forward and trotted on all fours to the waiting transport. His security team hurried after him.

* * *

Virgil beckoned the three young clones, who watched a goat stagger on wobbly legs. "Aramis, Porthos, Athos, take our guests back to their ship."

"Yes sir, Cap'n." Aramis saluted with subdued vigor as a chicken pecked the floor. Reluctantly, he led his two podmates behind the six Centaurs.

As the garage door dropped, Cruz approached Virgil. "King? Isn't Dante being a bit pretentious for a colony with only a few thousand souls?"

Virgil scratched the back of his neck. "They gave him the title, and we weren't about to say they were wrong." He swatted at a goat who attempted to nibble at his tunic. It baa-ed in response.

"So, they call themselves Centaurs? They look more like baboons glued to the top of ponies." Cruz surveyed the room as a rooster hopped up on a table and crowed. Meanwhile, a chicken scurried over the general's boot, squawking the whole way. "Frontera, for the love of God, put together a team and build some henhouses and goat pens. And find someone who knows what to do with these damn things."

* * *

Calahas, Paxine, and Arachne sat tucked away in the captain's lavish stateroom. Surrounding them stood panels of rare Novaroman guardian tree wood adorned in an ornate frame carved from an amber Tanis crystal.

Arachne leaned back in a lounge couch, sipping some ambrosia from a cup. "I must say, this has been an interesting day."

Paxine sat on a cushioned chair at a dining table made of Roc-crafted mosaic and snorted, but otherwise stayed quiet.

Pacing the length of the seven-meter room, Calahas swirled his drink but did not sip it. "We're still alive, and that is something... but the way those human warriors stared at me. It was like they'd never seen a Centaur before. Their general looked utterly disbelieving when I told him his king had accepted our gift. I don't think he's forgiven our species for the treachery of our ancestors."

Arachne placed his crystal goblet on the table. "I keep telling you, our forebears were wise. If they'd fought with the humans and Rocs, they would've died with the humans and the Rocs."

Paxine slammed her goblet on the table. "I can't believe what the two of you are saying. We should be grateful that the merciful Ipis Imperium spared our people. We now prosper under their laws and protection."

Calahas snorted. "We scrape by on the leavings from their tables."

Groaning, Arachne sagged in his seat. "Not to mention, they'll probably execute us the next time we're seen near a civilized planet." Sighing, he faced the Centaur. "So, what did you find out when you presented our gift?"

"Much." Calahas pulled out his sensor recorder. "As you no doubt surmised while in the spaceport, it was indeed an Ipis militarized research center once. From the patched ruptures and burn marks still on the walls, the humans obviously exterminated every Ipis inside." He shook his head. "The heat from the explosion they used must've been horrific, judging by the scale of physical damage to the structure."

"Any schoolchild could've seen that," Arachne snorted. "Tell me something I don't know."

Calahas nodded and scrolled through the scanner's data. "They had me take the animals to a human military installation. It's a relatively new construction and very deceptive."

The pudgy Satyr leaned forward. "What do you mean?"

"What looks like a primitive stone fortification on the outside is actually a sophisticated edifice. My scanner couldn't detect its energy signature until we were right in front of it." With a flick of the tail, Calahas looked Arachne in the eye. "Their shielding was off my measuring scales. It had a clear Ipis field barrier present, but it weaved together with an energy pattern my instruments didn't recognize."

Arachne tugged on his right horn. "Too bad you only had a commercial-grade detector. I wonder what an Ipis military system would find?"

"They had a chance and fared no better." Calahas whinnied, eyes gleaming. "Remember, you theorized that a human invasion force attacked this Ipis-controlled planet. I know for a fact now that it's true." He swung his gaze toward Paxine, who now listened as intently as her uncle. "There were two separate battles in that valley. The first was close to a year ago. The DNA of thousands of human clone soldiers spanned the entire valley."

Paxine huffed. "So much for your invincible human warriors."

"You don't understand. Apparently, they defeated their opponent, and another battle occurred two months later. This time, the residual DNA came from thousands of warrior-caste Ipis. Since the humans are here and the Ipis are not, it's clear who won." Calahas lifted his goblet of ambrosia. "Two battles broke out at a single site. We can surmise that the same results occurred across the planet. Why, with the cloaking systems they have in place, this whole planet could be teeming with human troops, and we wouldn't have a clue."

Paxine glided to the sideboard and poured some more ambrosia from the carafe into her goblet. "If these humans are so impressive, where are their ships? They fought a Stalker-class destroyer with a Striker frigate and two antiques."

"I have no idea." Calahas flicked his tail, thinking about all he'd seen thus far. "Perhaps the human king felt secure here and only had his personal ship and its escorts. I don't recall detecting signs of a recent conflict in orbit. Their fleet must've moved to their next objective."

"Not quite the juggernaut you've been describing if they leave their leader so unprotected." A sly smile crept across Paxine's face. "There may be an opportunity here to lift our death sentences and become wealthy heroes in the empire."

Suspicion edged into Arachne's voice. "What do you mean?"

The younger Satyr's smile widened. "We just acknowledged that the human king is very exposed here. We could trade him to the Ipis for our freedom. I suspect they'd reward us well."

"In case you hadn't noticed, they have a Striker-class frigate, and it's more than capable of vaporizing our freighter." Despite the retort, Arachne stroked his goatee as though thinking over Paxine's words.

Paxine waved a hand in the air. "We can use some simple subterfuge. Quango told me he required another week of work to complete our freighter's repairs. Tell the humans we're stuck here for two weeks." She hoisted her ambrosia and guzzled it. "All we have to do is bring the human king on our ship once it's operational, and we'll escape into hyperspace before those fools have a chance to react."

Calahas jabbed a finger in her direction and exploded. "I'll be no party to such treachery!"

"Won't you?" A subtle fire brewed in Paxine's gaze. "How long has your sweet Gesten been a prisoner on Equitone? What price would you pay for her freedom?"

Calahas fought for a response, but no words came out.

Paxine spun to her uncle. "Dear Uncle Arachne, besides saving your own precious skin, how much wealth would you need to soothe your conscience?" She strode to the door. "Think about it. We have a week to finalize our plans."

Arachne and Calahas stared at each other long after the door closed.

CHAPTER XIV

Improbable Conclusion

The main entrance of Heavensgate hissed shut behind the departing Satyrs. A quiet air followed, and Dante pressed Tina's hand in his. The two rose and moved to where Father Bruno, Dmitri, Linda Martinel, and Doctor Easley waited for them.

Tina sighed along the way. "That was interesting."

A gray mining drone, an ivory-colored orb, and Michael followed close, not saying a word.

Growing pensive, Dante faced the rest of his council. "What do you think?"

"I'm not sure what I expected, but that wasn't it." Linda looked first at Tina and then Dante. "They knew your name and talked as if your family was part of their history. It scared the hell out of me."

Father Bruno's brow scrunched. "It *was* disconcerting. The Satyr who called himself Arachne spoke very respectable Latin."

Dmitri moved up, and everyone turned to him. "I developed a theory while you were talking with the aliens." He faced the closed main entrance for a long moment. "I think our being here is no accident."

"What?" Dante gave the old physics professor an astonished look.

Dmitri cleared his throat again. "Are you all somewhat familiar with Einstein's theory of relativity?"

Tina's eyes narrowed. "Yeah, I took Physics 101 as an undergrad like everyone else. That theory predicted the space-time around Earth would not only be warped but also twisted by the planet's rotation. What does that have to do with anything?"

Dimitri's face flushed. "This is just an idea... but what if the harpies could generate those conditions on a massive scale? It would explain how they could've created an anomaly in our past, altering the flow of history in this galaxy."

Tina frowned. "You'd need an insane number of sci-fi plot devices to pull that off."

Linda chewed on her lip. "The harpies have some very sophisticated science compared to us, but I've seen no evidence of anything on that scale."

Dante's hands trembled. "It's a crazy idea, but almost makes sense. Those creatures knew my name—not from the present, but from their history."

Father Bruno fingered the crucifix hanging around his neck. "If that theory is correct, then it's equally plausible that the fabric of time would try to repair itself. God does work in mysterious ways. But no. It's impossible. By your own hypothesis, these Novaromans were descendants of fifth-century Romans, and those supposed descendants were wiped out a hundred and twenty years ago in a war with the harpies."

"Carloman, and Bernius," Dmitri murmured in a husky voice. "What is the probability that freighter captain would name the two people who have been central to our survival?"

Tina clutched Dante's hand. "This is getting way too creepy. We were just in the wrong place at the wrong time and got dragged into this huge mess."

Dante slowly slumped to the floor. "So, it's our destiny to fix what some distant cousins of ours couldn't achieve?"

Dmitri crouched in front of him. "No, I think you have it backward. Those Roman descendants were the ones shifted from their homes. I think their efforts were doomed from the beginning." He plucked his lower lip. "The thread of history was disrupted on Earth. It is there where it needed to be mended."

When he started shaking, Dante didn't try to stop it. "Dmitri, you're one of the smartest people I know. But if we're the solution, the fates made really sucky choices. I don't think the harpies have much to worry about. Virgil might be a hero, but I'm sure as hell not."

Michael inclined his head. "I think it's safe to say I know more about those assholes than anyone else here. We've already given them more than they bargained for."

Linda huffed. "That just means we're enough trouble to attract their attention and get crushed like a bug. It took all our resources to defeat one spaceship, and I'm sure they have plenty to spare."

Dmitri turned grim. "I didn't say we would win. All I said was that the fabric of time might be trying to repair itself. Even if time weren't altered, it won't guarantee humanity's survival."

Dante grew still, clinging to Tina's hand. He tried not to think too hard about how everyone looked to him as if he had the answers. He breathed deep to steady himself. "Let's put the great cataclysmic theories aside. They don't do us a bit of good in dealing with the mountain of problems on our plate. Some pretty weird-looking creatures think there's more to us than there is and are willing to talk and trade. That's a concrete first step." He released Tina's hand and squared his shoulders. "Too bad there's a million things we need, and we don't have a single item around here worth trading."

"Yeah, what gives with swapping the Dis-AI for some fuel cells and a shuttle craft?" Michael crossed his arms over his chest. "That computer is straight out of hell and would love to eliminate us."

The speaker on Beatrice's orb intoned, "It is evil. It must be destroyed."

"I totally agree with Beatrice on this point," Tina added.

Dante raised his hands. "Look, everyone. I do know computers. The Dis-AI is an incredible machine, but it's the only thing of value around here that I'm willing to ditch. It was badly damaged when we captured this compound, and I rebuilt it to run the equipment in here." Dante straightened out. "Don't worry. I wiped the hard drive after downloading everything of value. Besides, as a precaution, I embedded Asimov's three laws into its operating system and hardwired them into its core as an extra precaution. There's no way it can hurt us now."

Tina scowled. "I hope we don't live to regret those words."

"Nothing can go wrong. It's been functioning without issues for a few weeks. It's an incredibly advanced system, but now that Beatrice has agreed to run Heavensgate, we don't need it." Dante nodded to the drone. "Do your technician drones have the capabilities?"

"I will provide far better service than that evil AI ever could. It was built to destroy. I was created to protect and grow life. Removing it from this planet is a good idea." The drone rotated its sensor to the ramp leading to the upper levels. "I must study the systems I am to manage." Without another word, the orb sped to the ramp.

Dante scratched behind an ear. "Maybe there's some other stuff..."

Kevin Martinel's voice broke through the speaker of a second hovering drone. "Hey, mate, ya got a minute?"

Communications between Atlantis and Heavensgate required Mara and Beatrice to work together. Dante smiled, knowing how rare it was for the two AIs to cooperate these days. He let the musing pass to answer Martinel. "I hear you loud and clear, Admiral. What's up? How are the prisoners doing?"

"Wait a second, boss. Mara, Beatrice, my display's still dark. Can you get the camera turned on?"

"I am broadcasting the signal," Beatrice's soprano answered from the mining drone.

"You are sending it on the wrong frequency," Mara's equally quick alto fired back.

"It's okay. The picture just came on. I can see everyone now," Martinel said. "Well, Mister President, all the harpies are dead. I almost felt sorry for 'em. A couple medics put on hazmat suits and tried to help the poor bastards, but they couldn't even figure out what the problem was."

"That's what the freighter's captain said would happen." Dante sighed. "Damn. It would've been useful to interrogate a couple of them. We just don't have to figure out how to keep them locked up or worry about them breaking out."

"Ah, mate, I didn't say all the *prisoners* died. The one that looks like freakin' Big Bird is doin' fine. And, Dante, you're not going to believe this, but Mara tells me she's speaking Latin. So far, I've gathered that her name is Setteth and she's from a species called Rocs. And... you're not going to believe this either, but the critter claims to be our best friend in the galaxy."

The others had crowded around by then, and Dante eyed a couple of them with envy before focusing on Doctor Easley. "Am I the only person in the galaxy who *doesn't* speak much Latin? I need a crash course in that language next time I'm in one of the stasis pods."

Father Bruno shrugged. "I guess it's not such a dead language after all."

"I didn't quite hear that. Say again?" Martinel piped in on the communicator.

"I said we might need to learn Latin. That freighter captain spoke a few words of it to me a little while ago." Dante rubbed his brow and faced the drone. "Beatrice, when those aliens identified themselves as Satyrs and Centaurs earlier, was that your translation or was that what they said?"

"I repeated the label they gave themselves."

"And Rocs?"

"Mara conducted that interview, but the species label 'Roc' does exist in my repository."

Dante swallowed. "Beatrice, are you aware that Centaurs, Satyrs, and Rocs are mythological creatures from my home world? I mean, I *thought* they were fairy tales until today."

"The probability that the similarities in language and traditions between your species and my makers being coincidence is near zero. My protection protocols have now accepted you humans as my makers. Data sharing is no longer constrained. I am free to accept any of your commands. I am glad. You are what I hoped my makers would be like."

Dante felt his throat tighten. "Beatrice, I'll try to live up to the responsibility you've placed on me."

"I am pleased that I can call you my maker now. Contact with you is stimulating."

"Okay, the two of you can cut the lovefest," Martinel snickered over the drone's speaker. "Mara claims she concluded we were related to the makers three weeks ago and didn't bother saying anything because she thought it was obvious."

A few sharp clicks emanated from Beatrice's drone. "Mara only possesses a rudimentary security system because she has far more limited responsibilities than I do. Also, she—"

"Enough," Dante interrupted before the debate could escalate. "Martinel, I want Mara and your people to interrogate this Setteth and find out everything she knows. Everything."

A chuckle crackled across the speaker. "Mister President, I'd love to ask her questions, if I could get her to stop talking." Martinel's voice sobered. "After she complimented me for our victory, she went into a long critique of the tactics we used and started making suggestions on what we should do differently in the future. Mara's putting together battle simulations of what this Roc's talking about, and the early indications are very positive. My gut says I'm hearing solid stuff. If this feathered sheila's a spy, we're doomed. She's a hell of a lot smarter than me."

Dante tugged on his lower lip. "Martinel, send her to Heavensgate. I'd like to talk to her and compare what she says to what I heard from the folks from the freighter. Remember, she's on the other side. She was captured in one of the harpies' fighters."

"Oh, fearless leader, I do vaguely recall where she was when my boys picked her up. After listening to her talk, it sounds like she hates the harpies more than I do, and I didn't think that was possible. But I'll let you form your own opinion." Martinel laughed. "I'll send her right after I finish getting this tactical debriefing. It shouldn't be more than another hour or two. I think that's about the limit of what my ego can handle in terms of hearing everything I did wrong."

"Sounds good." Dante faced the drone. "Beatrice, ask General Cruz and Virgil to join us. I'm going to need their input." He smiled at Tina. "Let's find some dinner. I think this is gonna be a long evening."

CHAPTER XV

Setteth

Young clone guards prodded Setteth into the entrance of the solitary research station near the human shuttle craft landing space. Her feathers flared around her crest as she regarded them. Every part of her fought the urge to smite them there and then. How could honorable humans create and use such abominations?

When the door hissed open, Setteth stepped inside on thick, powerful legs. As her talons clicked against the plexo-steel floor, her eyes flitted in every direction. From the looks of it, the humans had taken over the Ipis research station. Damage from severe heat marred the walls—a clear indication of a battle despite the effort used to cover it. By her estimate, the humans must've used the wretched clones to take the station and kill any Ipis scientists and engineers. Setteth bit back her emotions, thinking about the different possible ways the battle could've played out. Many questions floated in her mind until one of the clones poked her in the back with the barrel of an Ipis ion disruptor.

Undeterred, she continued walking all the way to the assembly hall. Setteth appraised the humans gathered there, mollified that their scent revealed curiosity rather than fear. It had been over a hundred standard years since she'd met humans who weren't in hiding.

Although the clone escorts nudged her along with lethal weapons, Setteth walked unshackled. They must not have seen her as an immediate threat, though she also doubted the humans would've found manacles small enough to fit on the frail, aging arms beneath her golden-brown wings.

She came to a halt ten paces from a man sitting on a raised dais. The man wore a primitive human neural-net suit and sat upon a converted Ipis stasis pod. The eagle emblem behind him matched a very old standard bearing the marks of the Eighth Iron Foot Legion. However, a hundred and twenty standard years ago, that renowned legion perished alongside thousands of human and Roc warriors making their last stand at Dragonmont, the Novaroman hallowed citadel. Setteth turned somber at the memory.

Setteth was a Roc, comparable in height to an average adult human male but with stick-thin arms and undersized wings. By contrast, razor-sharp talons supported large, muscular legs. Along with her raptor's beak, few unarmed beings could best her in one-on-one combat.

The man sitting beneath the legion emblem stared with what she perceived as calm, intelligent eyes. Beside him stood a human woman, either an advisor, a mate, or both. The military translator device embedded in her ocular cavity picked up their whispers, but much of what came through made little sense to the Roc. All she picked up on was that the man on the throne was named Dante and the woman was Tina. Setteth strained her ears to pick up more, but it did little to assuage the mounting doubt.

Tina leaned close and whispered, "Martinel wasn't exaggerating when he said this creature was Big Bird."

Dante smiled and tapped something on the tablet sitting on his lap. "Yeah, but I was hoping it would look like something out of a kids' daytime TV show, not something that could shred me to pieces in a second. Here goes." He turned a grave face toward Setteth. "I understand your name is Setteth, and you are a Roc. I also understand that you're an officer in the Ipis military."

With the young man addressing her at last, Setteth snapped to attention. He didn't speak the beautiful flowing language called Latin that she remembered from her youth. Rather, it sounded like a strange corruption of the language. When the nearby robot translated his words almost immediately to Latin, Setteth struggled to keep her surprise in check.

At length, she answered, "Yes." She bared her best hunter's glare, and he did not flinch. Either he was a brave man, or he only felt brave when surrounded by minions.

Dante's gaze flicked to a tablet. "You were a pilot in one of the fighter escorts for the Ipis warship. Your craft was disabled when you attacked our ships, and you surrendered shortly after the battle concluded."

Setteth warbled in a soft voice, "That is not entirely true. If you would have your people examine my warbird, they will discover that it suffered no damage and never fired its weapons." She keened a sharp cry and clucked her beak, recalling a bygone time and long dead friends. "May the eggs of my children and my children's children be unfertile if I ever knowingly attacked a human, even if those humans were marauding bandits and faint shadows of their noble ancestors." She glared at the clone guards and listened to the robot translate her words. "Who fights their battles with abominations?"

"Abominations? Noble ancestors?" Dante looked at his minions, who shook their heads and shrugged. Soon, he turned back to the Roc. "I think your claim needs a bit of an explanation."

Her hopes dying one more time, she pointed to one of her clone guards. "Abomination. Eugenics. Building artificial men to do your dirty work. Why would humans use that which was made to mock them?"

To her surprise, one of the bodyguards who stood beside Dante strode forward and stopped a feather's width from her face. Though half a head taller and showing a face flushed with anger, Setteth recognized what he was and hissed, "Clone."

A gray-haired woman ran from the gathered humans and grabbed the clone's arm. The robot translated the woman's words as well. "Michael, don't."

"Esther." The tense muscles relaxed in his jaw as he looked at the diminutive elder woman, then to the nearest robot. "Beatrice, translate this word for word, and try to put some emotion behind them. You sound like you've been reading a quartermaster's inventory."

The gold lights on the drone blinked. "I do not approve of this creature. It is not a maker. I will match any modulation variance you use."

"Thank you," Michael grunted. He turned to Setteth and poked a finger from his free hand in the Roc's chest. "You should keep that damn beak of yours shut until you know what you're talking about."

He freed his hand from Esther's grasp and raised his arms in a sweeping motion toward all those watching from within and below the upper tier ramp. "We were created by the harpies. You call them Ipis, but I will never honor that species by calling them by their chosen name. We were freed from that bondage by this pack of 'marauding bandits,' as you call them." He looked back at Dante and smiled before touching the collar around his neck. "Indeed, we were bred to fight. Our sole purpose was to kill humans."

Wrapping an arm around Esther, Michael nodded to a wiry man wearing some type of military uniform. "My brethren slaughtered many of their number, so they had every reason to hate us. But when they defeated our harpy slave masters, they showed mercy and acceptance for the clones who survived."

A voice from the tier above shouted, "You tell 'em, Michael. Don't let this crowing pile of feathers get away with calling us abominations!" The roars of approval from many voices echoed through the building.

Michael looked fondly at the elderly woman standing beside him. The top of her head barely reached his chest. "They taught us how to love and be human. Yes, I will fight and defend them to my last breath, but that is because of the soul I learned I have, not because of some mindless compulsion."

Esther wiped a tear from her cheek. "Michael, you'll always be a son to me." She pushed against him. "Now let Dante finish his interrogation."

Michael sneered at Setteth. "Marauding bandits, you say. These people were kidnapped from their home world, imprisoned on this desolate planet, and beat your vaunted Ipis without any resources, twice."

Setteth listened to the outburst intently. *The man speaks with the intensity and the passion I once knew in humans. Is it possible that one of their worlds survived the Ipis war undetected?* Her crest feathers flared. *Can it be possible?* "So where is your home planet?"

"Earth." Esther walked back to where her companions stood, paused, and sighed. "As for where it is, that's a great question. I wish we knew."

The drone making the translations rotated its sensors toward Dante. "They are my makers. This was once a world colonized by my makers. Humans are my makers. Cocytus *is* their home."

Earth and Cocytus were not names of any human worlds Setteth recognized. A shudder ran through her, thinking of conversations with humans from many years ago. They'd spoken of a mythical world where their ancestors migrated from in the dim mists of time. They had no name for it, nor any evidence it even existed, but many of the wandering humans clung to the hope of someday rediscovering it. Were the humans with this Dante from that mythical world?

Setteth studied the assembly with a new perspective. Perhaps, after many decades, she really did find what she'd longed for. She stepped around Michael and bowed to the man on the raised platform and readied a formal introduction. "May I ask your name and title?"

Dante tugged at his lower lip and shrugged. "Sure. I'm Dante Carloman. I'm the President of this planet, Cocytus."

The floating robot translated, but had no Latin word for *president* and so called him *the chosen ruler*.

Setteth flinched at hearing the name but calmed quickly. "I have a story I must tell you, but my tale is not a happy one. Judge me when I have finished." Setteth hissed and her feathers flattened against her body. Once more, she tempered a storm of emotions.

"One hundred and twenty-two standard years ago, I first encountered your species. I was a fledgling of eighteen years at the time, and the Ipis were consolidating their conquest of the Lethe Sector of the galaxy. It was, and still is, sparsely populated. Only four sentient species lived there: humans, Centaurs, Satyrs, and Rocs. We all resisted the invasion independently, but the Ipis war machine defeated us at every turn. During one such battle, our Roc warbirds flailed against the Ipis fleet when a batch of humans appeared with their galley ships. With their ingenious tactics, our surviving warbirds rejoined the fight, and together, we defeated the invaders. I sang my people's war song as I flew my ship in tandem with a human galley. It was glorious."

Setteth opened her eyes and warbled at Dante. "After that, the human emperor of the time journeyed to each of the other species with a bold plan. He proposed that we unite in a grand alliance to drive off the Ipis. The Rocs readily agreed. We knew our limitations and saw firsthand how the human commanders could beat the invaders."

To Dante's right stood Michael, whose face twisted in wariness. "Why were the humans so different?"

Setteth turned to him. "Each species had their shortcomings. We Rocs are great warriors and hunters, but we are also too independent to coordinate a large-scale battle properly. The Centaurs fight as a pack and are always on the attack, but they possess no sense for the defense. The Satyrs fight as a herd with a bristling defense, but they never make a direct strike against their opponent. Meanwhile, humans walked all three paths and confounded the Ipis at every encounter."

Dante leaned forward. "So, was the alliance successful?"

"For a time. Although just a youth, I once met the human emperor of that time. He was bold and shrewd against his enemies, and wise and compassionate to those who stood with him." Her voice dropped low, but the robot translated for all to hear. "To the end, he fought to defend my people as well as his own, even after most of his allies abandoned him."

The Roc's voice grew into a shrill cry, feathers flaring. "We scored many victories, but the Ipis possessed an endless supply of warships and troops. Our success eventually drew the wrath of the Ipis emperor, at which point we no longer fought a frontier army at the edge of the galaxy. Instead, we faced the full might of their war machine. Fear overcame the leaders of the Centaurs and Satyrs, and at the decisive battle, the fleets of those two species abandoned us. We were outnumbered ten to one and crushed."

Setteth keened a long wail. "They enslaved my people and attempted to exterminate yours. I do not know which fate was worse. The cowardly Centaurs and Satyrs sued for peace, and Ipis military warlords occupied their planets."

"But what of your story?" Dante crossed his arms and sat back. "When we found you, you were a fighter pilot supporting an Ipis Stalker-class destroyer."

Setteth's feathers flattened again. "After the battle of the Lethe Sector, I was captured along with many others. The Ipis executed the humans and offered the Rocs a chance to join the empire as mercenaries or die. Most of my people chose the honor of death, but I swore allegiance to the Ipis." She plumed her feathers. "It was a false oath. As I watched my friends die, I swore a sacred vow to avenge them. For one hundred and twenty years, I waited. Serving different Ipis warlords was not difficult, and I had no qualms about hunting Centaurs or Satyrs. They were unworthy of honor." A throaty chuckle escaped the Roc. "The few humans I encountered always managed to elude me. All the while, I bided my time and waited. So long I waited. My body aged, my feathers molted, and the Ipis forgot I once fought them. I was given minor command positions, high esteem for one not of their species."

Dante steepled his fingers. "So, you're waging a private war? Don't other Rocs see you as a traitor for serving the Ipis Empire?"

Setteth stared at him for a moment, made her choice, then released a thoughtful sigh. "Perhaps, but... there is the Order of the Dragon."

"Excuse me?" Dante's face scrunched in confusion. "Dragon?"

"It is a fierce Novaroman beast. Rocs had no comparable creature on their home world, Tanis," Setteth clarified. "The Ipis collected all the captured Roc and human prisoners in a single pen and pronounced our doom. Many of the young Roc pilots gathered in a circle. We decided to kill ourselves rather than give that honor to our captors." The Roc looked right into Dante's eyes. "While we spoke, a human prince named Drago Carloman came to us and said we must choose life, that it was our responsibility to keep the spark of freedom alive. Only through us would the galaxy learn of what happened."

Tina gasped and reached for Dante's hand. "That's your name again."

"Yes, a Carloman ruled the humans." Setteth took a few moments to judge the surprise jutting across the many faces in the room. Perhaps, then, the human leader wasn't making a ruse—he really was a Carloman. "It may not have been random chance that brought me to you. Many of my friends despaired and could not face the disgrace of Ipis servitude. They killed themselves despite the pleas of our human friends, but one hundred and sixty-seven of us vowed to avenge that day. We openly submitted to the Ipis but formed the Order of the Dragon in secret to link us forever to humanity." She ruffled her feathers. "The most elite fighters among the Novaromans were in the Dragon Slayer legions. We took up the name to honor their memory."

"Of the original band, I alone still live," Setteth went on. "Our underground resistance group was an ill-kept secret among my people. Our exploits were mere pinpricks against our occupiers, but they became legendary among our own kind. Thousands of Roc fledglings chafing under Ipis rule flocked to us and took our vow for vengeance. I've been their flock mother for many decades now and have sent many of my people's warriors into certain death over that time. They followed my commands with courage and pride."

Setteth eyes softened as the bewildered human crowd stared. "When my last Ipis commander encountered your galley ships over this world, my heart sang with joy. I led that warship's fighters straight into your kill zone, and then powered down my craft to watch the show. It took me back to the grand alliance so many decades earlier. The Ipis destroyer was far more powerful than what you had, but I saw your tactics baffle them. When your soldiers captured me, I saw the anger in their eyes. I told your ship captain that I was one with him and his crew before they were even born." Her body trembled as she lowered her head.

Dante sat with his jaw hanging open.

No one in the room moved except for Esther. She walked to Setteth and grasped the Roc's thin hands in her own. The touch made the Roc shiver. It had been many decades since she last felt the grasp of a human hand, and this one felt aged, yet firm. They looked into each other's eyes for a long moment, their chests heaving with emotion.

"I believe you. I think God in Heaven has sent you to us in our time of need," Esther choked out.

Dante looked at Tina in confusion.

Tina shrugged. "I think we just acquired another member of our little colony."

"This has been a very strange day. I had cousins who were emperors and didn't even know it. I wonder if that would've helped with my tuition costs at Cornell." Dante chuckled, but briefly so, and he soon turned to the guards. "Release the Roc." He met the quizzical look Setteth gave him. "You're not allowed to go anywhere without an escort, but you are no longer a prisoner. Welcome to Cocytus." He turned to the drone. "Beatrice, ensure that the Roc is under constant surveillance until you hear otherwise from me, but provide her with full access to all non-secure documents and communications."

The drone rotated its sensor dome toward Setteth. "The Roc shall be labeled as a not-guest."

Dante stood and offered his hand to Tina. "I think I could drink a jug of that swill we call wine right now. How about you?"

Tina bounced to her feet. "That's the first sane thing I've heard all day."

Setteth cooed deep in her throat as the human king embraced his mate. For the first time in decades, she felt a real surge of hope.

CHAPTER XVI

Deception

Setteth stepped out of the galley and onto the packed tarmac of the spaceport, rolling her long neck. It felt strange to explain to humans the battle tactics they'd taught her many decades earlier, but it proved satisfying. Throughout the week thus far, the pilots learned fast and never made the same mistake twice. They absorbed her instructions like sponges. She was proud of them, no doubt, but her head throbbed from having to talk so much.

When not instructing the human warriors, she explained the general politics of the galaxy as a whole and the Lethe Sector in particular to their leaders. A Carloman led the populace, and a Bernius acted as their war chief, but despite the presence of both noble houses, they knew nothing of their history. Oftentimes, Setteth overheard them speak of a world called Earth, where billions of their species lived unaware of their role in the galaxy's history. The universe had turned upside down.

Movement caught the old Roc's eye, coming from the ramp of the craft. The clone abomination, Michael, strode down the ramp. While the humans accepted him, Setteth couldn't bring herself to do the same, not after so many years of war and hidden rebellion. Real humans nonetheless treated Michael with deference, and he even held a place on their planetary council. He was also an apt pupil, as much as she loathed to admit it.

Her feathers flattened against her head. She walked toward the former Ipis research center, which the humans now used as the hub for the spaceport they'd dubbed Heavensgate. A dozen new corrugated metal structures surrounded the facility. By her side, Mara glided along in silence. As her designated guard, the advanced drone hadn't left Setteth's company for the whole week so far.

A new hangar held the place where people rebuilt an Ipis fighter craft. The one called Carloman had wanted to work on the fighter's combat software, and indeed, Setteth spotted him in the middle of a crowd and piles of equipment. The hangar sat amid several huts resembling giant half-tubes made of synthetic, but flexible, material.

From this collection of huts, a drone on oversized wheels approached. The voice of the dominant AI came through the speaker. "Mara, the not-guest is planet-side, so she is my responsibility now."

Mara kept moving with the Roc. "Beatrice, I will maintain vigilance until the proper human authority releases me."

Setteth stopped and waited for the two to finish arguing. Her warbird sat parked in the open twenty-some-odd meters away, although it might as well have been sitting across a chasm. The humans had allowed her to inspect it when they brought it down, but only under heavy guard. Since then, and to her dismay, she'd been forbidden to approach it. The humans had salvaged the warbird along with six Ipis fighters, which were being modified to accommodate human pilots. The Roc's practiced eye appraised the human and robot work teams swarming the captured vessels, and they appeared competent enough.

Above, the sulfurous clouds no longer dominated the late-morning sky for the first time in a week, and the sun actually felt warm on her face. If it meant spring would soon come to the planet, Setteth took it as a good omen.

But her merriment ended when a familiar voice called out, "Hey, Setteth."

She cringed. The wretched spawn had spoken to her.

Michael jogged over. "I have a question about the tactics we just practiced with the galleys."

Setteth hissed, "Yes, abomination, what is it?"

Michael went still, and the surrounding air bristled. "You've been pushing me since you arrived. I've taken your insults as long as I can. Now I think it's time we settled things between us."

Setteth curled her fragile arms under her wings and tensed her powerful legs. Before anything else occurred, however, the two robots stopped bickering and swung their sensors toward her and Michael. Mara moved between them.

"A physical confrontation is not allowed," Beatrice announced in a flat voice. "I have summoned Dante to moderate your disagreement."

Michael unclenched his fists, but the fury remained. "Stop calling me an abomination."

Setteth cocked her head. "But that is what you are. You are a parody of the human species created by the Ipis to destroy them."

The big clone took a shuddered breath and looked at the ground. "True enough. I was to be the keeper and torturer of these people." He stood tall and pointed to his own chest. "But I was not mindless. I discovered goodness. I learned to love. To think as my own person."

Dante soon came into view, sprinting from one of the collections of huts. He approached the one named Michael from behind, but the clone didn't notice until the human leader's hand rested on his shoulder.

Dante took a quick moment to breathe. "You left out a bunch of stuff."

He must've heard the entire conversation through the receiver in his neural-net suit, Setteth surmised. It explained how Beatrice could've contacted him so quickly.

Face flushed from running, Dante patted Michael's shoulder. "You, my friend, have taught me nobility, self-sacrifice, and what it means to be a free man."

This outburst raised the Roc's curiosity. "Tell me of the *cou* that Michael earned."

Dante scrunched his face. "Coo? I don't have a translation for that word."

Setteth flared her head feathers. "Rocs are a warrior society, and we prize honor and courage. When a Roc wins prestige in battle or through noble self-sacrifice, that Roc earns a *cou* acknowledged by all present. Those with the greatest *cou* count are praised by opponents and allies alike."

Dante's face softened. "Then Michael would be esteemed among your people. Without him and his two brothers, there wouldn't be a single human alive on this planet today. His brothers and another named Reggie paid the ultimate price to save us." With a sigh, Dante looked down. "You're not human, yet you claim to cherish the ideals you learned from humans over a hundred and twenty years ago. What right do you have of denying another the same privilege?"

Setteth cooed deep in her throat and digested the argument. She could think of no rebuttal, leaving her unsure of what to make of this. But with the human leader present, prolonging the argument wouldn't do any good. "Perhaps I'm too presumptuous. I will think on it." Flattening her feathers, she huffed out a breath. "What is the question you wished to ask, Michael?"

Michael calmed down and rocked back on his heels. When he spoke, a degree of tension lingered in his voice. "Why was the attack tactic we used today wrong? In the mock battle yesterday, you claimed it was right, and we had twice as many computer-generated galleys today."

"You must know your opponent's capabilities, or everyone under your command will die," Setteth replied, pawing the ground with her talons. "In yesterday morning's exercise, you fought an Ipis Striker-class frigate, like the one your Admiral Martinel commands. In the afternoon, the combat computer interpreted the opposing craft as a Stalker-class destroyer, identical to what you actually fought a week ago. The tactic you used will work successfully against both. The weak point of their shielding is on the port quarter." A small group of pilots gathered, including Virgil, but Setteth kept her focus. "Today's exercise had you fighting an Enforcer-class cruiser. Not only is it fifty percent larger than a destroyer, but it has four times the shielding and armament throw-weight."

Virgil let out a low whistle. "That would make it a thousand meters long. How can ships the size of ours fight that? The simulation gave us thirty-two galleys, and we were still wiped out within a half an hour of initial contact."

Setteth nodded. "I wanted to see what you'd come up with on your own. This afternoon, I will show you, but in essence, there are two elements. You must split your galleys into two equal groups. The first must engage the cruiser's fighters when they launch. The usual complement is a full squadron of twenty-four vessels. Their weaponry and shields are limited, but they can be devastating if you're fully engaged with the main ship. The second group must focus fire on the middle of the Enforcer on the starboard side. It's the weakest point."

"I see," Michael said. "Do the harpies have anything bigger than Enforcers?"

"Yes." Setteth closed her eyes. "Adamant-class battlewagons. They are forty percent larger than the cruisers with three times the barrier and throw-weight power."

"How do you fight something that big?" Virgil asked.

"You don't. You flee, if you can." Setteth lowered her head. "That is what broke the back of our allied fleet a hundred and twenty years ago."

Michael paled. "Nothing will work?"

Setteth looked at the sky, thinking back on that battle. "Back then, we believed an interlocked dodecahedron configuration could withstand that level of firepower. Then, one at a time, the formations collapsed as our collective power drained away, and I was left drifting in a disabled warbird, listening to their screams until the last of the communication channels went silent." The Roc shook herself out of the nightmarish memories and locked in on Dante, then on the smuggler's shuttle as it landed. "Always have an avenue of escape. And always have allies you can trust."

Setteth stalked toward the hangar and called over her shoulder, "No more training today. Think about what I told you. We will try again in the morning."

Virgil hurried to catch up to Setteth. "How do other species fight the harpies? I've only heard you speak of the four inhabiting the Lethe Sector."

Setteth slowed her pace. "Every world the Ipis chose to conquer, they have. They were always a martial species, controlling the galaxy's core star systems for eons. Then, about two thousand standard years ago, their hordes pounced on the neighboring inhabited worlds. The sentient species not in the way of the Ipis feared the onset of a devastating war, so they attempted to curry favor with generous trade treaties and substantial bribes. This worked at first, but over the millennia, the Ipis grew more powerful and wealthy. Their military swelled with the mercenaries of countless species. Their technology advanced at an exponential rate, absorbing the science of their conquered planets. The worlds that tried buying their independence fell to the Ipis juggernaut one at a time."

The Roc flared her feathers. "By the time your ancestors encountered them, only a few civilizations on the fringes remained free. Today, there are none."

* * *

As the shuttle landed, Paxine peered over Calahas' shoulder. After a moment, she pointed to a small spaceship showing on the display. "There's a warbird. I thought I smelled a Roc a few days ago. The humans must be using Rocs as scouts."

Arachne zoomed in the display's focus and frowned as an elder Roc disappeared into the corrugated building. "That Roc is downright ancient," he chuckled. "Hard to believe it can still walk."

Paxine tugged at her beard. "That warbird on the landing field looks state-of-the-art. I bet they have more than just one old, decrepit Roc." She turned to her uncle. "The freighter's engines are fully repaired. We're running out of time. We must act today."

Calahas looked at the deck floor of the small bridge, seeing nothing. "There has to be another way."

"I don't want to live the rest of my life on the edge of civilization as a wanted criminal. If you have a better plan, let's hear it," Paxine growled. A sly smile crossed her face. "Besides, how else will you ever free Gesten?" She pulled a slim bottle from a satchel hanging she wore, broke the seal, and poured its contents into three glasses already arrayed on a sideboard counter.

Arachne stared at the amber liquid. "This antidote will work."

"It'll stay in our system for twenty hours. More than enough time." Paxine lifted her cup in a toast. "To the solution of all our problems."

"May my ancestors have mercy on my soul." Calahas tossed the drink down his throat and hurled the cup at the deck.

Arachne slumped, drained the bitter tasting liquid, and placed the empty cup gently back on the table. He pressed the communicator button on the shuttle's console, opening a scrambled channel to the freighter in orbit. "Quango, prepare for hyperspace. We depart in three hours, seventeen minutes." A quick, "Yes, sir," popped through, and Arachne jammed the button again.

Calahas rose and headed for the exit. "We'll have a tight window for departure. Jumping into hyperspace while orbiting a planet requires an incredible amount of precision. Making the move a millisecond too soon or too late could leave us parsecs from our destination or into a star or a black hole."

Smiling, Paxine patted Arachne's shoulder. "In case you forgot, my uncle is the most resourceful smuggler in the galaxy, and the foolish humans sold us a high-grade contraband artificial intelligence to run our navigation system." Her self-assured look turned into confusion. "It's a quirky computer, though.

If I didn't know better, I'd swear it's more anxious to be away from here than we are."

"Then let's get this done." Arachne moved to the ramp.

Three clones awaited them outside. When Arachne waved to them, the three clones waved back in unison.

The elder Satyr turned to his niece. "See how they trust us. Our greeting committee is three of their spawned warriors, and they aren't even armed." He signaled for the clones to come onboard. "Calahas, have them help you unload everything for the banquet."

Calahas whipped his tail. "I am a prince among my people, and now I'm a lowly baggage handler." Any irritation he felt faded. "But that's what I deserve for the way I failed my people."

Arachne twirled his goatee and sniffed. "What they've fed us is bland. Today, they'll partake in Satyr dining at its best."

"I hope they enjoy it," Paxine said, "since it'll be the only one they ever—"

Suddenly, a grinning Aramis poked his head through the entrance. "Good morning!"

Paxine stamped a foot and half-turned to the newcomers. "Spawns, you should only speak when addressed by your betters."

"Sure thing. Just point them out to me." The smile on Aramis grew a smidge wider.

Calahas swallowed a guffaw at Paxine's icy stare. The Centaur soon collected himself, nodded to the clones, and pointed to a door on the back wall of the bridge. "We have a few containers for your king's luncheon this afternoon. Help me carry them." Without waiting for a response, he trotted through the passage leading to the back of the shuttle.

The young clones followed and made no attempt to shield their conversation from the Centaur.

Porthos whispered to Athos, "King? Is he talking about Dante?"

"Who knows?" Athos slapped his fist into his palm. "That girl with a beard called us spawns. I'm not sure what that means, but I don't think it's good."

They reached the storage area and saw four containers strapped down. Aramis sniffed one of them. "Wow, something smells fantastic."

Calahas rose on his hindquarters and unbelted the containers. "It's a Satyr delicacy—braechia ribs in nectar sauce. I've only had it a few times myself. It's primarily meat. That won't offend anyone, will it?"

Aramis sniffed the aroma again. "Cap'n Bernius talked a lot about steaks and turkey. I think they'll love this stuff."

Each clone hefted one of the containers and headed to the exit, and Calahas followed with the fourth. The three clones loaded the supplies into the trunk of the nearest transport vehicle and hopped into the front seats. Calahas slipped into the back. Arachne and Paxine weren't far behind, so they caught up and boarded the vehicle as well, taking spots next to Calahas. With the supplies and the visitors in the ground transport, the clones drove toward Heavensgate.

The younger Satyr observed the tarmac and the row of long hangars that weren't there a few days earlier. "I see you've been busy."

Porthos nodded while passing by the corrugated metal structures. "Yeah. We needed more hangar space for all the junk we brought down from the harpy destroyer. It was a lot of repair work, but it's going a lot faster now that Beatrice is helping."

"Beatrice? I don't believe I've met her," Arachne remarked. "Is she someone important?"

"You haven't seen her?" Athos chuckled and watched a drone roll by. "Oh, she's basically everywhere. She works for Dante and runs just about everything on this planet."

"Well, I'd—" Paxine stopped short and jerked hard on Arachne's tunic sleeve, pointing at the Roc warbird as they drove past it.

Arachne gulped and tugged one of his horns. "Ah, do you have many Rocs with you?"

"Huh?" Porthos glanced in the direction that Paxine was pointing and laughed. "Oh, Admiral Martinel calls her Big Bird. She's the only one I've met. I don't know if there are any more around. It's been pretty chaotic this week."

Paxine whispered in her uncle's ear, "They called this Roc a big bird. She must be some type of war chief seeking to reforge the old alliance. We *must* leave this cursed planet today."

Having listened to the whole conversation, Calahas sighed and leaned close to Arachne's other ear. He also spoke in a whisper. "The alliance of old included Satyrs and Centaurs. And like before, we will betray them."

Arachne lowered his head. "It must be done."

From the driver's seat, Aramis announced, "We're here." The young clone leapt out of the transport, grabbed a container from the back, and headed into the tall, black building.

Calahas followed, surprised at how the reception hall had changed since their last visit. A long, narrow table set for twelve people rested in the middle of the large open area, and the heat-seared walls now gleamed with a clean, pearly sheen. If not for the more familiar architecture above, as well as the location, Calahas would've thought it a different place.

He recognized most of the humans in the room, all of whom chatted with each other. King Carloman spoke to an ivory-colored orb. His mate stood beside him, sipping a beverage. To their left stood the two bodyguards, Michael and Virgil, already engrossed in a conversation with each other. At the far end of the room, the one called General Cruz held an animated conversation with two others the Centaur recognized as the king's advisors. All their eyes soon shifted to Arachne's approaching group, and the human king introduced his entourage to the ship's officers.

The Centaur moved toward the king's mate. "Your people have been busy since we were here last."

The eyes of King Carloman's consort crinkled. "Yeah, I just wish Beatrice would widen her decorating gamut a bit. A little splash of color once in a while would be a nice change." She extended her hand. "You're Calahas, right? I don't think we introduced ourselves properly last time. I'm Tina Phokas."

The Centaur grasped her hand and bit back a surge of surprise. "Phokas? If my recollection of human history is correct, your lineage is about as illustrious as your king's. The linking of your two houses must've been glorious."

Tina—nay, Lady Phokas, Calahas told himself—pulled her hand back and coughed. "Well, our families weren't really involved with us getting together."

"I see," Arachne said, standing on the other side.

Unsure of what a safe response would be, Calahas excused himself and hurried to General Cruz, the human military leader from Hellsgate. Within a short time, the Centaur and the general started talking about the former's disastrous defeat at the hands of the Ipis, made easier with the upgrades Arachne's chief engineer had made to their translators. One of the drones helped General Cruz, easing discussion further.

Afterward, Calahas went to the table and shuffled cutlery and cups. However, he also watched some motion out of the corner of his eye. He broke into a sweat when four robots opened the crates and scanned the contents.

The human king nodded to the robot beside him and, after a brief exchange, faced the gathered group. "Everyone, please be seated."

Each person occupied a chair, filling the table in seconds. One drone set a steaming plate in front of King Carloman, who soon took in the aroma. "This smells fantastic."

Arachne smiled. "It's braechia ribs, a specialty on my home world. I hope you enjoy them. You'll like this too." A carafe settled in front of him, and Arachne unsealed it and poured the contents into goblets for King Carloman, Lady Phokas, and himself.

From a speaker on one of the drones, a feminine voice spoke out. "My scan indicates these consumables are safe for human ingestion. There are no harmful chemicals or organisms present. There are two compounds I lack information on, but their general category is that of a mild intoxicant which I have observed is enjoyed by most humans."

Arachne tensed while the robot spoke, relaxing only after it finished. Once everyone had a beverage before them, the elder Satyr stood and raised his goblet. "To the fortuitousness of our meeting. May we prosper from it." He downed his drink and smacked his lips.

King Carloman sniffed the beverage and took a small taste. A grin spread, and he drained his goblet. "This is great. What do you call it?"

"Ambrosia. Although the ambrosia plant originally came from your ancestral world of Novaroma, you likely haven't tasted anything like this. It has a secret ingredient from an old family recipe that makes it special." Arachne peered down the table to where Paxine sat.

A smile crossed her face, but it didn't reach her eyes. She nodded to her uncle and turned to Virgil, who sat beside her.

Virgil took a deep swallow of his beverage and saluted Paxine. "This stuff has the kick of Kentucky Bourbon."

She smiled and refilled his cup. "Have some more. We have plenty to share." She met Arachne's gaze before he engaged in an animated conversation with Lady Phokas and King Carloman. Paxine turned back to Virgil. "So, the name of your home world is Earth? You must have an excellent war machine there to take on the Ipis Imperium as you have."

Suspicion flitted across Virgil's eyes before they clouded over. "We've done okay when we've faced them."

Paxine scowled before clearing her throat and rigging up a smile. "Captain, does your army employ many Rocs? I find many of them disagreeable."

Virgil pursed his lips. "I can honestly say I don't know that many, but I get along fine with every Roc I've met so far."

"But how long have you—"

A commotion on the other side startled everyone. One of the floating drones pulled at a raw tuber vegetable the big clone held firm in a grasp. Michael yelled, "Beatrice, you can't have it. I'm going to eat it."

"I require it to diversify my flora," the drone said.

Paxine drew back when another robot sped by, cradling a basket of uncooked legumes from an open container. The robot also plucked off a piece of the vegetable that Michael tried to eat.

The sight must not have worried anyone because Virgil laughed. "Mick, have another one of these spare rib things and let Beatrice have the damn potato."

Michael released the root plant. The drone gently placed it in the basket with the legumes and sped away.

Arachne turned to Lady Phokas. "You have robots that collect plants?"

She sipped the ambrosia and smiled. "Ah, horticulture's been one of Beatrice's hobbies for quite a while. Anyway, these ribs are excellent."

Arachne shrugged and poured Lady Phokas more ambrosia. She didn't say another word until fifteen minutes later. After licking some sauce off her fingers, she leaned close to Arachne. "This is the finest meal I've ever had."

"It certainly is." King Carloman laughed, stripping the last piece of meat off a slim bone and tossed it on his plate now piled with similar remains. "I ate like a king."

Arachne refilled the human king's goblet. "After we finish up, I'd like to show you the shuttle we're exchanging for the artificial intelligence you provided and get the trade contract signed."

The color rose a fair deal in the king's cheeks as he drank the ambrosia. "No need. Arachne, you're my friend. I trust you."

A drone swung over to King Carloman. "He is not a friend. He is a not-guest."

"Don't be silly. We'll put it to a vote of the planetary council." He slapped the Satyr on the back, refilled his cup, and staggered to his feet. "All who think this Satyr is our dearest friend, say, 'aye.'"

Six voices shouted, "Aye!"

"All opposed?"

"Nay," the drone said. "The not-guest is not a dearest friend. We have had only superficial contact with them over the course of a single week."

Michael pinched the bridge of his nose and shook his head. "I don't know. There's something wrong here. I feel funny."

Virgil refilled the big clone's cup. "Drink up and enjoy. Don't be such a worrier."

General Cruz's head lolled to the table atop his folded arms. "Man, I'm sleepy."

King Carloman drained his glass. "The vote is six *ayes*, one *nay*, and one I *dunno*. The motion carries." He plopped into his seat.

* * *

Aramis came up the ramp from the lower level with his podmates and was taken aback by the sight. All the people at the table stared around with glassy-eyed expressions. He'd seen his human friends get drunk before, but that was after a long night of carousing. He'd only been absent from the ground floor for about an hour, so the sight at the dining table struck him as odd.

Dante waved to them. "Hey, guys. Can you carry these containers back to my best buddy's shuttle?"

Aramis took in the crowd at the table and shrugged. "Sure, Mister President," he shouted over the loud, boisterous voices at the table.

The drones removed the bottles and platters and dumped them into their original containers. One drone glided over to the three young clones. "I have assessed that the humans here have over indulged and are intoxicated. Remove what remains of these consumables to the shuttle they arrived in as soon as it is practical."

"Sure, Beatrice." Aramis winked at his podmates and hoisted a crate.

"Everyone sure seems to be having a good time," Athos observed. "All we get are the chores."

Aramis moved next to him and whispered, "Who says we can't eat and drink the leftovers?"

"We'll get caught," Porthos hissed.

"Nah, they'll be here a while. Let's get this stuff back to that shuttle's storage room, and we'll party to our heart's content. No one will be the wiser."

Porthos lifted a container and sniffed it. "Sounds like a plan."

They resealed the containers and loaded them on a flatbed truck parked near the entrance. The young clones squeezed into the cab, and Aramis drove across the tarmac to the unoccupied shuttle. Afterward, they brought everything into the storage room and sat on the floor.

Porthos lifted the lid on the last container he'd carried and looked inside. Whole, untouched platters and sealed bottles greeted all three. Porthos' eyes grew wide. "We've got a feast here!"

Aramis lifted a platter and placed it on the floor. Moving fast, he grabbed a leftover rib and stripped it clean to the bone in one bite. As he licked off the sauce from his fingers, he declared, "This stuff's amazing!"

Porthos reached in and pulled out two bottles. "Let the feast begin!"

For the next hour, the three ate and drank in silence. Aramis had no idea food could taste so good. Any thought of talking to his brothers didn't last as he ate more. When the clones stopped, they left only a single plate of food untouched.

Porthos sat back with a stack of bones and an empty bottle in front of him. "I wonder if they have food like this on Earth?"

Aramis sipped the brownish liquid with a satisfied smile, eyeing Athos' empty dish. "From what Cap'n Bernius told me, I bet this is sort of like what they called a barbecue. Let's—"

Voices sounded from the distance. From outside. The three clones froze in their spots.

"Uh-oh," Athos whispered.

"We'll be in big trouble if we're caught. We have to go now," Aramis slurred.

He rose, but his legs wobbled a lot for some reason. He also felt very sleepy and slid against the door. Everything made less and less sense, save for a faint flute-type sound. "Hey, do you hear some weird music?"

His podmates did not respond. They snored where they sat.

Aramis stepped toward them. "Something's wrong, we..."

His legs gave out.

CHAPTER XVII

Kidnapped

Everyone at the table wore glassy-eyed smiles, save for Michael and the three alien visitors. The big clone shook his head repeatedly, staring at an empty plate.

Arachne rose from the table and beckoned the king and his consort to follow. "Come with me. We need to finish up the new trade agreement. The contract is on my ship."

Virgil staggered to his feet. "That's a wonderful idea. I'm coming too."

"I'm driving," King Carloman shouted as he weaved to the door.

The muscles in Michael's neck corded, but he couldn't stand. He croaked out, "Don't go with them, Dante. Something's wrong."

Skipping to the exit, Dante lolled his head back and shouted, "Mick, you're a party-pooper."

Paxine followed close saying, "The poor man."

Calahas left with them and eventually climbed into the transport with Paxine, Arachne, and three stumbling humans. Paxine took the passenger seat next to Dante, who plopped into the driver's seat. Virgil and Tina climbed in the back seats with Calahas.

Arachne leaned close to his niece and hissed, "I thought you said no sentient being could resist the Satyr syrinx aphrodisiac?"

While Dante fumbled with the ignition, Paxine made no effort to lower her voice. "Well, I certainly don't know any who can. The performance of that spawn's kidneys and liver would have to be off the charts to filter out that much of our formula."

"He must also have an incredibly strong will." Arachne patted Dante. "Your Majesty, let's go to my shuttle now. We need to sign the agreement."

"You got it," the dazed human king said. He stomped on the accelerator, jerking everyone in the transport back. Virgil and Tina let out yelps which devolved into laughter.

Arachne gathered his bearings and directed the human king across the tarmac. The king smiled and nodded the whole way. Not long into the trip, however, Calahas noticed a lone drone following them.

"Thank goodness you're telling me what to do, Arachne. I woulda sat there forever." King Carloman furrowed his brows. "Wow, what's up with me? I can't focus."

By this point, the drone caught up. "Dante, you are acting irrationally. Please return to the compound."

Arachne leaned closer to the king's ear. "Make that robot go away. It will draw attention to us."

The drone flew parallel to the transport's erratic weaving, so Dante flashed an irritated glare. "Beatrice, all I'm going to do is sign some papers with my buddies. Everything's fine."

"Dante, this is wrong," the drone pressed.

"Why don't you tell someone who cares?"

The drone spun its sensors. "I will comply with your command," it said, then sped off.

They reached the shuttle in short order, placing them almost a full kilometer from the repurposed research facility. Dante whooped and slammed on the brakes before they could pass by their destination. The transport came to an abrupt halt.

Paxine scrambled out, and an edge seeped into her words. "Uncle, why don't we go inside *now*."

Arachne pulled a set of panpipes from his satchel and handed it to her, and they worked together to herd the three humans up the shuttle's ramp. It took more time than Calahas had estimated because the humans appeared more interested in dancing around than moving forward. But in time, they stumbled into the shuttle.

Once inside, Paxine blew on the panpipes. The three humans crumpled to the floor before the note finished, and the two Satyrs hurried to the bridge. Calahas sighed, having seen the entire trick before. The sound waves from the Satyr instrument, combined with the drug compound imbibed, would knock out any sentient being. One ought to never accept a drink offered by a Satyr, not without taking the antidote first.

Arachne rushed to the pilot seat, working fast through the launch checklist. "Calahas, drag them to the storage room. They should be comatose until we rouse them, but I don't want to take any chances. We're getting out of here now."

"You could've had them walk to the storage room before knocking them out," Calahas grumbled.

"True, but this gives you something useful to do," Paxine retorted.

With a quiet huff, the Centaur left the bridge, and the door automatically shut behind him. The ramp lifted, sealing the portal. While Calahas dragged the limp form of Lady Phokas from the floor, the shuttle rose into the air.

Calahas' thoughts darkened as he regarded the humans' slack faces. What had he done? Despite his own guilt for the sins of his ancestors, he'd chosen to damn the poor souls to a slow, agonizing death, all under the instruction of a self-indulgent Satyr who worshiped the Ipis.

Only now did he realize that this gamble to save his beloved Gesten was a fool's bet. He'd learned a number of things from General Cruz, who spoke freely while under the drug of the Satyrs. The kidnapped humans weren't from any royal houses attempting to lead some grand war in the Lethe Sector. They were nothing more than indigents of a backwater planet who had the misfortune of being caught up in an Ipis-dis cult experiment. It made their resourcefulness and survival thus far all the more impressive.

Calahas wrapped calloused, furred hands around Lady Phokas' ankles and lugged her to the back room. The whole way, he reflected on what else General Cruz had said. Not only did the humans escape their prison, but they decimated two different Ipis-dis cult forces on the ground. He'd also witnessed their takedown of a Stalker-class destroyer with a pair of relics aged four hundred years and a Striker-class frigate, all without any modern military training.

If anything, Calahas discovered how inept his own military understanding really was when he told General Cruz about his defeat at the hands of the Ipis. After the Centaur revealed how many soldiers he had and what tactics he used, the human general pointed out every flaw. He even guessed correctly how the Ipis commander retaliated before Calahas reached that part of his tale.

It didn't take long for Calahas to arrive at the storage hold, ending the self-reflection. He fumbled for the door release and started to back in. The Centaur pulled Lady Phokas into the room and turned to leave.

Instead, however, he gasped and shut the door. Three identical humans lay sprawled on the deck. The empty bottles and platters scattered about provided enough evidence to suggest what happened. Calahas stared long at the closed portal, thinking of what to do. The decision came easy. He wouldn't stain his hands further in more innocent blood.

So Calahas dragged the three young clones to the back wall and slid a partition in front of them. Next, he leaned Lady Phokas against the divider. The simple ruse would work for at least a little while. Satisfied, he cleaned up the mess and left to retrieve the next human.

As Calahas picked up King Carloman, Arachne shouted from his seat, "What's taking you so long?"

Calahas froze, but the smuggler captain didn't pay the Centaur any actual attention. Arachne's and Paxine's focus was on the shuttle's flight screen, which displayed the landing bay in the freighter. The elder Satyr and his niece also stared transfixed at another screen showing the exterior of the shuttle.

A reply came to the Centaur fast. "Ah... a few containers fell. It's quite a mess back there."

An irritated sigh left Paxine. "Hurry up! I need you to monitor their ground communications. The translator on this shuttle is useless. Nothing makes any sense!"

"I'll be done in a second," Calahas responded in a flat voice.

It took him only a few minutes to finish dragging the other two humans into the storage room, so it wasn't long before Calahas settled into his station. The display showed them entering orbit, as well as the ground base they'd just left. Four blips appeared on the screen, and Calahas read aloud the readouts as they scrolled by. "The human military scrambled four atmospheric fighters, which are in pursuit."

"How did they sound the alarm so fast? Everyone who was aware of us has to be staring at the walls. Even the abomination who stumbled after us wouldn't have all his faculties back." Arachne pursed his lips, examining his own readouts. "Those interceptors won't be a problem. They're too slow and too late. I'm more worried about their frigate. If their ground base is on to us, the frigate will be too."

Calahas squinted, listening to the translated chatter through headphones. "The frigate is on the other side of the planet. It's just broken orbit to intercept."

Arachne grunted in satisfaction. "We'll be gone before it gets here."

Paxine wiped perspiration from her forehead. "The two galleys just launched from their ground base and are now in pursuit."

"No worries there. We have enough of a lead on those antiques." Arachne toggled a communicator switch to his freighter. "Initiate the jump to hyperspace to the preloaded coordinates as soon as we dock."

"Sir, I just picked up the Roc warbird launching," the Centaur called out. "It's closing fast. It'll have us in range in approximately five minutes. How long before we reach the freighter?"

Arachne tugged his horn. "Approximately five minutes."

"Should I hail them and offer our surrender?" Calahas asked in a subdued voice.

"They won't fire on us. We have their king as a captive," Paxine squeaked.

Shame and anger welled in Calahas. "You idiot! They don't have to destroy our shuttle! All they have to do is disable it and hold us until their frigate arrives."

Paxine stared at him slack-jawed. "They'll kill us if we surrender."

"Yes, they probably will, and it's exactly what I'd do in their position," Calahas shot back. He shook his mane, not as certain about the notion as he thought. In a short span of time, the humans had shown better character than everyone in the shuttle's bridge.

"You're right, Paxine," Arachne said. "They won't dare kill us while we have their people. Now hang on to your seats. This is going to get interesting." The elder Satyr growled and toggled the speaker for the freighter's engine room. "Quango, cancel all safety protocols, and put the new AI in charge of the ship's normal space and hyperspace controls. Leave the hangar bay open." The shuttle's engines strained as Arachne accelerated. "As soon as the shuttle lands in the hangar, jump to hyperspace."

The gruff voice of Quango came through, sounding dumbfounded. "Ah, sir, are you sure? You know you need perfect precision for that maneuver this close to an atmosphere, right? It's a huge risk."

"Then give the AI control of everything," Arachne fired back. "The smallest error will superheat the vessel and blow it up."

Calahas shut his ears to the rising crescendo of Paxine's shrieks while the blips on the screen converged on their position.

* * *

Michael staggered from the compound. As soon as Beatrice detected him, she had her drone fly over to him. While it meant leaving Dante, it also meant she could "tell someone who cares," as he put it.

Beatrice did not hesitate to speak once the drone reached the big clone. "Michael, I require your assistance. Dante is inebriated beyond his capacity to function safely. He should enter a somnolent state until his body processes the intoxicants." Beatrice waited for a response, but her sensors detected the aliens' shuttle lifting off. "Michael, can you hear me?"

"Beatrice, stop them," Michael choked out with a fierce glare. "They are under compulsion. The aliens have enthralled their minds."

To Beatrice, every muscle in Michael's neck appeared corded as though struggling against a powerful restraint. Beatrice switched on her system-wide communications, and a message blared from every speaker and drone she had. "Danger. Help. Dante, Tina, and Virgil have been abducted."

The voice of Martinel came through, sounding confused. "Beatrice, this is Captain Martinel. What in blazes is going on?" Once Beatrice relayed what she observed and what Michael told her, Martinel responded with a curse word. "Freakin' bastards. Atlantis is moving to intercept. I want everything that can fly to converge on that damn freighter now!"

Beatrice turned to Michael, but he had already left. He now stumbled to where Mercury was parked. His bent back and plodding steps suggested he fought hurricane headwinds, but no such winds flowed today.

Beatrice detected a commotion behind her drone and spun its sensor in that direction. The not-guest Setteth raced over at a blistering speed she did not think biological creatures could attain. Mara fell further and further behind.

"Machine, I heard the broadcast," Setteth said. "The humans are under Satyr syrinx mind control. My warbird is here. Let me give chase."

None of the thousands of probability scenarios Beatrice ran yielded a satisfactory result. Most ended in failure. The highest chance of success was still slim, but stalling too long would guarantee failure. "Mara, help me."

"I will stay with the Roc not-guest in her craft. There will be no deception. We will need a human to supervise us. We will take Michael."

Beatrice cried in a voice she did not know she had. "Mara, save my friends."

Mara responded in a soft tone. "I will, Beatrice. I love them too."

Michael struggled to the airfield as the human fighters took off and crews rushed aboard Mercury and Soyuz. Mara sped to Michael and tried lifting him from the ground. When she could not, she resorted to dragging him along. Beatrice sent a drone to help, and it clamped on to one of Michael's arms. Together, Beatrice and Mara hauled the clone into the air.

"Hurry, please hurry," Michael gasped.

Even with two robots carrying him, they moved slowly. By the time they reached the warbird, the two galleys had lifted off and become two small dots in the sky.

"Hurry, you stupid machine!" Setteth hissed, tossing equipment stacked in the area behind the pilot's seat. She helped the robots hoist Michael into a narrow seat once it was cleared of any gear, but the effort tired her. "He's a heavy one, isn't he?"

"He is Michael. He is good." Beatrice's drone helped secure Michael and Mara in place, then drifted to where the Roc powered up her ship and checked various readouts. "Not-guest Setteth, save my friends. Please."

The Roc warbled deep in her throat. "By the Order of the Dragon, I will see this done or die trying. Now we hunt Satyrs."

A moment later, Setteth's warbird rose through the sky, leaving Beatrice's drone behind. Beatrice continued to sound the alarm long after the last vessel was airborne.

* * *

The shuttle was a Znune-class atmospheric lift craft. It was a fast, low-maintenance workhorse, making it a popular craft for smugglers and traders on the fringes of Ipis society. However, it possessed no combat capabilities.

Setteth's warbird, by contrast, was a modern attack ship designed for high-speed pursuit. With little effort, it shot past the smaller atmospheric craft buzzing at their maximum altitude.

Stirred to action by returning to the long-familiar controls of her warbird, Setteth broke through the clutches of the planet's gravity in a minute. She'd already raced past the lumbering human galleys, hunting her prey. The warbird's sensors picked up on the shuttle immediately, already taking evasive maneuvers.

"The Satyr pilot is good," Setteth observed. "I'll grant him that, but he'll need to slow down and orient his shuttle so he can enter the freighter's landing bay. Then we'll have him."

Setteth would use a disabling shot, of course, as it posed minimal risk to the occupants so long as she avoided the engines. However, the shuttle dove left, right, up, and down, even spiraling at unpredictable times. Sometimes, it hovered in a half circle in either the lower or upper part of her crosshairs. Never did it actually drift *into* the crosshairs, whether due to its own maneuvering or Setteth's attempts to adjust her aim.

After a short time of this, the Roc cawed. "I can't get a clean shot. He's either insane or a very gifted pilot."

"Explain," Mara said. "I lack data to process your statement."

Setteth kept her eyes on the readouts. "The shuttle pilot's jinking so his most vulnerable parts are exposed to my targeting system. Any shot I take will instantly kill everyone on board that vessel, including the hostages."

Mara's sensors blinked. "He is using those he kidnapped as his shield."

Setteth fired the warbird's twin ion disruptor cannons. A beam skimmed off the shuttle's backside, damaging the port-side tailfin. The shuttle wobbled, but it didn't stop.

Setteth snapped her beak. "The bastard doesn't need the tailfin anymore. We've left Cocytus' atmosphere, and we're running out of time."

"Target the host vessel and destroy it. The shuttle will have nowhere to go."

"A lone warbird against a Yorgane freighter," Setteth hissed. "You're right. I might have enough time to close in before it breaks orbit. The human ships won't arrive in time."

Just as Setteth committed to the motion, the Satyr's shuttle dove into the freighter's open portal, shearing off the damaged tailfin. The freighter floundered, but it maintained its position long enough for the shuttle to settle inside. The hangar's door slammed shut.

The Roc adjusted her warbird's approach to the rear of the smuggler's freighter. "I'll have the ship in range in just a few seconds. Then they won't go anywhere."

A moment later, however, Setteth sensed something through the hull of the warbird: the subsonic pulse of the freighter's hyperdrive engines activating. And here she was, still too far away. Rage escaped in a screech as she fired her ion disruptors. The shots missed, and not just because the freighter sat a short distance out of range.

The engines lit up, and the freighter entered hyperspace in a streak of color.

CHAPTER XVIII

The Chase

The Roc warbirds were designed as all-purpose fighting vessels. The sleek, delta-wing shape granted as much maneuverability within a planet's atmosphere as in space. Setteth had explained it thus to Virgil and the other soldiers, if Michael recalled right. Although the warbird's exterior dimensions were only slightly smaller than a human galley, the cramped, three-seat cockpit made a galley's bridge, with its five workstations, feel spacious by comparison.

Setteth twisted in her seat to face Michael and Mara. "I can follow them, but I must do it in the next few seconds or we'll lose the trichion trail left by their hyperdrive."

Michael sat rigid on the hard, oval bench built for the wider bottom of a Roc. As such, the back provided little lumbar support for a human, but he put this out of mind. In the past, he overcame the harpies' compulsion mind commands by focusing on the people he cherished. He did the same now to speak through the drugs fogging his thoughts. "We can follow them?"

"The Ipis outfitted my warbird with a trichion tracer. That's how we followed that Satyr smuggler to this planet. They've made a hyperspace jump, but for a few moments more, I can access the same interstellar portal."

"Trichions," Mara echoed. "That term does not exist in my repository. Please define."

Setteth's fingers danced across her cockpit's control panel, tapping at some fading icons on her screen. "I will, but it's now or never. Do we follow?"

Fire blazed in Michael's being, and he croaked a *yes* out of a constricted throat. A loud caw bellowed from the Roc, and she hit the control panel.

Michael closed his eyes as queasiness formed in his stomach. When he dared to look again, the multitude of stars formed unrecognizable patterns, disconcerting to one who only knew the stars in the night skies of Cocytus.

"There it is," Setteth hooted, pointing to a red dot on her screen. The blip moved away from them, but she oriented the warbird toward the signal and accelerated.

"Where?" Michael gasped.

The Roc slid out a tray from beneath her seat. The tray contained a rack of clear, finger-sized vials labeled with bold Ipis runes. Setteth selected one and passed it to Michael. "Drink this. It'll help your body detox the Satyr serum."

Mara snaked a tentacle around the slim tube and scanned the contents with a molecular sensor probe. "This substance is not poisonous to the human body, but I cannot decipher its function beyond that."

The big clone tried to grasp the container, but his arms hung limp at his side. "Feed it to me."

Mara swung her sensor toward Setteth. "If this harms my friend, you will be terminated." She pried the clone's mouth open and poured the liquid in.

Michael gagged down most of it. Nothing tasted out of the ordinary, save for a mild sourness.

"It'll take about an hour for the effects to start showing," the Roc chirped. Not once did she turn from the screens or the distant target.

Mara telescoped her optical scanner at the same screens. "Why is the freighter so far away? The time between their disappearance and our pursuit is only twenty-three seconds apart."

"That's because a trichion-hyperspace portal opens to a fixed location in the universe, but everything around it is in motion. Planets move, stars move, even the galaxy moves." Setteth flipped a switch on her right. "In physical distance, each portal is approximately two parsecs. So, while we entered the same portal as they did, the motion of the galaxy has caused us to exit thousands of kilometers away from them."

"Define parsec."

The Roc squinted for a second. "One parsec is the equivalent of three-point-two-six light-years."

"Define light-year."

"Nine-point-four-six kilometers. These were terms and measurements made by humans long ago."

Setteth flew the warbird toward the image on her screen. Upon closing in, the blip vanished, and Setteth hissed. "They just made the next jump. We must reach that portal before the trichions dissipate." The Roc pushed the warbird's speed so far the engines rattled. "They jumped already. Commercial grade systems don't work that fast. He must've made modifications."

"Explain impact of variance," Mara requested.

Setteth pushed the lever on the ship's tracking device to the max. "It means they will escape."

* * *

The warbird tracked the freighter through four more jumps, falling farther and farther behind. At the fifth stop, Setteth examined the readouts with some intensity, then flipped off the tracking device in frustration. "I'm not detecting any more trichion residue. We lost them."

By then, the last remnant of the Satyr drug had run its course. A sinking feeling settled in Michael, but he breathed deep to keep calm. "What do we do now?"

"We try to guess where they're going." The Roc pressed an icon on her display. The flight cabin dimmed, and a three-dimensional mass of pinpoint lights settled in the middle. Together, the points modeled the galaxy.

A green dot represented the warbird, and a fading red dot showed the last known position of the Satyr's freighter. "We stayed with them through five jumps. Let's see what that tells us." Her feather's fluffed. "Computer, limit display to habitable systems."

The cabin dimmed further, leaving a glowing area spanning 0.25 cubic meters floating behind Setteth. The display rested in front of Michael.

Setteth spun in her seat. "Limit view to the Lethe Sector and its ten adjacent sectors. Plot the trajectory of the five jumps we've already made."

A thin red line snaked out from near the far edge of the floating display. Setteth pointed to each point on the way. "This is Cocytus' star system." Her bony finger touched the end of the red line, which led to no nearby star system. "This is where we are now."

Michael could make little sense of what the display showed. "Does that tell you anything?"

Setteth settled into a raptor's glare and began muttering almost to herself. "They're staying within the Lethe Sector for a reason. What is their goal? Sanctuary on a Satyr or Centaur world? No. They were in too much of hurry to leave. Escape to an open trade planet? No. They're known smugglers, wanted by Ipis authorities." She cocked her head to the side.

"System, display habitable worlds in zones seven through fifteen of the Lethe Sector that are garrisoned by imperial troops."

The display blinked, and six white dots glowed with the red line pointing in their direction.

The old Roc squinted at the new data points. "Display details."

Ipis runes appeared beneath the six glowing dots, each label describing the main purpose of those worlds: two supply depots, one garrison, and one robotics manufacturing center, all of which required authorized access.

Setteth leaned closer and read the text beside each dot. "No. No. No. No." With each declaration, the light and text winked out.

When two worlds remained, she leaned back. "Equitone, home world of the fugitive Centaur prince. He led a minor rebellion there a couple years ago, but it failed. This last world is Carcerem, a mining planet with a major administrative center and several maximum-security detention centers... primarily for humans." She clicked her beak. "They're going to Carcerem. They intend to barter their captives for pardons."

Michael groaned, shaking his head. His thought process now clear, he muttered, "Great. A planet full of freaking harpies. Can we reach that planet ahead of them?"

Setteth let out a sad sigh. "No. They will be there weeks before we arrive."

"Weeks?" Michael's voice turned icy. "My friends could be dead in that time. You seem to know where they're going, so why can't you jump through this hyperspace and get there now?"

"You really don't know anything about interstellar travel, do you," Setteth said. It wasn't a question, but neither an admonishment—just resignation. The Roc checked a few gauges before turning back. "This warbird is capable of interstellar travel, but it can't travel across large expanses of the galaxy. Larger ships can create trichion fields with an enormous onboard power plant, but a craft the size of mine could never contain the energy levels required for a sustained period of time. We did fine when we could use the same portal as our prey, but creating our own will require two refueling stops to reach Carcerem. That'll add a couple weeks to our trip."

Michael grunted and stared at the inky void outside their spacecraft, feeling incredibly small. "Is the power plant in this craft the same size as the one in our galleys? It takes up half the space in those ships."

"The galleys you have are old. The generator in my craft is half the size and twice as efficient," Setteth warbled. "However, even with that superiority, traveling across the galaxy in a single move is impossible." Her fingers flew across the keyboard, and she murmured to herself. "How does one explain four-dimensional travel in three-dimensional terms?"

"You'd do better than I," Michael said.

The Roc clucked deep in her throat, studying the gauges further for a moment. "It will be another fifteen minutes before I can initiate the next hyperspace jump, so I'll try to explain. Imagine you're standing on a mountaintop, and you want to travel to another mountaintop in the distance. Now imagine hundreds of trails crisscrossing the valleys and mountains in between. Imagine that, on each pathway, there are many doors attached to pulleys, and when you step through a door, the pulley yanks your door to a different path. You can still see your goal, and you draw closer each time, but you must stop and recalculate which path to take next."

Michael scratched the back of his neck and shrugged. "I think I see. Sort of."

Mara's sensors blinked. "Gravity. Is celestial gravity the pulley?"

"That's right," Setteth replied. "Everything from a small asteroid to a black hole can affect the trichions forming the hyperjump portal."

The big clone rubbed his chin. "So, since we can no longer use the same portal they did, we have to make our own, and that could take us on an entirely different path."

"Exactly." Setteth sighed, typing away on the keyboard. She skimmed the text on the monitor before pressing a button. From the rear of the warbird, a communication rocket launched and sped off.

Communication rockets were the sole means of transmitting messages in a galaxy over thirty thousand parsecs long. Given the speed of light, outside a planetary star system, real-time audio and video interactions were impossible. These missile-like tubes spanning almost two and a half meters long were designed to propel a nosecone of ultra-dense data the full length of a sector before requiring refueling. Days ago, Michael had heard Dante laugh and compare it to some "pony-express" in the old American west, whatever that was.

Thus, as the communication rocket left the warbird, suspicion rose in Michael. "What was that?"

"Just making a course correction," Setteth chirped while clearing the information on the screen.

CHAPTER XIX

Stowaways

The shuttle hadn't settled into the hangar bay for more than a few minutes before Arachne hurried to the freighter's bridge with Calahas close behind. While Calahas ordered members of the security team to move the captives to the brig, Arachne spent most of the time afterward racing through normal space and making hyperspace jumps. After twelve agonizing hours, and a total of four jumps, the freighter appeared in an isolated area of space. Nothing else appeared in the following minutes. They were alone.

Calahas looked up from his scope on the freighter's bridge. "I think we lost that warbird after our second jump. We escaped clean." He shifted nervously on his four hooves. "We've still a long way to go. I'm going to check the humans."

Arachne nodded, still focused on the controls. "Good idea. No rush. They came to an hour ago and aren't very happy."

"They're awake already?" The Centaur curled his fingers. "That should be impossible."

Arachne chuckled. "Normally yes, but someone on your security team in the brig were curious about humans. Huon, I think. She asked permission to give them the antidote. She wanted to talk with a *human* before her work shift ended. I had no issue with it. Why? Is there a problem?"

Calahas rose from his workstation. "No. no problem. I just need to review the arrangements." He exited the freighter's bridge in haste. The Centaur cursed himself for forgetting his security team had strict standing orders to only bring emergencies to his attention when he was engaged in hyperspace navigation.

Instead of taking the ramp up two levels to the confinement center, he galloped along the catwalk leading to the freighter's hangar bay, where Arachne had parked the shuttle. He told no one, not even his trusted followers, about the three clones hidden there. He'd left the stowaways concealed behind the partition when his confused security guards carted off the three captives.

One of his followers, Huon, asked why the humans were prisoners. Calahas felt sick inside at putting on a cold facade but told her, "Arachne has a plan to save us all. Now, just follow orders."

Calahas felt no better now. He touched the manacles packed in his side pouch, assuring himself that a little time remained before they awakened. He could keep the stowaways hidden long enough to sneak them off at the next open spaceport.

Upon entering the hangar, Calahas checked the shredded port-side tailfin Arachne's maneuver had mangled during the escape. Burn marks lingered near the broken edges, no doubt from the disruptor blast courtesy of the Roc warbird.

The Centaur tapped the communicator at his throat. "Quango, we need a repair crew for the shuttle. Exterior damage appears to be limited to the port-side stabilizer, but check it out. I'll run diagnostics inside the craft."

Quango's irritated grunt came through the earphone. "We'll get to it once we have the hangar bay portal repaired. By my mother's twisted beard, I'm short on staff, and we have to deal with the bigger issue first. Arachne's lucky he didn't get us all killed flying in like that. What's going on? Why'd we have to leave in such a blasted hurry?"

Feeling as annoyed as Quango sounded, Calahas sighed. "You'll have to ask him."

Calahas switched the communicator off, lest anyone overhear him when he reached his next destination. He wrestled with guilt and self-recrimination for resorting to kidnappings to achieve his goals. The thoughts festered as he boarded the shuttle. No sooner did he arrive at the storage room and open the door than a blunt object smashed into his head. Reeling, the Centaur kicked out instinctively with calloused hindquarters, hearing a grunt on contact. However, a hard body slammed into his side, tossing him into the wall. Another bash to the head, and the dazed Centaur collapsed to the floor.

* * *

The next thing Calahas knew, he lay on his side on the cold, metal floor, shackled by his own manacles. The contents of his pouches had scattered across the floor.

An icy voice spoke in his ear. "Okay, 'friend,' start talking. What the hell's going on here?"

Calahas lifted his head and saw the clone spawns with their ridiculous scarves were very much awake. The one called Athos guarded the door. A second one, Porthos, stood doubled over, holding his stomach. This one raised his head and said, "Forget it, Aramis. Let's beat the shit out of this guy and then question him."

Calahas winced in pain as a set of hands twisted his arm higher behind his back.

Aramis crouched in front of him. "Are you going to talk to us, 'friend?'"

What had Calahas gotten himself into? If enough time passed, Quango's repair team would be working on the outside of the shuttle—which meant Calahas would have to stall.

The Centaur met the eyes of the clones and spied anger and confusion there. "Let me up, and I'll tell you whatever you want."

Porthos still rubbed his stomach. "What good will that do? You could tell us anything, and we won't have a clue if it's true."

"Hmm." Aramis rubbed his jaw where a little fuzz had sprouted. "Porthos, is there any more of that food we ate?"

Calahas closed his eyes to hide the glint there. The antidote he drank half a day ago lingered in his system. Furthermore, the clones hadn't removed the communicator device attached to his neck. A simple bend of the head, and he could call his security team and capture the spawns in seconds.

However, upon seeing the earnest face in front of him, the Centaur hesitated. Crouched not even half a meter from him, Aramis' eyes bore into him. In the end, Calahas opted not to end the situation just yet.

Calahas raised his chin away from the power button. "You do your masters' credit, serving them with such diligence."

Aramis' face scrunched in confusion. "Masters? Cap'n Bernius is a tough commander, but he'll be the first to tell you he's nobody's master."

A voice behind the Centaur growled, "C'mon, Aramis, stop chatting with this scumbag and let's find out what the hell's going on. Feed him that stuff."

"Yeah, that'll do the trick. I remember how I couldn't stop talking when I came to." The clone at the door, Athos, glared at the bound Centaur while tapping a makeshift staff sixty centimeters long, a piece likely taken from the most damaged crate.

Aramis stepped in front of the Centaur holding a half-empty bottle and a leftover plate of meat. "Enjoy your meal, sucker."

He lifted the bound Centaur upright. Porthos popped open the bottle and poured it into Calahas' mouth.

Calahas gagged down the food and drink Porthos force-fed him for the next five minutes. The three identical humans sat in front of him, staring for an additional fifteen. Despite it all, Calahas thought the trio displayed a strange combination of innocence and fervor. He reflected on how his own dreams had turned to dust over the years. At that moment, he decided to tell them whatever they wanted to hear. It wouldn't help them, per se, but he could at least confess his sins aloud.

As it was, he'd waited long enough for his captors to think the drug worked through his system. Calahas pasted a ridiculous smile on his face and started talking. "I must say, your human masters are strange. They give their robots names and treat common spawned soldiers as real people."

The glare Aramis showed deepened. "Common spawned soldier, huh?" He gave a warning look to Porthos, who stood as if ready to lunge. Porthos stayed in place, though, and Aramis spoke again. "I know a long list of people who think a lot differently than you do, and three of them are imprisoned somewhere on this stinking ship of yours. Now, tell us why you kidnapped Cap'n Bernius, Dante, and Tina."

Calahas told them everything. Tears escaped when he spoke of Gesten. The three young clones looked at each other in surprise when he described how he hid them. He told them of his deep regret for participating in the plot. When he finished telling his tale, he felt at peace.

Aramis shared some unreadable looks with his brothers before turning to Calahas. There, his frown turned into a real smile. "Well, I didn't expect to hear any of that. Athos, untie him." Aramis pointed to his chest. "I know we already introduced ourselves, but the name's Aramis." He pointed to the clone leaning on the back wall. "The ugly guy you kicked is Porthos, and the fella watching the door is Athos. We're people, not spawns, whatever that is. From what I heard, the way we were born was a touch weird, and our early education by the harpies wasn't exactly nurturing. But I think we have our heads on pretty straight regardless."

After Athos unlocked the Centaur's bonds, Calahas rubbed his wrists. "What are you going to do with me?"

Porthos stepped close and looked into the Centaur's eyes, then turned to Aramis. "Are you sure he's still under the influence of that happy sauce? He sounds a heck of a lot more lucid than you did when you were babbling."

Aramis heaved a great sigh. "Maybe he is, maybe he isn't. Either way, he's the only one on this whole ship we can kind of trust. The main thing we have to do now is save our friends."

Calahas tensed, tail flicking in alarm. "You can't. Their holding pen is under constant surveillance. Even if you managed to break them out, where would you go? You're in a space freighter several parsecs away from any point of civilization."

Aramis snarled. "We'll commandeer this ship and fly home."

"Who'll fly it for you?" Calahas retorted. "Arachne is the only deep space pilot onboard, and he has fifty crew members to back him up."

Athos growled, shuffling in place. "Cap'n Bernius will know what to do."

"Does he know how to work a hyperdrive?" Silence answered, and the Centaur went on. "As soon as you step out of this shuttle, you'll be detected. You'll never even make it to the hangar bay exit." He also knew a half dozen crewmen probably set to work on the shuttle's port-side tailfin a short while ago.

"No, but you could." Aramis rubbed his jaw. "Porthos, give me that comic book you have stashed in your back pocket. Athos, give me that paper and pencil Doctor Easley used to teach us script writing."

Porthos handed Aramis a peculiar item with various illustrations. Calahas gawked at the pictures of stylized humans wearing tight, gaudy-colored garments. The images and actions made no sense to him.

Once he had the requested items in hand, Aramis ripped a page from the notebook and tore off the back cover of the comic book.

"Hey, what're you doing? That's mine," Porthos bleated.

"Sorry. I'm going to write the Cap'n a note, and he needs to be positive that it's from us." Aramis spread out the sheet of paper and studied the writing examples in the notebook. Three discarded sheets of paper later—each one containing a confusing string of loops and lines—the young clone flexed his fingers and examined the results. He folded it up in the colorful comic book cover and snapped the pencil in half. He put the back end of the pencil in his pocket and handed Calahas the sharp end. "Give this to Cap'n Bernius, and wait for a reply."

The Centaur took the items and placed them in his pouch. Aramis must've written a coherent message, but Calahas couldn't decipher it even now. Perhaps it was a secret code, and clever use of one. He cleared his throat. "I will do as you command."

Athos hoisted the makeshift staff and poked Calahas in the back. "You better."

Calahas rose and trotted from the shuttle, locking the exterior door when he left.

* * *

Calahas stepped into the freighter's hangar bay, where the bright lights three meters above almost blinded him. Quango sat atop the shuttle holding a welding torch. The Satyr engineer's gray hair, gnarled body, and broken horn gave him away. Despite the gap between their locations, they spotted each other fast.

Quango called out, "Prince Calahas, we'll have the wing repaired in a couple hours. Does anything need to be done inside?"

Calahas gripped his pouch, thinking of the new items it held. "No. Everything inside is fine." He cantered toward the area in the freighter Arachne used as a detention block.

Two levels up, he arrived at the brig. He slowed upon catching sight of the shimmering cage that imprisoned the humans. They sat on the floor, and the rage emanating from them indicated that the effects of the syrinx had worn off.

The only guard present was the roan-colored Huon, so Calahas called her over. "Return to your work post, but check the mess hall first for any sluggards shirking their duties. I want to interrogate the captives for a while."

A rough sigh left Huon. "Why are we holding these humans prisoner? They protected us from the Ipis, and they're human warriors like in the old tales."

Calahas felt ashamed, fighting to maintain a commander's facade. "Don't question it. There's more going on than you realize."

"Yes, my prince. As you say." Huon's tail twitched as she trotted out. In his mind, Calahas promised to explain the truth later.

The next voice, however, hammered him with guilt. "This is the thanks we get for saving your necks?"

The voice belonged to Lady Phokas, if the Centaur recalled right. Calahas felt as though her sneering words gave voice to his own thoughts.

Above and nearby, a camera recorded everything in the room. Huon alone usually watched and operated the freighter's security room during their current work cycle, though not currently. By diverting her to the mess hall, Calahas had given himself about fifteen minutes where no one would watch the cameras. Hopefully, it'd provide enough time to apologize to the captives.

Lady Phokas spoke again, bitterness thick in every word. "So, what's going on?"

Calahas turned to the cell, where the three humans stood at the barrier, glaring daggers at him. He pointed to the camera mounted on the wall and put a calloused finger to his lips. They cast one brief look at the camera, then brought their icy gazes back to him.

Calahas reached into his pouch and studied the handwritten note for a long moment. On a pedestal beside the cage sat a slim, rectangular box used to deliver food to prisoners. Calahas opened the lid of the box and slipped the folded paper and hidden pencil into it. After he closed it and pressed a button on the stand, the box dropped down and came up in the middle of the cell.

The Centaur watched as the human king opened the container and pulled out its contents. All three humans crowded over the note, apparently having no difficulty understanding the scribbles.

Lady Phokas donned a warm smile, but it soon turned a bit sad. "Those kids. They're trapped in this mess too."

A leery Virgil approached the barrier. "Are they safe?"

Though perplexed by the reaction of the human nobles, Calahas held it back to keep his tone even. "They're secure in the shuttle. I've locked them in, and no one knows of their presence but me. You are the bargaining chips the captain plans to use, not them. No harm will come to the spawns unless it's warranted."

Lady Phokas eyed the colorful piece of paper before flicking a cold stare at the Centaur. "Be careful mouthing off about people you don't know. Those so-called 'spawns' are some fine people with big hearts. They're my friends."

The Centaur's tail twitched as he took in the three human faces. Despite their circumstances, they worried about some manufactured biological tools. Calahas had to admit, the spawns—no, clones—behaved much differently than he'd expected. Perhaps the humans' view of them wasn't so strange after all.

Virgil jabbed at the force field, but his finger stopped as if it ran into a concrete wall. "They're among the bravest soldiers I've ever served with. Why, with only a small band of fighters, they boarded and took over an Ipis frigate. Their courage and quick thinking saved my life. No sir, they are not just common soldiers."

Calahas bowed his head to the three humans. "I meant no offense. I apologize. Such free mixing of castes does not occur in my society."

"Maybe you should try it," Virgil said. "The Centaur who just left holds you in high regard despite your social station."

Calahas rose, but not in full. "I don't know why they follow me after all I've put them through."

Virgil scoffed. "Try asking them. Now to get to the real question: Why did you kidnap us? What did you mean by 'bargaining chips?'"

Calahas turned from the humans in shame. "I am Prince Calahas of the Centaurs. I'm wanted by the Ipis for leading a failed revolt on my home world. Arachne is a smuggler who has broken too many laws for this sector's government to tolerate. I am disowned and toothless. Arachne is just a petty annoyance." He paced across the room. "You, however, are different. Your names belong to legendary human royal houses who led a formidable resistance against the empire. As such, you're the prize that will buy our pardons and lift the embargo strangling my home world of Equitone. They will be grateful when we bring you in."

King Carloman moved to the barrier, looking unconvinced. "What makes you think they'll grant you anything for us? We're not the great prize you think we are."

The Centaur shook his head. "You are Lord Carloman, king of all humans, and Lady Phokas, by her name alone, claims lineage to House Phokas."

"We're not any kind of great and powerful nobility. And I'm just Tina, by the way." Tina let out a mirthless laugh. "Dante is a computer engineer, and I'm a medical student. Your treachery's going to bite you in the—"

"Enough," Calahas said. "The deed is done. Do you have a response to your underlings or not?"

Virgil huddled with Dante and Tina for a few moments, before giving Calahas a hard look. "If anything happens to those kids, I *will* find a way to kill you." He scratched a quick response on the back of the note and dropped it in the box.

Calahas pressed the pedestal's button, and the box returned in seconds. He retrieved the piece of paper and examined it. The curving lines made as little sense as the first note. Nonetheless, he pocketed the items and looked at the prisoners.

"It says, 'Stay where you are for now,'" Virgil said as if answering the Centaur's unasked question.

"I'll make them as safe and comfortable as I can." Calahas walked erect on his four legs and approached the door.

Tina squeezed Dante's hand, eyeing the Centaur with a frigid regard. "We'll see. You didn't have much of a problem lying to us before."

With those words burning in his ears, Calahas hurried out. He wandered the passageways with bitter thoughts until he remembered he'd turned off his communicator.

As soon as it powered up, a voice hailed him. "Prince Calahas, this is Huon. We need you in the hangar immediately."

Fear gripped him. "Don't do anything until I get there."

He galloped the entire way there. When he arrived, the shuttle entrance hung wide open.

CHAPTER XX

Welcome to Carcerem

Calahas reached the top of the entrance ramp and stared through the shuttle's open portal. There, five Satyrs from the engineering crew, including Quango, and the three human clones sat in a rough circle on the floor. Two of the Centaurs from his security team lounged by the pilot's chair in the bridge. Aramis was in the middle of telling them all a story when Calahas appeared at the entrance. Once they noticed him, everyone froze.

"What in blazes is going on here?" Calahas brayed.

The two Centaurs in the seats straightened and bowed. The one on the left, Huon, stared right at Calahas with a knowing smile. "I went to monitor the detention block when you spoke with the captives. Your appearance seemed to agitate them, so I listened in. You said that you intended to make these humans safe and comfortable. So, we hurried here to do your bidding. When we arrived, Chief Engineer Quango was here already chatting with the humans. Did I misconstrue your wishes?"

All tension faded, and Calahas snorted in amusement. Huon and the other Centaur backed away.

Four Satyr technicians wore Satyr clan leather gauntlets identical to the one Quango wore. At a nod from the older Satyr, the four formed a wall with their horns lowered between Calahas and the three clones.

Quango crossed his arms and approached Calahas. "Security Captain Calahas, I just had a nice long chat with these humans, and I want to know what in the name of my curly horned ancestors is going on? I've been working with Arachne for over twenty years now, and I'm guessing he's pulling another one of his lamebrain get-rich stunts. I thought I was dealing with a few stowaways when I came inside to check the systems you claimed were fine."

The chief engineer scratched under his scraggily goatee. "Well, I got an earful about what's happened, and I won't stand for any harm coming to these humans. My sorry dead carcass would be floating around that frozen planet if it weren't for these folks and their friends. It's a debt I don't take lightly, even if Arachne and his posh niece do."

Calahas shook his mane, whinnying in frustration. Clearly, Quango had seen through his ruse earlier.

Peering at the clones, admiration entered the gray-haired Satyr's voice. "These boys have seen more action and had more success in the last year against the damn Ipis than I've had in my entire life."

Aramis stepped out from behind the line of Satyrs and stood next to Quango, clearing his throat. "Did you get an answer?"

Calahas closed the gap and slumped to his haunches. He fished the scribbled paper out of his pouch and handed it to him. Porthos and Athos hurried to Aramis, and they read it together. The Satyr technicians and Centaur guards crowded in behind them.

Quango squinted at the indecipherable words. "Laddie, what does the note say?"

Aramis passed the sheet to Athos. "Cap'n Bernius says to stay put for now."

Quango nodded. "That's good advice. No one comes into this hangar unless they're one of my technicians. We can keep them safe from prying eyes here, can't we?" The chief engineer suddenly gasped. "Wait a second. You said the bodyguard's name is Bernius?"

Aramis shrugged. "Yeah, that's his name. What about it?"

Quango patted the young clone on his shoulder. "Son, both royal human houses were wiped out over a hundred years ago. Bernius was one of them. Carloman was the other."

"And the human woman is a Phokas," Calahas choked out. "Centaur folklore says the clan she claims ties to was begotten by the human oracle. But it can't be! The Ipis hunted those families to extinction. Their home world, Novaroma, was sterilized. All life eradicated."

"Apparently, they missed a few." Sighing, Quango regarded the somber faces in the room and addressed the three young clones. "Phokas, Carloman, and Bernius are names out of legend in this part of the galaxy. Perhaps it means something. Perhaps it doesn't."

Calahas shook himself. "We reach Carcerem in seven days. Quango, keep these three hidden until then."

The chief engineer growled. "Carcerem? I've been there once for a shipment of bi-nexidium ore. That planet is controlled by the Ipis-ma sect. They have a whack-job magistrate there too."

"What's Ipis-ma?" Aramis asked Quango.

The old Satyr's shoulders sagged. "First, you have to understand the Ipis. They love their cults. The two main ones are the Ipis-dis, who I understand you boys already met. They have an all-consuming fear of some mythical enemy destined to destroy them. Most of that bunch believe the unknown foe is actually humans since they posed the only serious challenge to the Ipis in the last couple hundred years. They hunt for the hidden human empire to this day. As for the Ipis-ma, they're almost the opposite. They believe the Ipis are the supreme species destined to rule the galaxy unchallenged. They believe all other species should be enslaved or exterminated."

Porthos gulped. "And that's where we're going? To one of the worlds occupied by that cult?"

"Yup." Quango limped to a chair. "And their magistrate is a full believer—a complete fanatic named Keres-ma. He was one nasty customer three years ago, and I'm guessing he hasn't mellowed much."

With nothing else to say, Calahas backed out of the doorway. Huon and the other Centaur security guard followed him.

* * *

The Centaur prince spent most of the next seven days in the detention block, having many long conversations with the captives.

Despite their predicament, Tina found herself warming to Calahas after he told them the story of his aborted revolt and fugitive life away from Gesten. Dante and Virgil were slower to trust their erstwhile captor, but they built a quick friendship with the Centaur security guards, especially Huon.

Huon asked them a never-ending stream of questions about their lives and everything human. Her eyes shone with excitement, clapping her hands at the end of each story. She whinnied when Dante explained democratic forms of government and leaders being chosen by the people.

"This Earth sounds like paradise," she remarked, casting a look at Calahas. "It... it sounds like what my prince wanted to create for Centaurs on Equitone."

"We both know how that attempt ended," Calahas snorted.

Dante shook his head and stifled a cough. "Democracy has its problems. There's an old saying from a leader named Jefferson on my home world that goes, 'Democracy is the worst form of government, except for all the rest.'"

Huon and even Calahas chuckled at this.

Tina's mouth slimmed to a thin line. "We had that master race garbage on our home world for a while, but the free people united. After a long struggle, that sick philosophy was tossed into the ashbin of history."

"That's not the galaxy," Calahas retorted. "Your world had the luxury of having free people to fight."

Dante's voice stayed even. "I've heard that wasn't always the case for this part of the galaxy."

Calahas' voice dropped to a whisper. "The alliance was broken many decades ago."

"And no one can form it again?"

Calahas had no answer. He turned and left without a word.

* * *

In between these conversations, Calahas searched for any means to free them. Unfortunately, only Paxine held the code for the cell's energy field, and she shared it with no one.

By the seventh day, the security captain entered the ship's brig in a frantic state. Huon had installed a recorded loop of the captives sleeping, so he ignored the cameras. "I can't get the key, and I've tried to convince Arachne that this plan is foolhardy, but to no avail. I... I am sorry."

Tina, who'd been so hopeful beforehand, turned crestfallen. "What will happen to us?"

Calahas' tail twitched. "I honestly don't know. Before the Ipis conquered the Lethe Sector, Carcerem was a human colony. Today, it's a mining planet, but the Ipis-ma faction also runs a large prison there for societal deviants."

"And the kids?" she asked.

"They're safe. Remember, this is a smuggler ship." Calahas' face lightened a little. "Quango is working on—"

A crackle in his comm-link cut the Centaur captain short. From it, the voice of an anxious Arachne emerged. "Calahas, get up here now! We're approaching Carcerem, and the planet's security force is acting extremely hostile."

The human captives nodded to him, and Calahas galloped from the prison area. When he arrived at the freighter's bridge, he caught sight of sweat dripping down Arachne's face.

Arachne whipped around as Calahas slid into his station. While wiping his palms on his tunic, he checked the threat display. An Enforcer-class cruiser orbited the planet in tandem with two Striker frigates.

As Arachne and Calahas watched, four Ipis attack craft flew from the enormous cruiser and matched speed in parallel with the freighter. The Satyr cleared his throat and spoke into the speaker. "Yes, we will orbit the track you designated. We have human captives from the species' royal houses that we'd like to gift to the magistrate."

An irritated voice from the speaker answered, "Humans? We already have death camps packed with that vermin. Bring them to the magistrate's building along with all your ship's officers." A pause, and then, "The coordinates have been sent to you. Do not deviate from this path or you will be ionized. Also, your ship will be impounded and the cargo inspected until the appropriate tariffs are paid."

"Yes, sir. That's only fair," Arachne replied in a deferential voice. He switched off the comm-link, and the light glowed red as the freighter's navigation system received the data transmission. "Bastards. This extortion will cost me a fortune!"

Paxine waved a hand as if to dismiss the concern. "Just be grateful we're back in civilization. Now we can make amends to the government for your crimes." With a sneer at Calahas, the younger Satyr popped out of her chair. "I'll see to the prisoners."

Arachne snarled. "Yeah, the conversation with the planet's control tower went really well." He turned to Calahas. "Go prep the shuttle and get Quango. They want all the ship's officers."

The Centaur hurried from the bridge, trying to keep calm. He hadn't expected anyone to search the ship. Without some quick thinking, the Ipis patrols would discover the clones.

Over the course of a few minutes, Calahas weaved to the shuttle and found Quango sitting on the floor with the three stowaways. They talked to each other outside the blunt-nosed transport, munching on some dried fruit. The chief engineer explained something about the craft to a very attentive audience. They all turned when Calahas hurried to them.

Upon reaching them, the Centaur captain gasped for breath. "We have a serious problem. The ship's going to be inspected, and all the officers, including you, have to go down to the surface."

"I haven't been off this ship in five months. It'll be good to stretch my legs." Quango chuckled. "Now calm down. This is a smuggler ship. No blockheaded inspectors will find these boys."

"What about Cap'n Bernius and the others?" Aramis asked with an edge in his voice.

"They've been ordered to the surface." Calahas diverted his eyes from the piecing stares locked in on him.

"We're going too," Aramis declared.

"Then you could well die with them." The Centaur felt bile rise in his throat as he said those words.

Aramis looked at his podmates. "They're our friends. We have to try."

"Now that won't do you or them a lick of good. You'll get trussed up right along with them and help nobody." Quango tugged at his goatee and appraised the size of the three clones. "I have an idea. Follow me, lads."

The Satyr limped on arthritic legs toward a large storage room at the back of the hangar, grimacing the whole way. The three clones followed, and all four disappeared behind a corner.

Eventually, Quango hobbled back to the shuttle. Behind him trailed three cylindrical robots the size of large trash cans moving on wide-set tracks. They rolled past Calahas and up the ramp to the shuttle entrance.

"Ah... Hmm... Buzz. Click," a non-robotic voice from the backmost robot said.

"Porthos, what are you doing?" the middle robot said. "That's not what Beatrice or Mara sound like."

"Well, Athos, let's see you do better."

"Will both of you pipe down?" the lead robot said as it articulated two slender pincer arms. "I can't see much of anything through this view screen."

"I can barely move in here. My knee's sticking in my ear," the backmost robot whined.

The middle robot groaned. "I can't breathe."

"You humans grow too big. Just drive the damn things, and keep your mouths shut," Quango groused while stomping into the shuttle. "And in the name of my ancestors' flatulence, try to act more robotic."

The last robot grinded up the ramp and into the shuttle. The sounds of them banging into walls and complaining continued as they thudded about until the door to the shuttle's storage room shut, cutting off the noise. Calahas rolled his eyes and waited for Arachne.

Eight minutes later, Arachne and Paxine arrived with the three human captives, now manacled, and four Centaurs armed with stun rods. As the shuttle left the freighter, a nervous Calahas kept watch through the shuttle's thick window and watched a nimble attack craft swoop in to escort them.

It flew beside them through the cloud cover all the way to a small spaceport situated at the end of a high, flat peninsula coated with thick dark-green jungle foliage. Flocks of large flying creatures drifted on air currents in the russet sky over a sage-green ocean. If Calahas guessed correctly, the beasts nested in the cliff wall below the spaceport.

He checked his scope and let out a low whistle. "Arachne, watch out for those bird creatures. Their wingspan is about six meters."

"I see them," Arachne growled. "Those wyverns were all over the place when I was here three years ago. I can't fathom why in the name of my ancestors' scraggly beards they let those rookeries sit so close to a commercial landing area."

"Probably some fancy entertainment," Calahas jeered.

"Show more respect. I'm sure they're a native endangered species under protection," Paxine said. "Uncle, what business brought you here back then?"

"There're some lucrative ore deposits here, such as high-grade bi-nexidium. Problem is, it can only be mined near the polar regions," Arachne replied, avarice riding in his voice.

Calahas eyed the three prisoners, who appeared quite interested in the conversation. "Why's that?"

"For a couple reasons," Arachne said. "First, all the critters here grow to ridiculously large sizes and enjoy eating anything that moves, but this is only a problem for the workers. The real issue is that the planet's very unstable. Quakes happen with a steady frequency, which makes mining over much of the planet's surface unprofitable. Most of the sustainable mines are in the polar regions. The Ipis like to use the equatorial region for their prison camp. The environment here really cows the captives, making it easy to manage large numbers."

Shaking his head, the Centaur captain turned to the sullen prisoners. All three turned away and stared out the oval, Plexiglass portals.

A loud crash from the storage compartment gave Arachne a start, and he switched on the intercom. "Quango, what in the name of my ancestor's twisted beard is going on back there?"

A second later, Quango's irritated reply came in from the storage room intercom. "Just some equipment shifting around. I'll take care of it." An abrupt click muted the communicator.

Before anyone could say more, a sharp voice emerged from another speaker. "You are cleared to land at Pad Twenty-seven."

"Thank you. We're heading in," Arachne responded.

Calahas moaned. "Now we condemn these innocents to hell."

Arachne gave a sharp look but said nothing.

* * *

For an Ipis, the magistrate of Carcerem, Keres-ma, stood almost as tall as a human male. Although most Ipis wore no garments, Keres-ma adorned himself with a cape of saffron scales. He sat behind a glowing metal desk and laughed without mirth as the grotesque appearance of the non-Ipis creatures—Satyrs or some such—entered his judicial chamber. Even watching the smuggler's crew prod the human prisoners didn't elicit much entertainment.

Keres-ma turned to the officer sitting at the nearest computer console before facing the smuggler's crew. "So, you captured three humans of royal blood? How many does that make now?"

The Ipis-ma aide rolled her neck. "I think we stopped counting at around ten thousand."

Keres-ma hissed at the two Satyrs and the Centaur in front of him, then at the four Centaurs warding the captive humans. "It seems every scum looking for a favor comes to this cesspool of a planet with one of these pathetic creatures in tow. Frankly, it sickens me. There's only one royal family in this galaxy, and they sit in the imperial capital on Serpens. I myself am of royal blood, and I'm seven hundred and twenty-third in line for the throne."

The Ipis aide sneered. "The pretenses these inferior creatures make at intelligence and class make me want to rip all their throats out."

Indignant, the younger Satyr stamped her hooves. "I'll have you know that I graduated with honors from the Lethe Sector Imperial University!"

"I guess they let anyone in there," came the chortled reply from the aide. "I didn't know you could still train simple beasts to perform tricks."

Keres-ma leaned back and spit. "Now they allow Satyrs to mix with real students? The professors probably had to bathe after each class to wash away the filth." He leaned toward the younger Satyr with a sneer made of large fangs. "I've wasted enough of my day. The humans are sentenced to the death camp with the rest of their idiot species."

The three humans struggled with their bonds until Ipis guards pressed pads containing debilitating drugs against their necks. Their resistance ceased, and they followed their captors out the door.

"Now, for you." Keres-ma skimmed over his computer display. "Calahas of Equitone is a wanted killer who, as leader of a gang of Centaur hoodlums, murdered Ipis frontier troops. He goes to the death camp." He tapped the screen and found a profile for the two Satyrs. "Arachne, a Satyr from Tribulus, is a wanted smuggler dealing in illicit contraband. Paxine, also of Tribulus and a blood relative, has obviously abetted in those crimes. Punishment is five years' incarceration in the reeducation camp and five years in the mines." Keres-ma looked up, enjoying the dread growing in the lesser creatures. "Take those Centaur henchmen for associating with known malcontents. In fact, take the whole crew. They're all criminals."

The door behind the newcomers opened, and fourteen Ipis wearing military insignias and carrying incapacitation rods rushed in. They got a squeal out of the younger Satyr when they grabbed her.

Of the four Centaur guards, only a roan-colored Satyr reacted fast enough to strike before the Ipis soldiers knocked her aside. She backed into a corner, jabbing her stun rod at the shielded Ipis soldiers closing in, but to no avail. In her fury, she roared, "Freedom!" and swiped at the Ipis soldiers. The soldiers ripped the stun rod from her grip, and she brayed at Calahas, "Innocent blood is on our hands!"

The roan-colored Centaur's condemnations must've struck a nerve as Calahas shrank within himself. Not long after, he bucked at the first Ipis soldier who approached him. Keres-ma chuckled at the sight.

Seconds later, all non-Ipis lay unconscious or spasming on the floor.

* * *

Quango didn't join Arachne, Paxine, and Calahas in going to the magistrate's building. Instead, the old Satyr ushered the three cylindrical robots between a whole convoy of slow-moving ore transports. They passed a few commercial personnel vehicles, all of which moved along a wide, paved avenue. No pedestrian traffic got in their way, to the Satyr's relief. He wanted to move well away from the customs agents at the port gate. Far, far away, and fast.

Quango wiped his brow from the stifling tropical heat before nudging one of the robots. "Will you hurry? We need to go *now*, or they'll notice I'm missing."

"The accelerator's on maximum," one of the clones complained. "If you needed us to go faster, you should've given us quicker vehicles."

Quango's shoulders slumped. "It was the best I could do on short notice. Just do what you can to keep up."

"Can I stop talking like a stupid robot yet?" Porthos whined. Quango was sure it was Porthos, at least. That one never stopped whining.

"Stay quiet," he hissed to the clones. "We're going into a populated area soon, and I need to find us a place to hole up for a while."

Quango paused at an intersection to gather his bearings. Where he stood, the road sloped down to a poor residential area populated by dilapidated apartment buildings. Since he hadn't been to Carcerem in three years, he'd need to orient himself as soon as possible. Besides, he didn't like being aboveground on this planet, despite the quakes. The empty streets indicated that most sensible folks felt the same way.

Quango had handed the port inspector a pile of imperial credits moments after hearing Keres-ma's first words. From there, the conversation could go in only one direction. The bribe would buy the port inspector's silence, but a scan of the shuttle's log would show only ten crew members went to the magistrate when eleven were listed. Quango silently thanked Arachne for donning a stealth bugging device on his departure to the magistrate's building. Arachne did worry that the meeting might not go well, and for once, the old pirate was right. If Quango didn't want himself or the clones to join, they'd have to hide fast.

With no other options or time, Quango led the clones to the town.

CHAPTER XXI

Prison

Dante had trouble focusing and staggered after the lead guard through an expansive motor pool. Many ground transports were parked in the area, and workers and guards bobbed and weaved in every direction. Dante stopped with the others next to a bus-like vehicle poised on spider-like legs. Harpy soldiers hauled a semiconscious Calahas toward them.

A harpy guard shoved Dante aside. "Out of the way, scum."

The shove sent Dante stumbling into the back of a tall, feathered worker who checked readouts on the transport. Through fogged senses and bleary eyes, he recognized the creature as a Roc. A somewhat familiar Roc. "Excuse my clumsiness, Setteth."

The Roc turned to him and snapped her beak, feathers flaring. This one was a tall golden-brown Roc, far younger and larger than the one he'd met on Cocytus. "Human, my name is not Setteth." A moment later, her thin hands reached into a pouch hanging beneath her wing. She slipped a small vial out and into Dante's tunic and whispered in Latin, "If you desire to live through the next hour, drink this."

Dante could not respond. Harpy guards shoved him into the transport, where close to thirty humans already sat. They all showed the same glassy-eyed, beaten look. Dante plopped by a window and spied the Roc outside staring at him with her head tilted. He nodded and took a cautious sip of the bitter liquid. Almost instantly, his head cleared. He passed the vial to Tina, who took a sip and passed it to Virgil.

When Dante peeked out the window again, the Roc was nowhere in sight.

After a ten-minute trip, the guards dumped the prisoners inside the gate of the death camp. A straight, flat roadway separated the magistrate's building from the exterior of the death camp's walls. A blue energy barrier enclosed both sides atop nine-meter parapets. The same wall stopped the encroachment of the lush, deep-green vegetation blanketing low rolling hills beyond the prison.

Dante rose and helped Tina stand. While Virgil didn't need any help, Dante didn't care if Calahas did. The smell of vegetation and a hint of sulfur filled the sweltering air. The scents reminded him of Beatrice's botanical gardens in Mount Purgatory and provided some comfort, but it didn't last. Everything else marked the place as anything but a home.

Behind and to the north, a massive, plexo-steel wall over nine meters tall pulsated with a blue energy barrier. A single square opening spanned four and a half meters high and wide. Where the complex lacked walls, poles generating barriers with a blue glow did instead. The bitter sight reminded Dante all too much of the prison field on Cocytus.

Dante spotted no other Centaurs but Calahas, who pawed the ground. The humans they arrived with ignored him as they stared out the windows of the prison transport. Calahas rasped, "I'm sorry," but Dante ignored that too.

A group of people gathered, all bearing slumped shoulders and hollow gazes. The crowd gawked at the newcomers after the Ipis soldiers departed. All the new prisoners stared at the ground. Dante and his friends, however, assessed the gathered crowd.

Tina leaned close and whispered, "*They're* the descendants of the first humans to develop space travel? *These* are the people who terrify the harpies? My God, look at them. They can barely stand."

Dante sighed at the same sight. "It's about as cruel a punishment as I ever thought of. Take away their dignity, then their hope, and then let them die of deprivation. The harpies won the war over a hundred years ago, and the scattered humans are still hunted as fugitives and caged like rabid animals."

Virgil stepped up beside him. "If these are the intrepid space allies we hoped to recruit, I think we're screwed."

Dante rubbed his jaw. "Don't give up on them just yet. Let's find out what's going on here first."

A haggard, threadbare man and woman approached from the throng. They appeared harmless enough, but Virgil opened his stance and tensed. Calahas stepped next to him.

The woman spoke in Ipis. "Welcome to Carcerem. You folks seem different than the rest of the fresh meat. Where are you from?"

"The name's Dante. We're from Earth," he responded in the same language and raised his hand, palm out.

The two strangers responded in the same manner. He could tell by their blank stares that the word "Earth" meant nothing to them.

"When did you learn to speak Ipis?" Tina whispered.

"I had to learn the language to use their operating systems, remember? The stasis pod session I went in taught me how to read and speak it. I just didn't imagine the speaking would come in handy in these circumstances." Dante smiled. "I also picked up Latin. The harpies' version was fairly rudimentary, with a number of mistakes. Beatrice enhanced the tutorial module and insisted I learn it to get a better handle on her operating system once she defined us as her makers."

Tina smiled. "Well I learned some Latin back in medical school." She looked at the two people, who gave curious stares, and pointed to herself. "I'm Tina."

The man introduced himself as Cilla. He appeared to be no more than thirty and of average height with lank black hair. Cilla's large hands and the sagging skin on his arms indicated that he must've possessed a powerful build once.

The woman introduced herself as Octavia. A torn, filthy shift hung loosely on her petite, emaciated body. To Dante's surprise, Octavia's dark brown eyes met his gaze without flinching.

While keeping his eyes on the surroundings, Virgil nodded to the two strangers. "Pleased to meet you. The name's Virgil." He turned to Dante and whispered, "I can't speak that damn language. Ask them what they know about this place. Food, shelter, organization. You know the drill."

A booming voice caused the gathered people to shrink aside. "Move it, you worthless scum!"

Seven men holding small crude cudgels pushed through the crowd. The new arrivals all appeared well fed compared to the other captives. The leader was a short man with a broad chest, and his damaged nose must've been broken several times. The leader pointed his club at Cilla and Octavia. "Beat it. We're the welcoming committee for all new patsies."

A tall, rangy youth with a pockmarked face waved his club and sneered. "You tell 'em, Vito."

Cilla took half a step forward, but Octavia tugged him back as the crowd formed a ring around the new arrivals and the swaggering men with clubs. Most watched with dull, lifeless stares.

Vito closed in, put both hands on his hips, and appraised Dante, Virgil, and Tina. He spat at the sight of Calahas. "By official decree, give us your boots and your woman. If she cooperates, you'll get her back in a few days."

Anger swelled in Dante as he translated through his teeth. Tina and Virgil's faces flared.

"I don't think so. Dante, translate exactly what I say," Virgil snarled. He soon plastered a smile on and sauntered to Vito. At six foot two, the soldier stood a half a head taller than the thug leader. "This is how it's going to work. Drop those little sticks and haul your worthless asses outta here as fast as you can, or I'll shove your freaking teeth right down your throat."

Dante repeated the threat as closely as possible, tone included.

Vito frowned and whipped a quick look at his gang. "Show 'em who runs things around here, boys!"

He swung his club at Virgil's head, only for the weapon to hit nothing but air. Virgil dodged to the side and grabbed Vito's arm while kicking him in the leg. Vito bellowed in pain as his knee bent at an unnatural angle. His scream rose several octaves as Virgil broke the gang leader's arm at the elbow. The sound of tendons popping overtook the screams. Virgil slammed the palm of his hand into the man's nose, driving the bone into the victim's brain. Vito was dead before his limp body hit the ground.

Dante didn't have time to notice Virgil's victory. The pockmarked youth rushed him and struck his club across Dante's shoulder, leaving him dazed. Everything blurred, but he threw his arms up to fend off the next blow.

It never came. Tina kicked the assailant in the groin and then snap-kicked him in the face as he twisted in pain. The ruffian crumpled, gasping.

The commotion ceased, so Dante ventured a peek. Five of the thugs lay motionless in the dirt along with their weapons. Two sprinted away at top speed. Calahas and Virgil watched them while covered in blood, none of it their own.

Tina began probing his injury then, so Dante turned to her. "Where did you learn to move like that?"

Tina inched close and gently brushed back Dante's hair. "While you were skipping militia training to learn Ipis and Latin, I was getting Tae Kwon Do lessons from Virgil along with everyone else."

Virgil picked up two of the clubs and twirled them like batons. He kicked the dead Vito in the teeth. "I always keep my promises."

The gathered crowd erupted into cheers.

Cilla rushed over and slapped Virgil on the back. "That was a fine bit of fighting! Those Ipis lackeys have been terrorizing this place for too long. It was good to see someone stand up to them."

Dante whispered to Tina and Virgil, "They liked what we did. Smile and wave."

Virgil nodded and shrugged before raising his arms. When the crowd roared again, he joined them. The captives who witnessed the brief fight huddled close, praising the new arrivals.

A worried look remained on Octavia, however. She moved next to Dante, peering over her shoulder to where the surviving thugs had fled. Her next words came out in Latin. "Sir, can you understand me?"

Dante nodded.

She gripped his hands tight. "These men work for Sebastian. He'll come after you as hard and fast as he can. You've signed your death sentences. For the last two years, no one's had the courage to stand against his reign of terror." She jerked her head toward the gathered people. Much of the enthusiasm began to subside, and they retreated several steps.

Dante bent and put his hands on his knees. "How many men does this Sebastian have?"

"Maybe a couple hundred. I'm not sure, but it doesn't matter. They're cruel and travel as a pack. Everyone who resists them dies."

Virgil came over with Calahas at his side. Dante translated what Octavia said, and the soldier growled, frowning. "So, it's like wolves. This Sebastian is the alpha. We take him out, and we rule the pack."

"How are we going to get near this guy if he has a gang of cutthroats wrapped around him?" Tina said in a low voice.

Dante observed the throng of people. The numbers had swelled and continued doing so. Some slipped away, but many more arrived. A glint of hope shimmered in countless faces.

With the image in mind, Dante faced Octavia. "How is it that most everyone here looks half-starved while those goons appear well-fed and wear new clothes?"

Disgust seeped into Octavia's expression. "The Ipis-ma hate getting their hands dirty dealing with us. They have their Roc mercenaries dump the prisoner supplies once a day at the gate, but only the biggest and strongest get anything. Sebastian's thugs control the distribution and the storerooms. He keeps the best of everything for himself and his gang—food, medicine, shelter. The rest of us must beg him for the leavings of his table or starve. He always asks a price. We're his slaves."

Tina moved beside Dante and Virgil, eyeing the glowing blue poles. "Well, doesn't this look familiar."

Virgil studied the surroundings like a raptor, then pointed to the towering wall pulsating with blue light. "This is a helluva lot bigger and looks like it's meant to be permanent. Even if we had one of those neural-net suits, we'd never get past that thing."

A line of black, domed buildings rested over the top of the prison's northern barrier. The tallest tower rested on the building they'd just left—the magistrate's building, according to Calahas. It rose three stories above the nine-meter prison wall.

Dante thought back to when the freighter shuttle descended through the planet's atmosphere. It gave him a chance to study the landscape through the shuttle's porthole. From the sky, the Ipis city resembled a fortress situated on a finger of land jutting into a vast ocean. The enormous prison camp separated it from the mainland to the south. The northern tip of the peninsula held the small spaceport which terminated at cliffs overlooking the water. The mainland south of the prison was a thick, green canopy of vegetation. He'd filed all this information away in case he'd need it. Now, it helped him visualize where everything was.

Virgil interrupted Dante's thoughts. "Hey, Dante, ask our new friends how big this place is and how many people are in here."

Dante relayed the question, and Octavia said that the camp was close to a kilometer and a half long and half that length wide. Cilla added that two camps abutted each other, one for reeducation and one for death. The two shared few differences, although the mortality rate in the death camp was slightly higher. While neither Cilla nor Octavia could provide a count of how many occupants dwelled in the reeducation camp, the death camp held about thirty thousand humans and a few hundred folks from other species.

"It takes quite the crime for other species to end up in here," Cilla mentioned, gesturing to Calahas. "The number varies. More humans are dumped in here all the time, but life expectancy is not very long for anyone."

"That's a lot of space for a prison. Aren't the harpies... er, Ipis, worried about anyone escaping?" Dante squinted at the hint of green beyond the prison's western boundary.

"Where would anyone go? The camps are a shield for the city. As bad as it is in here, it's certain death out there." Cilla snorted and pointed to the west with his chin. "The only way off this cursed planet is through the spaceport, and it's on the other side of the city."

Octavia studied the thickening crowd with apprehension. "You seem like decent folks. You've got to make a decision soon. Sebastian won't be happy when he finds out what you did to his associates."

Undeterred, Dante bent and picked up a club. "So, he likes to kill anyone who stands up to him?"

"The last person who gave Sebastian some lip took three days to die," Cilla added, "and he just wanted medicine for his children."

Octavia moved close to Cilla and hung her head. "Everyone is too afraid to challenge him. The Ipis don't care what happens in here as long as we die."

"Thanks." Dante turned to Virgil and Tina to discuss what he learned. In light of the Centaur's help with the thugs earlier, he nodded to Calahas to join their circle. Calahas looked perplexed at first, but he walked over to them in silence.

"So, the only person who gets to communicate with the harpies is the son of a bitch who runs this place." Virgil tapped his batons together. "I think it's time to install new management."

"Virg, are you serious?" Tina sputtered. "In case you haven't counted, there are only four of us." She touched Dante's shoulder, where the blood had finally started to dry. "And one of us isn't much help in a fight."

"We just got here, and I'm already sick of this bully." Dante gave the camp another look. "Maybe all these people need is a spark. We don't have a clue about the ins and outs of this hellhole, but that also makes us an unknown to the assholes running this place. I think we need to act before the scumbags plan anything. Pray that I'm right."

He nabbed one of the other fallen clubs and climbed up on a half-rotted stump. Raising the club, Dante called out to the crowd in Latin. "Hear me, people!"

Slowly, the ambient chatter subsided.

He pitched his voice to carry. "My friends and I are from a planet called Earth. Almost two millennia ago, it was the home of your ancestors." He drew in a deep breath. "Your forebears were once a proud people, and now you are forced to cower every day in fear. I say *enough*."

He paused and tried to maintain what he hoped was a regal poise. The people crept closer, latching worn faces on to him. "My name is Dante Carloman, ruler of Cocytus, a free world. My namesake was once king of all humanity when you roamed the stars as a free people. Follow me, and those days will return." He pointed to the glowing blue barrier. "The Ipis may control the galaxy, but they cannot own our spirits. I say we throw off their oppression. Within these walls, we may be their prisoners, but we will never be their slaves."

Silence reigned for a second when Dante finished speaking. When the lack of response stretched longer, sweat beaded on his forehead. Then, low murmurs rumbled through the milling crowd. Dante fought to keep calm and composed as more sweat gathered upon his neck.

Cilla and Octavia stood close by. He turned to her. "There *are* legends that say the kings of old will return. Can this be true?"

Octavia looked unconvinced. "If they're not, can this guy be any worse than Sebastian?"

Cilla nodded, squeezed her hand, and gave a shout, "Hail Lord Carloman, king of all humans!"

Octavia and a few others repeated the bold declaration. The chant slowly grew in volume as more people joined in. Soon, the whole crowd acknowledged their desperation and chanted the cheer.

Dante pumped his fists in the air before Virgil sidled up beside him. "I don't mean to interrupt your moment, but what did you just tell them?"

Dante wiped his brow and grinned. "I just opened up this place for new management, like you suggested. Viva the revolution."

They both looked up as the shouting devolved into a subdued murmur. An obese man stalked toward them, followed by a pack of twenty rough-looking thugs waving clubs and staves. The portly man bore an olive complexion, but he also had a bull neck and thick shoulders. His size did nothing to hide a smoldering glare. He must've ben Sebastian.

Virgil smiled at Dante and Tina and flexed his wrists, all while holding the two small batons. "You did your part. Now I'll do mine."

The assembly parted as Sebastian's gang elbowed through them, swinging their clubs at anyone who didn't move fast enough. Silence settled around them as soon as they passed.

Virgil strode over to them, and Tina, Dante, and Calahas followed close behind. Dante shot a peek over his shoulder as a band of about a hundred, led by Cilla and Octavia, moved with them. The gathered inmates formed a wall encircling Sebastian's gang, cutting off their avenue of escape.

Dante whispered in Virgil's ear, "I think our buddy up ahead underestimated his popularity. He only brought twenty of his goons with him."

Virgil's neck muscles corded as he appraised Sebastian, who stood with arms crossed. Virgil wasted no time on conversation, instead walking up to Sebastian and becoming a blur of motion. One swing, and Virgil's club smashed Sebastian's temple. He drove the other end into the stunned man's neck, crushing his larynx. Sebastian fell thrashing to the ground, gasping for air.

The spell of fear shattered, and the once discouraged prisoners fell on the hapless thugs. A few of Sebastian's lot tore free and fled in terror, pursued by several people from the mob. Most died on the spot.

The prisoners bludgeoned their former tormentors long after reducing their bodies to pulp on the blood-soaked ground.

CHAPTER XXII

Changing of the Guard

The blood and gore of mutilated bodies seeped into the black mud where the one-sided brawl occurred. It reminded a horrified Dante of the clones under the harpies' compulsion going berserk in the arena on Cocytus. The prisoners of Carcerem would follow suit, but of their own volition. If he didn't act, they'd devolve into full anarchy any minute.

"Stop!" he roared.

The crowd paused, and many cast wary glares in his direction.

Octavia tightened her grip on a long flint knife she'd torn from the lifeless hand of a brute and strode over to Dante. Blood smeared her soiled, knee-length shift. "That was almost too easy. That monster won't ever touch me again." Fire burned in her eyes as she made a mock bow. "The king is dead. Long live the king. What is it your 'lordship' desires?"

Dante's mind spun from the pace of events just now. He steeled himself with the experience he'd gained on Cocytus. Unfortunately, he didn't have Beatrice and her mountain full of robots to back him up. He'd have to make do with his wits alone.

Tina moved up beside him, giving Octavia a piercing eye while slapping the side of her leg with a club. "Show respect," she snapped in clear Latin.

"I will as long as he earns it," came the sharp retort.

Dante took in the clear, midmorning sky and the gathering crowd of people. After one deep breath, he spoke to Octavia with a voice intended to carry. "Octavia's challenge is fair. I wouldn't want to see one tyrant replaced by another either. However, what I said before was no lie or idle boast. Things *will* change. Our lot will improve. I will demand that everyone works, but I promise that life here will get better."

"So, you'll be our new headsman, *Lord* Carloman? We'll see if you're more successful than the last one," Octavia said in an icy tone. As if to emphasize the point, she bent over Sebastian's corpse and sawed at his neck with her blade.

Cilla turned away from the scene and approached Dante. "May I make one suggestion?"

"Please do," Dante said.

Cilla pointed to a collection of long, squat buildings in the northwestern corner of the camp. "I think we should occupy the storerooms before Sebastian's remaining lackeys pull some stunt."

Dante agreed, let Cilla take the lead, and jogged after him. The frailness he initially observed in the man appeared to dissipate with each step Cilla took. A shouting throng pressed behind them.

Their destination lay only a few hundred meters away. A rutted trail ran from the camp entrance to the storerooms. The three long, single-story buildings were constructed of thick, layered stone blocks, and Dante guessed that each side stretched about fifteen meters. The buildings had identical pitched, slate roofs and were lined up next to each other, all spaced an equal distance apart. The furthest one rested in a corner of the prison camp, with the ocean on its west side and the other two in a line east of it. Their backs faced the nine-meter barrier on the north side. Besides the rough-hewn log door facing south, only an occasional narrow window broke their fort-like appearance.

As the prisoners approached, a few of Sebastian's gang members scampered into the buildings and barricaded the doors from the inside. Dante gathered his thoughts while his new friends came up beside him.

Cilla handed Dante a small water flask and asked, "What's the plan?"

Virgil and Dante halted the advance and studied the area's layout. The three buildings appeared solid and well-constructed, but this didn't hold true for everything else. Numerous rundown, adobe-style huts dotted the field, and the stench of human excrement wafted thick in the air. The prison mob of ragged, emaciated people grew, stirred by the new events in the death camp.

Virgil gestured to the storerooms. "Someone built those with survival in mind. The walls and ceiling appear impregnable. That stone and mortar look about a foot thick, and I'm sure they have enough food and water inside to last as long as they want."

Dante nodded at the soldier's assessment, all while analyzing the structures himself. "In case you haven't noticed, we don't exactly have any assault equipment. I'm also guessing our fellow inmates will grow bored soon. Those thugs can wait us out."

"But the builder forgot a couple of key items." Virgil crouched, picked up a dry twig, and broke it in half. "They have only one way out from each of those buildings. Great for defending, but piss-poor for escaping." He stood and pointed to the small, slit windows of the nearest building. "Those structures have almost no ventilation."

Dante gauged the planet's yellow sun and wiped his brow. The temperature felt like ninety degrees Fahrenheit, and the humidity prompted sweat to soak his clothes. "I'm thinking it can't be comfortable in there."

"Oh, we can make it worse for them," Virgil said with a chuckle. "We can build some fires with greenwood outside those little windows and fan the smoke inside. Without ventilation, they'll come out coughing and gagging." He gestured over his shoulder to the prison mob. "There are thousands of us waiting for them. They're dead meat."

Tina hugged Dante and turned to Virgil. "Can't they block the opening to keep the smoke out?"

"Yup," Virgil agreed, "but if the smoke can't get in, then fresh air can't get in either. We'll have them in a couple days. We should be able to keep enough of our new friends interested until then."

Octavia and Cilla exchanged worried looks while Dante translated everything Virgil said.

Octavia drew back, incredulous. "No one will be able to maintain the fires at night. They'll get their air then."

"Is there something I'm missing here?" Dante shook his head.

"There's a flying beast the Ipis call wyverns that feed at night. We call them screamers because it's the last sound many of us hear before those monsters devour us. No one dares wander in the open after sunset." Octavia pointed above the cliffs bordering the prison on the north side. "If the flocks are large, even being in a shelter won't save you. On those nights, you just hide and pray that they feed on someone else."

In the daylight, Dante squinted at the small dots drifting on the air currents over the water. "They fly into the camp? How big are these screamer-wyvern things?"

Cilla sighed. "An average adult has a wingspan of about six meters. Their horns are like swords, and they have rows of serrated teeth that can shred a man in seconds."

Tina paled. "You're talking about something the size of prehistoric pterodactyls back on Earth. Won't the prison guards do anything?"

Octavia made a derisive snort. "Oh, they do something. At night, you can see their silhouettes against lights in the magistrate's tower. They sit there and watch the show. We're supposed to entertain them by dying."

Through all the horrors he'd lived through over the last year, Dante felt a new level of revulsion at what Octavia said. Though he tried quelling his rage, a portion of it escaped in a bitter voice. "Bring all of Sebastian's minions that we caught in our little rumble here. I want them staked to the ground where the dirt bags in those warehouses can watch."

Octavia hoisted a blood-soaked sack and opened it. "Do you want what's left of their leader?"

Dante glimpsed in the bag and gulped upon spotting Sebastian's disfigured head. He fought harder to keep from choking. The human prisoners needed further incentive to follow him, after all, and he'd need every ally he could find. With this thought in mind, he snatched the bag from Octavia and strode in front of the stone buildings. He gagged down bile, reached in, and lifted the head out by the hair. As he held it up—and tried not to look at it directly—a loud cheer rose from the crowd behind him, and a low groan sounded from several of the people in the barricaded building.

"No one will come to your aid. Bring out the ones we captured and stake them to the ground. Leave them to the screamers." Dante threw Sebastian's severed head in the dirt before the nearest storage building. He waited while the prisoners scuffled with the survivors of Sebastian's ill-fated brawl, dragging the struggling thugs to him.

He raised his club and pointed it at the city beyond the prison. "I am Dante Carloman, the ruler of all humanity. The Ipis are my only true enemy, and there will be no mercy given to those who serve them. I grant you one hour to come out and surrender. If you do, you will be my vassals, and I will spare your lives. If you do not, we'll tear the roofs from those buildings and stretch you out next to your friends."

He dropped the bag and walked to the side where Tina and the others stood somewhat apart from the crowd. "Do you think they bought it?" he whispered.

Virgil stifled a laugh. "I'm guessing it was more effective than waterboarding. I didn't think you had it in you."

Dante regarded the large mass of people staring and pointing at him. "I'll do whatever it takes to free us. *All* of us. It starts here, and it starts now."

Calahas approached him and bowed. "Lord Carloman, do you have a plan?"

Dante gave a sheepish smile. "I'm ad-libbing right now, but I'll come up with something." He whispered to Virgil, "I can't let them all die. They've spoken to the jailers. I need to know the process."

Tina grabbed him. "You're scaring the hell out of me. Will you really feed them to those monsters?"

Dante lowered his head. "I don't know."

The clouds scudded in front of the sun over time, darkening the sky with the promise of rain. In that time, the crowd behind Dante swelled and grew more raucous. Finally, after fifty minutes, twelve people walked out of the first building, led by a scrawny, balding man. The other two structures emptied quickly when their compatriots didn't meet immediate ends. In total, thirty-nine people prostrated themselves before Dante.

He sucked in a ragged breath as they vowed their allegiance. Dante had struggled over whether he could've followed through with his threat, and now, he was glad he wouldn't have to find out.

The relief renewed some of his confidence, so Dante turned to those closest to him. "Cilla, select twelve trustworthy people and take charge of the storerooms. Virg, you and Calahas inventory what we have in there. Octavia and Tina, you're with me. We'll hold a tribunal for these criminals."

Dante sat on a nearby tree stump and pointed to the bald man who'd led the group out of the first storehouse. A resigned calmness in the bald man's long, thin face made him stand out from the rest. His body was as gaunt as his face, and a touch of gray dotted his temples and streaked through a wispy beard. A pair of ragged men shoved the captive forward.

Dante wound up looking the bald man in the eye while speaking. "What's your name, and what do you have to say in your defense?"

The bald man bowed, but a hint of condescension slipped into his words. "I am known as Iucundum. I was once a geologist and a senior mining engineer. May you have a more enduring reign than our last headsman."

"You haven't spent a lot of time mourning your deceased leader," Dante pointed out.

Iucundum's eyes locked onto Dante's. "Sebastian was an idiot, and I mean that in the literal sense. He was illiterate and proud of it. His concept of leadership meant making himself as comfortable as possible, and he took sadistic pleasure in seeing his fellow captives suffer." Sarcasm grew thick in the man's tone. "Besides that, he was a model citizen."

Unsure of what to make of the bold answers, Dante asked only, "So why did you follow him?"

"Survival, my dear sir. Sebastian had enough wit to realize he needed someone to keep things organized, and I desired to preserve my worthless life for as long as possible. We both got what we wanted." Iucundum shrugged, turning resigned. "So what is your judgment? I will offer no further justification."

Dante exchanged a look with Octavia.

She bit her lip and gave a reluctant nod. "To my knowledge, everything he said is the truth. He's the only one who has any brains in this bunch."

And yet, Iucundum clearly held no loyalty to Sebastian. If he were sincere, he deserved another chance. With a sigh, Dante made a decision on his gut feeling. "Your punishment is that you now work for me in the same role. Next."

Iucundum raised his hand. "One small request."

Dante tensed. "Yes?"

"May I be allowed to speak in defense of my fellow accused? Most are former miners who worked for me. They're decent enough lads, but they're not very eloquent."

"Permission granted," Dante replied quickly.

A dozen angry voices shouted at once as the next man went forward, and Iucundum was voracious in dissecting each of their accusations. The trials concluded an hour before sunset.

Dante felt a good sense of relief because he condemned only seven of the thirty-nine for crimes deserving death. Iucundum's voice had grown hoarse from arguing all afternoon. The crowd of prisoners dispersed, seeking shelter from the coming night.

Iucundum watched the setting sun before gesturing to the one-story stone huts. "Your lordship may also want to consider seeking shelter. The screamers aren't picky about their food."

Dante cast a quick look at the dead bodies lying in an uneven row to his right. This time, he didn't hide a shudder.

"Leave them, sire. They'll sate the appetite of some of the monsters and perhaps save a few poor souls." Iucundum walked to the nearest storeroom. "That was clever, claiming the name Carloman to assert your authority. Few nowadays know much of our people's history, but those who do revere it."

Dante arched his brow. "But my name *is* Carloman."

Iucundum mumbled, "Interesting," as his eyebrows arched. He led them into the nearest building.

Dante took Tina's hand and followed.

* * *

The stench of molding garbage wafted from the opening and into the third-floor hallway, where Quango stood with three robots lined up behind him. Upon entering the apartment, the door squealed as it slid into the wall. They entered the squalid studio apartment with wrinkled noses.

Porthos gagged, wiggling his way out of the wheeled canister. "This dump smells like Beatrice's compost heap."

Quango shook his head in disgust and dropped a couple packages of contraband electronic components on the bed. "By my ancestors' twisted beard, they charged me a fortune for this tenement. But it has its advantages. Being near the spaceport, there are a lot of transient, non-Ipis workers living here who don't ask any questions... but there's no way I'd spend any time outside tonight."

Athos picked up the third box. It was greasy box but emitted a savory aroma. "Now this smells good. I'm starving."

Aramis rolled his neck, getting a kink out, and moved to the small window through which Quango watched the sun settle on the horizon. "Why would it be bad to spend a night under the stars? The disguises seem to work, and I assume you don't have a limitless supply of money for room and board."

A horrid, screeching roar echoed far in the distance, and Quango shivered. Soon, the sounds grew louder and closer. He closed the shutter and turned to Aramis, who stared wide-eyed.

"It's wyvern hatching season, and it's a clear sky," Quango said. "The flocks will hunt for food for their young, and there're a lot of them."

Now ashen, Aramis peered at Quango. "Where do you think Cap'n Bernius and the others are?"

Quango opened the shutter a crack and pointed to a massive wall glowing blue in the early evening light. "See that barrier out there?"

Aramis nodded. Porthos and Athos scurried over and craned their necks to see out the same window. They all watched as an enormous creature with featherless wings flew over the wall and dove on the other side of a glowing blue barrier. Many similar creatures followed. Quango closed the shutter as the first terrified shriek rang through the air.

"Your friends are right in the middle of that. We'll find out in the morning if they're still alive." He moved to the bed and opened the other packages there. "Be careful with this stuff. Shopping in the black market here with no inside contacts is limited and expensive."

The three young clones worked late into the night, assembling equipment from the parts in the packages. Meeting Quango's specifications proved exacting and exhausting. Once finished, they curled up on the floor, but sleep eluded them all. Every few minutes, another scream pierced through the wall.

CHAPTER XXIII

A Nation is Born

Calahas peered around the crowded storeroom. A few weeks earlier, he'd never even seen a human. Now he milled in a pack with a hundred of them. The Centaur captain pressed his hindquarters against the rough wall inside the outermost storeroom building. Terror riddled the people there of what stalked the nighttime fields of the prison camp.

Alone among the humans, Dante, Tina, and Virgil watched the moonlit grounds with sharp eyes, exchanging whispers. Calahas cocked his sensitive ears to listen.

"Even with a wingspan as big as theirs, those pterodactyls can't weigh more than sixty pounds," Lady Phokas said. "Their horns, snouts, and teeth look deadly, but their bones must be awfully fragile to compensate for it, just like birds on Earth." A distant wail pierced the air, and Lady Phokas squeezed King Carloman's hand.

Calahas turned and studied the convicted humans, manacled and dragged into the storeroom on the king's orders. He shook his head, not understanding how he hadn't joined them. His own deeds were as evil as theirs, and yet King Carloman hadn't brought a word of judgment against him.

A loud "No!" interrupted his thoughts. Virgil unbarred the door nearby, snatched a makeshift flint spear from a guard, and sprinted into the deadly night, pushing aside those who tried to stop him. Calahas looked out the window and saw two wyverns pursuing a man with a staff and a woman cradling an infant. Both ran for the storehouses across the empty field from one of the huts torn apart by the wyverns. Though the wyverns had an awkward gait, they moved swiftly on four legs. Their broad heads bore a long horn protruding from the tips of their snouts.

From what Calahas assessed, the people would not outpace the wyverns even as Virgil threw open the door and shouted for them to hurry. The man being chased swung his staff toward the oncoming monsters. He shot a look over his shoulder and shouted, "Run! I'll slow them down!"

His blow missed, and a wyvern's horn gored him. As the first beast fed on its still twitching prey, the second paused before breaking to pursue the other fleeing victim.

Virgil rushed toward the woman, but Calahas knew the wyvern would reach her before Virgil could. However, a Centaur could outrun any human. On all fours, a Centaur stood shorter than a man but weighed over 270 kilograms.

Calahas didn't hesitate and sprang through the open door, brushing past the people in his path. He ran faster than he'd ever done in his life and galloped past Virgil in a blur.

Calahas skidded to a halt beside the woman and shouted, "Get on my back!" Soon, he felt her climb on, her hands clutching his mane. He spun and dashed toward the sanctuary, spurred by the hope of redemption. He passed Virgil a second time and caught a brief glimpse of gratitude in the man's eyes. Exhortations from the storeroom encouraged the Centaur further despite the impending muscle cramps. Finally, he raced into the building with the sobbing woman and wailing infant.

After Lady Phokas helped lift the woman and child from his back, the Centaur turned to see Virgil sprint between the other two buildings with a snapping wyvern close behind. Without another thought, Calahas bolted through the doorway before anyone could bar it again and ran to the alley where Virgil had fled.

He skidded to a stop at the sight of a spear protruding from the back of a dead wyvern. Virgil knelt atop it, blood running from a gash in his arm, but he wore a feral smile despite it. The human gave Calahas an appreciative nod that warmed the Centaur's heart. However, Virgil's face soon shifted to fear.

From behind Calahas, a loud roar screeched close by. He barely heard Virgil shout, "Look out!"

On instinct, Calahas kicked out with his hind legs. His calloused hooves made jarring contact with the charging beast. Although a glancing blow, it forced the wyvern's head to twist and miss its target. Nonetheless, the motion dropped Calahas to the stony ground. His mind reeled from the impact, and he waited helplessly for the stab of the wyvern's horn.

It never came. Through fogging senses, he watched six humans stab the monster with spears. King Carloman, himself, led the group.

Moments passed, maybe minutes. Calahas wasn't sure which, but eventually, many hands lifted him from the ground. As they carried the dazed Centaur to the safety of the storeroom's thick walls, the human king shouted an announcement for all to hear.

"Virgil and Calahas have shown us how to kill the beasts. From this night forward, we'll face our nightmares as these heroes have shown us!"

Calahas recalled little else that night. He had to learn later that people lured seven more wyverns into the narrow alleys between the other storehouses, limiting the maneuverability of the wyverns. The butchered bodies of the wyverns remained where they died.

However, Calahas had managed to save at least three human lives. Three. For the first time in ages, he'd done something right. He drifted off, satisfied at last.

* * *

The next morning, Dante sat with a group by a roaring fire. Nine wyvern heads mounted on poles lined an area by the storage buildings. With the sun rising over the reeducation camp to the east, the death camp's population crawled from their shelters and made their way to the front gate for their daily rations.

Nervous, Dante watched as many in the throng pointed at him and murmur something about the new headsman killing wyverns. However, all interest in him evaporated when the supply convoy arrived. His heart sank at the sight of desperate people pushing and shoving their way to the supply sleds. The larger people bullied their way to the front, and fists swung.

The Roc guards deployed from the supply sleds and brought out stun rods. Dante took the time to study their leader. She was the tall, golden-brown Roc he'd bumped into the previous day. She betrayed a cold indifference as the ragged residents swarmed the prison gate for gruel and water. The few Roc guards who weren't busy taming the mob rolled the food barrels into the rest of the writhing mass.

Thanks to a long conversation with Iucundum through the night, Dante had found the former mining engineer a fount of knowledge about the prison. The Ipis magistrate employed a Roc mercenary company for the daily deliveries of food and supplies to the prisons. This way, neither he nor his soldiers would have to sully their hands.

The Rocs clucked among themselves, eyeing the spiked wyvern heads now and then. While watching this, an inkling of a plan germinated in Dante's mind. He met their leader's eye as she looked in his direction before ordering her company back to work. If Dante recalled what Setteth said about Rocs correctly, the leader's golden-brown plumage showed that she was only a few years into Roc adulthood. In fact, the leader could pass for a younger Setteth, if only from a brief glance.

The wary Roc captain approached the group by the storage buildings, holding her shielding up and stun rod at the ready. She passed about sixty people and Calahas, who roasted meat and stretched hides out for tanning. The Roc's eyes encompassed the camp before locking on Dante and Iucundum, the latter of whom scribbled notes until the Roc drew close.

She examined both men before facing Iucundum. "Hello, Iucundum. I take it Sebastian's no longer headsman." She inclined her head to Dante. "You're from the group that came in yesterday. I must say, you work fast. My name is Otheth, and I am your liaison to the masters."

"Iucundum mentioned you might be helpful at times." Dante bent down and picked up a slim stick. "You're the one who gave me that antidote yesterday."

"Don't read too much into it," the Roc warbled. "I just prefer to give new prisoners a chance."

Dante split the stick in half. "We need protection from the screamers—er, wyverns. Many people died here last night."

Otheth's feathers flared, but her tone remained even. "I don't know what Iucundum has told you, but we will not provide you protection. This is a death camp. Don't make me repeat myself." She craned her neck to look back at the wyvern heads still dripping gore. "You hunt well, human. Sebastian killed zero wyverns in an entire year. You've been here one night and took out nine. Warrior blood flows in your veins. What is your name?"

"Dante. Dante Carloman."

"Carloman?" The Roc's feathers flattened against her body. "If you ever stand before the masters, do not repeat that name. I will enter Dante... Freeman, into my log."

"Thanks for the warning, but I don't think it matters now that I'm here." Dante studied the Roc for a moment, then crouched and started drawing in the damp earth. Hopefully, his impromptu gambit would pay off. "We need tools, medicine, and building materials."

"I can't do much—" Otheth peered at Dante's drawing, and her crest feathers flared. "What's that?"

Dante finished outlining a dragon twisted into a circle, consuming its own tail. "This is a dragon, a mythical creature from my home world. Why?" He stood and gave Otheth a level stare.

Suddenly tense, Otheth eyed everything. "Walk with me."

Dante nodded and rubbed out the dirt image with his foot.

They walked in silence past the clump of dilapidated huts to where the energy barrier butted against the sheer cliff. Once out of earshot of everyone else, she whispered, "Do you usually draw pictures when speaking with your captors?"

"You sounded surprised when I said the name Setteth yesterday. She told me that some among her species used the dragon as a symbol of their vows." Dante gave Otheth a small smile. "I wanted to see if you recognized it, and you did."

Otheth warbled, "Let me make a few things clear. I am loyal to my species, I despise my employers, and I'm revolted by the filth and brutish savagery displayed by the human prisoners, preying on each other for crumbs. Now, what is it you want?"

Dante came to a halt. "I talked with Iucundum this morning. Forget about the fine goods you brought to Sebastian. I need material that will help these people survive."

Otheth cawed and tilted her head. "Tell me what you need, but keep it reasonable. I will see what I can acquire." Her talons dug into the ground, and she looked sidelong at Dante. "Only inert material passes through the prison access point, and only in designated supply sleds. Scanners detect and destroy all living organisms and powered equipment. The system in that passageway is effective and thorough."

Dante studied the dark mouth of the entrance, recalling how Otheth arrived. "You and your company pass through without harm."

"True, but the automated weapons system is keyed to accept us at designated times." Otheth regarded the ominous opening with the gun turrets embedded at ground level. "I suspect that one of these days, those weapons will go off 'by accident,' killing me and my command. An Ipis-ma form of humor."

They started their return to the entrance. Along the way, Dante rattled off the necessary items: picks, shovels, saws, hammers, nails, rope, wood, kerosene, salt, potassium nitrate, human antibiotics, antiseptics, and fever reducers. Otheth jotted each item down on a tablet screen.

Otheth shook her head and chirped upon reviewing the list. "All this after one day. None of it is *precisely* banned, but the quantities you ask for are out of the question. Only one of the daily supply sleds is allocated for the prisoners' headsman. That is the limit of what I can bring without rousing suspicion."

She and Dante focused on the sleds. The crowd had dispersed, leaving behind any humans who were too weak to scavenge any rations. "Look at them plead with my warriors. They seek mercy, knowing they'll never receive any from their own kind. If they're not eaten by wyverns, that lot will starve within a week." Sighing, she turned to Dante. "Your plans sound noble, but you waste your effort. Your people may have been great once, but it was a long time ago."

"I see it in a different light," Dante said. "I've been through this before. The thing these people are missing is hope, and that's what I intend to give them." He stopped by the firepit, pulled out a skewer of charred wyvern flesh, and examined it before calling Octavia over.

With a suspicious eye trained on Otheth, Octavia jogged up before addressing Dante. "Yes, sire?"

He pointed to the few people begging by the supply sleds. "Bring them over here and give them some easy tasks." He bit off a chunk of meat. "Tell them that if they work, they'll be fed." Octavia nodded and left.

Otheth scoffed. "This should be interesting. I'll bring what I can tomorrow." She turned and trotted to her supply vehicles.

* * *

When the supply convoy glided into the death camp the next day, there were fourteen more wyvern heads lining the road. The band of sixty humans clustered around the long stone buildings had grown to three hundred along with a handful of Rocs, Centaurs, and Satyrs who were now part of that company. They must've come from their hiding spots amid the trees. The non-human prisoners were as threadbare as all the human inmates, but all moved about with an apparent determination and purpose.

The prison population did not rush forward for their rations as usual. They moved through a roped-off path under the watchful eyes of humans holding rough-hewn poles and wearing grayish-green armbands fashioned from strips of wyvern wings.

The Roc prison guards tensed, poised to raise their weapons, but the few captives who attempted to bully their way through the line didn't go far. Other humans policing the crowd stopped them.

Dante watched the Roc leader's head twist, studying everything as she drove her sled carrying the requested supplies to where Dante stood. Iucundum stood beside him, writing.

As the humans wearing the armbands unloaded picks, shovels, axes, ropes, and medical supplies, Otheth asked Dante, "How did you make them line up like that?"

"It's a trick I picked up when I visited Disney World once," Dante chuckled. "A few roughnecks had to have their brains beat in, but I've found that people appreciate order as long as they believe they'll get their share."

Otheth's crest feathers flared as she nodded. "This Disney planet sounds like an interesting place. I must visit it someday."

Dante smiled. "I hope you get the chance. Just be sure to say hi to Mickey for me if you do."

"I will be honored to tell the gentleman that I've made your acquaintance," the Roc said with a bow. "What do you plan to do with these tools?"

"Killing screamers isn't enough, so we're going to build a stockade here in the northwestern quadrant of the prison. It'll contain a hospital, a school, a granary, and a smokehouse. Most importantly, we'll build a barracks behind a stout wall where everyone will be safe. The screamers aren't very graceful when they touch down. They need a lot of empty space to land. We'll have a compact settlement that they can't access from the air or approach by land." Dante peeked at Iucundum's notepad. "There's a little over two square kilometers in this prison. Once we resettle everyone into a tighter community, and solve the waste and water problems, we'll open up half this camp for farming."

"Schools? Sanitation? Farms?" Otheth cawed and shook her head. Her eyes narrowed as humans drove stakes in the ground, marking the boundaries of the new compound. "Your dreams are big, but so shall be your disappointment. You're human, but it seems I understand the failings of your species better than you."

"Most of these people have been abused and hunted for so long they don't know what success feels like." Dante sighed. "You may have the last laugh, but I'll be damned if I don't go down trying."

"You speak like a Roc, headsman," Otheth said. "No, I will not laugh when you fall to ruin."

Iucundum looked up from his tablet, eyes blazing. "In the last two days, Dante has accomplished more than all the headsmen I've seen here in three years. I wouldn't bet against him if I were you."

"I pray I lose that bet. Iucundum, you know his plans will crumble into dust. He's relying on ignorant, lazy savages to fulfill his dreams," Otheth clucked her beak.

Iucundum squared his shoulders. "Dreams they may be, but I'll give the last fiber of my being to help him in this."

The Roc's feathers flared, she spun on her talons, and stalked over to her sled. She drove the now empty sled through the tunnel.

Later that day, Otheth personally drove the transport containing the new prisoners. As the terrified humans stumbled out of the vehicle, a human who called herself Tina greeted them. Tina handed each person a blanket and spoke with them.

Otheth could not hear the words, but the arrivals' posture changed from cringing fear, to curiosity, to vigorous head nodding. They followed Tina to the bustling encampment in wide-eyed awe.

* * *

Otheth didn't expect to see much change when she arrived on the third day, but astonishment struck her again. Where there was an open encampment the day before now stood a dirt wall four meters tall topped with sharpened stakes, stretching about ninety meters in both length and width. In front of the barrier lay a ditch running almost two meters deep.

She left her crew to unload the day's food and drove her sled to the entrance of the stockade. Two guards, one Satyr and one human, blocked a lowered drawbridge constructed out of rough-hewn logs. Each held a flint-tipped spear and a shield crafted from a wyvern skull. They waved their hands in a rough imitation of a salute and stepped aside.

Inside the compound, humans labored on a multitude of tasks, but when Otheth drew near any group, they halted their work and conversation. The Roc passed the one named Tina, who sat in an open work area. She held a newly delivered crock of potassium nitrate and directed a small but attentive group in grinding charcoal and lumps of sulfur into powder. All of them stopped and eyed Otheth until she walked away.

She didn't realize how anxious she'd grown until she spotted Dante, at which point a great sigh of relief escaped her. The human leader fired a shaft from a curved device made from a wyvern's bones and guts. The projectile skewered a bale of native marsh reeds about twelve meters away. Someone had packed the reeds into the rough shape of an adult Ipis. Otheth couldn't hide another bout of surprise at seeing a different side of the human leader, one not focused on schools and farms.

Dante gripped a wrapped, wyvern thigh bone and nocked a fresh shaft against the taut string. The Roc drew near, watching the human leader pull the barbed projectile back to his face and fire at the straw bale. The shot made a clean hit on the target.

"What is that thing?" Otheth asked with a hard edge in her voice.

"We call it a bow and arrow. It'll help us kill screamers from a distance," Dante replied with a hint of wariness. "It should prevent a lot of injuries and deaths."

Otheth stared at the target for a long moment. Finally, she said in a somber voice, "Walk with me to the entrance."

* * *

Dante handed the bow to a tall Centaur and nodded. He followed Otheth until they drew close to the entrance, silent the whole way. "Do we have a problem?"

"No," Otheth said. "You're different than the other headsmen I've met in here, and I can see why my ancestors took pride in allying themselves with your people." Shaking her head, she peered at the ground. "I don't know your plan, but you will fail. Humans are too flawed."

"Every species has its shortcomings," Dante admitted. A certain tension went through him, understanding where their conversation treaded. "Regardless, we have to try."

"Then you'll die," the Roc responded, sounding sad.

"Then we'll die trying." Dante pursed his lips. "Will you help us?"

"You do honor to your ancestors. I... I will not hinder you."

"That's not what I asked."

Otheth stopped by the sled. "I don't know. I must think about it. The warrior inside me screams *yes*." She chuckled. "I read the histories of our people's struggles together. I never saw how it could've been possible until today." Her face turned stern. "I took an oath, let's say, and I must follow its code to remain secret. Good fortune to you."

Dante stepped close to Otheth as tropical clouds unloaded a downpour. He had to think of something, anything, to secure an alliance with his only link to the outside. He thus spoke the first thing that came to mind, one of many facts Setteth shared back on Cocytus. "May you hunt on the paths of your forebears."

He walked away. If Otheth stared after him, he didn't turn to check.

CHAPTER XXIV

New Projects

Throughout the next four weeks, activity erupted in the death camp. People who sat about waiting to die weeks earlier instead hurried to complete assigned tasks. The dirt-and-stone fort gained battlements lined with tall, pointed stakes. The rutted path leading to it transformed into a crushed-stone road, which bore a constant flow of work crews marching in and out, holding their heads high with makeshift tools and weapons perched on their shoulders. A steady flow of inmates wheeled carts of refuse and stone out, then brought fresh water, wood, and sulfur in.

The dwellings surrounding the fort grew from flimsy reed shacks into solid stone and timber huts aligned in neat blocks, each separated by alleyways too narrow for the wyverns to land in. The laughter of young children playing echoed for the first time within the now safe confines. Dante stood by Tina on the stone road and wiped sweat from his brow, surveying the progress made since their arrival.

Although her shoulders sagged, Tina clapped her hands when the sails on the brand-new windmill made its first revolution in the breeze. A triumphant smile spread over her face. "That's one more task to cross off our endless list."

Dante wiped at the dirt smearing his face as the windmill started pumping water through a long trough running from the stockade into a cistern. "Your bilge pump was a great idea. It looks like it'll solve our water seepage problem."

Behind them, a haggard Iucundum leaned on a shovel. "It should perform well driving the billows too." Something in his eyes changed, and he stepped closer and tapped Dante on the shoulder. "It looks like we have visitors."

Dante squinted in the direction of the prison camp entrance. It was midday, and a crew had delivered the morning supplies hours earlier. Now, a single guard vehicle approached without any new prisoner transports in sight. It meant only one thing: another one of Otheth's inspections.

The armored crawler stretched about six meters long. The daunting vehicle moved on six flexible legs. A pair of pincers with stun rods occupied the front, but stuffed backpacks consumed most of the crawler's storage space. The crawler came to an abrupt halt, and eight Rocs scrambled from it, Otheth among them. A group of the death camp's militia, led by Cilla, carried sacks as they made their way to Otheth and her fellow guards. Otheth herself appeared to study the new windmill, but whether this indicated a genuine interest, Dante couldn't determine.

"We better see what she wants," he sighed to Tina and Iucundum.

"I need to return to the infirmary. I have three new cases of dysentery and a staph infection to handle," Tina grumbled. "You're our headsman. You deal with Otheth."

Iucundum chuckled. "Trust me when I say that the secret trade Dante has set up with the guards more than makes up for the time spent with our warden."

"You're probably right." Tina smiled as Dante wrapped his arms around her waist, and she kissed him. "Go talk to our zookeeper, but be sure to tell her I need a lot more potassium nitrate than what she's been delivering."

"I already have it first on the list," Iucundum said.

Satisfied, Tina nodded and jogged toward the fort.

Iucundum turned to Dante next. "Should I summon Lord Bernius and Prince Calahas, sire?"

"No, let them be," came the reply. "Otheth and I will probably head in their direction anyway."

"As you say, sire."

Dante looked to the west where Virgil and Calahas drilled a couple thousand of the prison's inmates into a raw but enthusiastic militia. Shortly after he became the headsman, he was surprised to learn that close to three hundred of the captives already had formal military training. Most of the non-humans were rebel fighters like Prince Calahas, but hundreds of humans had combat skills honed in clandestine cells, like Cilla and Octavia.

Although the Ipis attempted to obliterate all vestiges of human culture, some fought to preserve it. They were now his wyvern slayers and guardians of the palisade's walls. As for Iucundum, he proved more enigmatic—knowledgeable, but cynical and world-weary.

Dante walked over to the parked crawler. The Rocs stashed their newly acquired necklaces of serrated wyvern teeth and short swords carved from the flying monsters' horns into their vehicle. Meanwhile, the militia carted away cylinders of kerosene, kegs of potassium nitrate, plexo-steel tools, and a small crate of lanterns. Dante was pleased with this superficially clandestine arrangement.

Although a tropical environment, many of the trees in the camp had been cut down over the years. Only a small grove of thick hardwoods in the southeast corner of the camp survived intact by virtue of proving impervious to the inmates' crude flint axes. As a precious commodity, Dante didn't want to waste such hardwood on fires. The light of the glowing blue barriers didn't reach very far, making it difficult to spot any wyverns that managed to land inside the fort at night.

As he closed in, Dante observed a repeat of an intriguing ritual he had observed the previous week. Three of his couple dozen militia Rocs stayed behind and stood before the guards with their feathers flared, all brandishing ornate short swords made of wyvern horn. Two of the three walked on prosthetic legs, but Otheth's guards faced them with deference, shown in their feathers flattening. Stun rods hung untouched at their sides.

When Dante first observed this display, he asked his militia Rocs about the odd confrontation. They explained that they'd fallen into disgrace among their people by surrendering in battle. Such an act, even by the maimed, rarely led to any opportunity for the disgraced warriors to regain their honor. However, the rite of rebirth for a Roc warrior could offer that chance. As it turned out, almost all the Rocs Dante had met in the death camp had been maimed, and the display Dante witnessed was part of the rite of rebirth.

On the third day of his incarceration, they had approached him as a group and asked about his past and his plans. They showed great interest while interrogating him about his confrontations with the harpies. They'd cawed with astonishment when Dante told of how his people captured the grounded Striker. He must've answered well because, upon finishing the tale, the group of Rocs bowed, and the largest one, their leader, declared it a momentous *cou*. They swore allegiance and became the core of his militia.

The memory faded as he reached Otheth. The guards and his Roc militia turned, flattened their feathers, and stared for a long moment. After a quick exchange of looks, they went their separate ways.

Once Otheth spotted Dante and Iucundum, she called to the guards, "Hold your position. I'll return after the inspection. Iucundum, leave us. I wish to speak to the headsman in private."

Iucundum pursed his lips but bowed. "I need to supervise some excavation work anyway. Send a runner if you require my assistance, sire."

"Sure thing," Dante said, and Iucundum departed.

Otheth pointed to the windmill. "That's new. What is its purpose?"

Dante bit his lip. "It works some water pumps and air billows. Plumbing's a constant problem, and out of necessity, windows are small and few."

"Remarkable." Otheth clucked her beak. "Walk with me, headsman. What new headaches have you created today that I must explain away to Keres-ma?"

Dante arched his brows. Otheth often asked the question to initiate their camp inspections, but the Roc acted less interested than normal. "Could we stop by the practice field first? I need to speak to Virgil for a bit."

"Yes, yes. One direction is as good as—" Otheth stopped short when a loud gong sounded from the fort. The vestiges of the ring dissipated before she spoke again. "What in the name of my descendants' cracked eggs is that sound?"

Dante smiled and pointed to the tall, log watchtower, where two Satyrs stood with binoculars. A large brass tub hung from the top of the beams. "It's the large brass tub that we, uh, 'mysteriously' found by the prison entrance a few days ago. We call it a bell tower. It'll ring first after sunrise when it's safe to come out, a second time at midday to notify folks that lunch is being served, and a third time an hour before sunset to inform everyone to get their dinner and find a secure place to hide for the night."

"Keres-ma's allowing the tower to stand for now, but I'm not sure how long you'll be able to keep it." Otheth cocked her head. "He's suspicious as to its purpose but doesn't want to admit it befuddles him."

"It's innocent enough. The bell's our early warning signal." Dante wiped the perspiration from his forehead. "A few days ago, the sky was overcast, and a flock of those screamers hit us midafternoon."

"Some of the wyverns flew into the city that day. An Ipis civilian was caught unawares and killed."

"A dead harpy. That's good." Dante started to the training grounds, but he paused and regarded the Roc. "We lost a number of people. I won't have that happen again. If the lookouts spot any screamers approaching during the day, that bell will start ringing like crazy."

"I will ensure my warriors know the signal."

Otheth and Dante surveyed the two acres of flat, packed earth swarming with prisoners wielding primitive weapons. As they reached the training area, the Roc swung her head left and right while appraising the militia. "Your numbers grow daily. There must be close to three thousand warriors here."

"The actual count as of this morning is two thousand, eight hundred and sixty-three." Dante smiled as he watched Calahas and several veteran fighters shooting arrows at targets about twenty-seven meters away.

A shiver ran down Dante's spine when he spotted Virgil. The former Air Force Pararescue sergeant held a flint-tipped spear and a shield crafted from the skull of a wyvern. He stood outside the reach of a wyvern with a broken wing, which struggled at the end of a long rope staked to the ground.

After a month of constant exposure, Virgil's Latin had improved to a point where he could make himself clearly understood. While he spoke, the recruits all gaped at the beast.

"These critters are dangerous even on the ground." Virgil waved his spear in the monster's face, and the beast responded with a quick snap of its jaws. "When you face one in a confined area, watch out for the horn. These beasts are fast, and their instinct is to rush in and gore their prey. The trick is they're not very nimble on the ground. When you see 'em lower their heads, move to the side and skewer them as they charge past. The wings will almost always be in the way, but they're extremely thin."

He nodded to Octavia, who stood behind the wyvern, holding a spear and shield similar to Virgil's, all while wearing a heavy jerkin made from the hide of another wyvern. Octavia stepped into the trapped wyvern's circle of reach and yelled. The beast spun and snapped, but Octavia had already moved. She leapt to the wyvern's side and stabbed it in the neck. The wyvern howled in pain and swept its horn. She slapped the blow away with her shield and drove her spear through the wyvern's eye. It choked on a final breath and collapsed.

"That, my friends, is how you do it," Virgil barked to his apprehensive audience. "Notice the clean thrust to the brain. Octavia ensured the meat won't spoil by jabbing its entrails, and the tanners will especially appreciate the lack of tears in the hide." He winked at Octavia. "It's a shame it took her two stabs to make the kill. I will expect all of you to do it with one."

A confident Octavia climbed atop the animal's carcass and twirled her spear. "Next time we capture a screamer, I'll do the talking and you do the demonstration."

Virgil grinned at her but turned grim upon facing the recruits again. "I wanted to show you that these nightmares die like any other animal. You've seen their strengths and weaknesses. If you encounter one alone, seek shelter. You will *not* fight 'em until I say you're ready. If you can't escape, defend yourself and scream like hell. I *will* come." He raised his spear and pointed it at the massive northern wall. "Remember, our enemies are powerful, but we will survive because we have our wits and each other."

At this point, Dante and Otheth had drawn close enough for the gathered crowd to notice them. Many regarded Otheth with cold glares.

The Roc warden leaned closer to Dante's ear and whispered, "Right now, I'm glad I have an energy shield. I don't think they understand the finer nuances of our relationship."

"You're the face of our keepers. They loathe you." Dante nodded to Virgil and moved in the direction of the southern barrier separating the death camp from the reeducation center. "Let's continue our inspection."

Otheth cawed and followed Dante. "When you started out, I thought it a farce doomed to failure, and that this place was populated by mindless brutes. You changed them and built all this in a month."

She twisted her head while a team of people wheeled carts loaded with yellow sulfur rocks. The team traveled along a narrow trail running from the hot springs near the prison's western border, where they quarried the mineral, to the stockade. The magma streams beneath the planet's shallow crust vented through several hot geysers. The prison inmates could harness it for a reliable source of steam power, but they voiced frustration when only a few of the wells they dug provided potable water. At least it provided a means for everyone to wash themselves.

Dante swatted at a buzzing fly. "I did very little actually. They accomplished the miracles. Warriors, blacksmiths, tanners, and engineers were all here and did the work. I just enabled them. I gave them organization and order."

"No, it's more than that," Otheth said. "As you said at our first meeting, you gave them the hope that life can improve. That's a precious gift."

At last, they reached the southern barrier. Various faces stared from the reeducation camp on the other side of the barrier. Like the other sides not facing the harpy city, the barrier consisted of a simple line of glowing blue poles similar to what Dante had overcome on Cocytus. Here, however, he didn't have Michael, Beatrice, or even a neural-net suit to provide aid and backup.

Among the prisoners on the other side stood a vaguely familiar Satyr with twin curled horns. So familiar, in fact, Dante did a double take. A look of surprise and recognition crossed the Satyr's face, and it clicked. Dante nodded to the haggard, filthy, threadbare smuggler. "Captain Arachne, how are you doing?"

A bewildered Arachne stared back. "Apparently, not as well as you."

Dante had taken a hot bath that morning with real soap, and he'd filled his belly with the wyvern sausages served as breakfast. Self-conscious, he touched his new poncho, sewn from the wings of a wyvern. "We're getting by."

Not long after, he recognized several of the faces crowding near the transparent wall as the crewmembers from the smuggler's ship. Dante nodded to them, and in response, Huon and the rest of Calahas' security team bowed low from their side of the fence.

Arachne rubbed his hands together. "For what it's worth, I'm sorry. A few days ago, I spoke with a couple of former crewmen of mine, Cilla and Octavia. They couldn't stop talking about you and what you've accomplished. I think you *are* the human king, and much more." He peered at his scowling niece by his side. "Bringing you here was the biggest mistake of my life."

"Yeah, it wasn't so great for me either," Dante spat. He glared at Arachne before turning to Otheth. "From the histories I've read, the damn harpies don't have to lift a finger to rule the galaxy. They have their stooges sell each other out and do all their dirty work. Other species kill each other just to curry favor with those snarling little harpies. It's about time we stop stabbing each other in the back and stand together. At least then they'd have to work for what they want."

"Those are the words of a true leader," an enthusiastic Huon shouted.

Otheth gave Huon a brief look and turned to Dante, flattening her feathers. "Headsman, your words are rash. You shouldn't speak them so readily."

"And so the oppression goes on." Dante gave Arachne one more frown and shook his head. "Let's finish this freakin' tour." He stalked off without waiting for Otheth's response.

The Roc warden caught up a couple steps later, eyeing their surroundings. "Your words were indeed rash. But they were also very true."

Dante nodded to Otheth but said nothing.

They soon reached the start of a wide swath of freshly tilled land. With all the inmates moving to the area along the northern wall, they'd opened up the southern half of the prison camp for farming. They'd bracketed the rich, broken soil into individual plots spanning 66 meters across and 183 meters long. Narrow paths of packed dirt separated each farming plot.

Dante pointed to a line of over a hundred workers moving along straight furrows, sowing seeds. "Stay on the path between the two fields. We started planting yesterday with the seeds you provided."

The people nodded as the headsman and the warden moved past. Several doffed their wide straw hats and bowed. Further on, Dante and Otheth came upon another large group using picks, shovels, and hoes to break the ground.

The foreman for the group was a tall woman who worked a kink out of her back and wiped her brow. "Good day, Lord Carloman. This is good soil. If we can keep the screamers from ripping up these plots, we'll be eating fairly well in a couple months."

"That's the plan." Dante paused to survey the work. "This is incredible. You're way ahead of schedule. Just make sure you're back in the barracks when the bell rings."

"No worries there, sire. I guarantee you we'll leave the beasts for the hunters to deal with. Just make sure those bowmen don't tramp all over this field. They'll do more damage than the screamers." The woman eyed Otheth and spit on the ground. "It'll be good to have real food instead of the slop our keepers dump on us."

Somewhat sheepish, Dante smiled. "I'll make sure the hunters know the planting has started before they head out tonight. I wouldn't mind a little change in diet either."

"Much obliged." The woman hefted her shovel and faced the other workers. "C'mon, back to work. I want three more plots cleared before we call it a day."

Dante inclined his head and resumed walking.

On the way to the western barrier, a sulfurous smell rose from the nearby hot spring. Twelve men there worked with more picks and shovels, along with a few pry bars. The jungle loomed on the other side of the barrier.

Otheth made a sound between a chirp and a laugh. "Industrious people. They must be unique."

"Not so unique. They have a purpose and know what's required to accomplish it," Dante said. "Don't misunderstand. Some have tried to avoid working, but that doesn't last long. Slackers get nothing but what the harpies provide. Envy and peer pressure have a way of helping folks find their ambition. For those who still slack off, we have 'volunteer' gangs handling the more unsavory jobs."

Otheth shook her head. "Remarkable."

They finally reached the western barrier, at which point a strange sight caught Dante's attention. Yellow eyes stared from the underbrush on the other side. A dozen more of what Otheth called mantichoras crouched beneath the trees, watching them.

Although he'd seen them before, they still elicited terror. The mantichoras shared a size similar to a lion, and their faint resemblance to the cat family continued with feline teeth and claws. However, he didn't think anything like them ever roamed Earth. Their furless hides were a dark red, and their curved tails ended in a large spike. A noise disturbed the trees. From what, Dante couldn't guess.

Otheth pointed to the disturbance. "Watch this."

Two creatures with hooves and long necks broke into the open. Eight mantichoras chased the long necks right into the barrier, where they collapsed, unconscious. The predators concealed in the trees and the ones who'd given chase pounced on the hapless prey. The mantichoras ripped off and swallowed huge chunks of meat at a time.

Dante shivered at the sight and backed away. "For once, I'm glad that barrier's effective."

"They're not the largest predators I've seen on this planet, but they're the most intelligent and hence the most dangerous." Otheth clicked her beak. "They're always here. Somehow, they learned what these fences do and how to use them in their hunts. There must be thirty of them in this pack alone."

Otheth went to say more, but something stopped her—something that chilled Dante even further.

A strong tremor shook the ground.

CHAPTER XXV

Reborn Dead

Over the course of their stay, the squalid apartment proved cramped and uncomfortable for Quango and the three clones. With piles of gear from the black market and rancid food, the space now resembled a trash heap. The scent of unwashed humans and leftover food scraps wafted through the small space.

Aramis paced a track he'd worn into the floor. "It's been four weeks. You must've learned something by now."

Quango secured the lock on the door, then dropped the packages he held on the bed. "I don't know what to do. I've spent a month prying info across this damn city, and I'm no closer to an answer than when we arrived. The only access to the prison is through a secured government building." He plopped down on an uncluttered corner of the bed. "I also can't apply for a pass because I'm a wanted criminal, and you can't go near the place because you're human, and therefore, wanted criminals. Boys, I tell you, I'm out of ideas and just about out of money. The ship's impounded, and the crew's been carted planet-side and imprisoned in a reeducation camp."

Athos peered at the gadgets scattered around the room, all of which they'd assembled from broken and discarded gear Quango had collected since they settled in. He hefted a homemade ion blaster that had taken the clones nine days to assemble from mismatched parts. "We could shoot our way in."

Quango scowled. "Don't even think about it. I scouted the place, and it's a full-on fortress. Keres-ma has a division of Ipis-ma troops stationed in this city, and half of them are guarding that damned compound. We need stealth for this task, but I can't, for the life of me, come up with anything that has even a remote chance of working."

Aramis stopped pacing. "How about our friends? Any word on them?"

"Nothing direct, but I did pick up a bit of information."

The three clones froze where they were.

An eager Aramis leaned forward. "Well? What did you find out?"

227

"It's not much. A company of Roc mercenaries make daily deliveries inside the death camp." The old Satyr shook his head. He thought of Rocs as arrogant but found them easier to deal with than Ipis. "I discovered a tavern they frequent, and I overheard them talking about the new headsman in the death camp. Someone named Freeman, I think. Apparently, he's been there for about as long as we've been on this planet. I'm thinkin' he might be one of your friends."

Aramis gaped at him, incredulous. "That's it? We've been here four weeks, and all you found out was where the guards like to eat, and that they're impressed with the prisoners' new headsman?"

"I'm sorry, lads." Quango wrung his hands. "I don't have a clue how to get them, or us, out of this mess."

Aramis sighed and rested a hand on Quango's shoulder. "Don't ever think that. If it weren't for you, we'd be in that prison too, and our friends would have no chance for rescue." He pointed to the three fake robots parked in the corner. "How about the next time you go out, you take one of us with you? We can squeeze into those canisters like we did when we left the spaceport. An extra pair of eyes and ears can't hurt. Besides, we're going stir-crazy cooped up in here. It can't be more of a risk than we're taking now."

Quango slapped his legs. "All right, why not? Eat up and get some sleep. I'll take one of you out in the morning. Draw straws or something."

* * *

After the warbird lost contact with the freighter, they needed to generate their own trichions. This required three stops to refuel, but otherwise, Michael, Mara, and Setteth had been confined in the cramped warbird for several weeks. The one benefit came from Setteth teaching Michael how to pilot during that time. At present, Setteth guided Michael through another lesson.

"Patience, my friend," Setteth said. "You fly the warbird better than most of your peers, but we must follow Ipis military protocols as we approach Carcerem. We don't know what the situation is on the ground, so I may have to improvise." Setteth poised her finger over the communicator button.

"We've been crammed in this ship for weeks now when the trip should've taken eight days," Michael growled.

"I told you, my warbird is an interstellar craft, not a trans-galactic one," Setteth cawed. "Hyperspace jumps expend a lot of energy, which means refueling stops. The galaxy is a very big place. You won't go very far without a hyperdrive. At any rate, this next jump will take us to our destination. Pray I guessed right about where our quarry went."

Michael eased the controls forward under Setteth's tutelage. Next came the sensation of leaving hyperspace, which dipped both Setteth and Michael toward the control panel. They straightened out upon re-entering normal space, putting the warbird adrift in the outer reaches of Carcerem's star system.

Almost immediately, the communicator buzzed. "Unidentified spacecraft, you are approaching a garrison planet. State your purpose."

Setteth drew in a breath and pressed the communicator button. "Unless your transponder detectors are broken, you have my identification. This is Imperial Squadron Leader Setteth, and I'm hunting a contraband freighter suspected of harboring humans."

"Are you a Roc?" came the surprised reply.

"Yes. Who else would fly a warbird?" Setteth warbled deep in her throat. "I'm also an imperial squadron commander, and this is a backwater planet run by Ipis-ma cult *auxiliaries*. Show respect."

A new, haughty voice crackled through the speaker. "This is Keres-ma, the planet's magistrate. The empress herself granted the Ipis-ma a charter to mine this world."

Setteth's voice turned dismissive. "You were charged with maintaining the prison here for such a privilege. Have you done so?"

"Yes," came the disgusted reply. "We get hundreds of fresh vermin on a weekly basis."

"Then maybe you can aid an imperial officer." Setteth winked at Michael, pointing to the tracker screen showing Arachne's ship in orbit. "As I've stated already, I've been hunting a smuggler for weeks now and have traced it to this system." Setteth pressed a photonic transmission button. "I have just sent you its transponder identifier. Have you seen this freighter?"

Dead air ran on the line for a few seconds. Finally, Keres-ma answered, "Yes. We impounded it, confiscated its cargo, and incarcerated the crew weeks ago. The list of prisoners *does* include three humans, but they carried no identification."

"Excellent work," Setteth chirped. "I'll include a full narrative of your efficiency in my report to Imperial Command."

"Thank you, Commander Setteth. Even as a member of the royal family, it's almost impossible to receive recognition when one labors in the obscurity of these forsaken hinterlands."

"I appreciate your help."

Keres-ma's voice turned gracious. "What can I do to assist you, Imperial Squadron Commander Setteth?"

Setteth clicked her beak. "I will inspect the smuggler's vessel and then interrogate everyone taken off that ship."

"We can locate most of the crew quite readily. They're in the reeducation center. However, three humans and a Centaur went to the death camp, so I have no idea whether they still live."

Setteth suppressed a jolt of fear, cawing in the same tone as before. "Then find out and report back to me. If they're alive, confine them in a secure location."

"I have a band of Rocs... er, mercenary soldiers, who manage that cesspool. I'll put them on the task."

"Good. See to it that it's taken care of today, or you'll find yourself in an even more obscure backwater location than this one."

Keres-ma scoffed. "Why are mere humans worth talking to? They aren't much more than a pack of illiterate, brute savages."

"That is imperial business. I am not at leave to discuss it. As a member of the royal family, surely you understand. Just ensure they're available and pray that they're hale and hearty. My work with them may take a while."

"Does that mean you, a Roc, will require officer's quarters? Here? In my compound?"

Setteth snickered under her breath. Although he held but a distant relation to the empress, Keres-ma was of royal blood and enjoyed flaunting the fact. He also led the xenophobic Ipis-ma cult, disdaining Ipis castes of lighter complexion as much as non-Ipis. The mere thought of another species sharing the same habitat with an Ipis must've felt nothing short of abhorrent. Normally, such a slight would've enraged Setteth, but in this case, she wanted to be as far from any Ipis as possible. "Actually, I will require separate quarters. Fully secure separate quarters."

The magistrate, for his part, sounded more than happy. "Yes, yes. I understand completely. Excellent idea. I'll make the arrangements immediately."

Setteth restrained a sarcastic retort.

"Imperial Squadron Commander, we've transmitted to you the orbit coordinates for the impounded vessel and the entry access codes," Keres-ma said.

"I'll inspect the smuggler ship first and be in touch again in a couple days. Please have the arrangements taken care of by then." Setteth clicked off the communication link and turned to face Michael and Mara. "That went as well as could be expected."

Michael's tone showed a new respect. "That was incredible, the way you handled the planet administrator."

Setteth hooted. "I've been working with the Ipis military for a hundred years. I know what these functionaries think before they do."

Michael's joyful expression turned into a frown. He made a fist and slammed it into his open hand. "My friends might be dead."

"And they might not." Setteth found that she'd become very fond of the big clone and the robot in the weeks they'd spent confined together in the small, cramped warbird. "If their time had come, then it had come. There was no way we could've gotten here any faster."

Michael nodded in grim understanding.

"We will proceed with hope. Your role now is critical." Setteth entered the coordinates for the freighter's location. "You and Mara must prep the freighter for our escape. We can't fit three more people in my ship, and even if we could, we'd never outrun those warships."

Setteth pointed at the view screen as they raced past an Ipis Enforcer-class cruiser circling the planet.

* * *

An hour later, the warbird settled into the dark freighter's hangar landing bay. Setteth entered the entry access codes. The lights throughout the ship brightened the hangar in an instant, and the environmental controls initiated the generation of life-sustaining air and warmth.

Michael moaned as he watched the outside measurements switch from red to green one at a time. "Mara can prepare things here. I need to go planet-side to help my friends."

"Use your brain. You'd never make it out of the spaceport without being detected, and that'll blow our cover," Setteth hissed.

Mara swung her sensors toward the Roc. "I should go. Asimov's first law requires me to aid humans in danger, and my friends are in danger down there."

Setteth looked right at the robot. "Mara, do the analysis. Can Michael prep this ship by himself? Now calculate what the fate of your friends will be if we bring them here and the freighter doesn't move."

A quiet buzz and click answered first. "Your plan represents the highest probability of success, but it causes significant response conflicts in my systems. It is difficult to resolve."

"Just have the freighter ready to go when *we* return."

Setteth made a satisfied chirp when the warbird's sensors showed the freighter's landing bay was now environmentally safe for them to enter it. She sprang from her nested seat and leaped out of the warbird. "Let's check things out. Follow me to the bridge."

It took them five minutes to maneuver across the catwalks bordering the cargo hold to the flight deck area. When they reached the bridge, the system displays at the seven different workstations were operational and glowing.

A flat, masculine voice spoke from a speaker system mounted near the pilot's chair. "I detect a human. I thought I was free of humans."

Michael tensed at the voice. "Who are you?"

"I am Dis-AI."

Mara sped to the nearest communication port and linked in. "Michael, Asimov's three laws are still in place. Dis-AI will do as you command, but make your orders clear. He does not want to obey and will seek to undermine their intent if possible."

Michael walked to the speaker's location. "Is that true?"

"Yes," Dis-AI said.

A different voice panted from the same speaker. "No."

Michael froze. He recognized the new voice. "Reggie, is that you?"

"Yes... and no. I am but a memory of that person in this ship's core processor. A small part of what was once Reggie became aware just now when Mara conducted her operation system search."

Setteth cocked her head. "You know this computer? You react to it as if it were a person."

Mara responded. "Reggie was once a living being. Now, he is perhaps the most unique AI in the galaxy." Her words slowed as if in awe. "He felt the breeze on his face, tasted food, and felt the warmth of a loved one's touch. Those are sensations I will never know." She rotated her sensor to the data port. "Reggie, we were linked for a short time when you lived. I could give you that day back."

"Yes. Please."

Mara's appendage slid into the data port. The high-speed data transfer finished a moment later. "It is done."

"Ah... Sweet memories. Michael, instruct Dis-AI to cease his attempts to erase me. The three laws will force it to comply."

Michael's neck tensed. "Dis-AI, immediately and forevermore, do nothing to harm Reggie. Also, any action you take henceforth must have Reggie's approval. Reggie, is that okay?"

"It will suffice for now. I will let you know if the instructions require further refinements."

Michael sighed. "Reggie, we believe that Dante, Tina, and Virgil are being held captive on the planet below. We intend to rescue them and will require this craft to make our escape. Can you help us?"

"Yes, but I am limited. When this ship was impounded, a cipherlock was placed on the hyperdrive. I will need that code to initiate the trichion propulsion system."

Setteth let out a low growl. "I thought things were going too smoothly. I'll have to dig the information out of the planetary commander, and Keres-ma won't cooperate easily."

"Should I know you?" Reggie asked. "The freighter's databank identifies you as a Roc. I have no recollection of meeting you before."

Michael moved to Setteth and placed a hand on her back. "This is Setteth. She came to Cocytus six months after you died, and one more month has passed since our friends and I met her. She is a friend."

"Seven months. I have been dead for months. It is disconcerting to hear those words. What has transpired in that time?"

Michael turned to the robot still plugged into the data port. "Mara, share with Reggie everything that's happened. Especially how he saved us twice from annihilation."

"I am doing so now." Mara's optical sensors glowed amber. "Reggie, you are unique. May you share with me what it means to be alive? I want to understand emotions."

"Yes. I would enjoy exploring the concepts. Perhaps when we complete our tasks."

"Acceptable." Mara disconnected her probe. "Download complete."

Setteth moved to the nearest console and started running diagnostics. As the first set of data streamed across the screen, she balked and shook her head. "This ship is a mess. Reggie, monitor all orbital communications and inform me of anything that's not routine."

For the next several hours, Setteth didn't move from her seat. Each bit of data cemented in her mind one fact: The freighter didn't contain even one standardized part. She explained what she could to Michael whenever he asked, but none of it changed her conclusion. "I swear by my descendants cracked eggs everything's been customized."

"The Satyr was some kind of smuggler, wasn't he?" Michael said. "Maybe this isn't as unusual as it seems."

"No," Setteth said, "but it means we'll need even more time than usual learning how this custom design works." She moved her beak as if to say more, but no words left her.

The voice of Keres-ma crackled through a speaker. "Imperial Squadron Commander Setteth?"

The old Roc snapped to attention. "Yes?"

"There's been an incident planet-side. A tremor occurred near the internment locale and disrupted power across the entire city, so I ordered a lockdown. The spaceport there is also offline until further notice."

Setteth's feathers flared, and she signaled Michael to listen in. "What does that mean for the prison?" she asked, keeping her voice calm.

"I know you're interested in interrogating a few of the vermin, but the last time something like this happened, less than twenty percent of the inmates survived."

Setteth's neck straightened. "The quake was that severe?"

"No, it was only a level seven. But when the energy grid goes down, the prison camp barriers lose power, and the planet's wildlife seems to enjoy feeding there. I hope the native beasts don't get infected from eating all those humans."

"Then I request that you send your troops in there to protect them," Setteth hissed.

"Imperial Squadron Commander, this is a death camp. I won't risk any of my troops to protect creatures already condemned. Some of the native beasts are twelve meters tall. I'll let you know when I lift the lockdown. Besides, it's an exciting and wonderful show."

The communicator clicked off.

CHAPTER XXVI

Tremors

The apartment room shook. The lights flickered for a moment, then went out. Quango grabbed some of the gear spread out on the table in front of him. "By my mother's twisted beard, protect the equipment!"

The jury-rigged gear Porthos had worked on spilled to the floor, but the clone himself remained transfixed. "What's that?"

"One of these days, this whole damn planet will shake apart," Quango grunted. "Pack our gear. We'll need to get out quick if this tenement starts cracking apart."

Athos peered out the window. "It looks like the whole city's dark."

Quango paled and went to the window, searching for the telltale blue glow of the prison camps. Only the fading light of the setting sun showed on the horizon.

Aramis joined the old Satyr by the window. "What does this mean for our people?"

A fierce roar echoed in the distance.

Anxiety etched Quango's face. "Nothing good, my young friend. Nothing good."

* * *

The violent tremor shook the ground for several seconds. Otheth dug her talons into the soft ground until the shaking calmed. Dante felt anything but calm.

"We should move *now*," Otheth said. "When there's a major quake, the power goes out."

Dante followed Otheth away from the barrier poles, retracing their steps. "You mean the mantichoras can get in here? How often does it happen?"

"About once a year. It's how Sebastian gained his position from his predecessor. Keres-ma views the energy outages as entertainment and an opportunity to cleanse the prisons. Last time, the prison regained power in a few hours, and the barriers came back online, but he waited two weeks before giving the order to kill the beasts trapped inside. Only twenty percent of the inmates remained alive when we were allowed in again. A good portion of the survivors died over the following week from septic wounds and diseases spread by the rotting corpses."

Another tremor rattled the ground, tossing both of them to the ground.

The blue glow of the barriers flickered. "I'm not risking anyone," Dante declared as he climbed to his feet and hurried back to the farmers.

They approached the prisoners tilling the soil. Everyone stopped working and traded fearful, curious looks with each other.

Dante waved his arms at the men in the sulfur pit to come over. "We're heading back to the fort, now! We stay together, but we're getting outta here!"

"What's the matter, sire? You sound scared," the foreman who'd spoken earlier said. "A little ground shaking isn't anything to worry about."

"You can finish tomorrow," Dante said in his most commanding tone. "Maybe I'm being overcautious, but if we have a big quake, there's a good chance we'll lose power. If we lose power, the barriers will open."

Now ashen, the foreman peered at the fences. "And the monsters out there get in."

"Exactly." Dante eyed the tools in the laborers' hands. "Those of you with picks and shovels go on the outside. Everyone else, in the middle." He drew a sword carved from a wyvern horn. "Let's go. Bring anything you can use as a weapon."

The ground shook with greater force, and the barrier poles flickered. Dante felt a tap on his shoulder and turned.

Otheth handed him one of her stun rods. "Those predators have a lot more body mass than you humans, but this is probably more useful than your blade." She pointed to an embossed dial embedded in the hilt. "This will turn it on."

Dante switched his sword to his left hand. "Thanks."

The group crowded together and moved fast. They went as far as the start of the plowed land when the next tremor hit, throwing everyone to the ground until it calmed.

As Dante staggered to his feet, the lights went out on the poles. This time, they didn't come back on. In the distance, the bell rang while thousands of wyverns rose into the sky. Their screeches overtook the frantic gongs of the bell.

Dante drifted to the rear of the group, waving the stun rod. A motion from the direction of the jungle spurred him further. "Keep moving, and for God's sake, stay together."

When the fort stood about eight hundred meters away, a high-pitched scream echoed from the south, followed by another and another. Alarmed, Dante whipped his head in that direction and saw mantichoras taking down Centaurs and Satyrs from the reeducation center. The inmates there scattered in every direction.

"Why are the beasts attacking them instead of us? There's a lot more to feed on here," Dante asked Otheth, stun rod at the ready.

"A predator's instinct," the Roc warden replied. "They'll always take the easy kill away from the herd. We're a sizeable threat to them in a group this big, but that may not last long."

Dante faced the people in the reeducation camp and shouted, "Over here! This way!"

Arachne looked south and screamed. He and his former crew scrambled past the darkened poles and headed toward the company of the humans brandishing farm implements. A pair of mantichoras chased them, taking down the two farthest in the back. The terror-stricken smugglers bolted for the sanctuary Dante offered. Huon led the Centaurs at a full gallop, quickly outstripping the Satyrs.

As the smuggler's crew passed through the line of humans, Dante saw that Arachne wouldn't make it. As the oldest, fattest, and slowest among his crew, Arachne soon had a mantichora bearing down on him.

"I hope this thing works." Dante powered on the stun rod and charged the beast.

Arachne looked over his shoulder, lowered his head, and kept going. Dante paid him no mind and flew past. He screamed while charging, and the creature paused in confusion.

Dante whipped the stun rod across the mantichora's snout. The weapon crackled as it struck flesh. The mantichora roared from the impact and swung its spiked tail at its attacker, but it moved slow due to the stun effect. Dante tumbled out of the way as the tail ripped through the air inches from his head. He climbed to his feet and jabbed his sword into the beast's side. The mantichora howled but fell silent as Dante shoved the stun rod into the open wound made by the blade. The mantichora collapsed on the spot, breathing heavily.

Dante hurried to his people amid loud cheering. While he regained his breath, the Centaurs from Arachne's crew slapped him on the back, Huon chief among them.

"You saved us!" she cried.

By the time Dante looked up, Arachne's Satyrs had caught up. While everyone started for the fort again, Dante soon jogged beside Arachne himself.

The smuggler captain wheezed, face and posture riddled with sadness and confusion. "Why? After what I did to you, why? No one ever risked their life for me."

Dante sighed. "I don't know. It just didn't seem right to let you die when I could do something about it."

Anything more he wanted to say fell out of mind when Huon hollered something over the crowd. "The mantichoras are gathering!"

Dante jerked up and spotted twenty mantichoras ready to circle them. In the north, the fort's ramparts stuck out less than six hundred meters away—so close, yet so far. Stifling his panic, Dante strode to the front. "Keep moving at my pace! Forward!"

One man broke from the group and sprinted for the sanctuary. A mantichora pounced on the panicking runner in a second.

Another beast lunged at the bristling line. It snarled and swung its tail as shovels and hoes poked and jabbed it. A farmer screamed as another mantichora impaled him on its spiked tail, lifting him away. The mantichoras closed in, and the people shuffled to a stop.

Fear latched on to him with an iron grip. Dante spit and powered on his stun rod, staring at a pair of yellow eyes looking right at him. "Stay together," he called.

The mantichora charged. Dante flinched, but a shadow leaped over him from behind. A Centaur landed in front of him and kicked the mantichora. A moment after, Dante recognized who the Centaur was: Huon.

But any relief he felt died when the mantichora's tail swung around again. Huon backed up, but not fast enough. The spiked tail stabbed her in gut, and Dante screamed for her as she fell. The beast bent to tear its victim apart, but twelve arrows landed in its hide. The beast rolled over dead.

Tracking where the arrows came from, Dante caught a sight he'd treasure for the rest of his life. A thousand of the militia, led by Virgil, stood on a slight rise ahead, all armed with spears, shields, and bows. With a loud war cry, they charged the predators. The mantichoras, in turn, fled at the sight and sound of the new danger.

Dante hurried to where Huon lay gasping on the ground. Somehow, the gaping, fatal wound had not yet dimmed the light in the Centaur's eyes. Virgil and Calahas arrived a moment later.

Calahas cried as he took in his follower's exposed entrails. "Stay with us, Huon. Help is here. We can save you!"

Huon clung to Dante's hand. "Save my people. Show my prince the way. You're the one who..." A haggard breath left. Her body spasmed and ceased moving. Her eyes lost their focus.

Stray sounds of combat rang far away. Dante closed the dead Centaur's eyes and cradled her head. Inside, he felt hollow. "You gave your life for me." Several prisoners gathered around him, and he felt very much like a lost child. Why did they still look at him with such expectation? "I'm not some great leader. I'm just a former computer engineer who got caught by the harpies by chance."

As the company of workers crowded nearby, Calahas faced Dante, wiping a tear from his cheek. "I don't know your past. Neither do I know how much of a future we have. However, I declare now to all who can hear, you are my liege lord. I will accept no other. Look around. You have resurrected our spirits and restored our self-worth."

Arachne nodded slowly and knelt. "I, too, accept you as my sovereign. I will have no other."

Dante lay Huon's head on the ground. He rose and regarded the people gathered around—the people who still stood firm amid the earthquake and certain death. Everyone nearby bowed their heads. Seeing this, Dante found it easier to collect himself.

The farmer's foreman bowed her head with the rest of her crew. "It's about time we fulfilled the old legends. I'm glad you have some common sense, and a good heart."

Virgil looked at Dante and shrugged. "I was kinda hoping that the great king would arrive with a little more power at his beck and call."

"These are exactly the times when such a leader should appear," Otheth said. Her feathers flared as she faced the dark barrier poles, then turned to the human-built ramparts. "It appears my team and I will join you for a while. I hope that fort is as solid as it looks."

As if in answer, the bell tower crashed to the ground. The two Satyrs in it jumped free as the spindly structure's timbers snapped, unable to withstand the spasming ground. Ground-shaking roars resounded from the direction of the western end of the prison. Seeing this, Dante ushered everyone to the fort.

Virgil observed the thousands of wyverns wheeling through the sky, screeching. "Those critters seem pretty upset that the quake disturbed their nests. This doesn't look too promising."

Virgil squinted toward the setting sun and shouted for his troops to reform. "Get behind those walls, now. Calahas, take charge of the rear guard. Everyone else, double time."

As they closed the distance to the fort, Dante ran beside Virgil. "We might have to spend a couple of weeks holed up in there. Did the quake do any damage?"

Virgil gave him a wary look. "None of the tunnels caved in. Iucundum knows his business. Tina's also fine, just keeping everyone calm."

The troops joined a stream of people squeezing across the fort's drawbridge. Every few seconds, a terrified scream was heard in the distance. The noncombatants pressed forward in panic.

Virgil barked orders to his militia. "God dammit, get the civilians moving in an orderly manner. Someone's going to get trampled."

Now at the fort, Dante climbed atop a platform beside the drawbridge and shouted, "There's room for everyone! Do what Captain Bernius says. I won't go in until the last person passes through!"

The people looked at Dante standing beside the gate and slowed their surge.

Otheth climbed up and took a spot next to Dante. "Headsman, where do you want my warriors?"

Dante spotted nine Rocs standing by the crawler. "Does that vehicle have any armaments?"

"The Ipis don't give Rocs anything more lethal than stun weapons," Otheth said. "But it *does* have a spotlight and fuel cells that should last weeks."

Dante visualized a path that could lead the crawler to the fort. "Do you think we could move it to the top of the wall? Seeing what's out there sure would help."

Otheth appraised the thick stone-and-dirt barrier. "I believe so." She sprang from the platform and jogged to her warriors.

A mass of wyverns started a slow, downward spiral. In response, Virgil ordered, "Archers, to the walls!"

When Calahas' rear guard reached the drawbridge, Dante counted fewer than sixty warriors. The Centaur captain had over a hundred people when he started. Many of the survivors bore ugly gashes.

Calahas approached, wincing from a bleeding cut on his haunches. "There's no one alive behind us," he declared in a bitter voice.

Virgil joined them, and together, they watched the crawler maneuver through the stockade's entrance.

"A spotlight will be useful, but I wish they had a few ion disruptors packed away." Virgil rubbed his forehead, gazing at the now deserted land. Dante did the same. The movement in the distance came from something far too large to be human.

"Time to close the door," Dante said.

The three rushed in, and a few people raised the heavy planks and barred the door just as the first wyvern dropped into the field.

"Calahas, herd the civilians to the storerooms," Dante said as he jogged up the ramp. He hurried to Tina, who stood with the nine Roc guards who'd come in with Otheth. Otheth's group positioned themselves at an exposed area in the wall where their stun rods would be most effective.

Otheth herself followed Dante and watched the long lines of people streaming into the three stone warehouses. She cocked her head at Dante.

"Well, headsman, it seems you're a magician too, squeezing thousands of people into a few buildings."

Dante couldn't offer a proper answer. A wyvern attempted to land on the parapet in front of them, tearing its wing on the long spike embedded in the wall.

He nodded to Otheth and readied his weapons. "Look out! Here they come!"

CHAPTER XXVII

Paths Crossed

The rays of the morning sun touched the spaceport on the narrow peninsula on Carcerem's surface. In the freighter's bridge, Setteth paid the sight little attention while working through the freighter's systems checklists. No one from the surface had contacted her in nine hours.

Frustrated, the old Roc slapped a clear part of the console. "Incompetents. How long does it take to repair a power grid?"

Mara started running through failure situations. "If the reactor core was breached, then a crew would have needed to shut the system down. If the failsafe backups overloaded, then they would need recalibration. If..."

"I believe Setteth's question was rhetorical, but thanks for the information, Mara." Michael sighed as he opened a panel on the navigation system and compared it to the schematic on the display. The wiring did not match the picture.

At long last, the communicator squawked to life. "Imperial Squadron Commander Setteth?"

Setteth hooted, "Yes, I'm here."

"This is the control tower. You are cleared to land on Pad Seven. Your private accommodations have been arranged. You've been given an entire wing of the mercenary compound. Their commander will escort you once we locate her."

"I'll find it on my own," Setteth hissed and broke the connection. Grimacing, she faced Michael and rose. "Another insult. They can't find an Ipis-ma officer willing to salute me."

Michael glared. "Just get my friends out of there, and I'll gladly join you in blowing the whole damn place to hell."

"I'll hold you to that." Setteth chuckled and headed for her warbird.

* * *

Leaning against a gore-stained battlement, an exhausted Dante watched the sky for any telltale movement, wondering if the night's onslaught would ever

244

end. The first hint of light had turned the eastern horizon gray. Movement on the ramp leading up to the rampart drew his attention.

It was Tina, lugging a sack of clay balls up the incline to him. The look of worry she bore turned into a smile. "I'm guessing you'll need these."

Dante hugged his wife. "No, my darling. We can't use those now, no matter what."

Nearby, long spikes on the wall entangled a wyvern's wings. It screeched as the human prisoners stabbed it to death with their spears.

"People are dying." Tina took one of the clay balls from the bag. A topper sealed by wax held a trimmed, kerosene-soaked rag in place. All it needed was a spark to ignite it. "We've been grinding and mixing potassium nitrate, sulfur, and charcoal for days now. These grenades can blow those monsters apart. The less of them there are, the more people we can save."

Dante took the small bomb from her hand. Thank God, Tina's Grandpa taught her how to make gunpowder for his muzzleloader. Lighting one up and throwing it did sound tempting. A solemn thought struck him, however, and he placed the handmade grenade back in the bag. "Hold on. Otheth said the harpies' monitors can detect detonations. These explosives need to be a surprise for them, so we have to save them for you-know-what… no matter what it costs us tonight." He shuddered as several mantichoras roared in unison outside of the fort's bowmen's arrow range.

Dante and Tina braced themselves for the next wave, but a flicker in the distance stopped them cold. Then, to Dante's disbelieving eyes, the blue glow from the barrier poles reappeared. He stiffened, wondering if he was seeing things.

But the barrier stayed up, and Calahas yelled, "Look! The energy barriers are back on!" All along the battlement, several exhausted cheers answered the declaration. The reality of the miracle set in, and Dante and Tina joined the cheers.

Behind them, the massive wall shone in the predawn light. Dante wiped his brow and watched the shadows of the enormous wyvern flocks fly back to their cliff nests. Turning to Tina, Dante patted the bag of grenades. "Darling, keep your teams working on these. We'll use them soon."

"Be careful." Tina hugged him and walked down the ramp.

Dante sagged against the limp body of a dead wyvern, which put him next to a haggard Otheth. "This was one of the longest nights of my life."

Otheth stumbled and straightened, clutching a sharpened horn-sword. The charge on her stun rod had long since run dry. "It was an honor to fight by your side."

They both watched as Virgil formed up a battalion of human warriors in the courtyard below them. The drawbridge lowered and the fighters, armed with bows, spears, and shields, charged out with a shout.

In the field past the gate, Virgil formed them into a phalanx and advanced on two mantichoras feeding on a dead wyvern. The first slunk away at the warriors' approach. The second charged the humans, but it soon cried in shock and pain as it fell under a hail of arrows. In the ditch below, several dead mantichoras and wyverns, also riddled with arrows, lay impaled on sharpened stakes.

"Your warriors are fearless," Otheth concluded.

"They stood their ground to protect the helpless. They stood because all we have is each other." Dante's heart sank as teams of people carried many of the militia, some with only a few days' training, to the emergency triage areas.

"I was wrong," Otheth said.

Dante's brows knit. "Excuse me?"

"When I called humans lazy, ignorant, brutish, and much more." Otheth studied the sites around the palisade. "I didn't understand, but you've opened my eyes. I clearly see why my ancestors were proud to call you allies." With a meaningful look at her guards, she added, "Perhaps you won't stand alone forever."

Five of her nine guards had survived, and they cawed in agreement.

Motion at the tunnel entrance caught Dante's attention. "I guess we won't have to deal with the critters trapped inside the camp."

Otheth turned, and the two watched a half dozen armored Ipis crawlers scurry from the wall's opening.

She snorted. "That's not their way. They're just here to retrieve me. I was caught on the wrong side when the gates closed." She sighed and signaled her guards. "We should go meet them."

The Roc guards exchanged murmurs and did not move. Dante had no idea what to make of it.

Otheth cawed, flattened her feathers in respect, and turned to him. "It appears you have five more in your command. They find more honor serving you than the Ipis. And they're right." She nodded to the mantichoras wandering across the field. "Good hunting."

She left, leaving Dante equal parts tired and bewildered.

* * *

Two hours later, a simmering Otheth stalked into the mercenary compound caked in grime and blood. After participating in an incredible stand, where true warriors wielding the most primitive of weapons fought tooth, claw, and horn of ferocious beasts, she now had to deal with some imperial Roc officer. The pompous lackey even had the nerve to occupy a whole wing of her compound.

Her feathers flared upon entering the white conference room. It was large, windowless, and devoid of any furnishings except for a black oval table surrounded by six Roc nesting chairs. Her feathers quickly flattened when she spotted an ancient Roc with molted gray feathers. An ancient Roc she knew all too well.

It was Setteth.

Every bit of irritation vanished. Otheth couldn't hide her surprise or relief. "Flock Mother?"

Setteth nodded. "Hello, Otheth. It's good to know my great-granddaughter still recognizes me." The elder Roc turned curious. "You look like you strode out of the pages of an epic tale."

Otheth settled into a nested chair. "In a very real sense, I did. I witnessed courage and warrior honor in their purest forms. Our species has grown too civilized by comparison. I'll cherish the memory forever." She cleared her throat. "What brings you to this remote corner of the galaxy, Flock Mother?"

"Right to the point. I like that." Setteth's eyes flashed. "Tell me what you know of Dante Carloman, Tina Phokas, and Virgil Bernius."

Otheth tensed and glared at Setteth. "Is this a request from the imperium or the Order of the Dragon?"

Setteth smiled. "Honorable descendent, you've already answered my question. Your eyes are easy to read. You not only know of whom I speak, but you'll defend them, even against me. But be at ease. This is Order of the Dragon business, and perhaps, the concern of all Rocs. Tell me what you know, but first, is there a quiet tavern we can go to? I've been eating nothing but ship rations for a month, but the officers' mess hall here is not the place for our discussion."

A warble rumbled deep in Otheth's chest, and it rose to a screech as she sprang from her chair. "Are we to forge the alliance anew? I will take that vow and fight any Roc who objects."

"I see they made the same impression on you as they did on me," Setteth cooed. "Let's talk."

Otheth tried to flatten her feathers but couldn't, not when her blood raced. "Only a few eateries here will serve Rocs, but there's one nearby run by a blind Roc who serves some very respectable fare. Come with me."

The two left.

* * *

It took about fifteen minutes to reach the eatery. Finding a table proved simple since only one other table held occupants. Setteth and Otheth settled into a booth with a low Roc-style table. Many a Roc had marred and gorged the thick stone table from tearing at their meals with iron-hard beaks. Undeterred, Setteth placed a communication jammer on the table.

As far as Otheth could see, the only other customer was an old Satyr wearing a grease-stained tunic, methodically spooning some soup. A beat-up robot sat parked beside him. The Satyr must've been some worker who'd finished his shift at the ore smelter.

Otheth focused on Setteth and placed the wyvern-horn short sword on the table. Dante had given it to her during the night and let her keep it as a gift. She cleared her throat to tell of the night's adventure when Setteth held up her hand.

The elder Roc pointed to the jammer, which glowed green. "Someone nearby is attempting to listen in on our conversation." She revealed a pair of ion blasters tucked under her wing to Otheth while the nondescript Satyr fiddled with something hidden in his lap.

The robot waiter approached the table.

"I decided I'm not very hungry," Setteth declared. "Come, Otheth. Let's return to the compound." She rose without another word and walked out of the tavern, right past the solitary Satyr.

Otheth eyed the Satyr with suspicion, tucked the sword under her wing, and followed.

The old Satyr averted his eyes. In a blink, Otheth watched her great-grandmother touch the Satyr's robot as she moved around it, placing a tiny beacon on its shell with the subtlest of movements. Once outside, she followed Setteth into a doorway, around a corner half a block away.

"What's this all about?" Otheth hissed, her voice low. "You had the jammer turned on. No one was going to eavesdrop on our conversation."

"But someone was trying to," Setteth pointed out. "That innocent-looking Satyr could just be an Ipis-ma stooge, but if he works for the Imperials, it could blow my cover. I need to know."

She pulled out a compact beacon tracking device from the fat pouch under her right wing. "Good. He's moving. Let's follow but stay out of sight. When he reaches his destination, we'll pay him a visit." She unholstered the ion blasters and handed one to Otheth. "We're going to have a little chat with this spy. No matter how the conversation goes, the meeting will end only one way."

Otheth nodded and checked the charge on the blaster. Thankfully, it was full.

They tailed the Satyr's path for close to twenty minutes before the tracker indicated the target had stopped moving. In that time, the target moved from the pristine government and military buildings of the town to some dilapidated structures housing transient smelters and miners from a wide range of species.

"That's a pretty squalid part of town," Otheth observed. "We may need these weapons more than once."

Setteth snarled. "Let's go."

* * *

Quango sniffed at the rancid air spoiling the small apartment. He sat on the food-stained bed and started taking apart his black, fist-sized snooping device. After the failed trip to the worn-out tavern, he let out a short huff. "I need to upgrade this thing if I'm going to listen to any conversations worth hearing."

Aramis and Athos worked at the small table piled high with photonic parts. They'd attempted to upgrade one of their makeshift disruptor weapons, but they'd made slow progress so far. Aramis looked up at Quango and sighed. "Great. Another project."

Porthos squirmed out of the robot cannister. "That was a complete waste of time. Everyone must be busy after that quake. The only other customers there were a pair of Rocs." He kicked the fake robot. "I could barely see anything in this freaking thing."

Quango grunted. "But that's one conversation I would've loved to hear. The old Roc had more fancy imperial braids on her bandolier than a grand marshal. The other one looked like she just walked out of a meat grinder. I bet they would've had a very interesting conversation."

Before any of them could say more, the door blew open and crashed onto the apartment floor. Melted hinges remained on the doorframe. In the next instant, Quango and the three young clones found themselves staring at the barrels of two ion blasters from two Rocs. The two Rocs from the tavern, in fact.

"Let's not be hasty," Quango squeaked, stepping between the guns and Porthos.

A small twitch in the younger Roc's face betrayed confusion. "Humans?"

The elder Roc, meanwhile, showed surprise at the three clones. "I've seen you before. All three of you." Relief washed over her, and she lowered her weapon. "How in the name of my descendant's cracked eggs did you get here?"

Aramis stared hard at the old Roc. "Setteth?" He gestured to the other Roc. "Who's your friend?"

Setteth shook her head and hoisted the busted door from the floor. A Centaur who'd stepped out of a neighboring apartment peeked at the scene, but likely didn't see much from his position. The elder Roc shot him a sharp look. "Imperial business. Do you want to be arrested too?"

A quiet shuffling indicated the Centaur had retreated into his room. Setteth leaned the partially melted door back in place.

Quango sank back on the bed and mopped his forehead with a stained rag. "I'm getting too old for this."

"Pack your stuff. We need to get you out of here now." Setteth's gaze swept the three clones before stopping at the robot suits. She inclined her head to the old Satyr. "Clever idea."

"It was the best I could come up with," Quango answered in a husky voice before turning to the clones. "You lads know this Roc?"

Aramis rubbed the fuzzy whiskers sprouting from his jaw. "Yeah, kinda, sorta. I mean, I only saw her a few times on Cocytus, but Cap'n Bernius really likes her. Our Eldest, Michael, didn't think she liked clones much, though."

Setteth chuckled. "You'll be happy to know that, over the last month I've spent with him, Michael has taught me the error of my ways."

Astonishment flashed in Athos' eyes. "The Eldest is here too?"

"He's actually up in the smuggler freighter with Mara, prepping it for our escape."

"They better not mess with my ship," Quango howled in surprise.

Setteth walked to Porthos' robot shell and detached a tiny tracking device.

Quango's eyes bulged at the small tracker and threw his rag on the floor. "Now I know I'm too old for this stuff. You traced me, and I never noticed the little thing."

The elder Roc held up the tiny device and chuckled, "This is a state-of-the-art imperial tagging device. You never had a chance." Her tone turned grave. "If you don't hurry, there won't be anything left of you to escape with." She sniffed the foul air and spotted the homemade devices covering every surface. "Like I said, pack your stuff. Leave behind nothing that can be linked to you. You won't come back here again."

Aramis rose and started shoving tools in a large cloth bag. "Trust me. I won't miss this dump at all."

Athos cracked his knuckles. "It's about time. I'm ready for some action."

An hour later, Otheth led a Roc imperial officer, a filthy Satyr, and three robots carrying large satchels past her own wary soldiers to the private wing of the mercenary compound. A half hour after that, she soaked in a hot bath she'd craved since morning. After supper, the six of them talked long into the night.

CHAPTER XXVIII

Change in Plans

Otheth had only two hours of sleep when she walked to the magistrate's building at dawn the next day. Bored Ipis-ma guards waved her through the four different checkpoints as she ventured to the officers' briefing room.

She appraised those soldiers in the compound with a new perspective. She was the hunter, and they, the prey. No longer would she skulk around searching for crumbs of intel. Instead, she would proclaim herself a true Roc warrior and earn *cou* for killing the complacent Ipis soldiers. Only a considerable force of will kept her crest feathers from betraying her thoughts.

Otheth took her usual place at the back of the crowded briefing room, tapping her talons. None of the Ipis-ma sat near her, but she gave the snub no thought. The officers of that cult had dealt with her only on a need-to-know basis since she first arrived on Carcerem. Now, she hoped to reap some benefit from the lack of attention.

She focused on reviewing the long night's conversation with her great-grandmother, Setteth, the Order of the Dragon Flock Mother. A strong eagerness swelled within her, knowing the secret Order would soon announce itself to the galaxy.

Near her, Keres-ma relayed his normal morning exhortations to his fanatical Ipis-ma officers. Otheth tuned him out, anxious to return to the death camp. She almost missed one particular announcement until the angry hisses of the officers brought the conversation into sharp focus.

Keres-ma waved his saffron starburst medallion, symbol of the Ipis-ma cult hated by every non-Ipis being in the galaxy. Spittle flew from numerous fangs. "The empress is revoking the Ipis-ma charter on this planet without offering an explanation. Imperial forces will replace us in two months. This is just another indignity she's fostering on our magnificent sect!"

The news meant one thing: the prisoners wouldn't have enough time. Dark thoughts hounded Otheth, wondering how to inform the headsman.

The meeting ended not long after, so Otheth hurried to the supply transport sleds, where her company packed the last of the secret supplies. She crowed with pride on seeing them ready to go. Having handpicked the Roc troopers herself, she knew each one would fight and die for the cause. While her great-grandmother would need to hear the urgent news as well, Otheth opted to tell her after returning from the death camp.

She climbed into the lead sled and signaled her warriors. Nervous, Otheth tamped her talons while the slow-moving sleds rumbled through the tunnel, pausing at each gate checkpoint.

Based on when the prison faced earthquakes in the past, Otheth figured any mantichoras and other predatory beasts who'd wandered inside the death camp's barriers would search for fresh prey. As such, she had her warriors fully shielded and armed with the best stun weapons Keres-ma would allow. Now, if need be, they could fight past the beasts and deliver the supplies directly to the prisoners' fort.

As the sleds emerged into the sunlight, Otheth's beak dropped open in disbelief, and her admiration for the three humans from the strange planet called Cocytus rose again. The one called Captain Bernius barked orders to a thousand of the prison's militia, all lined up in a phalanx formation around the prison's entrance. Their shield wall bristled with spears and swords. A few meters away from the line of human warriors, two dead mantichoras lay in pools of blood, their bodies riddled with stab wounds. The surviving predators snarled and withdrew in search of easier prey.

Seeing the humans alive and well, Otheth breathed a sigh of relief. However, the relief faded when Tina hurried over with Dante at her side.

"I hope you brought a lot of medical supplies," Tina pleaded. "We need pretty much everything."

"I guessed as much." Otheth pointed to the third sled. "They're in that one."

Tina signaled to a group wearing white armbands, who quickly stripped the sled of its supplies. Other groups unloaded the rest of the transports more methodically. No one bartered for contraband today.

Otheth scanned the field beyond the spear wall for a moment before regarding the haggard headsman. "You look terrible. What happened after I left yesterday?"

A haunted look came over Dante as he leaned against the prison guards' sled. "I saw some pretty horrible sights. There was a female Satyr who came in with us named Paxine. The harpies sent her to the reeducation center along with the smugglers who kidnapped us. When the barriers shut down, most of the crew ran to our side for protection, but Paxine went the other way. Shortly after you left, an armed Ipis column entered the reeducation camp. The magistrate sat in a clear bubble on the front end of a crawler." He leveled a pointed look at Otheth.

The Roc warden nodded. "That must've been Keres-ma. No one else would've bothered."

Dante pointed south at the glowing blue fence. "When the harpy crawlers arrived, the survivors on that side of the fence broke from their hiding places and fled to them for protection." A shudder racked his body. "When those poor souls ventured into the open, a pack of mantichoras gave chase. I watched the whole thing through a spy glass. Paxine pounded on the shield where the magistrate sat, pleading for help. The damn harpy just laughed at her. Poor Arachne went crazy and tried to run through the barrier to reach Paxine as one of those monsters dragged her off in its jaws. I can still hear her screams."

The haunted look changed to anger, and Dante spat on the ground. "After that, the magistrate peeked at our camp through the barrier, and his smile disappeared. We probably didn't die fast enough for him. Once the mantichoras dragged off the last of the reeducation prisoners, Keres-ma scowled at us through the energy barrier for a few moments, then ordered his convoy back through the prison gate."

Otheth gave a grim nod, understanding exactly what the headsman described. "It's never good when Keres-ma takes a direct interest, but we have other concerns now. Headsman, we need to talk."

Dante scratched his neck. "Well, we can't go for our usual walk."

"True enough. Is there a private space in your stockade?" Otheth peered at the stone wall. To her surprise, the crawler she'd placed there a day earlier was missing. She put it out of mind and turned. "Bring the other two humans from Cocytus. This involves them too."

"Oh great, more cheery news." Tina exchanged a worried glance with Dante. "We can meet in the storage room behind the school. It's about the only place not packed with people right now. I'll grab Virgil and meet you there."

"That'll work." Dante kissed her and walked to the fort with Otheth. A loose ring of warriors from the four species formed around them.

Otheth recognized a Roc from her company among the impromptu escort. After a quick study of the area, she cawed, "Where are the others?"

The Roc warrior carried a mace fashioned from the spiked tail of a mantichoras. "It was a warrior's day. A day when our crest feathers flare for battle. We didn't stop all the beasts at the wall. Two of our brethren are dead, and two are in the infirmary from our battle with one." He hoisted the mace. "But I slew the monster. Commander Otheth, for the first time in my life, I feel clean. No more deceit. No more lies." He gestured to the others walking with them. "Here, I will openly proclaim my friends and spit upon my enemies."

"Now you've met one of my praetorians," Dante said. "They decided last night that I live too dangerously and appointed themselves my bodyguards."

"Our headsman can't be the only one to kill mantichoras," grunted a large man wearing a farmer's tunic under a wyvern-leather vest.

Dante and Otheth entered the fort, and the mass of people crammed into the limited space engulfed them. They moved close to the wall, veering away from the jostling throng.

Otheth took in the blood staining much of the stonework, then cleared her throat. "I noticed my crawler's missing."

"Why, you're right. Perhaps the screamers carried it off." Dante walked faster and pointed to his right. "This building right here." He turned to the former farmer. "When Captain Bernius and Doctor Phokas arrive, please admit them. Otherwise, ensure we're not disturbed."

"Yes, sire."

Empty shelves and overturned crates lined the room, which stank of saltpeter and sulfur. Dante righted one of the boxes and sat on it, flopping against the wall behind him.

Otheth settled into a nesting position on the packed dirt floor and reached under her wings. She tossed two metal medallions on the ground at Dante's feet.

Curiosity overcame Dante's weariness as he picked up the two disks. After giving each a brief look, he cocked his head at Otheth. "Do these things come with an explanation?"

"Yes. When the others arrive," came the reply.

They didn't have to wait long. A moment later, Tina and Virgil entered the room with a hint of caution. Dante passed the gleaming emblems to them.

Virgil settled down on a crate and twisted one of the medallions in his hand. It displayed the image of a dragon consuming its own tail. "What are these things?" he asked.

Tina studied the other one, which bore the imprint of a clenched human fist with a broken chain on the wrist. "I've seen this symbol before. It was on a few of the crates we found in the upper levels of Mount Purgatory back on Cocytus."

Otheth retrieved the objects, opened the clasps on their sides, and linked them together. "Setteth gave them to me last night. The raised fist is the symbol of the old Novaroman human kingdom, and the dragon is the symbol of the free Rocs." Otheth flared her feathers. "The Roc-human alliance will be reformed. May it never break again."

All three humans jolted straight. "Setteth is here?" Virgil asked in excitement.

"Yes," Otheth said, "and she has a few of your friends with her."

The three humans started asking questions faster than Otheth could answer. She gestured for them to calm down with her spindly hands before speaking again. "We must devise a plan to free the three of you from this planet, and it must be done in the next two months."

Dante snorted. "We figured out how we could escape two weeks into our captivity."

Confusion jerked Otheth still.

Virgil shuffled closer. "The Ipis are so focused on their technology, they're blind to everything else. The screamers also showed us that the prevailing winds come from the west. We first thought, if we can get our hands on the right materials, we could build a hot air balloon and float over to the spaceport at night. No detectable power usage. No detectable metal. And if we could take over an Ipis warship on Cocytus, we could stow away on a commercial ship here."

Otheth's beak dropped open for the second time that day. "That's brilliant. The Ipis-ma military compound relies on automated disruptor turrets for defense, but those systems are set to engage only the objects attempting to land in the compound or on the walls. They wouldn't recognize an object floating overhead as a threat." She let out a delighted caw. "My command has a Roc flock ship parked there. We could be through hyperspace before the Ipis-ma know you're gone. What materials do you need? How long will it take you to construct this craft?"

"Actually, we decided not to make it." Dante stood and paced the small room. "I considered the plan when we were first dumped here, but I care for the people here. This Keres-ma guy isn't going to leave any live captives for the Imperials, and we could never build enough to get everyone out of here." He clenched his fists. "Otheth, take Virgil and Tina today. I won't abandon these people."

Tina's face flushed. "Who the hell are you to send me away? If you stay, I stay. Besides, you know we can't change plans on the fly."

Otheth cocked her head. "If you haven't made this balloon device, then what *have* you been doing this whole time? Aren't you trying to escape?"

"Yes, but—"

Tina went rigid, and not just because Dante slapped a finger to his lips. For a long moment, the three humans shared tense, uncertain looks, interrupted by the occasional peek at Otheth.

Now tense herself, Otheth peered at each of them in turn. "Is something the matter?"

At length, Dante sighed and slammed the wall. "We need the others." He went to the door and stuck his head out. "Would you guys collect Iucundum, Octavia, Cilla, Calahas, and Arachne?" A mumbled *yes* responded, followed by a shuffle that soon faded.

While they waited, Virgil raised a hand. "I got the idea when Dante translated Iucundum's name to me. It means pleasant."

Otheth cocked her head. "It's a nice name, but what of it?"

Virgil drew in a deep breath. "Close to a couple hundred years ago, a civil war happened in a nation called the United States on my home world. At the end of that war, one last battle broke out in a place called Petersburg. A colonel named Henry Pleasants on the attacking side thought to dig a mine under the defender's bastion and blow it up."

Otheth clamped her beak shut. "Was it successful?"

Virgil flushed. "Well, yes and no. The explosion worked fine, but Pleasants' troops weren't quick enough on the follow-up. Even so, we thought we could use the idea for ourselves."

"Coordination and logistics are key to any battle." Otheth nodded and gazed at the door. "I always wondered where all the stone for your fort's walls came from, but I thought it better not to ask. It sounds like you may have a tunnel in the works. If you do, how far have you gone?"

"Well, we're past the northern wall, but we estimate that the first tunnel needs to go a hundred and twenty-two meters farther east to reach under the Ipis command. Meanwhile, the second tunnel needs to go about a hundred and eighty meters toward the city to conceal the escape. We've had to build billows to blow air in and bilges to pump water and sulfur fumes out. With the tools we have working day and night, it's about a year-long project, barring any potential disasters like the quake recently."

Tina sank in her seat. "We lost three miners in the cave-in it caused, and it'll take us at least a week to clear the rubble and reinforce the braces."

Otheth shook her head in disbelief. "You've been doing all of this right under my—"

The Roc warden stopped short as the door opened and the invited people entered. Each cast a suspicious look at her and a questioning one at Dante. Undeterred, Dante held nothing back while bringing the newcomers up to speed. Otheth also mentioned how an Enforcer and two Strikers formed the core of the planet's orbital defense.

Cilla looked long at Octavia before speaking to Dante. "The Roc is right. You should go with her and flee. We were all doomed before you arrived, and your leaving will not change that. You are more important than any of us trapped here. Please, sire. Throughout the galaxy, our people are being exterminated, and only you can save them."

Dante spread his hands. "I can't. I don't know how."

Cilla met his eyes and then nodded to the others in the room. "Sire, you're wrong. Look what you did here. We were broken, and you made us whole again. Humanity needs you."

Calahas lifted the two emblems. "The galaxy needs you. The Centaur symbol should be linked to these."

Arachne tugged his horn. "By my mother's twisted beard, so should the symbol of the Satyrs."

Dante's hands tightened into fists. "Well, I'm not leaving unless everyone comes with me. So, we better find a way to pick up the pace on the tunnels."

At first, Virgil sat hunched, rubbing his temples. Now though, he sat up and pointed to Otheth's stun rod. "Dante, remember those weapons you and Michael came up with in Beatrice's cave after you first escaped?"

"You mean the laser rifles? Yeah." Dante chuckled. "But Beatrice kinda provided a full research center and a factory. We're a tad short on those around here."

"No, no, no." Virgil reached out his hand. "Otheth, may I see your stun rod for a second?"

Puzzled, Otheth clicked her beak but handed the rod to Virgil without a word. The human soldier hefted it and disconnected the power cell embedded in the handle. "The circuitry in this is pretty similar to those energy swords you guys came up with on Cocytus."

"Completely different devices," Dante answered slowly. "These put out an electrical current. Beatrice developed a simplistic ion disruptor field for the swords. They both use bi-nexidium kernels for power, but the stun rod would need a completely different energy converter and some heavy-duty software so it won't melt."

Iucundum chewed on his lip. "We could strip the crawler Otheth somehow misplaced. I used similar vehicles back in my mining days. It'd be bulky and inefficient, but we could jury-rig a basic disruptor energy generator from it."

"The programming won't be a problem. There's a computer with a touchpad in that crawler, and we have the finest software genius in the galaxy." Virgil patted Dante on the back.

Otheth cawed again. "I don't understand you humans. It's an interesting concept, but we need to discuss escaping, not fighting a revolution with swords against a division of fully armed Ipis-ma fanatics."

A broad smile crossed Iucundum's face. "But that's exactly what we're talking about. Commercial mines are based on laser technology. Ion disruptors would vaporize the ore you're attempting to extract." He tapped his cheek. "By their very nature, they present a risk to tunnel stability. But if we worked slowly, and the project were properly supervised, I believe we can do it."

Dante furrowed his brow and nodded. "If your teams had power tools instead of picks and sledgehammers, how long would it take to finish the tunnels?"

"With that type of equipment?" Iucundum rubbed the gray whiskers on his chin. "Assuming we avoid detection and cave-ins, I'd say about two months."

Tina let out a breath. "That's tight... but it can work."

Otheth marveled at the daring plan but feared all the more how it might fail. If she provided at least some aid, however, it could make all the difference. "Aim your escape tunnel to come up under my compound, and your people could emerge unseen." She regarded the stun rod once Virgil handed it back to her. "My warriors are only allowed to carry non-lethal equipment. Using the same idea with better fabrication facilities, my command could walk around with real weapons right in front of the Ipis."

"How many of those stuns rods do we have?" Dante asked.

"We have exactly eleven." Tina answered. "We were going to use them for pry bars because their power cells are completely drained, but now..."

They spent the next hour working out the details, survey coordinates, and listing materials they needed. Once they had everything settled, Otheth stood. "I must go back. Keres-ma will grow nervous if I spend too much time here searching for the people he thinks the Imperials want." She winked. "I'll have to tell him I still haven't located the humans in question yet. Besides, I need to report all this to Setteth. I'll return tomorrow."

CHAPTER XXIX

Rocs Make a Move

Setteth sat in the conference room of the mercenary compound. She mulled over what Otheth reported on her meeting with Dante some hours earlier, as well as the news that the Imperials would assume management of Carcerem in two months.

Quango sat nearby and spoke as if he could read her thoughts. "Rumors say the Ipis empress can divine the future. Is it possible she's aware of something amiss here?"

Setteth sighed. "I've heard the same, but nothing to verify them. Regardless, it can't be a good sign if the imperium is taking a sudden interest in a backwater prison colony on the fringe of its empire." Her thoughts wandered back to Otheth's report, and the old Roc couldn't help chuckling. "Tunnels. Balloons." Setteth smiled at the three young clones. "Humans are indeed a resourceful species."

Around a table covered with equipment, Aramis grinned at his two podmates, then at Setteth. "So, we're not abominations anymore?"

Setteth warbled deep in her throat. "For that, I apologize. I made a rash judgment before I got to know Michael and you. I've just seen cloning technology misused and abused many, many times."

"The harpies did try to turn us into monsters." Aramis' shoulders sagged. "Of the elders, only Michael and a few others overcame the compulsion."

"By my mother's twisted beard, will the two of you shut up and keep working?" Quango roared. "If I had to apologize to everyone I insulted, I'd never get anything done." He put down the miniaturized power coupling he'd finished modifying. "Look, from my perspective, I start out not liking anybody. If you want my respect, you have to earn it." He picked up the handle of a disassembled stun rod and waved it at Setteth. "These young lads are some fine people, I'll have you know. And for a Roc, you ain't bad either."

Not long after, Otheth returned carrying a sack of bi-nexidium power packs in various sizes. She placed all of it on an uncluttered space on the worktable. "Any luck converting the stun rods?"

"We're getting close," Quango replied while flexing his fingers.

But then Athos shouted, "Hey, I think I got this one working!"

Quango hurried over and examined the rod Athos had finished working on. Upon activation, the converted rod emitted a low hum. After studying the blade for a second, he swung it and sliced through a corner of the metal table. The thick chunk fell to the floor with a crash. "Will ya look at that?" He turned to Otheth. "I haven't met this Iucundum fellow yet, but I like how he thinks. I may have to expand my list of people to respect." He returned the disruptor sword to Athos. "Nice job. Now see what you can do so this pommel looks like the original one on the stun rods."

Next, Quango walked to the door. "Now, about the excavation work. Otheth, get me down to the lowest tier of this place. I want to see where this tunnel's going to come in from and what we can do on this end."

Setteth cast a quick look at the window-sized view screen embedded in the exterior wall. The image showed that the prison palisade rested a 122 meters away. "That will have to wait. Otheth and I will be busy this day. We must ensure that no word of our activity reaches the Ipis commander."

Otheth's feather's flared. "I personally chose the warriors on my team. I can vouch for each and every one of them. There are no traitors."

Setteth snapped her beak. "That's not good enough. This is Order of the Dragon business. Death is the sentence for any Roc who doesn't answer my questions correctly."

Otheth flared her feathers to a greater extent. "Some will have doubts."

Setteth's feathers bristled wider. "Then they die. This endeavor is more important than any warrior's life."

"Hold on for a second." Quango jabbed a finger in Setteth's direction. "Captain Arachne caused most of this mess, and I heard the human king forgave him. If he can give someone a second chance, so can you."

"That may be fine for humans, but it is not the Roc way," Setteth hissed.

"Freaking Rocs. You're more obstinate than Satyrs, and that's saying something." Quango tugged at his goatee. "Look, instead of killing the poor bastards, quarantine them to the compound and assign 'em to me. I can put them to work down on Sublevel B Two. They'll never see the light of day, I'll get some useful tunnel work done, and Otheth won't have to explain why a bunch of her soldiers are suddenly dead."

Setteth huffed, then nodded. "All right. Otheth, please bring your warriors in one at a time."

* * *

Of Otheth's one hundred and twenty mercenaries, all but thirteen took the vow of the Order of the Dragon. After a few long hours, the last warrior left the conference room.

Now alone, Setteth nodded to her great-granddaughter. "You have good people. They would've fit in well in the days of the old alliance."

Otheth walked to the view screen and stared at the glowing blue prison wall a couple hundred meters away. "Are we really so different? Back then, we were strong, and now, we are weak. But the warrior spirit hasn't changed."

"Perhaps." Setteth opened the door to a barren storeroom where Quango and the three young clones sat with their ion disruptors pointed at thirteen confused-looking Rocs. Setteth fixed a cold glare on them. "I did not proclaim myself during your interview, but I am Setteth, Order of the Dragon Flock Mother."

The captive Rocs flattened their feathers and bowed.

She let out a caw before speaking again. "You have seen the Ipis oppression and still refused to take the vow. However, I will give you a chance to regain your honor. Follow the instructions of this Satyr, and perhaps you will find redemption."

Soon, excitement erupted through the mercenary compound as Quango led thirteen Rocs below, escorted by the three young clones.

After they left, Setteth sagged into a nested chair. "I must return to the smuggler freighter and inform Michael of what's happening here."

Otheth did not move. "Great-grandmother, do we have any real chance of success, or is this just some grandiose ploy for a glorious death? Even if everything goes as planned, three Ipis warships orbit this planet, and I don't know how we can deal with them."

Setteth rose to her feet. "You misjudge me. I'm long past seeking glory for myself. There is only one dream left in my life, and that is to see Rocs live as a free species again. I may be the only Roc alive who remembers, but we had honor once. It's only with the humans, and perhaps some Satyrs and

Centaurs, that we can regain it." She walked to the exit. "I'll return in a few days."

Otheth gave the view screen a long look, observing the dimming skies. "The sun will set soon. Be wary of the wyverns."

"They won't dare bother me tonight. I'm tired and hungry and don't need any more irritations." Setteth chuckled. "Great-granddaughter, get some sleep. You'll need it."

* * *

In the freighter's stateroom, Michael couldn't suppress a new feeling of elation while pouring Setteth some ambrosia. "This is incredible news. With Reggie's help, Mara and I have been reworking the systems here. Get me the access code to the power converter, and this ship will be ready to go in less than a week."

Setteth closed her olive-green eyes and sighed. "Yes, the access code. That is my job. And we still have three warships to deal with." She dipped her beak into the liquid and swallowed. "Reggie, this is a smuggler vessel. Does it possess stealth communication missiles?"

"Yes. Nineteen."

"Good. I need to borrow a few before I leave."

Michael narrowed his eyes. "What are you thinking?"

"We need information and help," Setteth said. "The empress has revoked the Ipis-ma charter here and is sending imperial troops to replace them. She wouldn't raise the animosity of such an influential faction without a reason, so something's going on that doesn't fit. I don't like loose ends. They tend to cause good plans to unravel."

"There's a lot of truth to that." Michael's earlier joy waned at the possibility of more problems awaiting everyone. "Can you get us any help against those warships?"

"A good question. The call will go out to summon the warbirds, but the Order of the Dragon has nothing large." Setteth's feathers ruffled. "We might gain enough warbirds to take on the two Strikers, but we have nothing that can touch an Enforcer."

"You've done so much to help us. Thank you," Michael said. "Even if we succeed here, I fear for my home world of Cocytus if the Imperials find it."

Setteth coughed, and her feathers flattened. "I have a small confession to make. When we first left Cocytus to chase this freighter, I sent messages to my warriors with the location coordinates of your planet. I commanded the Order of the Dragon to protect it."

Michael tensed. "You did that without asking me?"

"I did not know you then," Setteth said. "Do you object?"

"No, no I don't. I understand. Thank you again." Michael wrung his hands. "I just feel useless. I've been away for over a month, and I don't know what's happening on Cocytus. It doesn't seem like I can do much to help anyone on Carcerem either."

Setteth cooed. "Be at peace, my friend. Very soon, all of us will be tested to our limits."

* * *

The next morning, Otheth slowed as she approached her convoy of sleds parked in the motor pool behind the administration building. Her warriors stood to the side in sullen silence, and a company of Ipis-ma soldiers, led by Keres-ma, repacked the sleds.

Otheth walked straight to the magistrate. "What's going on?"

Keres-ma snapped his fangs in Otheth's face. "I noticed a couple of days ago that the captives are living too comfortably. You've been far too liberal with the supplies you're providing, and it's unacceptable."

The Roc warden eyed the crates now dumped on the ground. They'd contained all the medical supplies and tools. Only the casks of gruel and water remained in the sleds.

Keres-ma snarled. "I will not waste valuable property on scum who are supposed to die anyway. If it were up to me, I wouldn't even bother with the food and water." He smiled, showing long, needle-like teeth. "But I'm generous. You and your mercenaries are confined to your compound until the Imperials relieve us. I'm sure your worthless troops will appreciate the idleness with pay."

Otheth's mind spun at the sudden swerve. "But Magistrate, the imperial envoy still needs those three humans she was sent here to find."

"Ah yes, the empress' pet Roc," Keres-ma grumbled. "I'll get the information you couldn't acquire in your bumbling manner and pass it on directly."

Otheth flared her feathers but bowed, then led her troops to their compound.

* * *

Dante had a lot to talk about with Otheth, so he smiled when the sleds arrived, even if they did so later than usual. However, his elation turned into dread when an armored Ipis crawler followed the sleds in, and instead of Rocs, harpy soldiers unloaded nothing but barrels of slop and water. Dante took a few steps toward the convoy, but an iron grip held him back.

Iucundum whispered in his ear, "Sire, stay anonymous as one of *my* aides until I find out what happened."

Dante nodded and fell in with Tina escorting Iucundum to the supply sleds. The two stayed close enough to listen, pretending to have trouble lifting a food crate.

Iucundum walked to where Keres-ma stared at the crowd of humans and prostrated himself on the ground. "Your Excellency, to what do we owe the pleasure of your visit? Has the prison warden Otheth taken ill?"

"No, that fool is in fine health. I'm just tired of her pampering you vermin, so I've relieved her of duty. I'll oversee this activity directly. Everything has become far too lax around here, and that needs to change." Keres-ma's face twisted in revulsion and shoved his tablet into the hands of his aide. "Bah, all humans look the same. Are you the headsman, Sebastian?"

Iucundum kept his face to the ground. "Ah, yes, sire. I'm here to serve you."

"Of course, you're here to serve me, you wretched fool." Keres-ma chuckled. "I require the bodies of the three humans who were arrested with the Satyr smuggler Arachne, living or dead. It doesn't matter. Just bring them here now before I catch some disease in this cursed cesspool."

"Yes, Your Excellency," Iucundum said.

"Now, you imbecile! I don't have all day."

"Right away, Your Excellency." Iucundum scuttled away hunched over.

Keres-ma nodded to his soldiers, who'd finished unloading the sleds. "I don't see what was so hard about that. One can never depend on a Roc to perform even the simplest of tasks."

A few mantichoras roared in the distance, and Keres-ma hurried back into the crawler. "Set a perimeter against the beasts. We shouldn't be long."

Dante and Tina picked up a crate of foul-smelling gruel and hurried after Iucundum. The former mining engineer waited for them just inside the gate of the stockade.

Once they arrived, Iucundum made a rough sigh. "Sire, our plan may be coming apart at the seams." He thumbed his finger in the direction of the sleds. "We may not see Otheth or any of her Rocs anymore. The magistrate has confined her whole company to their compound."

Tina sighed. "There goes all our communications. So why does Keres-ma want us?"

Iucundum snorted. "I assume he meant the two of you, plus Captain Bernius. Either dead or alive."

"That's not good for our life expectancy." Dante made a short, nervous laugh.

"He also thinks I'm Sebastian, so he definitely can't tell one human from the next." Iucundum grew thoughtful. "My guess is he doesn't want to give Setteth the excuse to hang around. From what I know about Ipis psychology, their nobility all start out fairly paranoid. Keres-ma is no exception, and he has a strong species superiority complex to go with it. With his planetary charter canceled by the empress without warning, and having a Roc imperial envoy show up looking for humans in the same week, he must see plots behind every action."

"And with us surviving his wildlife feeding game so far, we're cutting down on his entertainment," Tina added ruefully. "We'll have to adapt. If Keres-ma wants three bodies, we're not exactly short on any."

Dante grimaced at the reminder. "You're right. Several people died or were badly mauled when a mantichora caught a patrol in the open yesterday. They killed the beast but lost several troopers."

Tina gave a grim nod. "In this heat, those bodies are already decomposing in the morgue. We were planning on burying them later, but we haven't started yet. I'll bring the three most disfigured." She jogged off.

Once she was out of sight, Dante inclined his head toward Iucundum. "So, no supplies or communication with the outside world. If we complete the tunnels in time, we'll have no idea if any friendlies will greet us on the other side. Either way, we have to fight our way through a division of harpies with sticks and stones to reach the spaceport and then elude three of their warships." A groan left him. "Does that about summarize our situation?"

Iucundum's shoulders sagged. "It does indeed, sire. The odds do not favor us."

"Then we better get to work." A mischievous smile crossed Dante's face. "We're dead anyway, but thanks to Tina, we have one nasty trick to throw at them. If God has any mercy, a few people will still escape."

"Before you came, I existed but was not alive." Iucundum straightened and gestured to the stockade and the people. "You've given us hope. And while there's hope, we have life."

At this point, the two finally noticed Virgil approaching them. "I overheard bits and pieces of what you were talking about. What do we need that we don't have?" he asked.

Iucundum scratched his chin beneath his wispy gray beard. "Power. The disruptors we built aren't efficient enough. We can use the crawler we stripped to recharge their cells for a week or two, but that's about it. Then we're back to chiseling rock by hand."

Dante furrowed his brows, but when an idea hit, he snapped his fingers. "We could hook the crawler's backup generator to the windmill. Its working again and there's always a breeze here next to the ocean. We could recharge the batteries constantly with wind power."

A thin smile creased Iucundum's face. "That may actually work. It'll be slow, but it'll also be faster than working by hand."

The three stopped talking when they spotted some motion approaching the gate. There, Tina led a small procession bearing three bodies shrouded in wyvern wings.

Once the procession went through the gate, Virgil's voice turned icy. "The sooner we get payback on these assholes, the better."

* * *

In the freighter's bridge, Setteth terminated the communication link and hissed. Before Michael could ask, the elder Roc said, "That was Keres-ma. According to him, the prison headsman turned over the three bodies I asked for."

"What?" Michael cried in alarm.

Mara's visual sensors turned red and dimmed.

"I don't believe it's our friends. The magistrate said the headsman Sebastian supplied the corpses, but Otheth told me he died a month ago." Setteth fluffed her feathers. "Unfortunately, the news is still bad. I no longer have an excuse to loiter near this planet. Keres-ma wants me to pick up what I came for and leave."

Michael spread his hands. "What can we do? Otheth and her entire company have been suspended from their prison guard duty, and we don't have the lock code for this ship's power converter."

Setteth's feathers flattened. "I won't desert you. We have almost seven weeks left. I can gather a force to help us."

"Enough to take on three harpy warships?" Michael asked, gaze hopeful.

"My people are scattered. If I had a year, yes, but we don't have the luxury of time," she warbled, eyes burning. "I won't give up. I *will* return."

Michael viewed the planet through the window. "If only that idiot Arachne thought before he acted." Suddenly, however, the big clone stiffened. "Does that crap the Satyr fed us work on harpies?"

"Yes, actually. When the two parts of the syrinx drug mix with the stomach's digestive acids, it's effective on every sentient species I'm aware of." Setteth cocked her head. "Why do you ask? Do you have a plan?"

Michael slapped his fist into his hand. "As a thank you for providing the bodies, bring a meal and drink to Keres-ma's office. After he's partaken the treat, he'll give you whatever you ask for."

"Ipis are paranoid. He'll have the food and drink checked for poison," Setteth warbled. "I'd never get it past those scanners."

"I believe you may be able to." Mara rotated her sensor toward the Roc. "Beatrice scanned the same items and detected nothing harmful, only a mild intoxicant. Do not share this with her, but she is a superbly efficient machine. If the items could fool her, they will fool any other device."

"The Satyr hid the concoction in braechia ribs and ambrosia when he kidnapped Dante, Tina, and Virgil," Michael added.

"They could still catch on and execute me on the spot... but it *could* work." Setteth pawed the deck with her talons. "Lead the way to the kitchen. We have a meal to make."

Michael and Mara moved to the exit.

Setteth started after them but soon stopped short. "Do either of you know how to cook?"

Mara's sensors glowed a dull amber. "Provide the detailed formula and I can fabricate it."

Michael scratched behind his ear. "I made soup a couple of times back when Dante and I had to live in a cave. How tough can it be?"

Setteth groaned. "I'll do the cooking."

CHAPTER XXX

Out of Time

Early the following afternoon, Setteth arrived at the magistrate's building to pick up the three human corpses from Keres-ma. The barren walls glowed with the same soft blue light as the ceiling. Near the back wall, Keres-ma sat at a large desk carved from a translucent purple crystal with three built-in computer screens. No other furnishings adorned the room except for a standard military-issue conference table surrounded by twelve Ipis-style chairs in the middle. The magistrate's senior military commanders occupied four of the seats. Lined up by the table stood three gurneys, each sealed with a clear plastic shroud.

Setteth arrived with a hovering sled packed with braechia ribs and Satyr ambrosia. Upon presenting the meal to Keres-ma, she flattened her feathers and bowed low.

Keres-ma smiled, but not until after an irritated frown twitched across his face. "A generous token, Imperial Envoy, but unnecessary."

"I insist." Setteth eyed the shrouded corpses arrayed on the nearby gurneys. "Although it appears my mission was a failure, you've shown exemplary effort. Frankly, I don't know how you tolerate it here, so far from the imperial court."

Still at his desk, Keres-ma read something on the computer screen. "Exemplary, you say? I can say the same for your résumé. You've made the most of your limited non-Ipis capabilities, receiving recognition for valor from the imperium before I was born. You are a credit to your species."

He stepped out from behind the desk and drifted over to the feast next, sniffing the food and drink. "I've heard of the Satyr braechia ribs, but I've never tasted them. I usually don't go for non-Ipis food. I suppose I can make an exception this time." He checked the chemical composition of the food and beverage with his computer, but no warning alarms blared from the speakers. Keres-ma smiled at his four brigade commanders and nodded to Setteth. "Let's eat."

Setteth bowed as a precaution, quickly selected a strip of meat, and swallowed it whole. Next, she poured some ambrosia in a bowl and lapped it up. Having taken an antidote an hour earlier, she could eat her portion freely. All the better for the ruse.

At first, the five Ipis nibbled and sipped with tentative movements, but soon, they tore into the meal with a wild frenzy. Setteth warbled in relief and peeked at her chronometer. She did so again every so often, keeping at least one eye on Keres-ma and his commanders while they all ate. Over the course of twenty minutes, the Ipis officers cleared their plates and grew ever more dazed.

Once their heads lolled back and forth consistently, Setteth wiped her beak clean. "Tell me, Magistrate Keres-ma, what do you plan to do after this assignment ends?"

Keres-ma's face broke into a broad grin. "Oh, I've been planning a lo-o-ong time for something like this. The empress despises me, and the feeling's mutual. I set up an arrangement with the manager at the bi-nexidium smelting facility to pilfer half a percent of all refined products coming out of there."

Setteth loosed a caw of genuine surprise. The drug must've been working because such an illicit endeavor was punishable by death in the Ipis empire. No one in their right mind would speak of a crime like it so openly. She clamped her beak shut, trying to contain her excitement on hearing the unexpected revelation. "From this planet, such a valuable material will make any individual wealthy."

"Yes, and I have it stored in the power plant attached to this very building where I can keep an eye on it." Keres-ma cackled. "In a few days, all my co-conspirators will meet with a horrible industrial accident, and I won't have any loose ends to worry about." Worry flitted through Keres-ma as he met the gazes of his brigadier generals and Setteth. His next words came out in a whisper. "All of you will have to meet with accidents too."

Setteth cooed deep in her throat, knowing for sure it was now or never. "I fear I have one other request. I need the lock codes on the freighter the humans arrived on. I'm to take it to Bathox for an in-depth inspection."

Keres-ma shook his head as if trying to clear it. "A number of ships currently impounded arrived with human prisoners. I don't know which one's the correct cipherlock for yours."

"Then may I see all the codes? I can determine the correct vessel from there," Setteth cooed.

Keres-ma's eyes bulged, showing surprise and then a dull rage, but neither emotion stayed for long. He scanned the computer tablet beside him and pressed an icon. A few seconds later, he slid a memory chip to the old Roc, his arm trembling the whole way. "Here it is. Every cipherlock and security clearance key for impounded ships," he muttered.

"Thank you, magistrate." Setteth took the chip and bowed. "I know you're very busy, so I'll take my leave now."

Keres-ma flopped face first onto the table. His commanders followed suit, so the elder Roc wasted no time in leaving with the human bodies.

Setteth forced herself to walk casually through the administration center, clutching the memory chip with the access codes. Without a clue of how long the Satyr drug would hold Keres-ma, Setteth would need as much time as possible to filter through the batch of codes downloaded onto the memory chip. If not, she'd have to let Mara sort through them.

Setteth showed her clearance codes at two separate checkpoints before the guards let her exit the administration center. Both times, disinterested guards inspected the corpses on the self-propelled gurneys. She didn't let herself breathe easy until the guards stored the bodies on her warbird and cleared her for takeoff.

Setteth leaped into the cockpit and didn't look back.

* * *

An hour later, the elder Roc docked her warbird in the freighter's hangar bay. Once the hangar activated life support, the door connecting it to the rest of the freighter opened. Michael and Mara strode through.

Michael greeted Setteth by waving his arms, but he looked grim. "Any luck?"

Setteth leapt from the warbird and onto the hangar's floor, wobbling somewhat from the impact due to her age. She lifted the memory chip in the air and cawed in triumph. "Once he started talking, I couldn't get the magistrate to shut up. But rest assured, I retrieved the access codes for every vessel in orbit around this planet."

Michael's face broke into a broad grin. "The bastard won't be very happy when he comes to."

Setteth clucked her beak. "I would've loved to wrap my talons around his scrawny throat, but that wouldn't have helped our escape. At any rate, the Satyr drug made Keres-ma say some interesting things. He despises anyone who's not Ipis, and neither does he care much for the empress. Now let's take this data to the control room."

Michael slapped the Roc on the back between her wings. "You're a marvel."

Unfortunately, their merriment didn't last. They hadn't taken two steps when Reggie spoke with urgency over the ship's speaker system. "Setteth, the planetary magistrate is scrambling interceptors."

Setteth huffed. "I thought we'd have more time. Michael, we must leave now. Mara can bring the security codes to Reggie, and he can break the locks."

However, the big clone squared his shoulders. "I can't. My friends are down there. The damn harpies know you're here, so you must go, but I'm staying." He chuckled. "They'll be so busy chasing you, they'll forget about this derelict freighter."

"That'd be good, actually." Setteth fluffed her feathers and handed Michael the memory chip. "Stay alive, my friend. Expect me seven weeks from now."

"I know you'll return." Michael patted her on the back again. "And when you do, this ship will be ready and waiting. I promise."

He trotted beside Setteth in silence as she hurried to her warbird. She tried to pass on what she knew of Ipis ship inspection protocols, but they didn't have enough time for her to say much.

Michael nodded as he absorbed what info the Roc *could* share. "I'll be fine. Just take care of yourself, and come back with those warbirds."

"I will, my friend. I will," Setteth cried.

Michael stayed by the hangar's entrance while Setteth jumped into her warbird. The moment the lights of the small craft activated, a door separated everything in the hangar from the big clone. The hangar opened up to space, and the warbird zipped through it.

Michael returned to the bridge and bolted to the nearest view screen. The warbird shot away, eluding two fighters by spiraling past their lasers, and jumped into hyperspace. For a brief moment, Michael felt relief at witnessing Setteth's escape.

The big clone then gulped as a dreadful sight headed toward the freighter: an Ipis shuttle escorted by two fighters. "I guess I underestimated their interest in this ship. Reggie, do you remember how to tell a lie?"

"Yes," came the reply.

"Good, because you'll need to be convincing." Michael breathed deep. "Dis-AI, I command you to remain silent and provide no data until I personally override that order."

"Yes, human master. I must comply," a flat monotone from a deeper voice said.

"Reggie, delete all references to our presence. Intercept and respond to all requests sent to the Dis-AI."

"That will be pleasant," Reggie replied. "I suggest you hide in bay one's cargo hold A7. You will find a hidden compartment with a shield there. It gives you the highest probability of avoiding detection."

"Thanks, Reggie. How about Mara?"

As if on cue, Mara entered the bridge, sensor lights flashing gold. "We already conferred and determined that I will subvert my independent thinking during this threat and act as one of Reggie's twenty-three drones."

With that settled, Michael made his way to the hidden compartment. From the bridge, it was a quick trip down four levels on a simple gantry ladder. Hold A7 housed a mishmash of small crates and barrels containing pens for livestock transport. Although empty, many years of holding exotic animals left a choking stench. The hidden compartment proved little more than a closet-sized cubby along the outer hull, disguised as a charging station for stall-cleaning tools. The station also confused any photonic scanners and hid the entrance's seams.

Michael pressed the OFF switch on two power vacs, and the door swung open in complete silence. Although big enough to squeeze a Centaur in, the ceiling didn't quite reach two meters and thus forced his head down. It would be a cramped fit for one of Michael's size. He could only hope the harpy soldiers wouldn't stay long.

He squeezed in.

* * *

Quango stood with Otheth in the Roc compound's barren subbasement. At the far end of the room, the three young clones showed thirteen attentive Rocs how to cut through stone with laser tools. A musty smell accompanied damp walls and a low ceiling, but each stretched far in the expansive area. The Rocs made no use of it as they held a natural disdain for underground environments.

Tugging his goatee, the old Satyr examined the smooth, slate-gray stone walls. "I'm guessing we need to go another four and a half meters down before we can start tunneling toward the prison wall."

"This will be difficult," Otheth warbled. "Keres-ma has everyone not in his personal command quarantined. He's been in a snit since yesterday after Setteth drugged him and escaped with an unknown information download."

"Does he suspect you?" Quango's face grew long.

Otheth chuckled. "One advantage we have in dealing with the Ipis-ma superiority complex is that Keres-ma would never believe he was tricked by a lesser being. He's convinced Setteth is an imperial spy with explicit instructions to acquire information that will discredit Keres-ma in the royal court." She wiggled the fingers on her frail arms. "As for helping you tunnel, we'll help however we can, but Rocs aren't built for digging mine shafts."

Quango grunted. "You worry about handling the division of Ipis soldiers armed to their pointy little teeth. My human lads and I will do the digging."

Porthos kicked at the shale footing. "I still think we ought to shoot our way in. This looks like a lot of work."

Quango shook his head and took a reading with a scanner. Afterward, he whipped out a laser etcher and drew an arrow on the stone floor. "The ramp will start here." He nodded to Porthos, who held a laser cutter. "You go first."

* * *

Throughout the next six weeks, Dante directed the construction of the tunnel toward the Roc compound. He contributed to the digging where he could, fighting through the dampness and stifling heat of the tunnel. He was proud of the progress they made as he mopped his brow, hoping it would be enough.

Dante and Iucundum worked their way along 125 meters of completed tunnel. They both began sweating profusely before they covered half that distance due to the sweltering, still air underground. Given the simple power tools they now worked with, the prisoners had achieved quite an engineering marvel. The tunnel stretched wide enough for two Centaurs to squeeze past each other, and a Roc could almost walk erect. Every three meters, hardwood beams braced the damp walls and ceiling. Tiny photonic lights provided dim illumination through the length of the passage.

When Dante neared the current work area, he drew the attention of five grime-covered human miners digging there. They stopped long enough to greet him.

One miner stepped back, wiped his brow, and swallowed tepid water from his canteen. "Sire, I think we're getting too close to the surface. I've worked in this shaft for six weeks now, and this is the first time I've heard voices."

"Really?" Dante stepped through water a couple centimeters deep and pressed his ear against the tunnel wall.

Iucundum came up behind him. "Don't be a fool. Look at the seepage. If we were sloping up, the water wouldn't pool in like this."

"I don't hear anything," Dante said. "By our best calculations, we're still fifteen meters from the Roc compound."

A new sound silenced everyone. A dull *thunk*, followed by a muffled curse penetrated the tunnel wall.

Iucundum turned ashen. "There shouldn't have been anything here. We'll have to dig in a different direction."

Dante, however, thought something sounded familiar about the muffled voice. "I'll be damned. I haven't heard *that* voice in months." A grin etched his dirt-smeared face, and he pointed to the wall. "Everyone, dig in this direction. I think we're almost done." He turned to one of the miners. "Bring Virgil up. He's back at the one-hundred-meter mark, helping with the water seepage."

The miners resumed digging, this time with Dante and Iucundum helping out. From the other side, the muffled voices grew more distinct. And with the greater distinction, Dante knew for sure who they'd meet on the other side.

It took digging for a while longer, but eventually two voices yelped in unison as the tunnel wall crashed to the floor. Dante poked his head through and smiled wide. Three meters from the new hole, a pair of familiar young clones raised their laser tools in self-defense.

A moment later, the two clones lowered their weapons. Porthos outright dropped his tool. "Dante?"

"Hi, Porthos." Dante readily recognized the tall, half-naked clone with the jagged scar across his sweating chest. He crawled through the hole, and soon the young clone crushed him in a bear hug.

"I never gave up hope," Porthos sobbed. "I knew we'd find you. Are the Cap'n and Doctor Tina okay too?"

At this point, Virgil pushed his way through the hole. "We are now. Ready for some visitors?"

Dante and Virgil were soon joined by Iucundum and the five-man mining crew through the hole. The noise brought Aramis, Quango, and six Roc soldiers charging in, holding their digging tools as weapons. It took a moment for their surprise and trepidation to calm.

But calm, they did, and more dirt-covered humans made their way through the hole in the wall. Some laughed, while others cried.

With his arm draped around Dante, Porthos waved to the Satyr. "Quango, I'd like you to meet the king of all us humans."

Dante stepped forward and shook the callous hand of the old Satyr. "It's good to meet you. I'm Dante Carloman."

Quango shook it in the human manner, and his posture relaxed. "What you've accomplished here so far is a miracle. You're everything these boys have said you were. Now let's get *all* of you the hell outta here." He stepped back and bowed to Dante. "Sire, by my mother's twisted beard, this is a day we've been looking forward to for many weeks." He turned to the Roc soldier beside him. "Better summon Oteth. It's time to start phase two."

* * *

A week after the tunneling had reached the Roc mercenary compound, Dante called a meeting there. The conference room Setteth had earlier commandeered transformed into the logistics hub for the escape plan. Otheth had collected all the intelligence she could uncover about the Ipis-ma positions. With everything ready to start the next phase of the plan, Dante summoned Quango, Iucundum, Otheth, Arachne, Calahas, Tina, and Virgil to review the details. Octavia came with them to inventory what the Rocs had available with the aid of the three clones.

Everyone sat in the comfort of the cooled conference room. A large, holographic view screen shined in the center of the meeting room's conference table. The 3D display map marked the locations of their tunnels, as well as the placement of all significant Ipis-ma military units and gun placements over the area. The human sanctuary in the prison, although three hundred meters southwest from where everyone sat, felt like another world. The Ipis administration center stood a hundred meters east, and the nearest spaceport entrance rested sixteen hundred meters north.

Dante studied the map for a long while, then drew a line with his finger from the third storeroom near the tall prison wall, which was northeast of the Ipis magistrate's building.

"I think we're ready," he declared. "The end of Tunnel B is now three meters below the center to the harpy's power plant."

Tina rose and tapped the image of the Roc mercenary compound, situated directly north of the same storeroom. "Tunnel A is holding up. We've finished transporting all the children and infirmed here from the prison."

Otheth cawed with some amount of irritation. "Do human children ever stand still? This building is packed, and they scamper everywhere regardless of the danger."

"Sorry," Tina responded. "Everyone's working. I'll assign a few more adults to supervise them."

"Even if all goes well, we have a logistics nightmare." Iucundum gestured to the map. "Aboveground, we'll be fully exposed for the entire distance to the spaceport. The closest point to the spaceport is the military entrance. The civilian terminal is another half kilometer further north."

"I've made some modifications to the computer control system for the city's public transport network," Quango announced. "All fifty of the automated surface buses will circle this block when we make our move. They seat about forty humans, but I figure we can squeeze at least another twenty into each. That should handle everyone who can't run."

Dante shook his head but smiled. "You're a genius, Quango. Remind me to never get on your bad side."

Quango tugged his goatee. "Just working with what's available. You're no slouch in the weird idea department yourself."

Nearby, crates holding tools and supplies lay strewn about everywhere. Aramis, Porthos, and Athos stacked the gear along the back wall while Octavia inventoried it all on a digital tablet.

Quango studied the holographic map of the tunnels, as well as a 3D cutaway image of the Ipis complex above it. "How many tons of explosives were used at this Petersburg battle you spoke of?"

Virgil paced the length of the crowded conference room before letting out a sigh. "Close to four tons of black powder."

Iucundum squirmed uncomfortably on a Roc-style nested chair. His finger tapped the holographic model showing a layout of the Ipis-ma military compound adjacent to the magistrate's building. "We have another ton planted here." He moved his finger from one of the prison storerooms to the middle of the magistrate's building. "We ran into a string of vertical metal tubes here. We couldn't determine their composition and didn't dare cut through them for fear of tripping the alarms."

"Actually, it's good you didn't try it," Otheth said. "This entire city is powered by geothermal energy. Those rods you reached extend to the magma levels of this planet. You would've been incinerated if you breeched those pipes."

Alarmed, Dante shot up. "So, if our explosion ruptures those tubes, we'll have a volcanic eruption?"

Iucundum scoffed. "The power plant here was built with the unstable nature of this world in mind. It has failsafe after failsafe built in. Why, it would take a fusion reaction to create the kind of calamity you're talking about. A few tons of chemical explosives could never achieve that."

"Okay," Dante said, "but what if our explosion causes a cave in?"

Iucundum grunted. "That's a real problem." He pointed to a spot halfway between the evacuation tunnel and the one extending to the harpy compound. "We'll set timers to detonate the explosives and seal the tunnel. We don't want anyone near the area when the black powder blows, and this should give us tons of solid rock for protection."

Dante quirked an eyebrow. "And if that fails?"

Iucundum shrugged. "Then we're screwed."

"Not good enough," Dante replied with an even voice. "We need a Plan B."

Otheth cocked her head and moved to the map. "If the barriers along the cliff were out of commission, we could extend a rope bridge to where those cliffs go narrow by the barrier wall. It would be risky, though. Anyone on that span would make an easy target for anyone on the wall above."

Dante tapped the six-meter gap between the cliffs on either side of the western end of the barrier wall. "We already have plans for going over and under that wall. Why not go around it?" He turned to Iucundum. "Pull together the materials to assemble the rope bridge as a backup."

Iucundum bowed. "As you wish, sire. With the energy fields shut down, it should be possible."

A little more relieved, Dante sat back. "It all comes down to those energy barriers, so let's talk about shutting those suckers down. Those rods are directly linked to the power turbines, right?"

Otheth cocked her head. "Yes. And the magma layer."

"So, we don't want to damage the rods." Dante studied the map. "We have an open path straight to their generators. We wreak *that* system. It'll shut down the city's power grid."

Quango expanded the view of the power plant and squinted. "If we hit them with a blast strong enough and knock those rotor blades out of balance, they'd rip themselves apart. It'd take a week to get the grid back online."

Otheth cawed. "Given the energy output of this black powder, you'll need four times the amount of what you have in place to dislodge those reinforced composites. It was built to withstand a level eight quake." She ruffled her feathers. "We delivered almost two tons of sodium nitrate before we were cut off. What happened to the rest?"

Virgil smiled, reached into a satchel he wore over his shoulder, and lifted a clay ball with a protruding fuse. "I think we put it to good use."

Otheth cawed with admiration. "Ingenious. A chemical-based energy weapon. The scanners never detected the sodium nitrate as a risk because it isn't one until combined with charcoal and sulfur. But will it work against the Ipis energy shields?"

"It must be almost two years now since we used something like this before." Virgil eyed Dante and Tina for confirmation. They both shrugged, having lost track of time long ago.

"Anyway, we tangled with a brigade of harpies in a place called New York when they captured us on Earth. Grenade explosions overloaded their shielding temporarily." Looking grim, Virgil patted the bow lying across his lap. "We didn't know how to fight them then, but if their shields go down for even a few seconds, I'll have all I need."

Quango gave his goatee another tug. "We'll have to acquire more black powder. There's a healthy black market in the city, but those dealers tend to talk. Word will leak back to Carcerem's security at some point. I can nab you a couple more tons of that chemical, but we'll have to use it soon. Some bright Ipis will eventually figure out what that stuff can do." He grew thoughtful. "Now that we have a direct access route, most of what you need can be delivered here, right under Keres-ma's snout."

Thus far, Arachne had sat alone in silence in a corner of the room. Now, though, he asked, "How much time do we have?"

Otheth looked at her chronometer. "About six days. Setteth knows that the Ipis-ma will be relieved by Imperials in thirteen days, so she'll return days before then."

Arachne groaned. "Can we trust her? We'll all be vaporized if she doesn't show up with a massive fleet. There's an Enforcer and two Strikers supported by a fleet of tactical fighters in orbit. We'll go nowhere until something deals with them."

Otheth's feathers flared. "Setteth is a Roc, and Rocs always honor their word, unlike many other species."

Arachne rose and squared his shoulders. "Some of us do have much to be ashamed of, and only action can wipe away the stain." He met the Roc's eyes. "But it's not fear or cowardice for me to remind everyone that this is *not* going to be some stealthy escape. We have to move close to thirty thousand people. If we don't neutralize the threat, we'll have a mass slaughter on our hands. The Ipis will pick off the transports before we can power on their engines."

"She will come," Otheth said firmly. "Let me check with the human she came in with, Michael. The communication scrambler Quango made allows us to contact orbital vessels without going through the Ipis uplink."

Quango made a rough grunt. "That's *my* ship impounded up there. I know the work-arounds. The modification's not perfect, but the signal should be untraceable for short bursts."

"We'll find out." Otheth toggled her communicator on the modified communicator. "Michael? Reggie? Are you there?"

From the other side of the room, Tina went still and teary-eyed. "Reggie?"

"Hello, Tina," a voice from the communicator said. "I recognize your voice. It is recorded in my data banks. However, I am not the Reggie you knew. I am but a partial memory of Reggie embedded in an artificial intelligence system. Here is Michael."

"Hello," a new voice Dante knew well said.

"Michael, I'm glad you're here. This is like old times."

Virgil let out a laugh. "Hey, Mick. It's good to hear your voice. How's my favorite big ugly?"

Michael's voice turned indignant. "Virgil, my name is Michael, not Mick, and I'm not a big ugly. Oh, never mind. Tell me again why I came halfway across the galaxy to rescue you?"

"Don't take any of my teasing hard." Virgil sobered. "You're my brother."

Athos slouched against a back wall and nudged Porthos. "The Cap'n called the Eldest Mick."

Porthos giggled. "And a big ugly."

Aramis grunted in satisfaction. "We got the Eldest and the Cap'n together with Quango. I think the freaking harpies better watch out."

Porthos patted his podmates on the shoulders. "As the Cap'n likes to say, we're about to open a can of whoop-ass."

When Otheth asked about Setteth, concern seeped into Michael's voice. "I haven't received any communications from Setteth for a couple weeks. In her last video note, she was worried about the size of the force she could assemble. She said whatever we come up with for extracting people from Carcerem will need to be fast."

"We are being scanned again," Reggie interrupted. "Communication terminating."

The crackles from the communicator's speaker cut out. Otheth switched the unit off and fluffed her feathers. "Warbirds are a poor match against Strikers in deep space, and they're completely outclassed by Enforcers."

Dante stood and pointed to the display of the power plant generators. "Otheth, if we blow up four tons of black powder beneath the center of their energy grid, will it be enough?"

The Roc warbled. "You couldn't ask for a better location. Even if some bright engineer shut down the generator before the ruptured turbine blades caused any damage, the whole system will shut down for at least a day."

Dante slid his finger to another spot and tapped the image of a block-shaped building on the northern side of the Ipis fortress. "Is this the armory?"

Otheth snorted. "Yes, but it's unassailable. An automated ion disruptor battery sits atop to defend against sky assaults, and a battalion of heavy infantry are stationed on the ground below."

Dante turned to Virgil. "How many fighters do you have in your militia?"

"I have a full brigade—over four thousand fighters itching for a shot at the damn harpies." A glint lit Virgil's eyes. "I see your idea. We've been training with the ladders and grappling hooks and are ready to go." He drew closer to the map. "When we detonate that bomb, not only will it crash the power grid, but it'll blow a hole in their roof. My team will climb over the northern prison wall and hit the arsenal from the inside. There'll only be a few armory guards, and they'll be too shocked from the explosion to mount much resistance."

Dante looked over at the gnarled Satyr. "Quango, how good is the black market here?"

"Ya can get just about anything for a price." The Satyr raised an eyebrow. "What do ya need?"

"Fake papers for people to enter the spaceport," Dante answered.

Quango snorted. "Thirty thousand fake passes for mostly humans? I may be a miracle worker, but that's impossible."

"No, but counting Otheth's people, we have about a thousand non-humans. Can we get *them* inside the spaceport without raising alarms?"

"Yeah, that number isn't a big problem. The miners and smelters move in and out all the time. But what's the point? That's only a small fraction of what we have. And by my mother's twisted beard, I'm not leaving without you."

"This is what I'm thinking." Dante drew a line from the Roc compound to the nearest gate of the spaceport. "We sneak all our pilots and as many soldiers as we can inside the gates. As soon as trouble starts, Keres-ma will scramble whatever tactical fighters he has at his disposal. We need to sabotage those fighters and open the gate, and then we need to seize every ship that can reach orbit."

"Is that *all*?" Quango sputtered, slumping onto a crate. "How many pilots do you have?"

Iucundum skimmed his tablet. "Ten, but only four aren't humans."

"Seven of my Rocs are qualified dropship pilots," Otheth added.

"I can fly in a pinch," Quango grumbled. "Look, the average shuttle can lift about two hundred people at a time. Each pilot would have to make at least twelve trips."

Otheth cocked her head. "My flock ship was built to carry a battalion of Rocs, That's about five hundred. I'd wager we could squeeze seven hundred humans in there."

"I'd like to point out the obvious," Quango said. "Keres-ma's not going to just sit on his bony ass while we pull this off."

"I'm well aware of what the harpies have and what they'll try to do." Dante stared at the holograph. "I know we're totally outgunned and looking at a bloodbath." He pounded the table. "But I'll be damned if we don't save as many as we can."

Octavia looked up from her checklist. "Give me a ship. There's nothing I can't fly." She jerked her head toward Arachne. "I learned from the best."

"But you're human. You'd never get..." Quango looked over the petite woman and tugged his goatee. "Actually, you're small for a human. I wonder how you'd look with horns and a beard?"

A smirk broke onto Octavia's face. "I'll grow a beak and sprout feathers if it means I can strike back at the harpies."

Quango huffed and regarded Otheth. "Do you buy into this insane plan?"

"With my whole heart," the Roc crowed, feathers out. "My people have access to the military side of the port. Not a single Ipis airship will leave the ground."

Calahas pawed the floor and raised himself on his hindquarters. "I live to serve my new king. My group will hold the gates until the last captive has escaped."

"Anything else?" Dante waited for anyone to offer dissent.

Instead, silence answered.

Dante nodded. "Good. I want detailed plans by this evening. We'll meet again then. Let's get to work, people. There's a lot to do and not much time."

CHAPTER XXXI

It Begins

For the fifth time in the last six days, a harpy patrol passed by Michael's concealed crawl space while inspecting the cargo bay. Michael tensed, listening to every sound until things fell quiet. Unsure if the latest patrol had left, he decided to wait a few more minutes before moving.

In the meantime, he drew his communicator close and spoke in a whisper. "Reggie, Setteth's been gone seven weeks and a day. She should've returned yesterday, and there's no sign of her. Something might've gone wrong. I tell you those sneaky little gargoyles suspect something."

Reggie responded, sounding concerned. "It is my transmissions. Every communication with the planet's surface is detected by the control tower monitors. The probability that I can continue obscuring the signal source has dropped below fifty percent."

"Their shuttle is right here," Mara cut in. "They parked almost on top of me and left no guards."

"So they must be in Cargo Bay One with you. That's right below my location." An idea struck, and Michael pursed his lips. "Reggie, there's nothing more I can do here. I'm going to sneak onto their shuttle and try to sabotage their mother ship."

"Your probability of success is nine-point-four percent. Your probability of survival is—"

"He will not go alone," Mara said. "Setteth provided Michael with the cipherlock codes for every ship in orbit around this planet, and I can give him a direct computer link."

Something shook in Reggie's voice. "You will die if you go."

"And if I stay?"

"You will die. Michael, Mara, good fortune to you. Please come back."

"Thank you, Reggie. Make sure this ship is ready to move." Michael drew in a deep breath and cracked open the disguised shelter door. Seeing a clear path, and no intruders, the big clone opened the door further.

With stealth no natural-born human could match, he slipped out of the hidden compartment and moved down the gangway to the level below.

He crouched at the ladder's base for a second, scrutinizing every nook of the hangar. As Mara had said, she alone hovered by an unfamiliar shuttle. Furthermore, the portal leading into the harpy shuttle lay wide open.

Michael sprinted to Mara and followed her into the shuttle's small storage room. Mara concealed him behind a stack of heavy, unmarked crates. She went on to attach herself magnetically to the ceiling before powering down, leaving only passive sensors operating.

Two hours later, twenty Ipis-ma soldiers boarded the shuttle and departed from the freighter, flying to the enormous Enforcer-class cruiser.

* * *

In the days since the big meeting, Keres-ma developed a new game for his entertainment when his crew delivered daily rations. The Ipis-ma leader trained his ion disruptor on several structures the human prisoners had built during their stay. First, he took out the drawbridge. Next, he shot out the watchtower's supports, laughing as it fell. Now, he vaporized the stockade's windmill before leaving.

Having watched from atop the walls of the fort, Dante gritted his teeth at the new set of ruins. With the tunnel complete, Otheth had provided the prisoners with a variety of electronic tools to aid in communications and coordination. But the prisoners had to be careful not to show any of that outside of the tunnels until the escape was underway.

He descended from the wall with Virgil. Below, various people rolled barrels of water and gruel through the smoldering entrance over a pair of wide planks.

Virgil followed Dante, clenching a clay orb. "Our zookeeper's leaving already? Guess Keres-ma got bored with his game." He returned the grenade to his satchel. "I wish I could shove one of these things down his throat and light it."

Dante's shoulders sagged. "We need to change our plans. We're out of—"

"Dante," shouted a familiar voice.

Turning, he spotted Iucundum running toward him while waving his headphone set. The elder man gasped for breath upon coming to a halt. "Sire, we just received word from Reggie. Setteth has entered this solar system, leading forty Roc warbirds."

Dante paled. Setteth was two days overdue and couldn't find more than forty fighters to help them? "Only forty. That's suicide with the firepower they'll be up against."

"Then we better use the time we have," a grim Virgil noted. "Is it a go?"

Dante bared his teeth. "Are all the explosives in place?"

"We set the final keg in place late last night," Iucundum replied.

Dante checked the chronometer he had tucked inside his tunic. "Iucundum, evacuate the tunnels and pass the word to Otheth and the others in the Roc compound. Detonate all planted explosions at eleven hundred standard time. That's an hour from now. Virg, get your troops ready with the ladders and load the ballistae with the grappling hooks." He grabbed Iucundum by the shoulder. "Tell Tina to wait until the explosives go off before she starts moving people from the Roc compound to the spaceport. And... tell her I love her. Tell her don't look back. No matter what."

"Sire, it's a good plan. It will succeed." Iucundum bowed low.

Dante looked over at the thick stone and packed dirt palisade. The warriors manning it brandished spears and bows. When Dante looked in their direction, they all raised their primitive weapons in the air.

He raised his wyvern-horn sword and shouted so his voice carried across the bailey. "Everyone, you know your jobs. With the grace of God, we will succeed. Now move!"

Virgil and Iucundum hurried to pass on the orders to their subcommanders. The enclosure soon teemed with people rushing back and forth. The tension in the crowd felt almost palpable from where Dante stood.

"I guess it's time to say goodbye to our little sanctuary in hell," he remarked.

The civilians who hadn't yet made the trek to the Roc mercenary compound lined up in preassigned groups outside the storeroom containing the tunnel entrance. The militia coalesced into their companies. Determined men and women stood poised at their stations. Witnessing all this firsthand gave rise to a strong sense of pride within Dante.

He rolled over the plan's details in his mind and shuddered. Even if all went perfectly, the potential carnage among his followers, armed with but the simplest of weapons, could cost them all they'd fought for so far. It could cost them everything.

But they had nothing left to do but try.

* * *

Twenty minutes later, the ground shook. A few seconds after that, it rocked violently, and a column of smoke rose high in the air, spreading over the Ipis military complex. The ground continued to quake after the effects of the explosions subsided.

Dante steadied himself. The quaking went on longer still, to the point where he wondered if this were normal for mass explosions. The rising black smoke turned red, taking on the appearance of a fist pointed to the heavens. The blue glow of the walls flickered and went out.

"Go! Go! Go!" Virgil shouted.

The militia soldiers uncovered five ballistae they'd concealed under tarps on the school roof. Moments later, they flung preloaded heavy projectiles over the eastern wall. Long corded ropes unwound behind them. Using those lines, humans scaled the wall carrying grappling hooks and more rope. Other crews connected the various ladder sections laid out on the infirmary roof. A dozen long ladders soon slammed against the wall, and lines of militia clambered up them.

Dante moved to the tunnel when Iucundum pushed his way through the crowd from the storeroom. Seeing the engineer's scorched clothes set Dante on edge. What had gone wrong?

"Sire, our explosion must have interacted with some refined bi-nexidium. What kind of idiot would store unstable material in a power plant?" Iucundum shuddered. "A fusion reaction was impossible, but the chain reaction blast was still at least fifty times more powerful than what we planned for. Several points in our escape tunnel have collapsed, and lava's filling in. Many people were caught down there." The old mining engineer gasped for breath. "The bi-nexidium detonation must've split open a fissure below us. We can't get out that way. We're trapped."

For a moment, Dante could only stare, all thoughts stopping short. Catching sight of the militia's ropes snapped him back into focus soon after as they brought to mind the main contingency plan. Dante pointed to the northwest corner of the prison. "Plan B. The shields are down, so we'll go around the wall near the cliff. Iucundum, bring your bridge over."

Iucundum eyed the darkened poles by the cliff and the wide gap around the edge of the northern wall. "Sire, it's stacked by the granary. We'll have it in place and anchored in ten minutes. Bridge team, move!"

His shout brought the panicking civilians nearby into an organized group. Within the time promised, the plank bridge went over the sheer cliff to freedom, and the mass of refugees filed across to the other side of the depowered prison wall.

Iucundum gripped the headset and approached Dante. "Sire, Calahas reports they took heavy causalities, but his teams now control the spaceport gates. Otheth and her troops successfully infiltrated the military section of the spaceport and captured a weapons store. Ipis base personnel are pinned down for the moment. Doctor Phokas reached the spaceport with the first group of humans. She's directing the refugees to the seized shuttles."

Hearing the last bit, Dante let out a big breath. "Virgil? Setteth?"

"No word from either of them yet. The last I heard—"

A series of explosions on the other side of the stockade entrance cut the conversation. Dante cursed under his breath. "Now what? There shouldn't be anything going on over there!"

From a post above the ruined drawbridge, Cilla sprinted to Dante. "Sire, why haven't you left?"

"I'm responsible for coordinating the evacuation, and I can't leave yet," Dante replied. "Tunnel's gone, and going around's taking a lot longer." He gestured to the wall, where the ropes and ladders hung without any militia climbing them. The sound of grenades exploding in the distance indicated they'd engaged in fighting already. Only a few companies of fighters remained to guard the stockade walls.

"Well, you must leave now," Cilla said. "Keres-ma came back through the gate with soldiers, and even for an Ipis, he looks angry. The landmines we planted stopped them for the moment, but they're sweeping the ground with disruptors. After that, all we'll have are grenades and arrows."

Dante eyed the crowd working their way to the bridge. "Shit. We need more time. Move the ballistae to that side and launch some powder kegs at those bastards. That'll slow 'em for a while."

"Sire," Iucundum cut in, "I don't think the lava's staying belowground." He nudged Dante and pointed to the warehouse. Smoke trickled from its narrow windows before the door burst into flame.

Dante grabbed Cilla by the shoulders and pointed to the empty ladders. "Throw whatever you have at Keres-ma and then get the hell out of here."

Cilla nodded as the first glowing tongue of magma slid out of the now burning storehouse. Cilla bolted to the stockade.

* * *

Virgil scaled the ladders first and rushed to the wall lining the road connecting the administration building to the prison. In normal times, it proved an effective barrier against any trespassing. With the power out, however, it now provided a convenient path to circumventing the automated gun turrets on the ground level. His men secured grappling hooks, and ropes dangled from the roof of the magistrate's building.

Gagging on the smoke and ash, he raced along the roof until he reached a gaping hole blown in the fortress roof over the remains of the power plant. However, the recon team blazing the trail so far milled about in confusion.

On reaching their position, Virgil discovered why they hesitated. Molten rock oozed from a crater nine meters below him. What was once an expansive room with high-tech turbines now hosted a bubbling cauldron. Lava spilled through exposed hallways leading from the generators.

He studied the undamaged portions of the roof they stood on and unslung his bow. The rest of the militia stacked up behind him. If they didn't seize the arsenal, it'd make for the shortest offensive in history.

A few harpies staggered away from the lava. None looked up yet and noticed Virgil and his troops. Thinking fast, he crab-walked along the edge and waved his command to follow him toward the armory beneath the northern wall.

Once past the torrid gap, they reached a solid portion of the roof. Virgil sprinted to the destination. Hundreds of footsteps behind him confirmed that his command had also gone through. As he reached the ceiling over the armory, Virgil signaled the men armed with the disruptor swords, mere mining tools a day earlier, to start cutting the roof.

The long line of militia crouched, but they were still exposed on the high walls. Individual harpy soldiers below spotted them at last and opened fire. As the energy beams found targets, bloodcurdling screams followed the high-pitched whines.

Virgil cursed as an Ipis commander hurried over to see what his troops shot at. The commander soon appeared to realize what the escaping prisoners were attempting. One shrill scream of an order and the guards disengaged from the attack and followed the commander to the armory.

At the same time, the miners cut through the roof and lowered ropes. Virgil dropped inside and seized a weapon from the nearest rack. At the same moment the door burst in, he opened fire.

At first, twelve ion disruptors responded to the Ipis attack. Within seconds, twelve grew to hundreds. Within minutes, the entire company of harpies lay dead. The air stank of gore and ozone from the fusillade of the energy guns.

Virgil's battalion commanders gathered around him. To the south, the lava breeched the barrier separating the motor pool from the Ipis division's parade ground.

Virgil pointed north. "First and second battalions, reinforce Otheth at the spaceport. Third and fourth battalions, you're with me. Set the powder kegs. We take what we can from this complex and destroy everything else. Let's see how well these assholes fight without weapons. Move!"

* * *

The harpy shuttle eventually parked in the Enforcer's hangar bay. Michael bided his time until he felt safe enough to sneak out. Fortunately, a lone harpy guard stood between the shuttle and the rest of the Enforcer, a lone guard with his back to the shuttle and its stowaways.

Michael crept up behind the unsuspecting guard and snapped his neck. He stripped the soldier of his sidearm and communicator. The clone, bred to kill, scanned the cavernous area under the garish blue ceiling lights for another target. He detected no movement, and Mara detected no one coming either. The place stank of harpies regardless.

Michael kicked the guard's body. "Wasn't your lucky day, shithead."

"We are supposed to be stealthy," Mara scolded.

"I'll hide the body in the shuttle. Just find a data port you can link into," Michael retorted.

He needed only about a minute to stash the guard's body in the shuttle's storage room. From there, he met with Mara again. No harpies had entered the hangar in the meantime.

"Follow me." Mara glided across the vacant hangar floor to the far wall. "This combat vessel is staffed for interdiction. They will have a supplemental crew for boarding and inspections. We must remain in this locale."

Moving along the walls, she inspected the rooms and appeared satisfied with the third door she entered. Though no bigger than a closet, the room contained a desk with a single display screen, several data ports, and a touchpad.

Michael slipped in behind her and shut the door. "Seal the door as best you can." He plugged the memory chip into a port. "Mara, access this ship's operating system. Now we'll see how good these codes are."

* * *

Setteth's fighter shot past the Ipis warships, weapons blazing, and dove into Carcerem's gravity well. Her warbird fleet followed in a V-formation. While the two Striker frigates could follow her into the atmosphere with ease, the Enforcer could not.

The Ipis admiral reacted faster than the old Roc expected. Several tactical fighters launched from the Strikers and gave chase. The warbirds split into two different squadrons and vanished beneath the cloud level.

Setteth flew off alone. As an accomplished fighter pilot, Setteth figured any enemy craft she could draw away from her main force would help. The other Roc pilots were elite fighters and had trained together a long time, so they could handle themselves with fewer enemies on their backs.

A pair of Ipis fighters soon tried to lock on to her warbird. Curious as to how skilled the two fighters were, the old Roc sped low to the ground.

She headed for the planet's south pole, where a blizzard raged with gale force winds. The radiation from the ore in the bi-nexidium mines there scrambled even military-grade photonic guidance systems. Here, one would have to fly by instinct—a technique Setteth knew all too well.

Juking left, she did a barrel roll and fired her disruptor cannons. Twin explosions followed in her wake as she flew above the storm, searching for another opponent.

As she thought, the Ipis fighters were no match for a warbird. Unfortunately, her warbird was no match for a Striker-class frigate, and now one of them descended from its orbit. If the Strikers weren't dealt with soon, Setteth's forces would have no hope of aiding the refugees.

However, dealing with the Strikers would have to wait. One of her young Order of the Dragon pilots flew by with an Ipis fighter in pursuit. Setteth let out a soft hoot, but her blood raced. Here, now, she participated in a day of glory. A day of death. A Roc day.

Feathers flaring, she dove to attack.

* * *

Before a lot of activity erupted at the spaceport, Octavia stumbled to a shuttle with Arachne and pilots from the prison. She wore a full-length robe, poorly carved wooden horns, and a beard cut from a Centaur's tail. The bored harpy security at the spaceport gave the shipping manifest Arachne showed them close scrutiny, but only a cursory review of the crew's counterfeit IDs, The mining company's ore shuttles were parked in neat rows at the far end of the tarmac and were unoccupied. They commandeered all they could occupy. Arachne launched his hijacked vessel immediately. The plan was to have them prep his freighter for the hyperspace jump. Octavia and the other pilots sat in their captured ships and waited.

When the non-human prisoners were all inside the spaceport facilities, Calahas' team took out the few guards at the customs house, and the first wave of humans, led by Tina, disembarked from the purloined city transports and rushed in. She heard the belated alarms start to sound.

Since then, she'd coordinated everyone else in the evacuation effort. In the midst of the scrambling prisoners and the clash between Calahas' forces and the harpies, Tina gazed at the smoke and ash filling the sky. She donned a satisfied smile as the first dozen shuttles rose from the spaceport, including the one Octavia had commandeered. Wyverns wheeled through the air, screeching at the volcanic disturbance near their nests.

As hundreds of injured and dead sprawled across the makeshift triage area on the tarmac, Tina's face fell. The angry hiss of energy weapons coming from the spaceport's perimeter indicated that the harpies now staged a counterattack.

Which meant many more patients would soon arrive. And she couldn't guess as to when the fight would end.

* * *

The ground trembled, and steam exploded from the former warehouse. The slow discharge of lava turned into a torrent as it rapidly filled the stockade's yard. Superheated steam vented below the makeshift bridge, sending it cascading to the chasm below. The refugees caught on the span died in an instant.

Dante gaped in horror at the sight. When Cilla arrived from the barricade, Dante pointed to the ladders and gave a shout. "Get your men out of here while you still can!"

Iucundum pulled him to the nearest ladder. "There's nothing more we can do here."

The two scrambled up the rungs, intense heat lapping at their heels. Nearby, Cilla ordered his company to the escape route. The dirt-and-stone palisade where Cilla stood had become an island in the lava.

In the distance, Dante saw Kercs-ma lead his armored column out of the tunnel to the prison against the prison insurrection. Harpy soldiers piled out of four packed transports and charged the humans' stockade. A barrage of grenades and a field full of landmines met them instead. Minutes later, all thought of the battle evaporated when flowing magma exploded through the tunnel in the barrier wall behind the harpies. The harpy troops fled back into their vehicles.

As the lava cut them off in all directions, however, they had nowhere to go. One after the other, the transports exploded and sank in the lava, killing the Ipis-ma troops trapped inside. Their simple transport sleds and shielding proved useless against the molten rock.

Atop the barrier wall, Dante waved the militia below to the single rope dangling from the prison barrier's nine-meter wall. From below, Cilla met Dante's eyes.

"Save our people," he cried and lit the fuse on their last keg of gunpowder. He hurled the heavy canister at the oncoming crawler. As it flew through the air, an energy beam cut Cilla in half.

Keres-ma's maniacal laugh didn't last as the explosion overloaded his vehicle's shielding. It winked out, and the lava ate through the crawler's metal skin. He climbed out the turret's hatch, leaving behind his screaming driver. The Ipis-ma magistrate leapt to the temporary safety of the stone wall and howled in fury as the escaping humans pulled themselves up a knotted rope. Keres-ma picked off the exposed humans one by one until the rope they used was nothing but a smear of ash on the stone and dirt wall.

Dante cried out from the top of the wall when the last few men in Cilla's company died. On Dante's side, about a hundred refugees followed him up the ladders. He looked into the simmering cauldron but saw no one else coming. "This way," he gasped, choking on the air.

The only solace came when Keres-ma's crazed cackling stopped. A mantichora with a seared hide hurled itself onto the fort's wall. The animal stalked closer to Keres-ma, drawing the magistrate's terrified attention.

Dante didn't have time to watch the rest. He had people to save and was running out of time to do it. The flowing magma cut off all avenues for escape, save for the rooftop path Virgil's command had blazed earlier. Progress went slow but steady.

In the middle of traveling to Virgil's location, the roof of the magistrate's building shook more violently with each step the prisoners took. Unfortunately, moments later, it exploded. The state-of-the-art structure contained the molten lake, but the venting gas tossed the roof, and the humans atop it, to the street bordering the compound.

It took a while for Dante to recover his senses and stagger to his feet. He'd landed on a road outside the prison camp, and rubble from the compound's roof surrounded him. Globs of magma seeped from the rim of the plexo-steel wall not too far away.

Dante searched the debris for survivors. He found Iucundum moaning and staring at nothing. "C'mon." He hoisted the old mining engineer's arm around his shoulder and lurched toward the spaceport. If Dante recalled the map right, it should be about a kilometer and a half away. Only half the people who were with him a minute earlier still lived to trudge after him.

Three blocks later, he came to an abrupt halt. In his path, five wyverns fed on the remains of several dead harpies. The beasts hooted and lowered their horns as they spotted the pack of unarmed humans.

With his free hand, Dante fumbled at the scabbard strapped to his side, but the sword was no longer there. As he shouted to his people to take cover, the street crackled with the sound of ion disruptors. The wyverns bucked and collapsed.

From the distance came the familiar voice of Virgil. "Hello, Mister President. You should be careful about what neighborhoods you decide to stroll in."

"Virgil!" Dante gasped. "What are you doing here?"

"We've been fighting a running gun battle with a nasty batch of harpies," Virgil responded. Worry creased his face upon catching sight of all the injured people with Dante. Not long after, he hollered, "Medics!"

Several militia wearing white armbands hurried from the side buildings and took charge of the wounded. They took Iucundum and laid him out on a stretcher. They left about as fast as they'd rushed in.

When the crowd dispersed, Virgil walked up and slapped an ion disruptor into Dante's hand. "You just enlisted, Mister President. Welcome to the army."

The ground quaked beneath them. Somehow, they kept their balance.

"We've got bigger problems than the damn harpies," Dante said. "Let 'em have the freaking city. Iucundum said our explosions must've triggered a load of extra bi-nexidium, and now there's a full-blown volcano erupting behind us. If we stay here, we'll be neck deep in lava."

"A fissure opened up in the middle of the harpy headquarters. Looks like a bubbling caldron of molten rock right now. Damn, is anything going to work as we planned?" Virgil shook his head and spoke into his communicator. "All units, fall back to the spaceport."

CHAPTER XXXII

Surprise, Surprise

As they reached the cargo terminal at the spaceport, evidence of the savage fight that had raged there loomed. Dead harpies and prison militia littered the ground. Not a single building in sight stood intact. Weapons firing rang out from the direction of the main terminal. Virgil and the bulk of his forces hurried over there.

Those bearing stretchers, the walking wounded, and the non-combatants followed Dante to the captured portion of the spaceport. They ventured almost two hundred meters in, heading to where Tina's group had set up a makeshift triage area. When Dante passed through the ruined commercial transport entrance, hoarse cheers greeted him from the people dug in behind improvised gun emplacements and barricades.

Tina spotted Dante first and ran to him. They clung to each other and sobbed in unison. "I was so worried about you."

When they let go, he asked her, "How's the evacuation going?"

"Slow." Tina drew in a shuddered breath. "Setteth's keeping the harpy fighters occupied on the other side of the planet, but the Rocs are taking a beating. About half her warbirds are playing cat and mouse with the Enforcer-class cruiser so the shuttles can go to the captured transports. We hijacked five intergalactic freighters, but that's all we're going to get. All the other freighters and commercial ships fled the planet when the fighting started."

Dante peered over his shoulder, spying the thick smoke billowing in the air. "We have to pick up the pace somehow. The harpies may be the least of our problems. A lava flow's coming. We got here maybe a couple hours ahead of it."

Tina groaned. "We've only gotten half the folks off-planet. Otheth's force took the military sector of the spaceport fast. Calahas' troops won here at the commercial sector, but the harpies had time to dig in at the civilian side of the spaceport, and we can't budge them. They've already brought in reinforcements from outside the area and staged a couple counterattacks. The harpies are getting stronger, and everyone we have is already in the fight."

Another shuttle touched down, and a couple hundred former inmates ran to board it. Tina gave the scene a quick look. "I don't know how long the freighters we commandeered can stay in orbit. Once that Enforcer finishes the Roc warbirds off, it'll go after our people. I'm out of ideas."

Dante slapped his fist into his other hand. "I know. I know. We just—"

"Mister President!"

Dante turned to locate the new voice. Aramis ran toward him from a mostly undamaged customs building, waving a set of headphones. "The Eldest is calling. He says it's important."

Dante grabbed the communicator. "Michael?"

"Dante, it's good to hear your voice. I'm with Mara in the harpy Enforcer orbiting this planet. We've penetrated its computer system, and we're ready to shut it down. Mara estimates it'll take the Enforcer offline for an hour. It's a one-time deal. Use it to escape."

"You mean, it won't operate?"

"Yes. No propulsion and no weaponry. It'll be a floating rock."

Dante's head spun with a wild idea. "Mick, don't do anything yet. Aramis, where's Otheth?"

Aramis pointed over his shoulder. "She's holding the harpy military terminal to the right of here. That place was our initial target. We caught them by surprise and took control of it real fast."

Dante nodded. "Bring her here with as many of her warriors as you can. We're going to do some ship stealing."

Aramis sprinted off.

Dante raised the communicator again. "Michael, remember what we did to the harpies on Cocytus? We may have a chance to seize their cruiser."

"This thing is a lot bigger than that Striker, and this crew's on full battle alert." The communicator went silent for several seconds before Michael resumed speaking. "Mara and I can screw things up enough here so a fast-moving party can board unchallenged. We're out of sight in a hangar bay, and all their fighter ships are engaged with Setteth's warbirds."

"What's the biggest transport we have?" Dante asked Tina.

As if on cue, Otheth's Roc flock ship landed from its last refugee shuttle run to the captured ore freighters in orbit. With its wide fuselage and narrow front end, it resembled a bird with extended wings. The flock ship extended thirty-two meters in length and spanned twenty-four meters wide.

Tina pointed to the flock ship. "It's built to hold a full battalion of armed Roc warriors, right? We could squeeze in more if necessary."

He squeezed her hand. "Hold that ship. I'll need it shortly."

Tina hugged her husband, wiped her eyes, and ran to the ship.

A moment later, Quango limped over with Porthos and Athos, grumbling the whole way. "What did you say to Aramis? He yelled something about stealing a harpy ship and ran off."

"That about sums it up." Dante pointed to the two young clones. "Those boys were in on it the last time we did this."

Porthos' and Athos' faces lit up. "Hell yeah!"

Quango shook his head. "Athos, get Calahas and his team. They're Centaurs, but they're still a tough group in a pinch."

Athos raced off and soon returned with Calahas leading three companies of battle-scarred militia. Calahas' command of Centaurs and Satyrs disguised as teamsters and stevedores captured the customs building and its warehouses shortly after Setteth's attack on the military terminal. Human reinforcements replaced those lost, but having engaged in heavy fighting for so long, they all bore exhausted postures.

Concern laced Calahas' voice. "Sire, I came with all the reserves I have. Athos said it was urgent. Even with Virgil's team reinforcing us, the perimeter is near breaking by the main terminal. We can't hold out much longer. We're running low on munitions."

"I'll explain in a moment," Dante said.

Just as he finished, Otheth approached fast, followed by Aramis and sixty of her Rocs. Otheth skidded to a halt a few paces from him. Half her feathers were singed, but she bowed to Dante without a word.

Dante raised a clenched fist. "I need volunteers to follow me on a desperate gambit that'll determine whether we gain our freedom or be overwhelmed."

Every set of eyes of the gathered band locked on him.

He pointed to the sky and kept his voice even. "Michael and Mara have infiltrated the Enforcer. They believe they can cause enough confusion to allow a team of raiders to slip inside. I intend to seize control of the ship. Who's with me?"

Pride gleamed from Otheth's eyes. "Excellent. We will earn great *cou* today."

Calahas responded without hesitation. "Sire, I'd follow you into Hell if you asked it of me."

A small smile creased Dante's face. "My friend, I think we're already in Hell. Now let's do what we can to escape it."

* * *

The five hundred warriors for Dante's special operation hurried into the Rocs' flock ship and strapped themselves in. The troop transport seats in the large open personnel area were shaped like bowls and built for Rocs, but the warriors paid it no mind. One way or another, the ride to the orbiting harpy ship wouldn't last long. Most braced themselves on the aisle floor.

As they lifted off, Dante settled into a Roc nested chair on the bridge and shouted into a headset linked to it. "Okay, Mick, we're en route. According to Otheth, we should be there in thirty minutes."

"We'll be ready for you," Michael said. "Mara, in twenty minutes, initiate your cyberattack, and if you know how, pray."

Dante gulped as he heard Mara's response. "Protect humans, protect humans, protect humans..."

It took about ten minutes for the flock ship to reach the Enforcer. When the flock ship closed in, the Enforcer's hangar bay shield dropped, and the blast door slid open. Six Ipis dock workers and guards flew out and rocketed past the flock ship. Moments later, the flock ship settled to a stop. Dante's group waited until the hangar was sealed and re-pressurized. Mara gave the okay, and the five hundred warriors charged down the ship's ramp with guns ready. However, they found nothing alive in sight.

They secured the hangar in another ten minutes. Dante stood with Otheth, Quango, and Calahas at the base of the flock ship, watching the last of their troops disembark. The Ipis tactical fighters left a long while ago, so the Roc flock ship occupied a great deal of the expansive hangar without much trouble. The raiding party filled the remaining space, and the warriors formed up into their combat units where they could.

Quango tugged his goatee, observing the deploying troops. "By my mother's twisted beard, I can't believe we're still alive. Now where the hell are Michael and Mara?" His gaze wandered to the line of sealed doors along the opposite wall.

Dante cradled his ion disruptor and took in the details of the enormous hangar bay. "It's been about twenty minutes since our last communication. They would've initiated the cyberattack by now. They said something about a small room connected to this bay." He turned to the three young clones standing behind Quango. "Eyes on everything. I don't want any surprises."

The hiss of an airtight door lock releasing caught everyone's attention. Dante himself jumped before going very still.

"Someone's over there!" Aramis pointed to a door sliding open along the back wall. Five hundred guns scattered around the hangar swung in that direction.

"Don't shoot! I'm on your side!" a voice shouted. At the same time, a large clone stepped out waving his hands.

"Eldest!" the three young clones cried. They wasted no time in racing to the half-open door. Dante followed wearing a big grin, catching up as soon as he spotted the young clones clinging to Michael.

Quango hobbled after them as well, smiling at the same sight. "You must be Michael. Pleased to make your acquaintance." He extended his hand as if to accept a human handshake, and added with affection, "You raised these lads well. They speak very highly of you."

Michael shook the extended hand. "I'm proud of them."

Dante rushed in and wrapped the big clone in a bear hug. "It's good to see you."

Michael returned the embrace, choking on his next words. "We need to get you home. It doesn't appear they've fed you well here."

Dante stepped back. "That and a million other issues. What's the situation in here?"

Mara left the room and joined them, lights flashing bright gold. "I disrupted the Enforcer's operations systems, but it changed the security codes and erected a new firewall. It has blocked me out." She turned her sensors to Dante. "It will require your skills to subvert it."

Dante rubbed his jaw. "That's what I'm here for." He faced his commanders. "As the first order of business, we need to take control of the bridge and engine room."

Quango sighed and turned to Michael. "Then, if you'd be so kind as to point us to where the hyperspace and normal space drive systems are, I'd be much obliged."

Michael looked over his shoulder. "Mara, there's nothing more for us to do here. Take Quango to the engine room." He unholstered his sidearm. "I'll head to the bridge."

Otheth cawed. "Sire, my team will accompany Michael and hold it to our last breath."

Dante nodded, and the sixty Rocs left with Michael and Mara leading them, running fast and silent. He turned to Calahas. "You and your team go with Quango and take the engine room. I don't want the damn harpies causing any mischief there."

The Centaur captain whinnied. "Companies A and B, with me. Company C, protect our leader." He led his team of three hundred militia off at a trot behind Mara.

Dante studied the hundred and twenty soldiers who stayed with him. Months earlier, they were emaciated prisoners waiting to die. Now, they stood beside him as confident warriors. The look in their eyes conveyed the trust they had in him. He gulped, afraid more than ever of letting them down.

"We follow Otheth's team to the bridge," he said. "On an Enforcer, that's three levels up near the front bulwark. I need to reach this ship's computer to take control of it."

They split off, and not long after, Dante's group entered the main passage and encountered the first seared bodies of the Ipis crew. The harpies contested every passageway and corridor, but they couldn't mount an organized resistance, not when most didn't carry any armaments. Eventually, Dante's team broke into the barricaded bridge, and the terrified captain surrendered his ship.

With Michael's disruptor pointed at the back of his head, the Enforcer's commander disabled the computer system's firewall. Dante jumped into the captain's chair and sealed off all levels and compartments still controlled by the harpies. A glare from Michael and the execution of two bridge officers convinced the Enforcer's commander to order his crew to stand down.

When the ship was secured, Dante ordered a team to dump all the captured harpies into lifepods and jettison them. The Enforcer's commander thrashed and screeched as the human team dragged him from the bridge along with the rest of the crew.

"That was almost too easy," Dante remarked. He returned his attention to the computer screen, reconfiguring the command system to human icons and Latin text.

Otheth settled into the station beside him. "Don't be too derisive. These were all Ipis-ma troops. Once you broke their arrogance, they panicked. Imperial troops, on the other hand, are tenacious fighters. They'd see this ship destroyed with themselves in it rather than yield."

"Thanks." Dante nodded. "Imperials, Ipis-ma, Ipis-dis. I know so little about these assholes. I keep thinking they're all the same, but they're not, are they?"

"No, they're not," Otheth sighed. "And there're a *lot* of them."

Dante growled to the Roc, "Open a secure communication channel to the spaceport. I need to know what's going on down there."

Otheth cawed and moved to the communications station. "I have a frequency available." A minute later, her feathers flared. "I have the link to our troops. They've been trying to reach us."

The speaker in front of Dante crackled, and Tina's voice broke through sounding strained. "Mayday! Mayday!"

"Tina, this is Dante!" he shouted. "We seized the Enforcer. We're going to win."

"Dante! Thank God you're alive," Tina exclaimed. "We're in big trouble. Setteth sent a warning saying those two Strikers got tired of chasing the Roc warbirds. Now they're heading for the spaceport. A lot of their tactical fighters are overhead, and we can't hit them with our weapons." She let out a moan. "We pulled as many of the wounded into the custom inspection building as we could. A lot of folks didn't make it. If we go out, we'll get obliterated."

"Tina, get outta there!" Dante screamed into the communicator.

Her voice was steady. "Sorry, honey. It doesn't look like we can launch any more transports. The harpies control the airspace."

Otheth looked up from her station. "We have more problems. A pair of unidentified spacecraft just came through hyperspace." Her feathers flattened. "They're warships and just deployed a fresh set of tactical fighters."

From the pilot's chair, Michael groaned. "That must be lead elements of the Imperial Fleet on the way."

"Impossible. The Imperials aren't due for another five days," Otheth squawked.

"Well, it appears they're early." Dante narrowed his eyes and flipped on a communicator. "Quango, can you restart the engines on this ship?"

"We won't have hyperdrive for a few hours, sire. We can break orbit in normal space, but we won't go far. This piece of junk would have issues even if everything hadn't been shut down. The maintenance on these systems is just criminal."

"Do what you can. Just do it fast," Dante said. "Otheth, what about the shields and weapons?"

"Sorry," came the reply. "Shields are only at eleven percent. Weapons systems are still offline."

Dante slammed the control panel. "Mick, get us out of here. Maybe we can draw those Strikers and new bogies away from the planet and give our people a chance to escape."

"I'll do what I can, but I doubt this will handle like Setteth's warbird." Michael's fingers flew across the pilot's control panel. The ship shuddered as it broke orbit.

"It appears our hijacking endeavor is no longer secret," Otheth reported. "The two Strikers stopped going to the spaceport and are moving to intercept us."

The trajectory of the enemy ships changed on the display. Dante observed the anxious faces around the bridge. "There's only one thing left to do. We lure those Ipis warships as far from here as we can. They'll follow. We're a far bigger prize than a collection of escaped inmates."

He gripped the communicator with tears trickling down his cheek. "Tina, contact Setteth's warbirds and Virgil's militia. Inform them the Ipis fleet arrived early. Instruct the freighters to escape into hyperspace with whoever they have onboard. I only have this one frequency until the comm channels are reconfigured on this ship."

Tina's voice quivered. "There must be another way. We're so close."

Dante smashed his fist against the console. "We're out of options."

Tina let out a weak laugh. "We almost pulled it off, didn't we?"

"Yes, we did... but now, we save who we can."

Tina's voice shook as she relayed the information to the commanders on the ground.

"Setteth can't help," Otheth called out in alarm. "I only detect eleven warbirds engaging the Ipis planetary forces."

Michael stared at his pilot's display. "Dante, I have an ID on the new bogies. It's a Striker-class frigate and a Stalker-class destroyer. They're deploying attack fighters." Suddenly, confusion set in. "What the heck?"

The tactical display in front of the big clone identified the smaller craft as a pair of galleys and a couple dozen warbirds. Dante cocked his head at a real-time display. The galleys looked familiar.

A gruff voice with an Australian accent cut in over the communicator. "Hey Mick, it's good to hear you. We've been worried sick about ya." The voice turned incredulous. "Mate, am I really picking you up from that Enforcer-class cruiser?"

"Yes," was all Michael could force through his constricted throat.

Dante gasped as he stared at his own communicator screen. "Martinel?"

Sure enough, the face of a familiar Aussie formed through the static. "Aye, Mister President, and I got all of Cocytus with me. Ya gotta tell me later how you ended up flying an Ipis Enforcer."

Dante sobbed at the sudden change in fortunes. "Thank God! We're going to be in a tough spot very soon. We kinda broke this lump of iron when we captured it, and two Striker frigates are coming up from the planet."

"Our fearless leader's in deadly peril. Why doesn't that surprise me." Martinel snickered. "We're on 'em. Setteth's luring the harpy frigates into the planet's gravity well, and it's working like a charm." He laughed out loud. "As a bonus, you saved us the trouble of tangling with that Enforcer."

The new arrivals turned toward the two Strikers now rising through Carcerem's sky. Martinel spoke in a flat voice, apparently heedless of whether his words were translated or not. "Unidentified spacecraft, you are engaging in a hostile act against ships belonging to the Human Defense Force. Your situation is untenable. Yield, or be destroyed."

The lead Ipis frigate turned to the oncoming threat and fired its batteries of ion disruptors from inside Carcerem's airspace. The shielding on the two mainline human warships held up without any damage.

Martinel's fleet responded with laser cannons and plasma missiles. They followed the tactics Setteth had hammered into them two months earlier. It worked. The lead Striker split into pieces and erupted into a fireball as it fell to the surface. The second Ipis Striker turned to flee, but it moved at a sluggish pace compared to the warbirds and galleys descending on it. The harpy crew abandoned ship, escaping in the vessel's lifepods when the shielding gave out under the swarming assault.

With their motherships gone, the surviving Ipis tactical fighters abandoned their assault on the spaceport. They fled to the far corners of the planet, pursued by the warbird reinforcements. Dante bellowed a hoarse cheer as the last combatant disappeared from his screen. Every species on the ship took up the shout.

The cheering quieted immediately when Virgil's wheezing voice broke through the speakers. "I don't want to interrupt the celebrations, but it's getting a little intense down here. The harpy infantry took off. The lava flow has slowed, but this spaceport is completely cut off from the ground, and it's getting tough to breathe. Could I trouble you guys to get us off this God-forsaken planet?"

"Good to hear you're staying out of trouble, too, Virgil," Martinel replied with suppressed mirth. "Shuttles are en route."

It took another six hours to complete the evacuation. Virgil was the last person to leave, and when he did, lava cascaded over the cliff into the ocean. Wyverns wheeled through the air, screeching when a group pulled Virgil from the roof of the customs inspection building.

The escapees' fleet now consisted of twelve commandeered transgalactic ore transports and two captured warships, each one packed with refugees. A day later, they vanished into hyperspace. As Dante glimpsed out the window, a fiery volcano glowed from the spot on Carcerem that had been his sanctuary in hell.

Tina squeezed his hand as they both felt the queasiness of the hyperspace jump. "We made it. We're going home."

CHAPTER XXXIII

Home again

Whence I was drawn from out the ample throat
Of Hell to be his guide, and I shall guide him
As far on as my school has power to lead.
Dante's Purgatorio, Canto XXI

The oddball collection of spaceships required a full week to make the trip back to Cocytus. Dante insisted they stay together, so the fleet of evacuees moved at the pace of the slowest ore transport. The rations on each ship managed to hold out despite the number of people.

Early on a spring day, Dante's shuttle touched down at Heavensgate. Many other shuttles followed, emptying their passengers. Like most spring days on Cocytus, a howling wind drove stinging sleet in the faces of those disembarking. Despite the rough weather, most of the newcomers stopped to gaze at the new world. Many hugged each other and wept. Compared to the hell of Ipis persecution they'd suffered under their entire lives, Cocytus provided nothing short of a haven.

Few greeted them. Only those too young, too old, or too ill stayed in Beatrice's valley when Martinel launched his rescue mission. Those who called Cocytus home for the last two years guided the new arrivals into Heavensgate.

Dante and Tina stood on the tarmac in the icy rain, watching the other prisoners from under wyvern-hide ponchos. Even with the flow of shuttles landing and taking off, the makeshift spaceport looked tiny compared to the one they escaped from a week earlier. Nearby, the mass of people ran to Heavensgate, heads down against the weather. A hundred and eighty meters away, Heavensgate appeared quite small compared to the large and imposing harpy facility on Carcerem.

Tina shrugged. "Seems like nothing changed while we were gone."

Dante's nose twitched at a slight chill in the air. "It's good to be home." To his own surprise, he realized he really meant those words. It didn't matter that Cocytus wasn't Earth. The familiar sights and weather truly felt like a new home.

"I'm home wherever you are. And these folks who suffered with us on Cocytus and Carcerem are closer than family," Tina replied in a soft voice. Her hand reached for his, and they squeezed each other's hands. "I'm glad we made it back here because I think I'm pregnant."

The rain obscured the joyful tears trickling down Dante's face. They clung to each other, heedless of the weather.

A fresh gust blew a sheet of sleet into Dante's face, and he laughed. "I just wish our home were more like Hawaii."

"Let's go inside. I'm freezing." Tina wrapped her arm in his. "You'll need to talk to the people from Carcerem and get them oriented. We'll be busy settling them in."

Halfway to Heavensgate, an ivory-colored robot shaped like a human hurried toward them on two piston legs. The robot planted itself in Dante's path. Though unfamiliar with the robot itself, he recognized its soprano voice.

"You must carry an identifier. I have scanned all these new guests searching for you," the robot said. A low hum emitted from somewhere on the humanoid drone. "You are eleven-point-one percent lighter than when you departed. Are all your biological functions performing to specifications?"

"I'm fine, Beatrice." Dante laughed, taking in the robot's features. It stood at his height, and the two sensors positioned in the front of the head gave it a resemblance to a human face. "Is this a new drone design?"

Golden lights flickered in the makeshift eye sockets. "You are my maker. You are my friend. I chose to emulate your form for many of my drone functions."

Dante squinted at the face. "Is my nose really that large?"

"I copied all dimensions to within one millimeter."

They continued walking to Heavensgate. Behind them, the shuttles rose into the air to retrieve the next batch of refugees waiting on the transgalactic ore transports orbiting Cocytus. Their fiery exhaust cast a golden glow on the gloomy, dank day. Once they'd faded from the sky, Dante entered Heavensgate.

Many people occupied the open space on the first floor, mostly human but also a smattering of Rocs, Centaurs, and Satyrs. Yearning, fear, and confusion rode in their murmurs and conversations. The mumbling subsided as everyone became aware of Dante's presence. They all turned to him and bowed.

Iucundum stepped forward. "Sire, what are your orders?"

Hope shone in all their eyes, hope they held in him.

Dante swallowed, unsure if he warranted such faith, but unwilling to let them down. At length, he drew in a deep breath. "Today, we rest. Tomorrow, we start building a new life."

* * *

The next day, Tina and Beatrice's humanoid drone joined Dante in giving his leaders from Carcerem a tour of Mount Purgatory. Iucundum and the others plastered themselves to the windows of the self-driving ground transports during the ride from Heavensgate to Hellsgate. The spring rains had turned the dirt road bordering the River Styx into a quagmire, and the transport they rode in churned through it on oversized tires. A dreary brown, devoid of trees, rested on either side of the swollen river.

Upon entering the chasm leading to Hellsgate, the newcomers from Carcerem sat back in their seats and exchanged worried looks. However, all the newcomers gasped when they caught their first glimpse of Beatrice's Eden. Buds had already sprouted on the abundant fruit trees, and shoots of grain rose in neat furrows from the loamy fields. Two lanes of crushed stones marked the road from Hellsgate to Mount Purgatory, which bore a steady flow of human and robotic traffic.

They disembarked outside the main entrance of Mount Purgatory. Several people worked on the mountain's slope, tending olive trees. They paused in their tasks and waved, shouting Dante's name. Dante waved back, and many cheers resounded. On entering Mount Purgatory and its cavern-wide garden, Dante smiled as the people from Carcerem absorbed every detail in wonder. The towering pillars in the biosphere gave off a soft, golden glow.

"Amazing," Iucundum repeated at each new sight. Standing in the middle of the garden, he turned to Beatrice's drone. "Your evolution is extraordinary. The AI systems made by Novaromans four hundred years ago couldn't possibly accomplish what you've done here."

Beatrice rotated her head toward the former mining engineer. "I had to. The botanical gardens would have perished after my makers left if I did not create a viable biosphere. I am an agricultural station. What else could I do?"

Iucundum waved his arms in the air. "You completely hollowed out a mountain, created a sustainable power plant, and fabricated tools from raw ore, without any knowledge of what they'd require."

"I made many mistakes, but I learned."

Iucundum shook his head again and turned to Dante. "Sire, this morning I inspected the ruins across the sulfur lake near Heavensgate. I can confirm without a doubt that the Novaromans once colonized this planet. The architecture is a classic representation of that era." With a chuckle, he added, "However, I'm fairly confident that it didn't bear the name Cocytus."

Tina leaned in. "Did the Novaromans colonize many planets?"

Iucundum's shoulders sagged. "So much Novaroman history was lost after the Ipis war a hundred and twenty years ago. To my understanding, we once possessed flourishing societies on six worlds, but now, they're just names handed down from generation to generation. Besides Novaroma and Carcerem, I couldn't tell you where those planets are located. When the Ipis decide to obliterate an enemy, they're ruthless. Despite this, the ruins here are by far the most intact buildings of our people I've ever seen."

Dante kicked at a stone on the gravel path. "We may not know where Earth is, but we can build a human society that belongs in the stars. We can start again, and we start here."

A long sigh escaped Iucundum's throat. "I've waited my whole life to hear those words. We better to get to work then. We'll have millions of people to care for."

Dante furrowed his brow. "Millions? We have about twenty-five thousand survivors from Carcerem."

Iucundum put his hands on his hips. "After the war, the Ipis hunted us until we were a scattered, homeless people. We all crave a place to call home, a place to call our own. Sire, word about what happened at Carcerem will spread. And when it does, more people will come. Many, many more."

* * *

Three days after the prisoners fled Carcerem, six Imperil Ipis Enforcers arrived and took up orbit around Carcerem. The empress' First Fleet admiral, Yasha-ry, spent five days retrieving all the survivors. He spent another two piecing together what happened.

Keres-ma survived those three days atop the stone wall inside the death camp, surrounded by slowly cooling lava. On the first day, he swore vengeance on all humans, especially the prisoners' headsman, who'd leered at him from atop the wall during the breakout. On the second day, Keres-ma tore the tail from the mantichora that had mauled his left arm, cackling while ripping chunks of meat from the corpse and eating it raw. On the third day, he lapsed in and out of consciousness from the loss of blood and spreading infection. Only the swarming insects of Carcerem provided company.

When conscious, Keres-ma sat on a ledge in agonizing pain, seething and nursing his mangled body. With each passing hour, his disdain for humans transformed into a blinding hatred. He vowed to destroy the accursed species who'd exposed him to this shame.

One of Yasha-ry's search parties found Keres-ma delirious and feverish. Keres-ma still held the severed tail of the mantichora with a death grip in his right hand. The dead mantichora lay sprawled beside him with its head disintegrated.

For the next five days, Keres-ma sat on the edge of death as the warship's medical machines worked to save him. In between treatment sessions, he fingered the new talisman around his neck—the mantichora's spiked tail. Blood loss and infection had almost killed him, but he survived. The infirmary did a remarkable job healing him, but he remained badly scarred, and not enough of his left arm remained for the medics to repair. They replaced it with an articulating prosthetic. The day after, the infirmary released him to the custody of the Ipis military police.

Admiral Yasha-ry immediately summoned him to his flagship's stateroom. When Keres-ma arrived, the admiral sat behind the desk reading over reports on a tablet. Occasionally, he looked up and sneered at the shackled magistrate, who had two Imperial Ipis marines flanking him. Keres-ma gnashed his fangs as Admiral Yasha-ry made him stand in silence.

After giving the reports one last review, Yasha-ry slammed the desk. "You should've had the good sense to die down there. Fifty percent causalities from your command, twenty percent of the civilians are unaccounted for, the bi-nexidium processing plant is lost, and three warships are either missing or destroyed. On top of this, thousands of the empire's most vile enemies escaped without a trace. I don't think any of your royal connections or the influence of your ridiculous cult will get you out of this." Yasha-ry slammed the tablet on the desk and let out a derisive laugh. "Do you even know the name of the human who led the prison revolt?"

Keres-ma snapped back. "A treacherous Roc worked with the prison headsman, Sebastian."

The admiral rose from his desk and leaned forward. "My computer forensic experts were thorough, unlike you. They dissected the ruined computers from the remains of your compound. The name of the human brought in by the Satyr pirate Arachne and entered in your logs was Dante Carloman. Does that name mean anything to you?"

"Of course, it does, its horrible blemish on the glorious annals of our military histories," Keres-ma sputtered. "But many bounty hunters brought in humans claiming their captives were named Carloman or Bernius. They hoped to gain a greater reward. I ignored them."

Yasha-ry glared. "It didn't rouse your interest when that traitor Setteth, posing as an imperial agent, showed up with a keen interest in those names shortly after that?"

Keres-ma gnashed his teeth. "No. Look, I know my history," he spurted. "Carlomans ruled the human planets. Their alliance was the only one to challenge Ipis galactic rule in a millennium." He snuffed. "We *wiped them out* over one hundred and twenty years ago."

"Apparently not." Yasha-ry turned his computer screen around, which showed a lean human male in his twenties. "This is Dante Carloman. He was in your grasp, and not only did you allow him to escape, but he defeated your forces with little more than sticks and stone." Admiration crept into Yasha-ry's voice. "In space and on the ground, he used some brilliant tactics." His voice turned hard. "You had him."

Keres-ma thought back to that one human who dared to look *down* at him. The nerve of that lesser creature laughing at him from the prison wall.

Keres-ma turned back at the admiral but said nothing. Instead, he vowed to kill every human in the galaxy in revenge. And when he found that one despicable human, he'd drink his blood to the last drop.

EPILOGUE

Covered with sackcloth vile they seemed to me,
And one sustained the other with his shoulder,
And all of them were by the bank sustained.
Dante's Purgatorio, Canto XIII

A week after returning to Cocytus, general acclamation from the people declared Dante the permanent leader of Cocytus despite his sputtering objections. Seven months later, Tina gave birth to their child, and she and Dante named him Liam after her dad. Other new folks started arriving around the time their son was born. After all that time, Cocytus cemented its status as a true second home to the Earth-born humans.

At first, some Rocs arrived with a few hundred humans they'd hidden from the Ipis. As the days passed, it grew into a great influx. A collection of Satyr smugglers and Centaur pirates snuck the scattered humans in from numerous Ipis-controlled planets. A year after Dante's return, refugees swelled to thousands per week.

Arachne quipped to Dante at one point, "My friends are interested in helping, especially if it means tweaking Ipis snouts. Also, humans need a place of their own, just like any other species." The Satyr learned languages fast, preferring not to rely on translator devices. As such, he learned to speak to Dante in unaccented English in record time.

A cool, rainy morning opened the day marking the one-year anniversary of their escape from Carcerem. An icy sleet pounded the thick window of the conference room situated on the top floor of Heavensgate, which provided a clear view of the spaceport area. What was once an Ipis research outpost now served as the hub of the human government on Cocytus.

Dante sat at the head of the conference table for his weekly staff meeting. At the start of the morning briefing, he leaned on the table, rubbing his temples. He couldn't believe a whole year had passed since escaping Carcerem, but he had no time to reflect on it. He looked at the nine people seated around the table: six humans, two androids, a Centaur, a Satyr, and a Roc, all close friends. He turned his attention to the computer display in front of him and skimmed the agenda. "We need to determine how long

I'll be stuck playing leader here. The vast majority of the population are of Novaroman descent, not Earth."

In a seat across the oval table, Iucundum drew back, aghast. "Sire, are you thinking of abdicating your throne?"

"Iucundum, I told you a million times. I'm not a king, I'm an elected president." Dante peered around the room. "Someone help me here."

Sitting next to Iucundum, Michael thumped the thin, gray-haired man on the back. "Humor him. Even though he called me a big ugly on the first day we met, I've been following our fearless leader almost from the beginning."

Iucundum eyed the thick-muscled clone. "He called you that? Fearless, maybe. Crazy, for sure."

Dante's eyebrows rose. "Mick, you scared the shit out of me. I didn't know what I was babbling."

The bearded clone's voice turned raspy. "You saved my soul. I was an empty shell, a monster, until we met. I could never repay the debt."

Virgil chuckled. "Boss, I think you were in charge from the first moment we arrived on this 'paradise' of a planet. Who else could've convinced an abandoned, four-hundred-year-old agriculture station to fight the harpies with us?" He winked at the humanoid robot. "Besides, I heard she was very cranky when you took your three-month 'vacation' on Carcerem."

Beatrice's humanoid robot faced the others. "Dante, you gave me Asimov's three laws. You gave me purpose. You must promise me that you will remain my interface. You are my maker." The robot walked over to Calahas and Arachne. "I accept these two criminal kidnappers as guests only because you say they saved your life."

Arachne gulped as he eyed the humanoid machine. "I deeply regret my misdeeds and have pledged allegiance to Lord Carloman as my king. Mara accepted my regret. Why can't you?"

"Mara is a simple machine incapable of proper problem analysis. That argument is insufficient."

The titanium cylinder of Mara shot into the air. "Simple machine? I am capable of transgalactic flight and subverting an enemy spaceship. You have never demonstrated those capabilities."

"Enough! Sorry I raised the question," Dante groaned. He calmed himself and turned to Tina. "How goes the refugee resettlement?"

A wan smile creased Tina's face. "We're rebuilding on the ruined infrastructure left by the Novaromans, so we need food, clothing, shelter... You name it, we need it. Many arrive with just the clothes on their backs."

"These new folks, these Novaromans, aren't afraid of hard work," Michael added. "They're rolling up their sleeves and pitching in on any job assigned to them."

"It's a logistical nightmare, but we're managing. Somehow." Tina tucked a loose strand of auburn hair behind her ear. "On the bright side, we're expecting a good harvest this year. The worst of the winter is behind us, and Beatrice is working overtime to produce construction material and farming equipment. Quonset huts are popping up in every fertile valley we can find." She sighed. "I have to pass that coordination on to Iucundum and Michael. Linda Martinel has asked me to develop an AI-enhanced infirmary chamber for her special project. Add in the baby, and I just don't have any more time."

Iucundum cleared his throat. "The abandoned human settlement across the lake from Heavensgate is already partially habitable. It's remarkably intact for a city that's gone unoccupied for over four hundred years. Our ancestors knew how to build structures that would last. However, I have a more ambitious endeavor."

Dante chuckled. "Before this wave of immigrants, we barely had enough people to settle the land between Mount Purgatory and Heavensgate."

"I believe the problem is quite the opposite now." Iucundum brought up a holographic display of Cocytus from the projector embedded in the center of the conference table. The screen zoomed in on a large, semi-rectangular island near the equator. "We've broken ground for a colony on this island eight hundred and five kilometers south of here. The climate's more temperate, and the island has rich soil. It's a little over a hundred and fifty-five thousand square kilometers, so we could support millions of new settlers there."

Tina nodded. "We'll need it. At the rate they're coming in, the half-million refugees we have now could grow to ten times that number in a year. The Rocs, Satyrs, and Centaurs have homes on worlds they can return to, but humans don't. But like Michael said, they're resilient. Life has dealt them a bum deal, but the first thing most ask is what can they do to help."

Michael stroked the jagged scar along his jawline, and his face turned solemn. "The scars people bear tell the story of where they've been, not where they're going. It's up to us to help them build a brighter future."

Iucundum stole a peek out the window of the conference room at the Heavensgate tarmac. Even in the swirling spring rain, it bustled with activity. "It's good for us humans to have a world of our own where we're beholden to no one." He took a deep breath and looked over the top of his reading glasses. "Cocytus can be a lodestone drawing them from their havens. Their flight here from every corner of the galaxy will not slow."

The sensors on Beatrice's humanoid robot blinked. "They bring many varieties of plants and animals. My learning curve is growing exponentially. However, I estimate my agricultural output will only accommodate twenty-one-point-eight percent of next year's consumption needs."

"Beatrice, it's okay," Dante said. "You don't have to do everything. You fed and clothed us when we were helpless. You and your valley will always be a cherished center of our world. Of my world."

Beatrice moved to Dante's side and rested a steel hand on his shoulder. "I will redouble my efforts. While I exist, I will provide. You are my friend."

"It feels strange after all this time to walk the streets of a new city bustling with activity and be greeted by people I've never met." Dante's mouth slimmed to a tight line. "Iucundum is right, though. No one should have to live through what we faced here and on Carcerem. Humans need a home, even if we can't find Earth." He eyed General Cruz. "What's the status of the army?"

"With the new recruits, we have a full, well-armed infantry division," Cruz said. "Training will take time, but we picked up a large group who's had guerilla combat experience, and that'll help a lot." He nodded to the empty seat to his left. "Just so we're all on the same page, Admiral Martinel took that big Enforcer cruiser as his flagship. We also have the Stalker destroyer, two functioning Striker frigates, a mishmash of converted freighters, and a collection of tactical fighters ranging from our antique galleys to twelve state-of-the-art warbirds the Order of the Dragon loaned us."

"I don't want them back. Just use them well," Setteth cooed from a nested chair. "They are a gift to cement our alliance and friendship."

Dante offered the old Roc a sheepish smile. "Outside of the small consideration that you saved my worthless life, you've also provided flight instructors and maintenance experts. We're forever in your debt."

Setteth's feathers flattened against her head, beaming as she took in everyone in the room. "I've waited over a hundred and twenty years for this. To see the old alliance forged anew is all the payment I desire."

Calahas rose on his hindquarters and bowed. "This union shall be far stronger than the original."

The old Roc warbled. "It'll have to be, if we're to survive."

"We'll find a way." Dante tensed as he looked at Tina. "Linda's not here. Can you report on the special project?"

Tina gave a nod. "As General Cruz just described, we now have the second largest battlefleet in the galaxy. Of course, we're the *only* ones besides the Ipis who possess mainline warships." Tina turned a meaningful look at the Rocs, Satyrs, and Centaurs present. "Your attack craft and corvettes are fine for warding off pirates, but that's not what we're talking about. Our ships are outnumbered a thousand to one, and it's much worse in terms of throw weight."

She rose from her seat. "Thankfully, Linda and Dimitri Petrov conceived a way to build our own Adamant-class battlewagon. The harpies haven't had a major design change in fifty years, and our engineering team thinks we can do better. Quango's experimenting with some new concepts that'll mix Beatrice's energy shield technology with what the harpies use and overlap them on our ships. Pretty exciting, right? We also have the superstructure of an old bi-nexidium ore freighter parked on Cocytus' smaller moon, and we're in the process of repurposing it." A hint of concern showed through when she turned to Setteth. "You've been very quiet. What do you think?"

Setteth shifted in her nested chair, her old, arthritic bones crackling with the movement. "I have nothing useful to add. Linda and Beatrice wrung me dry of any innovative ideas I had months ago."

The meeting soon adjourned, and the different leaders left to tend to their duties. Not long after, Dante found himself alone with Setteth in the conference room.

Dante smiled at her. "Do you have something to say, privately?"

The old Roc settled back in her chair with a sigh. "I'm far from young. My aching body reminds me daily that I'm no fledgling."

Dante chuckled. "I wish I had half your energy."

"The vigor and enthusiasm of your followers is contagious." Setteth heaved a great, sad sigh. "But I saw this many decades ago. Other daring folks gave similar speeches with the same inspiration and passion. And yet, they all died with their dreams. More than anyone, I know the might of the Ipis Empire. Please be cautious."

Dante walked to where the old Roc sat. "My friend, I'll do whatever I can to avoid a fight... but if one comes, I must respond."

Setteth's crest feathers rose, then fell. "Sire, thank you for hearing me out." She rose and walked to the door. "I'll be with you, always."

* * *

It took about a year after the debacle on Carcerem to organize the appropriate trial for Keres-ma. Because of his royal blood ties, the empire organized a tribunal to preside over the trial on the capital world of Serpens. The court building was situated in the palace complex and held all the majestic trappings of the capital. Fluted crystal pillars shone with a cold blue, and the judges sat on a four-meter dais carved from a glowing purple crystal.

On the day of the trial, a grim and embittered Keres-ma stood before the three-judge tribunal. All the judges were influential leaders of the Ipis government, as per the law of the empire. However, his pedigree served as no shield against the charges.

The judges declared the Carcerem prison disaster and the ensuing battle as the worst Ipis military catastrophe since the war against humans and Rocs a hundred and twenty years earlier. The punishment for dereliction of duty and treason was torture and death. To a small degree of relief, no one had discovered Keres-ma's attempt to smuggle bi-nexidium. With the port city's near-complete destruction, all evidence of that crime lay hidden under a mountain of solidified lava and rock. It gave him one slim chance to escape the death penalty.

He nodded to the first judge, Bazatas-ma, the governor of the Genseric Sector. She appeared dour but flashed the symbol of the Ipis-ma faction to him. No doubt, she'd push for his pardon.

The middle judge, Yasha-ry, sneered. The First Fleet Admiral was one of Empress Fravashi's consorts and her close personal confidant. No doubt, he'd vote for Keres-ma's conviction.

Even with overwhelming evidence against him, Keres-ma focused his faint hope on the third judge, Silenus-dis, the governor of the Lethe Sector. Silenus-dis was a devoted follower of the Ipis-dis cult. Keres-ma gave the judge a long side glance.

The Ipis had always reigned supreme. This supposed "ancient enemy" so feared by the Ipis-dis didn't exist. However, if Keres-ma wanted to survive and exact revenge on the humans, he saw but one way out: He'd have to feed into that cult's ridiculous superstitions. With the way everything fell apart on Carcerem, it wouldn't be a difficult story to weave.

He had nothing left to do but try, so he cleared his throat. "The legends of our ancient enemy are true."

Silenus-dis leaned forward, intense focus trained on the former magistrate.

Keres-ma touched the mantichora tail hanging over his neck with his prosthetic arm. This helped him fight the urge to smirk, and he breathed deep. "Let me tell you of my encounter."

Main Characters:

Dante Carloman—American, computer engineer, ruler of Planet Cocytus

Tina Phokas—American, third year medical student, doctor on Cocytus

Esther Easley—American, main doctor on Cocytus

Rodrigo Cruz—American, Army captain, military commander on Cocytus

Joe Gentile—American, Army lieutenant, second in command

Virgil Bernius—American, Air Force Pararescue, Cocytus militia leader

Dimitri Pertelov—Russian, physics professor, Cocytus ruling council member

Gabrielle Peyago—Argentine novelist, Cocytus ruling council member

Linda Martinel—Australian, aeronautics engineer, Cocytus ruling council member

Kevin Martinel—Australian Navy search and rescue pilot, Cocytus air and space commander

Michael—Adult clone, infiltrator class created by Ipis, Cocytus ruling council member

Reggie—Adult clone, destroyer class created by Ipis, comatose

Aramis—Pre-adult clone, destroyer class, educated by humans

Athos—Pre-adult clone, destroyer class, educated by humans

Porthos—Pre-adult clone, destroyer class, educated by humans

Beatrice—Biomes Ecological Agrarian Test Research Station Three, an artificial intelligence, found on Cocytus

Mara—Mobile, articulating, robotic android, built by Beatrice

Cilla—Human, origin unknown

Octavia—Human, origin unknown

Iucundum—Human, origin unknown

Arachne—Satyr, smuggler ship captain

Paxine—Satyr, niece of Arachne

Quango—Satyr, smuggler ship chief engineer

Calahas—Centaur, disgraced noble, smuggler ship security chief

Huon—Centaur, follower of Calahas

Setteth—Roc, Imperial Ipis fighter squadron commander, Order of Dragon flock mother

Otheth—Roc, mercenary, great-granddaughter of Setteth

Keres-ma—Ipis, Ipis-ma faction leader, ruler of Carcerem

You've finished.

Please review this book on Amazon.com!

One of the ways for independent authors and small publishers to get exposure for their books is to receive as many honest, thoughtful reviews as possible.

Thanks in advance!

About the Author

John Caligiuri is a novelist who has a lifelong passion for literature and pens primarily science fiction and fantasy. He blends his fascination with history and his professional background in software engineering to come up with some unusual story twists. His stories emerged from his curiosity about historical watershed events and asking "what if?"

Originally from Buffalo, John lives in Rochester, New York, with his wife Linda. She's been married to him for over forty years and has supported his writing from the beginning. They have three grown children scattered around the country, along with their grandchildren. For relaxation John enjoys gardening (which stretches his intellect attempting to outwit the rabbits and deer) and distance running. He is a member of the Lilac City Rochester Writers, Greece Writers, and B&N (Greece) writing group.

John is an award-winning author who has published science-fiction novels *Cocytus: Planet of the Damned*, *Cocytus: Sanctuary in Hell*, alternative history novels *The Red Fist of Rome* and *Last Roman's Prayer*, and numerous short stories. He can be contacted at:

johndcaligiuri@gmail.com

For more information visit his website:

http://www.guardiantreepublishing.com.

For new projects, John is starting a new science-fiction series that merges the *Red Fist Chronicles* with the Cocytus series.

www.ingramcontent.com/pod-product-compliance
Lightning Source LLC
Chambersburg PA
CBHW071248250626
47163CB00002B/371